Changing Places

Changing Places

Rosamund Ridley

PIATKUS

Acknowledgements are due to the following
people, for their professional advice:
John Dugdale B.A. F.I.B.M.S.
Dr John McIver M.D., F.R.C.P., F.R.C.Path

First published in Great Britain in 1994 by
Judy Piatkus (Publishers) Ltd of
5 Windmill Street, London W1P 1HF

*A catalogue record for this book is available
from the British Library*

ISBN 0-7499-0260-4

Phototypeset in 11/12pt Times by
Computerset, Harmondsworth, Middlesex
Printed and bound in Great Britain by
Biddles Ltd, Guildford & Kings Lynn

To R.R.E.E. and L.

Chapter One

Christopher Marlowe wasn't sure he still existed. Life hadn't worked out according to plan at all. Self-doubt began long ago, when the Vatican deleted his name-saint. St Christopher, patron of travellers, hero of a billion or so tacky medals and car plaques, was a mere legend, a pious hijacking of Atlas. So far, Marlow had achieved none of the things proud parents want for their children – fame, riches or happiness – least of all happiness. He'd been unhappy for too long to remember anything else.

There was the real Christopher Marlowe, extant when the saint was still bona fide, dead correctly young, romantic and gay at twenty-nine, with three pages in the *Oxford Dictionary of Quotations*. His namesake was ten years older already, straight, and had written nothing memorable yet. This wouldn't matter if he were a brain surgeon, or a fireman, or a happy housewife. It seemed to matter a great deal, because writing was Marlowe's job. His parents should have resisted the temptation to saddle their first-born with Christopher, but initially it had certain merits, like the name of a famous father. Christopher Marlowe, *enfant terrible*, earned more than useful pocket money, freelancing at thirteen, writing poetry, a latter-day Chatterton. At fourteen, he had his own weekly column in the local paper. A year later, he was broadcasting, securing, through sheer audacity, a ten-minute interview with Tolkien. As a sideline, he edited the school magazine, and passed ten subjects at GCE, all at grade one.

Then his career veered off course. He sat the Oxford entrance exams, recovered slowly, if never completely, from

1

the shock of failure. Shy and insecure, he'd never taken success for granted, but the school and his parents had expected a scholarship, nothing less. A month later, he accepted a place at a currently fashionable campus; fashionable, but definitely not Oxford. His school reserved the Honours Board for Oxbridge.

Chastened, Marlowe learned to re-invent himself, made no mention of his illustrious past. Fairly soon, sided by the theatrical name, he attracted attention once more, campus hack and bar-prop by day, hard secret slogger by night. He was reading Politics. With a certain prescience, he made the Eastern Bloc his special option. He liked the mystery of his craft, made friends with very long names, like Wladislaw Sienkiewicz and Erzsébet Szent-Györgyi. In vacations, he contrived to explore forbidden Eastern Europe, returned suavely expressing a preference for Czech beer, at 2p a pint, and Czech women, at an undisclosed price. Restored glory was confirmed, the year of editing the campus paper. First class honours were an unexpected bonus. Congenitally nervous still, he hadn't dared to apply for a BBC traineeship. he liked attention well enough though, wanted his own part in changing an appalling world. Journalism was the obvious choice, his track record impeccable. Trained, decreed competent, he found editors willing to pay him. A column headed Christopher Marlowe commanded attention, even before people read what he had to say. He enjoyed a year or two in Manchester, moved on, uncertainly at first, to London, and the posh broadsheets. This being all he'd ever wanted, he felt brave enough to fall in love, and very nearly settle down.

This was a mistake. It showed, soon enough, in his work. The woman was difficult, cared altogether too much for her own more brilliant career. She wouldn't, for instance, entertain the idea of marriage. Lapsed cradle Catholic, Marlowe suffered occasional pangs of guilt, though never of faith. Overlooked once too often, he moved to a new venture, hoping for a fresh start. He knew something was badly wrong when the milkman called him Mr Grey. His worst suspicions were confirmed when he found himself described as Annabel Grey's husband. Unfit for anything else, he tried working harder, hoping the niggling pain would go away if he ignored it long enough. On the other hand, he was running out of time, pleading, *O lente, lente, currite noctis equi.* Success, Bel stated, came before thirty-five, or not at all. She herself was well on the way, able to say such things without a qualm.

Marlowe wrote about life, the everyday kind, all over Europe, including the East. He didn't deal in political tantrums, domestic or international. He wrote best about the many pains and occasional pleasures of daily life, success, failure, poverty, life on the dole or in a Docklands penthouse. He was equally good at both, and a smattering of the Slavonic languages gave him an entrée into those parts of Eastern Europe mere English graduates cannot reach. It was a decent enough career. He was by no means famous, and his name proved all too easy to forget after all. Bel, Dr Annabel Grey, was far better known. If she wrote for a magazine, it was her name, not the subject, that went on the front cover. She'd published three very clever books, already prescribed texts. She'd been on *Question Time*, was consulted on *Today* and the *World at One*. She was also extremely beautiful, and she refused to have him at the birth of their second, and unwanted, child. For a journalist of his ilk, this was a double blow: rejected as a birth partner and deprived of good copy. The birth of their first-born, Luke, had been uplifting, and a nice little earner too.

Marlowe sat anonymous, reading his own words, written by a stranger. The paper was yesterday's, left in the hospital waiting room after some other drama. The scrawny boy opposite stood up, paced the room again, then riffled through the rack of magazines, unread, new-minted all. No one came here to read. The boy roamed again, stood with his back to Marlowe, staring out of the rain-lashed window. There was nothing at all to see, only tarmac, a scatter of parked cars and the clutter of signs, Greek to him: orthopaedics, paediatrics, pathology. Fumbling in the pockets of skin-tight pale jeans, he turned to face Marlowe. There were tears in the pale-green eyes, an explosion of ache around his mouth. Above a child's lips, red and softly curving, there was the merest shadow of a moustache. He said, shy and uncertain, 'Excuse me. Would you have any matches?'

3

Marlow shook his head, pointed to the *No Smoking* signs on every wall, then added, compassionately, 'Sorry. I don't smoke. Would you like a coffee? There's a machine somewhere.'

The boy shook his head, tried, furtively, to wipe his eyes on the sleeve of his leather jacket. The hospital allowed emotion. Marlowe extracted a tissue from the box of Kleenex Mansize on the coffee table. Shameless now, the boy helped himself to more, let the hot tears flow. Marlowe, detached, professional, allowed the child his privacy, read on. It was an account of his old friendship with Jerzy Zeromski. British born and bred, Jerzy had taken his MBA and his equally Polish wife back to Poland, to retrieve his grandfather's business in Gdansk. In his first letter, Jerzy had ended, wryly, that Polish has no real word for 'efficiency'. And Jerzy's first child had been dressed in parcels of Luke's Mothercare cast-offs. From anecdote, the article moved into real time, Jerzy's anticipation of Baltic emancipation. Jerzy, no romantic, had timed his move well. Feliks now dressed in Benetton and other international uniforms. Baby Piotr still wore Mothercare, but Jerzy's wife ordered it new.

Marlowe turned to the women's page, but it was tedious, only fashion. In another day or two, there would be letters from sour feminists, bewailing time and space wasted on such trivia. Bel would laugh at them, sneer gently, curling her carefully painted lips. Annabel had no pity for women so scared of their sex that they dressed in mere coverings. Annabel liked to be beautiful, as much as she enjoyed being clever. This was one reason why she loathed pregnancy. It destroyed, from within, the female, curving body she lived in. It invaded her, something alien, made her into a *woman with child*. After Luke, she'd said, cool and precise, 'I don't think we'll have any more.'

Marlowe, astounded by his son's perfect male body, had pleaded for one more. He wanted a daughter, the miracle again but another sex, his very own woman.

Bel weaned their son, took her pills, went back to work, and that had been that, for thirteen years. She stayed with Marlowe from habit, and because he met her standard for male beauty, being dark, lean, touching six foot, with grey

4

eyes and a dislike of shaving that preceded designer stubble. At weekends, he never shaved. Bel reserved sex with him for weekends. Monday to Friday was her business.

Outside in the corridor, heels clacked and the door opened. A nurse with an encouraging smile peered round. 'All right?'

Marlowe nodded. The boy turned away, ashamed of his wet face. The woman smiled again, for both of them.

'If you'd like to . . .'

Marlow folded the paper and said, coldly, 'Thank you, but Annabel doesn't want me to be with her.'

The woman stared at him, dismayed, then said, in her nurse's voice, 'Some ladies do say that, but we find they don't really mean it. If I come with you . . .? It's Mrs–?'

'Dr Annabel Grey. Before you say it, I'm not Mr Grey. My name's Marlowe. Bel doesn't use my name, and we aren't married.'

She patted his hand, officiously maternal. 'It's quite all right. We've moved with the times, you'll find. One week, we didn't have a single married lady in the ward. It's all *partners* these days, if we're lucky.'

Marlowe left his hand where it was, strangely grateful for any human contact now. The nurse must be in her mid-fifties, his mother's age when she died. He managed to find courtesy, an explanation she would understand. 'It's not my choice. If she'd have me, I'd be with her. Bel didn't want me to see her in labour again.'

'Then it isn't your first?'

Marlowe closed his eyes, remembering the first cry, then that little moving body. His son. He wanted Luke here now, for comfort, but that was taboo. The hospital considered itself modern, came out well enough in *The Good Birth Guide*; they did water births, stools, bean bags, birthing rooms, but they had to draw the line somewhere. Twelve-year-olds watching second-stage labour wasn't on, yet. They'd allowed a Burmese cat once. Bel had chosen this place via friends and the Kitzinger bible.

Marlowe found his eyes closing again, forced them open. The nurse was still with him, definitely maternal now.

'If you could get some sleep. . . If she really doesn't want

5

you around, why not go home to bed? We'll ring as soon as there's any news.'

Marlowe checked his watch. It was four fifteen, ten minutes and fifty seconds since last time. Almost, he could hear Bel, sarcastic, mocking, the day the little band of blue confirmed this pregnancy.

'Yes, of course you want the bloody baby. You would. All that shared-pregnancy crap. All those bloody pathetic tears. Turn down Vivaldi, pass the camcorder, and a right tearjerker for the paper before they've even cut the cord. The bilge you came out with when Luke was born made me want to throw up. I had a *baby*, for godsake. Most women can. I'm sick to bloody death of men going on about the most beautiful moment of their lives. You try nine months of throwing up, feeling vile, looking worse. Piles are a pain in the bum. Backache's not a few twinges, more like a knife through to your guts. One idiot gynaecologist says the kicks don't hurt. Luke near enough broke my ribs kicking. On bad days, near the end, you throw up because the little bastards work out on your stomach. Anyway, I'm not having it. If Murphy turns agonized papist on me, I'll go private.'

He'd won, or he wouldn't be here now, waiting for this unwanted birth. He'd pleaded with her, proud of her beautiful, clever body that made babies for him. After Murphy refused to sanction the abortion, Bel booked a clinic, but Marlowe had used low cunning, played devil's advocate, disturbing her own moribund conscience.

'You'd better get fixed quickly, before it starts to look human.'

Bel, as he intended, had brought out the pictures of a ten-week foetus, complete, transparently human, and she'd carried this second child full term. Now, she was giving birth as she intended, alone.

Looking up again, Marlowe discovered that the nurse had gone. The boy sat facing him, staring bleakly at the posters on the wall. Two condemned smoking, before or after birth. The rest proscribed most other pleasures. Marlowe thought the Aids poster skull slightly tasteless for this venue. On the far wall, there were advertisements for cervical cancer smear tests and breast examination. There were free leaflets on a stand. He'd read most of them in the first hour. All found some reason for diagrams of the female reproductive organs. The boy, who looked illiterate, had helped himself to a few.

'Turns you up, doesn't it?' he said suddenly. 'If they really looked like that . . . I heard you talking. Mine doesn't want me with her either. I wanted to be there with her, see the kid born, but . . .'

He stopped, lost for words, fighting tears again. Marlowe, amused by his own prejudice, had expected a sub-Cockney accent and no grammar, but the boy's voice was classless, no glottal stops, not mid-Atlantic whine. He had very clean, deeply grooved fingernails. He was in control now, the tears a shared secret.

Marlowe, on impulse, said, 'How old are you?'

The boy smiled, looking for a fleeting moment, almost proud. 'Sixteen. Seventeen next month. So is she, but three days before me. I go for older women. We're both doing A levels. You see fewer social workers if it wasn't underage sex – one thing less they can get you for. Her parents are keeping the baby. Rabid Catholics, the pair of them, so they can hardly whinge about birth control.'

Marlowe smiled back, aware that he was old enough to be the boy's father.

The boy laughed, looked younger still, fledgling, and nobody's father yet. 'It was supposed to be safe sex. Like it says on the old death's-head over there. Rubber johnnies landed us right in it. Could have been worse, of course.'

He paused, to gauge Marlowe's reaction. He too had measured the years, but women had made them equals. Seeing a faint smile, he laughed again, glancing at the Aids poster.

'Holy Mother Church got it right after all. One faithful partner for life, complete with the blessing of Her Majesty's government. I won't risk a rubber johnny again. A baby's one thing. Anyway, there wasn't anyone else, only her. Now she doesn't want to know. Won't even speak to me, won't let me buy things for the kid. Someone at school told me she'd come in.'

Marlowe, trapped, saw no way out of it. Besides, the boy had honoured him with equality. Anywhere else, the very

7

young regarded their elders as barely human. They moved in other space, arrogant.

The electric clock jerked down onto the half-hour. Bel had been in labour since yesterday morning, about half past eight. Close on twenty hours of pain . . . He couldn't imagine it, failed even in the attempt. After Luke's birth, she'd tried to describe it, but no words evoke pain, except for the sufferer.

He said, gently, 'How did she feel about the baby?'

'Sick. Sick with fear, then sick as a dog, for months. They said it would stop, but it didn't. Even last week, she was still throwing up. You feel a right bastard for landing them in it.'

Marlowe thought of Bel removing the long mirror from their bedroom, dressing in the bathroom, disguising the swollen body with all the artifice her money could buy. In no way did she look pregnant, until the seventh month. Then, she'd been so beautiful, with a child's clear skin and a woman's lovely, rounded body. The fierce kicks delighted him, watching and touching unseen movement.

This second baby was more vigorous, kicked harder, had made Bel sicker, heavier. She'd suffered more from the disorders of pregnancy, defying even her own body, she'd stayed at work until the day before yesterday. She'd left in the middle of tutorials to be sick: she had sat up writing lectures or marking assignments through stabbing backache. At weekends, when they should have been free, she worked longer hours still, on her own data, writing papers into the small hours. Levy, her professor, was moving on to a chair at his old Cambridge college. Bel's track record was good. She was the obvious choice, a respected teacher, but she hadn't published quite enough, taking too much time out, before Luke. This second, unwanted child wouldn't be allowed to wreck her chances. Marlowe wondered if she suffered more for rejecting it so wilfully; her body or the child's exacting revenge. As for the baby . . . he'd read somewhere that the mother's hostility could be communicated, affecting the child for years after birth. He'd had a bad pregnancy too, nightmares that left him sick and shaking, stillbirth, cot death.

'Penny for them?'

Marlowe looked up, saw the clock; quarter to five. Surely it must be soon now? They didn't allow long labours these

8

days . . . No *Queen Jane lay in labour/For nine dayes and
more* . . . He said, dry-mouthed, hoarse, 'Only wishing it was
over. Shall I get those coffees?'

The boy nodded grateful. 'Black, please. One sugar.' He
offered a handful of coins.

Marlowe shook his head. 'My round.'

When he came back, the room was empty. He left the plastic lid on the boy's coffee, hoped that the news had come and
was good. Bel wouldn't agree; her position on this subject
was stubbornly Malthusian, laced with guilt. The score was
bad, both these births unplanned, unwanted. Bel's guru as a
student had been Paul Ehrlich, modern Malthus, *The
Population Bomb* her bible. She'd once, on Channel 4,
applauded the Chinese one-child family. Population figures
were her favourite numbers game. She wrote and lectured
with fervour, convinced nine tenths of her own students. She
had, moonlighting in one of the posh glossies promoted Luke
as her chosen only child. Marlowe, remembering, marvelled
again that he had been able to talk her out of an abortion.
Correctly, as it happened, he decided that the choice had been
hers after all. Bel, strictly logical, argued that she could do
what she liked with her own body. The baby was not her own
body, therefore, she had no right to destroy it; Q.E.D. Bel had
given up religion more thoroughly than most, didn't come
even when he took Luke to church at Christmas. Marlowe
suspected her insatiable curiosity. She couldn't resist seeing
what would happen if . . . Nor was she a quitter. This pregnancy, a paper toiled over in the small hours, or even their
long years together. Closing his eyes again, Marlowe remembered, with love, the first lyrical days.

He'd been a makeweight at the Cambridge ball, fifth
columnist, there to expose gilded youth, throwing up in their
hired finery. Bel, Primavera, in gauzy green had agreed to be
quoted and photographed. Bel allowed the camera to record
in calculated detail the rose and white of her perfect breasts.
The same night, or rather, in grey and drizzling dawn, she'd
taken him to bed. Unasked, he would never have presumed.
Bel chose all her lovers, then and now. A year or so later,
though, it was Bel who suggested they move in together.
Fidelity, let alone monogamy, had never been part of the deal,

9

but Bel, like any other human creature, needed somewhere she could feel safe. For two or three extraordinary months, they'd both been in love, until she became pregnant with Luke. Pregnant, she'd turned on him, catlike, appalled by the assault on her beautiful body. Female, though, she wanted a safe place for her child. He was that safe place. It was as simple as that. There were invitations, veiled or direct, from several women, some men. He ignored them, wanted only Bel. Luke must have been about six months old when Bel said, in her detached, clear-sighted way. 'I've stopped loving you. At least, I'm not in love with you any more. I care more about Luke.'

For Marlowe, the process had taken longer, many years longer. Luke, growing from infancy to wounded childhood, failed to understand, then understood all too well. Bel liked and enjoyed sex very much. They still made love, now and then – which was why he was here. Bel could have had the pregnancy terminated, but had chosen to see it through. He admired her still for that, for her courage, her honesty, her ferocious intelligence. There was also the small matter of her exquisite body. Most men would have endured a good deal, to share Bel's bed, even occasionally. Sometimes, they'd made love regularly, two people, getting through life together.

He hadn't heard the boy return, turned round only as the brown plastic cup was lifted from the table. There were tears again, and at first no words at all. Marlowe held the boy in his arms, let the tears wet yesterday's shirt, sticky with the night's sweat.

'She's alright.'

In his arms still, the child trembled, struggled to check sobs. Marlowe made him sit down, made him drink. The coffee had been scalding, was still hot enough. Only now did he register the boy's fear. After silence, he said, 'The baby?'

'A boy. Three kilos something – I can't remember. A son. I'm a dad.' He began to cry again, freely now, past caring, his face red and blotched like a child's.

Marlowe finished his own coffee, afraid now for Bel, who had been in labour too long. Presently, there was a knock at the door, and a woman came in. She stood there, uncertain,

10

then came straight over to the boy and held him close. There was no likeness. She must be the girl's mother, only mid thirties herself; their story, and nothing to do with him.

Marlowe withdrew to stand in the chill corridor, lit only by two dim overhead lights. He walked to the far end, stood by the glass doors, watching the night. Here, he could see the wraith shapes of naked trees, moving too much in a night of wind and rain. There was a pool of water by the doorway, starting to seep through, soaking the coir doormat stamped with the hospital logo. He should tell somebody. Outside, a slate crashed to the ground, then another, with a sound of shattering glass. Outside, too, a car arrived at speed, braked sharply, sweeping up a great wall of water. Watching, he saw the dark shape of a man run to the front entrance and hammer on the door. A nurse came out, followed by a porter with a wheelchair. They covered the swollen woman with blankets and wheeled her in. Marlowe, voyeur, recalled Bel's incoherent fury. She loathed the passivity of childbirth, raged when it was said, of some gravid female, *they've taken her in*. Bel had driven here, grimacing through the pains, walking in herself, walking to the labour ward, alone.

A nurse approached, fair, too young. 'Mr Grey?'

Marlowe agreed. It saved time.

'Congratulations. You have a little girl. Three kilos, two hundred grammes.'

'Bel?'

'She's fine. We did a forceps. She's tired, but you could stay a minute or two.'

Marlow drove home, father of two. It was dawn, without sun, and the city hideous. There were no quiet hours now, no silent streets. Girls on thin legs propped up more girls, or men, he couldn't tell. The party season lasted all year, but had more excuse in winter. In mid-October, Christmas looked even sillier: lights strung across shop fronts, and fat men in red selling anything. The streets were empty, the roads clear.

He circled back to the City Road. Bel wanted a free entry in the *Independent*: 'On 18 October, to Annabel Grey and Christopher Marlowe, a daughter.'

She liked free offers, saved money-off coupons, filled in absurd questionnaires, to be rewarded with money off cat food and dishwasher powder. They had neither. Cunning, she would buy all the necessary packets at once, wouldn't waste time with dribs and drabs, risk the offer running out. They had six ice-cream shaped fridge magnets, nine mock vintage vans, five aprons in bright pvc, a Cadbury's shopping bag, and a fleet of submarines that worked with bicarb. Marlowe recalled a superior model from his childhood, blamed defence cuts, and made her laugh, even in the eighth grinding month of pregnancy. She liked these toys better than ten per cent extra, or coins in the post. Willing to please, he munched through sacks of cereal, suffered the overpowering scent of each new detergent. Bel kidded herself that this hobby was efficient, the real suckers being those who saved and missed out, for want of one special voucher.

Away from her temper and her angry body, he would still feel fond of her. Pale, tired, otherwise entirely herself, she'd said one word when he saw her: 'Satisfied?' And then she had turned over to sleep. They'd allowed him to hold his daughter, plastic-tagged, umbilical cord clipped, and dressed in swaddling white. He was still reeling from the shock of it, the assault of love for her. Luke's birth had been about pride, cliché-ridden joy in a first-born son. Bel had said, coldly, that more males were born, adding, truthfully, that she'd wanted a girl. Now she had a girl, and didn't want her at all.

Luke was staying overnight with his aunt Sarah. Marlowe, with time on his hands, decided to pay for his own birth announcement, in the *Guardian*, which his father might read. He'd written for the paper often enough, and Dad would have a copy, lovingly proud of his children. Marlowe chose his own, less austere words: 'On 18 October, St Luke's Day, to Annabel Grey and Christopher Marlowe, a welcome daughter, sister for Luke. D.G.' Only his father would notice or care for the D.G. which stood for Deo gratias. Bel would most certainly quarrel with 'welcome'.

Stopping for a pee, he saw his haggard and unshaven face in the mirror. Cold water improved things a little, but the day and night had left him ten years older. Leaving, he all but collided with a man who passed for a friend. Probably, they loathed each other, but had never put it to the test as women might. Laidlaw's wife, overweight, blonde with perpetual dark roots, worked as a secretary in Bel's department.

The man said, cheerfully, 'You look bloody. How's Bel?'

Marlowe straightened his tie, buttoned his grey wool coat. 'Is that better? Annabel is fine, thank you.'

Laidlaw grinned. 'Sue tipped me off. How's the baby?'

Marlowe saw her crushed-rose sleeping face and the dark-blue eyes trying to focus on him. He said, 'She's fine, too. Born at quarter to five this morning.'

He reeled then, unprepared for Laidlaw's thump between the shoulder blades. 'Nice one! Girls are best. What happened to the squeaky-green-one-child family?'

Marlowe made no answer. He could think of plenty, even unrehearsed, smug or ribald, but not for Laidlaw.

'Wet her head this lunchtime?'

Marlowe nodded, made his escape. Outside, he felt very odd, disconnected. Walking, he was too conscious of the action, every move an effort. Driving home he had to brake sharply, avoiding a taxi, almost too late. The abuse was all he deserved, or less. He'd slept badly the night before. Luke had woken from a nightmare about birth, derived from his taste for lurid science fiction. They'd talked, father and son, long into the night. Marlowe, drugged with sleep, discussed the stages of labour, the absolute normality of Luke's own birth, some thirteen years ago. They were supposed to learn all this at school or on *Blue Peter*. Luke was convinced his mother would die, and afraid of handicap, for Bel was no longer very young. The truth was that he knew too much, amniocentesis, chorionic villus sampling, genetic counselling. Bel, as it happened, had left nothing to chance. The baby, so far as anyone could tell, was normal. She'd elected not to know its sex.

When Luke slept at last, it had been four o'clock and Bel was already restless, getting up three times for the loo, one more curse of late pregnancy. At six, she was up for the fourth time, came back to announce the show. After that, his role was defined, and horribly limited. Only absolute shits avoided the birth now, but Bel didn't want him with her. At seven, her waters broke, cue for driving Luke to Sarah's house in Islington. The contractions hadn't started though, didn't really get under way until after eight, while they sat in a jam, Bel driving. At the reception desk, she'd dismissed him, walking away briskly, between pains. When he caught up with her and tried to argue, she'd smiled, as if amused. She said, 'You can't have the thing for me. I really don't see the point.'

Chapter Two

Marlowe let himself in, kicked aside yesterday's post and two free sheets, retrieved yesterday's milk, six free-range eggs and four organic yogurts. The milk float was three doors down, on the other side. Shivering from exhaustion, Marlowe stood waiting, tried to remember when they last paid him. Hideously cheerful, the man was heading for him already, eight bottles threaded between his half-gloved fingers.

'Missus alright?'

Marlow nodded; so much for London anonymity.

'Next door but one saw you go.' He waited, expectant.

Marlowe cursed Bel for being so bloody negative, trying to kill his joy. He had a daughter, alive and perfect, *'sole daughter of my house and heart'*. Balancing eggs, yogurt and three pints of semi-skim, he said, exulting, 'A girl. Beautiful. Masses of dark hair.'

'Magic. New babies are magic. I delivered one once.' The milkman grinned, proud father himself, gap-toothed as a six-year-old.

Bel ranted about tooth decay, bewailed the appalling working-class diet, the way their kids gobbled sweets. The sheer inefficiency made her angry. Bel thought the world could be perfect, if only people used a bit of nous and self-restraint.

Marlowe thought the gap-toothed grin engaging. He craved the simplicity of being a milkman, one skill to master and an image the Saatchis would charge eyeteeth for. Milk, yogurts, eggs and babies, delivered with a smile, old ladies saved from hypothermia, and all before sunup. He needn't

15

have wasted time on the announcements either, common property now, at least in their patch of Clapham.

The man fished out two fifty-pence pieces. 'Cross her palm . . .'

Marlowe looked blank, then realised he hadn't a free hand. He put the milk and eggs down on the doormat, shifted the yogurts to his left hand. 'Thanks very much. But what do we owe you?'

'Zilch. Zero. Your missus paid up. My ma's north country. Cross a babby's palm with silver, draw the curtains for a death. She'll not change. It's good luck. You won't be wanting today's.'

'But we didn't cancel –'

'Let you off. You'll want more soon, christening and all that. Anyway, all the very best.'

Marlowe, deeply envious, watched the little man go, skipping down three steps, up three more, back to the float, up and down, happy and glorious, an English milkman on his round.

Yesterday's supper dishes were still in the sink. Bel insisted it was efficient to wash up once a day, after breakfast, when the economy-rate water was at its hottest. Dishwashers were proscribed, planet enemies, not worth it for a small household. She bought medium-sized yellow rubber gloves, which would fit them both. Marlowe washed up, his brain still somewhere else. Halfway down the bowl, he met Luke's take-away tray, still smeary with curry and grains of rice. Luke ate on the move, absently; he looked after himself all too well. Occasionally, for matters of life and death, he was given to Sarah. Otherwise, he had a key, and money for take-aways. He could use the microwave and the fan oven, never invited too many friends in, never wrecked the place, or smoked or drank. At least, he left no evidence. Luke and his friends lived unparented, moved from house to house with videos and CDs. Most had parents, but these were clever, with full diaries. When Luke was born, Bel hired a nanny, but loathed having someone else in the house. Later, they'd taken turns to collect him from child minders and feed him on boiled egg with Marmite soldiers.

When the baby was two weeks old, Luke's last child min-

16

der would take over. Bel planned to hand her over each day en route to the university. A full time nanny was out, never to be endured again. They'd no room, unless they gave up the study, never mind the appalling cost. Last week, hands across her tight belly, she'd raged at him over some asinine filler on Channel 4, where an earth mother of four was sounding off. The gist of it was, he recalled, that 'the feminist whinge of *affordable child care*' meant paying some other woman peanuts to look after your kids. Filling the second sink, for rinsing, he recalled a slammed door and noisy retching. Bel didn't like the truth, that was her trouble. Pregnant, she resorted rather too often to the tactics of Violet Elizabeth Bott.

Three mugs to hang on brass hooks, gaudy on the eco-sound waxed pine wall. Bel never bought mugs if she could help it. Anything paid for leaped to the quarry-tiled floor, smashed itself to deliberate smithereens. There were a dozen sloganned mugs, free with petrol, chocolate, tea, soup, and two tankards, free with the nastiest alcohol-free lager. Cat's pee . . . but Bel had sworn off alcohol, before Luke. A fair minded woman, she'd made the same sacrifice for the unwanted daughter. In the same spirit, she refused pills for her sickness, pain relief in her long labour. Filling the kettle, to make tea or coffee, he reconsidered Bel. If they met now, they wouldn't spend a night together, let alone fourteen years, on and off. The years had taken them in different directions.

The trouble was Bel's hardness and ambition.

Marlowe roamed about a bit, restored order. There were ready meals in the freezer; Luke's clothes for the next week in labelled piles, including three extra pairs of socks for rugger and hockey. After nine, Marlowe made phone calls to Bel's mother, his father, the office, assorted friends. He accepted congratulations, promised to be in tomorrow, then rang his sister. She brought Luke to the phone at once. There was a peak-rate silence. Coaxed and cajoled, the boy stayed resolutely dumb. At last, she gave up, let him go back to a small cousin, male, but with shoulder-length fair curls. Sarah had girls, too, red-haired, spikily cropped. She worked at home, designing vibrant, appallingly expensive hand-knits

17

and hand-painted silk dresses. She employed outworkers, paid fair wages. The results were stunning, the enterprise an economic disaster. Bel said she should sell her designs to the mass market, or pay less. Sarah only smiled. Years ago, they'd agreed to detest each other, but peacefully. Sarah was married to a GP, who volunteered to treat winos and street kids. Marlowe, spectator, suspected they did very well together; they looked happy. The house was an agreeable tip.

Luke had the phone back, having found his voice at last. 'Dad?'

He sounded not thirteen but six, pathetically young. The young were terrifying, first that child father, then his amazing daughter, now Luke. It could not be borne, so much frailty, so much he couldn't save them from. His newborn daughter was scarred already, bruised by the forceps that had lifted her into the world.

Luke said, uncertainly, 'Is there a baby?'

If only the boy were here in his arms, or, better still, both of them, and Bel safe in their own bed . . . Marlowe said, cheerfully, 'Yes. A girl. And Bel's fine.'

Silence again.

Sarah took the phone back. 'It's no use. They simply won't, not at this age. Babies are embarrassing. I think kids invented the gooseberry bush to spare our blushes. When?'

'Quarter to five this morning.'

A pause for calculations. 'Twenty-one hours, ye gods! Poor old Bel! The girls were a couple of hours each. Mark took a bit longer, two and a half.'

Cue for flattery. Marlowe said what he must. Sarah, seven stone four, made an unlikely earth mother.

In smug sisterhood, she added, 'Poor love, she must be shattered. And you.'

'She's very tired. I only saw her briefly. I was going to come over for Luke.'

'Don't. Go to bed. What on earth would you do all day? I'm running him to school. We were only waiting for news. You could've rung earlier. He prowled round the house all night, worried sick.'

'About Bel?'

Marlowe, guilty, knew he'd been wrong, off-loading Luke

18

like that. They should have been together. He couldn't remember Sarah's birth – there were only two years between them – but he'd seen Frances at once, five minutes old, naked still, and his mother Madonna-proud. Frances was out of his life for ever, a nun, running a mobile clinic around the Sudan.

Sarah was still talking. 'Bel? Of course. And he was worried about you, on your own.'

Marlowe said, suddenly resolute, 'I'll pick him up from school. He can come with me this evening. I'll be round for his things later.'

Sarah didn't object, didn't beg for another day of her nephew. She had an enviably level-headed approach to children, slotted them into her life as if they were people. She'd given birth to all three at home, and whisked them round Sainsbury's barely two days later. Sarah knew exactly who she was and where she was going. He'd seen a feature on her designs in a magazine in the dentist's waiting room, a fortnight ago. Bel, on free treatment, had been peeved when there was nothing to do, as if cheated of her NHS rights. He wished, not for the first time, that she'd get her politics in better order. Of late, she'd seemed far right of the Bow Group, except for thinking all defence folly – which was rather like taking on Catholicism without the Pope. Once, in a local council election, she'd voted Green because she liked their ruthless views on population. On education, she was a shameless elitist, thought the masses might as well leave school at fourteen. And she'd said, coldly, 'If there's anything wrong, they can just let the sprog die. Survival of the fittest.' She'd agreed to every single test they suggested, afraid of letting a mistake through the system. Bel thought the unfit who did slip through should be sterilised. She would, of course, be sterilised herself. Marlowe had offered, but she'd said no. He might want a child with another partner, whereas she most definitely did not; another child, that is.

Marlowe made tea, added yesterday's milk, read the morning paper. This week, it was the *Independent*. Bel kept changing their order, didn't want to get typecast. Once, it was the *Sun*, which he'd rather enjoyed. He turned to the announcements. Too early for his daughter, of course, but he

19

checked out the births, so many sons and daughters, name-less. They hadn't discussed a name at all. The baby had been due on Friday, and he'd fancied Freya. Bel, very likely, would have objected.

He thought of food, but a day without food or sleep had killed his appetite. Dead beat, he ran a bath, stripped off, revolted by the smell of his own sweat. Obediently, he put the discarded clothes in the correct linen basket, according to wash temperature, then lowered himself into blessed healing water. Twice he fell asleep, woke the second time in a cold bath lined with grey scum. Then he had to shower, to remove the scum, and clean the grimy bath. Bel never bathed; she showered twice a day and washed her sleek fair crop every morning. Marlowe washed his own, then faced the last grisly ritual. Bel, who didn't always like the truth, had chosen rose-tinted glass for the bathroom mirrors. Today, he was glad of it, scraping away the squalid stubble. His mouth felt foul, tainted. He brushed vigorously, remembering the old bedtime ritual with Luke, Punch and Judy strawberry toothpaste and nursery rhymes, for the two minutes' struggle. At three, Luke had enjoyed the old horror:

> *Quick, quick, the cat's been sick,*
> *Where? Where?*
> *Under the chair.*
> *Hasten, hasten, fetch a basin.*
> *Great Scott! What a lot!*

Giggling, Marlowe splashed cold water on his face, tossed his towel towards the third basket, and made for bed.

Luke lay carved in stillness, his skin grey, eyes closed in mar-ble death. Marlowe, without tears, watched as Bel carried their son to his coffin bed. Then she tried to screw down the lid, but she was using the wrong screwdriver, as usual: she needed a Phillips. She never looked first, never made the slightest effort to put a plug on properly. The brilliant Dr Grey had to ask, every time, which was neutral. He rum-maged in the toolbox, found the right one for her, watched as she sealed the coffin, as Luke woke, screaming till the sky split, and he was alone, without Bel or Luke. On the horizon, he could see Bel, walking behind the coffin; he heard her manic laugh as they threw the coffin over cliffs, falling sheer ... He wanted to run, stood transfixed, until the abyss ...

Marlowe woke, drenched in sweat, reached out for the comfort of Bel's arms, then remembered. Luke was at school, Bel and the nameless baby in hospital. Then he saw the time, bright green, three twenty-three; threw off the duvet, searched frantically for clothes, car keys, sanity. He found the keys at last by a laundry basket, fallen from yesterday's trousers, and reached the school at twenty to four. Luke didn't know he wasn't going back to Sarah's. This term, he'd been allowed to make his own way home, with his own key.

Marlowe parked, prudently, two streets away. The Astra lacked style; Luke wouldn't want it seen. Nor were people his age collected from school. Dropped off in the morning, yes, but after school he expected to be free. But there were a few parents or au pairs. Luke and many others didn't qualify for a bus pass. It was cheaper, though not greener, to pick them up by car. Very few went willingly from school to their own homes. Luke came by bus or tube, if it rained, came home by degrees otherwise.

At four o'clock, bells shrilled and the young were released, scruffy, strident, fearless creatures. Luke was in the centre of a scuffling group, cuffing each other, fighting happily, exactly like puppies. Then Luke caught sight of his father, freed himself, became individual. They walked to the car, at first in awkward silence. Presently, Luke began to talk about a rugger match on Saturday. Marlow tried to remember if Luke had ever said *Mother* or *Mum*. Bel preferred her given name. Luke was quite right. Bel was nobody's *Mum*.

Driving to the hospital that evening, Marlowe tried to make conversation. Luke sat very still beside him, said nothing until they were almost there. The question came as Marlowe edged his way through three sets of lights. He didn't answer at first. The boy's voice rose, insistent, repeating the same words; maddening. It worked, though. Next time Luke stonewalled, Marlowe resolved to try the same tactics.

'Where are the flowers? And grapes? And a present for the baby? I bet you're lying. I bet she's dead. Women die, having

21

babies. And the baby's in special care. We did birth at school. There's a video, and you see them, all tubes and monitors.'

Marlowe came through the last lights. He drove on, watching for signs and somewhere to park. he said, contrite, 'You're right. Where do I get flowers at this time of night? Or grapes?'

Luke considered. 'Someone's garden? I know where there's black grapes, on a house near the British Museum. Only, maybe we'd have to ask, and they'd say no. Anyway, Bel doesn't like grapes, except the titchy ones with no pips. You should've remembered flowers. You're supposed to give women flowers, all the time. You never do. Maybe that's why she –'

Marlowe said, quickly, 'And a present for the baby. I'm useless, aren't I?'

He was trying to follow arrows that seemed to head for cones and orange netting. A JCB blocked his way. He reversed, cursing, almost hitting a white Mercedes, containing another father and a small child. They got out, found no damage, said things. On the back seat of the Merc, there were flowers, pink lilies, stephanotis. The child clutched a beribboned parcel. The man was festooned with Mothercare bags.

Marlowe said, brightly, 'Maternity?'

The man nodded. He'd cut himself shaving, wore odd socks, and there was a smear of something dark on his pink tie. Blood brothers, they reversed between cones and netting, and found the temporary board that said *Maternity* lying on its back, the arrow indicating any of three routes. Marlowe led the way, found himself in a cul-de-sac of reserved parking spaces, consultants only. The third time, he got it right, but dawdled, made a great fuss of locking up rather than be seen empty-handed by Mercedes man. Outside the ward, he found a barrow doing a smart trade in dahlias and blowsy chrysanthemums at pink-lily prices. The baby would have to wait.

Bel had just finished her supper, or, rather, finished with it. She'd left emerald peas, three inches of cold batter, flabby chips and a slab of sponge cake in congealed custard. She said, peevish, 'I'm starving. What did you bring?'

Luke sat on the bed. 'Flowers. No grapes, nothing for the

22

baby. We'll get something tomorrow.' He inspected the fish-tank cot, leaned over and touched one hand. Tendril fingers closed about his. Being male, Luke succumbed at once, but he added mendacious, or embryo diplomat, 'We needed to see what she looks like, before buying a present.'

Bel, amused, lifted the baby out and introduced her children. 'And what does she look like?'

Luke considered. The baby still gripped one of his long and rather grubby fingers. He stroked silky dark hair, tender, amazed by what his mother had done.

'She's pretty. She's not like a baby. I've seen babies. They're bald. We'll buy something tomorrow.'

Bel moved her pain carefully. The bastards had cut her about, insisting on forceps when she was beyond speech. Almost, she regretted banning Chris. He might have been useful. On the other hand, overawed, appalled by the squalor of birth, he might have colluded with them, allowed drugs, begged for a caesarean. Also, he would have seen her in pain, animal. Delivered, she was his equal again.

She indicated the congealed food. 'I can't eat that muck. Bring me something from a deli. Luke can stay here.'

Marlowe wanted to hold his daughter, unfold her, see again miniature humanity, but Bel looked dangerous. She was writing in a cheap reporter's pad, the kind she always used to draft lectures, tore out a sheet.

'There. Get what you can. I expect you haven't any cash?'

Marlowe checked his wallet; one fiver, three cards and a phone card with one unit left. Forty-seven pence in his pocket. 'I'll get some.'

Bel, impatient, handed him twenty pounds. 'Go now, or they might not let you back.'

He returned as eviction bells rang, pounded up the ward against a tide of banished men. Bel was feeding the baby, the dark head half the size of her milky breast. On the bed was a copy of *Mother and Baby*. She'd been reading it, tenderly absorbed, for all the time allowed. She was so ruthless with herself. She'd read *Mother and Baby* just once before, the week Luke was born, instead of *Cosmopolitan*. He wanted to stay and watch over them both, but Bel reached for the carrier bag, inspected its contents.

23

'It'll do. I've written you a list for tomorrow. And my laptop, and if my proofs come, bring them in. They insist on a week, after forceps. Bloody waste of time. She's fine, so am I. You'd better go. Medusa over there's glaring. Don't forget nappies, and use the vouchers in my freebie bag.'

Marlowe kissed her. He couldn't very well not. Leaning over, he could smell birth: milk, sweat, blood and damaged flesh. He felt absolutely no desire for Bel. Awe, yes and a measure of fear, but no love or lust. That was over, and he was free at last. His daughter was something else. There were no words for so much love.

The bells clanged again and Luke tugged him away, embarrassed by the sight of so many newly delivered women. They had stitches, hurt, down below. It was all on that video. Babies' heads tore the stretched perineal flesh, or doctors came, with giant scissors. Birth was appalling, if it weren't for the babies. His sister was the most beautiful thing he'd ever seen.

The day before Bel's release, Marlowe blitzed the house, made chaos to restore order. Sarah had offered to take Luke again, but this he refused. It was easy enough to slot in time for the school run. Also, he disliked, intensely, living alone, responsible for no one. Luke provided so much; company, comfort, love and an excuse to stay in. Child-free friends were a nuisance, still drinking and partying as if nothing had changed. They hadn't noticed at all.

His theme this month was poverty – black, white, endemic. He'd collected the continental data already. Two weeks before the baby, he'd joined the bizarre African settlement around Termini station in Rome. They stood in falling rain, exotically thin; sold, or didn't sell, carved things, spread about their feet on gaudy cloths. At night, they cooked in the Metro tunnel, where the bag-snatching beggars preyed. Three long days later, in Filipino Oslo, he found the underclass of Scandinavia; not the cherished nomads of the Arctic, but boat people and street cleaners. They staffed the cruise ships of the North Sea, the fishing boats and canning factories. Like all the poor, they had too many children. Last week, in Brixton, he'd shopped all day in a seedy supermarket. Every

24

move confirmed the sins of poverty, from the chained coin-in-slot carts to the locked lavatories. Border guards impounded shopping bags, released them only on production of a till receipt. Inventing a desperate small daughter, he'd asked about the loos.

'Drugs,' a guard explained, laconic, hostile.

Marlowe had followed the sordid little story up, sought out the manager. Too many syringes and, only last week, a fifteen-year-old overdose, dying in the hospital, thank God, not in his store.

Cruising about, Marlow had inspected carts; white bread, white sugar, baked beans, frozen chips, lurid toys, half price; the stuff of poverty. Queues for cigarettes, special offer, none for the fruit or vegetables. At the checkout, from behind a swollen woman, he watched the family at the next till. Shaven-headed, gaunt in his flapping overcoat, the father was West Indian. Thin and fair, the mother, ringless, looked no more than twenty, and seven months pregnant. A baby sat in their cart; another, in summer clothes and barefoot, slept in a shiny new pushchair. There were two more children, all under five. They lived on the usual staples. Marlowe, running out of time and devious, waylaid them. The ensuing sob-story was well worth his trouble. The father, twenty-three, had lost his job as a hospital cleaner two years ago, when the work was contracted out. Two children were asthmatic. With any luck, the tear-jerker would net them decent clothes for the kids, or even the offer of a job.

Marlowe detested poverty, must grub it out, root and branch. There was, for instance, no need these days to breed child after child. The tattered Africans shouldn't live on the streets of Rome, nor should the Filipinos scavenge for scraps of the Scandinavian good life. The Marseilles Arabs accepted abuse as the price of a living wage. Jerzy's story gave him some comfort. From nothing, from dereliction and chaos, Jerzy was creating order, paying his workers well enough, making the future for Feliks and Piotr.

Bel detested poverty quite as much, but she lacked pity. Bel favoured mass sterilisation programmes for the world's poor, dared to say so on screen and on air. She hadn't yet, or not in public, suggested sterilisation for British claimants, but she certainly approved. Bel was attracting more attention than ever of late. She prescribed greater control over the poor, would tackle the problem at source; supply housing, heating and food vouchers, and they could fritter the rest away on fags, beer and tacky fashion for their kids. She would add, sententiously, 'You never see *them* in Oxfam, do you?'

Bel was a self-righteous, arrogant, borderline fascist bitch. Three weeks before giving birth, she'd enjoyed herself immensely, hired by the BBC as maverick right-winger and token woman on *Any Questions*. Now, in a ward full of joyous mothers, she sat aloof, correcting proofs, grudgingly fed the baby if it wailed. Why the hell did he live with such a woman? He knew various answers, in no particular order of importance. Bel was very beautiful, she was Luke's mother, and they were used to this arrangement. The baby was his. As Bel assured him it couldn't be her current lover's: Sam had been to the vet, years ago.

Last night, ferrying in Luke, grapes, sheep's-milk yogurt with honey, smoked salmon paté, unsalted Welsh butter and sourdough bread baked in a stone oven, he'd considered names all the way. Parking, he'd settled on Felicity or, if Bel objected too strongly, Elizabeth. Filching grapes, he had said. 'About names . . .'

Bel had reached for her handbag and handed him the mean little form with no details, the kind issued free by the registrar. 'Done. They came this morning.'

The baby had been registered as Caroline Sophia. He felt cheated. It wasn't that he objected, per se, to Caroline. Sophia was another matter, but merely second; no one need know. He'd loved Felicity, wanted her for his daughter. Bel had no right . . .

She said, superb, '*I* did all the donkey work. You chose Luke and *Benedict*, for godsake. Caroline is a perfectly respectable name. I suppose you wanted something ridiculous.

Marlowe, discouraged said nothing, agreed to Caroline. The only associations he could think of were unfortunate: Lady Caroline Lamb and the appalling Caroline of Brunswick. By way of compensation, he held her all visiting time, even changing her dirty nappy. The sweet milky smell

26

of it disturbed memories of Luke, newborn, frail and alarming. He knew better now; wanted to take her, run with her for ever, over the hills and far away.

Bel said Caroline had her heel-prick that morning, for phenylketonuria. The idea of his daughter in pain hurt.

From eleven till two he worked, completing the Brixton feature, then faxed it in. The sun shone, hard and brilliant, gesticulating at smeared windows, cobwebbed corners. In the bathroom, there were traces of green slime, and a large hairy spider in the bath. He rescued the spider, tackled the windows at speed, slopped bleach on the slime, watered cyclamens, cleaned the bath and shower. Ten minutes with the Hoover, Luke's sci-fi comics chucked in the magazine rack, and the house was back to Bel's standard.

That night, Luke was quieter than ever. He'd eaten almost nothing, sat still and pale through visiting time. Marlowe dreaded a chuck-up in the night – the shivering, vomiting child; his own nausea, clearing up. He didn't offer more food, and allowed Luke to stay up, watching anything, all the way to *Newsnight*. All evening, people died, en masse, alone, in fact or fiction.

Luke, extraordinarily, reached for his father's hand. He said, 'In religious and social studies, we talked about marriage. Will you and Bel ever marry, do you think?'

Marlowe shook his head. 'No. Bel certainly wouldn't want to. What's brought this on? Someone at school?'

Luke said, 'Likely, isn't it? You've been together longer than lots of married people.'

'There you are, then. A meaningless piece of paper, as Bel always says.'

Luke said, shrewdly, 'But what about you? I know she sleeps with other people. I've known for ages, so you needn't pretend. I heard you talking about whether the baby's yours. Anyway, I don't care whose she is. She's beautiful, and she's my sister. Actually, I think she looks like you. Sam's a troll.'

Marlowe could think of nothing at all to say.

Luke continued, entirely reckless now, 'I think, maybe, you shouldn't stay together. I wouldn't stay with a girl who cheated on me.'

Marlowe tried to find words, reminded himself that Luke

wasn't quite thirteen, he said gently, 'Caroline is mine. And I wanted her.'

Luke persisted. 'And Bel?'

Marlowe held his son close, too thin, too frail. He said, uneasily, 'I don't know, Luke. It's for her to decide. It always has been. Most relationships work like that, you'll find.'

Luke said, unexpectedly, 'Last week, we talked about prayer. Some people in my class pray. Could I, do you think? In case I die?'

Marlowe touched his son's cool forehead. No cause for alarm. When Luke was small, he'd lived in fear of meningitis or leukaemia destroying his child. He feared being miles or days away from home, and hearing of Luke's death. It happened, and people lived with such grief.

'If you like. In October, when I was a kid, we had to say the rosary every night. We all had our own rosaries.'

Luke said, puzzled, 'What's a rosary? Anyway, I'd feel a bit of a prat, praying. Wouldn't you?'

Marlowe agreed, and diverted the conversation to easier ground. Religious and social studies was the bane of his life. Luke confronted eternal truths every Tuesday, for forty minutes. Next week, it would be euthanasia, and the week after, eugenics. Marlowe, apostate, watched as his son, as part of his homework, wrote out the Lord's Prayer, *ancien regime*, and proceeded to write his own commentary. Luke's school was wholly secular, chosen for academic excellence. He'd been baptised, to pacify grandparents, but his Marlowe grandfather knew religion was off limits. Besides, he hadn't seen Luke since May; he lived two hundred miles away.

Luke said, 'It's the only one I know. Mrs Allen taught me, and *God bless everyone*. I used to say it in bed, after you'd gone. Not any more, of course. I like the words though. *For thine is the Kingdom, the power and the glory. . . .*'

'Mrs Allen?'

'The childminder. The one who gave me that badge on my birthday, when I was six.'

Marlowe remembered it well, hearts and flowers, and in wobbling capitals, MY CHILDMINDER LOVES ME Evidently, they'd got off lightly. It might have been Jesus. Perhaps the desire to worship was innate? And God was still

28

invoked. Unthinkable grief was explained as His will, like the stillbirth in the next bed to Bel. The very worst mayhem was His doing too, floods, cyclones, earthquakes, Acts of God all. God, presumably, allowed terrorism, war, and Aids. Luke looked better now, faint colour in his cheeks. Perhaps he wouldn't throw up after all. Marlow touched the boy's hand, 'How about bed, old man? I'm shattered.'

The boy shook his head, said, very low, 'Not yet. I couldn't sleep last night. Will our baby die? Sunil had a baby sister in July, but she's dead now. She was dead in her pram, last week.'

Marlowe wished Luke could be small again. Little children were easy, loved totally. Their trust was terrible. Luke, almost thirteen, wanted the truth. He said, taking the boy's hand, to make it easier. 'Some babies do die. Nobody knows why. We'll take great care of her.'

Luke nodded. 'I'll watch her, all the time. I could stay off school, if you like. Could I stay off tomorrow? I'll go to bed now. Could I borrow your *Lord of the Rings*? We're doing the sixties in English.'

Relieved, Marlowe got up, searched for Tolkien and left Luke in the safe Shire country. Downstairs again, he fell asleep, alone. When he woke, it was morning, the day he could bring his daughter home.

Chapter Three

After the health visitor had left, Bel mixed Caroline's next feed, undiscovered in her lie. She liked to preserve some illusions. Let the wretched woman write that Caroline was fully breast-fed. It hadn't been true for a week, but Bel had her own ideas about truth.

The past few days had been noisy, all roaring despair. Marlowe, trying to work at home, plugged his ears with cotton wool, then went to plead for his daughter. Bel, back zipped, sleek and sinister in crushed black velvet, forced the silicone teat between Caroline's soft lips. The baby gagged, choked, vomiting back saliva and formula. Bel had taken good care to wear an apron, swaddle her helpless daughter. Marlowe watched unhappily. It was 30 October. The next morning, Bel intended to be at work, conducting seminars with her chosen few. She had her eye on two or even three potential Firsts. Like anything human, they needed goading. She'd no intention of coming home to breast-feed the little sucking thing half the night. She had work to do, research, marking. Tomorrow, Caroline would start with the child minder, who needed a baby she could bottle-feed tidily anywhere. Lying to the health visitor minimised hassle, useless battles with birth women, who classed her as a contracting uterus, lactating boobs. Bel whinged, these post natal days, about the expense of the lochia, said too often, too freely that the necessary towels should be on prescription, free, like any other hospital dressing. She was still in howling agony from stitches.

Marlowe, who had the reward of his daughter, and no pain,

humbly kept quiet, cooked for Luke and waited for Bel's anger to subside. It would be better once she was back at work, no longer called 'mum' or 'dear' by women in navy blue. He felt guilty because she'd suffered and he hadn't. She'd been sick, swollen, labouring and cut. His second, man-sized guilt was that he'd wanted the accidental baby. Motherhood wasn't her job. She wasn't cut out for it at all. He considered writing, and even drafted an article on this theme, the ultimate sexist crime.

Bel loved Luke well enough, on her own terms. He was intelligent, a son to be proud of. Really able women had children as well as top jobs. At four years old, walking by the river, Luke had stopped by a greenish bronze statue and explained oxidation. Luke recited the alphabet at eighteen months, counted to twenty at two, read simple books at three. At eleven, he'd won a scholarship to the right school. He studied hard, won prizes *and* house colours for sport. He knocked about with likeable kids from homes not unlike his own. Luke read the papers and discussed the day's increasingly depressing news, but liked science fiction and fantasy better. At weekends, he played rugger well, ran better, discovering a talent for cross-country. In bad weather, he took himself off to the museums, returned only at closing time.

Bel approved. Bar the rugger and running, this mirrored her own childhood. She could be a good mother for him, treating him as a younger equal, which was exactly the way she treated her students. She would encourage him to excel, win prizes, *summa cum laude*, but heaven help him if he didn't.

Marlowe, at the keyboard, searched for the cruel truth. The first time, she'd cried in his arms at night, trapped in her swollen body. She ate the barest minimum, read studies of undernourished women in Africa and wartime Holland, who gave birth to normal babies, made that her target. The result pleased her well enough; a healthy baby, and her own slim figure a week after birth. The starved women ran short of milk; so did Bel, but she didn't care, and didn't need to. 'My wife is, for want of a longer word, a lousy mother, won't feed her baby, pays another woman peanuts to change nappies and wipe bottoms.' He looked at what he'd written, imagined it in

31

print, perhaps next week, guessed the reactions, including Bel's. Then he jiggled the mouse, cleared the text, and the words were gone, as if they'd never been. Not that it wasn't true. Bel wasn't ill, not suffering from post-natal depression, or puerperal psychosis. Bright with energy, she'd been working on a report for the Health Education Authority. Bel, newly delivered, had her mind firmly on the underclass, prostitution among the young homeless of both sexes. She'd taken leave to give birth. Now she was raring to go, before the insidious hours and days made a mother of her after all.

Rifling through the box on his desk, he found the right disk, watched as yesterday's work came up on screen. He killed five minutes or so, correcting spellings, tinkering with words, then worked, heedless, until Bel had her arms around him, three hours later.

She kissed him, expertly, on the back of his neck, where the birthmark lay hidden by dark hair. She'd said, somewhere else, long ago, 'No one else knows. . . .'

Marlowe, face down in the flowery meadow, had taken her hands away for kisses, 'I expect my mother does. And other women.'

Bel, laughing, had traced the heart shape again with one cool finger. 'What other women?'

And then, of course, they'd had to make love, for their own different reasons.

Taking her hands now, he reassured himself; it was Bel who'd chosen him, insisted on living together, parallel lives. He said, carefully, 'It's very quiet. What have you done with the baby?'

Bel came to sit on his knee. It was painful still, but she wanted to, as if they were lovers. She had, already, an inkling of the future, but it frightened her. Sam would never trust, never forgive, possessed her as of right. Better to pretend . . .

'Asleep, would you believe? Five hours solid yelling her silly head off. Then she saw sense, slurped the lot down and went off, ten minutes ago. Are you working?'

The screen had gone dark. He brought the text back, let her read it.

'Well?'

'Well what?'

32

Marlowe brought his hands up to her breasts, full, still, from birth, heavy with milk.

'Jerzy and Ewa. Are they the future? Nice little earner, by all accounts. Taking on more staff. The Finns are more than ready to do business, since they lost the Russians. They're nervous. Scandinavia's been in trouble all round. OK, Jerzy and Ewa are the future. Where does that leave us? Given half a chance, the Baltic states will have the Hanseatic League up and running again while the EC falls apart bickering and the Balkans waste the next fifty years killing each other. Jerzy says it's a good time to be Polish, for the first time in five centuries.'

'What happened then?'

Marlowe kissed her, excited by the heavy breasts and straining, soft velvet. 'God knows. The Russians or Lithuanians, I suppose. Or some kind of Germans. When in doubt, invade Poland. It must be very unsettling. Nobody invades us except the Japs, if we grovel enough and offer the right sweeteners. The point is, Jerzy and Ewa are *happy*. The future looks good. God knows why. . . . They've little enough. I suppose it depends where you're starting from. Jerzy wanted to go to Gdansk, and so far, it's no regrets. Whereas . . . He spread his hands, wordlessly, eloquent.

Bel chewed his ear, enjoyed the reaction, quick and passionate. She said, softly, 'Luke won't be home till five. Caroline's asleep. What are we waiting for?'

Marlowe was kissing her, forcing his tongue between her lips. Bel, as she always did, freed herself.

'Not here. And you should be working. Is that finished?'

Marlowe corrected two spellings. 'One reference to check.'

Bel stood in the doorway, out of reach. 'See to it, then. I'll be upstairs.'

Then she was gone. Marlowe, thwarted, searched through his files, found what he needed, a date for Zygmunt August. The Jerzy and Ewa saga was becoming tedious. It had begun as a neat little 'them and us', had run its course. Jerzy was doing nicely. The scrawny, asthmatic kids in a Brixton supermarket were further down the heap than any of Jerzy's workers.

Marlowe printed off his own copy and faxed in the work, horribly aware of his own overpowering boredom. He disliked the narrow little room they called the study, furnished too cheaply, years ago, when Bel was only working part time. The desk was from MFI, fake teak veneer peeling off chipboard, the bookshelves nasty metal struts, supporting more chipboard. Half his library of paperbacks was on self-destruct, strewing pages like confetti when he opened them. The bottom, widest shelf sagged under the weight of files and reports he'd never read again. There was a tatty paper wallet full of his juvenilia. Bel, cheerfully drunk, had read them aloud at their house-warming party, three months before Luke. He should have burned them, but there'd been no fire, only anonymous warmth.

The phone shrilled. Russell, his immediate boss, wanted him to scoot up north to extend the theme of home-grown poverty. One of the local radio stations was running a week-long series, interviewing survivors of the Depression. Russell said, well fed and infuriatingly cheerful.

'Is it or isn't it? No one can tell till it's over. Like the Hundred Years' War. All grist to the mill . . . They've got one priceless old darling, fourteen kids and on the game to keep them. Only, she never did . . .'

'Never did what? . . . Oh, I see. Sorry. It's all these two-a.m. feeds'

Russell laughed again, a rich bearded rumble. 'Devout Methodist. Before, er, delivering the goods, she'd burst into tears and plead the starving kids. Most paid up, tanner to a quid. Best-fed family in Ancoats, and her virtue intact.'

Marlowe said, only slightly amused, 'If you know all that already, why am I going up?'

Russell became serious. 'A three-generation study? Rags to riches and back again. Jarrow revisited.'

'Jarrow's northeast. Manchester's in the west.'

Russell, third-generation Weybridge, said, easily, 'It's all the north, isn't it? Add erudition. Class structure – Pareto and all that . . . Circulation of something or other.'

Marlowe agreed to go. Bel would complain, but Russell's voice had enough edge to convey the subtext; write something good, or else. Marlowe had been tempted to point out that Pareto dealt in elites, not the underclass, but had the sense to resist. Then he remembered Bel, waiting upstairs, but when he reached her, she was asleep, and the baby howling.

He lay in bed, idle in morning darkness, watching Bel dress. Five thirty was a revolting time to get up, fit only for farmers and kids delivering papers. Bel switched on the light, stood on one leg, then the other, easing on seamed tights. Then she sat on the edge of the bed to fasten her bra. It was too tight. She was, incidentally, in some pain, her breasts hard with milk, for weaning Caro so cruelly. Marlowe thought it served her right, watched, unkindly, as she rummaged in her drawers, found a stretch bra, lined it with pads to soak up the sticky milk. Since yesterday, and Russell's call, he was in disgrace for not coming to her. Quite what they would have done, he didn't know. It was too soon for much, with her body so cut about. Bel had written a whinge for *Woman's Hour*: caesareans rated too much ready sympathy, hideous perineal slashes not enough. She, Bel, suggested that a neat seam across the belly might be a darned sight less painful than jagged cuts below. Other women suffered in silence; Bel got the BBC to pay up. Marlowe had read the script. It was funny enough, borderline decent, would do just as well in the *Guardian*. Half-dressed, she looked sexy enough, her waist almost normal, her belly flat, as if she'd never been pregnant. She paused briefly in front of the full-length mirror, inspected herself sideways. Marlowe, supine, thought she looked good, but felt no desire at all. This was disturbing. Bel was a stunningly attractive woman, and chose to live with him, most of the time. He should feel something, surely? An erection, at least? She put on more clothes. She'd never cared for power dressing, aimed to be all woman, in liquid, lovely clothes. The colours of this dress were jewel bright – garnet, amethyst, jade – in frail velvet. No expert in these matters, he thought it belonged rather to the night. Then she added a sweater – cashmere, cyclamen pink – and the dress became a skirt.

She said, complacently, 'Will I do?'

Marlowe rolled over in bed. 'Fabulous.'

Bel came over to kiss him. She switched on the radio, and the alarm squawked. 'You're so quaint. That was thirty years ago.'

'What do people say now?'

She kissed him again, calculatingly lascivious, 'I haven't the faintest idea. It was "wicked" once, but that was an age ago. Invent a word. I must be off.'

Marlowe, naked, sat up in bed, hugging the duvet around his bare chest. In better days, she'd approved of his lean, almost hairless body. Sam was Neanderthal, with jutting eyebrows and chest hair up to his neck. Marlowe felt inferior now, simply for being in bed while a newly delivered woman marched out to work. He said, aggrieved, 'Why the rush? Seven-o'clock classes? Since when –?'

Bel collected papers from her desk, which was in the alcove they'd walled in, made into her study. Everything in Bel's study was crafted by a master joiner, in 1987 hurricane wood. Her shelves fitted the slanting walls, tailored and fine. She fastened her Gladstone bag and came back.

'I can work better there. I see the first kids at nine. They expect a seminar on "Elites in a classless society". The department printer is better than ours. I need to run off some notes for them. If I take the kids in, I'll be rushing in at five to.'

'I see. And what about me? Doesn't it matter if I crawl in late, with sick down my shirt?'

Bel put on her coat, which was black, vaguely Regency, and her hat, which was quite unnecessary. In amber velvet, its wide brim curled back, framing her clever face. He thought there should be a feather, imagined it there, and Bel, smiling, Gainsborough lady.

She said, altogether casual, with no real thought for him, or the children, 'Russell wants you at ten, right? No use going in earlier. Run Luke to school, settle Caroline with the minder. There are wipes if she's sick. Could you pick her up tonight?'

Marlowe lay down, craving sleep and old memories of holding Bel in his arms, years ago. The radio was well past the shipping forecast now. He woke up, suddenly, roused by an accident on the M6, near Knutsford.

'But I'm going to Manchester. I'll be away all week.'

Bel swore, crudely. Academics swore all the time, worse than most journalists dared. Caro would copy, then she'd be sorry.

Bel didn't look sorry at all, bending low before the mirror to apply more brown mascara.

'You might have told me.'

'I did. Several times. You were reading the paper.'

Bel adjusted her hat again, scowled at her own face, stuck out her tongue. 'Scumbag. I didn't hear you. Oh, very well. I'll have to pick them up myself from Mrs Thing.'

'Allen. The child minder is called Mrs Allen. And it's not them, it's just the baby. Luke lets himself in.'

'Of course. I forget how old he is. Mrs Allen makes me nervous.'

'She taught Luke the Our Father once.'

'How very odd. Still, I don't suppose it did any harm. They were always doing Eid and Diwali at primary school. Odder still, because there were about five black kids in the whole school. Take her a few hundred nappies. They came yesterday. And half a dozen tins of SMA, and the sterilizer – it's still in its box – and the bag of clothes. I'll come at five.'

Then she was gone. Marlowe pulled the duvet over his head, tried to pretend, for thirty seconds, that he could sleep, make love, rise at ten, shamble out to an eleven o'clock lecture, twenty years ago. Then, in quick terror, he flung back the duvet, ran naked to the nursery, where Caroline slept in her fairy-tale cot.

She lay, pink as almond blossom, on white linen, sucking one shell-tipped finger. She breathed, lifting the satin and lace cover, and her lips moved, sucking. Bel, illogical or consumed by guilt, had blown three hundred quid on the new cot, another hundred on bedding, a frightening sum on the multi-function buggy. All Luke's things had been given away or sold. Sarah and Paul slept with their sprogs until they were big enough for a real bed. Bel thought the idea revolting, and said, as Marlowe hadn't dared, what about sex? They'd merely laughed. Sarah had bequeathed a bundle of baby clothes, mostly female. Bel had taken one look and passed the lot on to Oxfam. Sarah washed with phosphate-free detergent, pea green. It might remove actual dirt, but Bel had her doubts. Caroline started life with six of the best of everything, in virgin white. Marlowe looked on satin and the three-hundred-quid cot, wishing it was Luke's second-hand wicker basket with the chewed leather handles. His daughter looked unreal, cut out from a catalogue. To use nothing old or borrowed seemed unlucky. Still naked, he thought of the milkman's silver, fetched the two fifty-pence pieces from the Peter Rabbit porringer where he'd put them. Then he crossed her palm, waited for the blessing. Her fingers closed round his, frail as threads of steel.

Luke said, 'Gone native, Dad?'

Marlowe looked for a towel or something, then realised this would be ridiculous. Bel used to walk naked, years ago, before Luke. Since childbirth, she guarded her body better, dressed coyly in the bathroom or in half darkness. At first, he'd thought this idiotic, sharing a bath with his baby son. When Luke was three, asking about pubic hair, they stopped bathing together. Marlowe felt now that his body was ridiculous, animal, without even the decency of fur for a covering.

He lied, 'I heard Caroline crying and there wasn't time to get dressed.'

Luke inspected the baby. 'But she didn't cry. I keep coming in, in case she's dead.'

Shivering, Marlowe wanted to hug his son, kiss the pale cheeks, stroke the shaggy dark hair, but it was too late. He said, 'All right, I confess. I had a cot-death panic and ran straight here.'

Luke tenderly took the baby's hand in his own, kissed the soft cheeks. He said, anxiously, 'I keep her safe. I know about cot death from television and Sunil's sister.'

Marlowe went to find his clothes, appalled by the weight of responsibility. Luke shouldn't know about sudden death, or fear.

He dressed with more care than usual, for Russell, packed for the days ahead. No suit – he wasn't a rep or an MP. He'd long ago settled on a kind of uniform; shirts of black or white, trousers called taupe, camel or stone, meaning beige. Long ago, in Berlin, the day after the Wall came down, he'd bought a black leather jacket, long in the body, single-breasted, *Echtes Leder*. His overcoat was outlandish enough, long cherished; a naval officer's greatcoat, vintage 1943, brass buttons gleaming.

Marlowe fastened his tie, toyed with the idea of designer stubble, knew exactly what Russell would think of that. Why the hell couldn't they come up with something like the pill, cut out the dreary business? Women had periods, but only once a month. He should be so lucky.

Luke sat down on the bed, just missed seeing slight blood-stains on the sheet, could hardly miss the packets of maternity towels and breast pads. He didn't look embarrassed. Luke no longer thought birth terrible, but magical, a holy mystery.

Marlowe, his privacy invaded, said crossly, 'How many times have I told you not sit on the bed? Stop lurking about and get dressed for school.'

Luke lay on the floor, spread-eagled, grinning. He said, cheerfully, 'Keep your hair on. It's a no-uniform day. You wear what you like, and pay fifty pence. Starving Africans, this time. Why are they always starving? Last time, it was new maths books, and tons of parents wouldn't pay up. I *said*, where's Bel?'

'She went out before six, to do some work for her students.'

Luke climbed on the bed again, with Bel's black silk camisole on his head. 'Then who will drive me to school?'

'I will, of course. And Caroline to Mrs Allen. Now scram. Go and make some toast. Just get out of here.'

Luke went. From the doorway, he said, 'Jules's mother had a late baby, but she packed in work to look after it. Didn't go back from maternity leave.'

Marlowe listened for any note of reproach, but there was none. On the other hand, his daughter was yelling, not merely reproachful but in a flaming temper. She must get it from her mother.

Chapter Four

In the safe locked cell, driving north, he could cry in peace, let the tears flow until salt water ran down inside his collar. After the first hour, he tried to stop, but the tears came still. The act of sobbing had become part of him, natural as every breath, forty years, near enough, of unshed tears. His mother said, washing gravel from raw two-year-old knees, 'Big boys don't cry.' She repeated the words, her mantra, when he started school, when his dog was run over, when the class bully broke his glasses and claimed his pocket money with a Chinese burn. She'd nothing better to say when his best friend was killed, cycling down Princes Parkway, twelve and a half, James MacBride, first love. Not her fault, only the cruel code of her own parents. The rule was, no tears, except for the alien, weaker sex. His mother had managed better with Sarah and Frances, but they weren't close, never touched or kissed with easy grace. Only in black and white did they even stand together; the camera's lie. Dad was the loving one, gentle.

Fifty miles south of Manchester, there were no more tears. He pulled into the services, went to the loo and washed his salty face. Salt crusted his lenses. He removed them, cleaned them carefully and put them to soak. Bel, superbly practical, had insisted on a spare pair, the day he washed one down a hotel washbasin in Gdansk. She was right, as usual. He'd been in one hell of a mess, couldn't drive, squinting one-eyed for days. Bel was always right. Leaning over the cracked basin to insert the second lens, Marlowe corrected himself. Bel was right, if you accepted her ruthless code. Today, for instance, absolute priority had been given to her work. Her two-week-old daughter and her son were expendable. Bel had no time to waste, and it would be hard to blame her. She knew exactly where she wanted to be; a chair now, a move to Oxbridge or Paris within five years. The children weren't her fault, or not entirely. He was as much to blame.

Luke had to be left at school early, with the morning version of latchkey kids. The cherished arrived later, with a parent, or from tubes and buses. Cheapskate parents dumped the kids en route to work and had the younger ones picked up by child minders. Luke was used to the women they hired to mother him. Older now, he relished the freedom of his own doorkey. He ate what he liked, watched what he liked – snuff videos, for all they knew. On balance, Luke didn't want Bel there to welcome him with love and questions. For an hour or two, sometimes much longer, the place was his. He could foresee a time when this freedom could be put to even better use.

From Luke's school gate, Marlowe had driven on to the child minder. Caroline, slate-eyed, watched his hands at the wheel, watched the world as he carried her up the Allen steps in her child seat. Obedient, he ferried in bales of nappies, then the tins of milk, the neat bag of new clothes. Luke, if pressed, would say Mrs Allen was nice, give or take the Lord's Prayer. She was on the approved list, and they paid the going rate. The baby was in expert hands.

Walking back to the car, grieving, Marlowe fought hard against the urge to turn back, snatch his baby, run with her, for ever. A hundred miles later, he'd admitted the truth. The grief was for himself, child-free, at a price he'd agreed to pay.

He would leave the motorway, head for the Pennine hills. It was a day of small light, and that all but gone. In the wilderness, he could pay to be a tourist, pay the ferryman for a journey into darkness, far below the world; see things turned to stone, by magic or some other alchemy. He'd been back once, with Bel, when Luke was a year old and Bel no longer loved him.

Dwelling on the past was a mistake. One furtive sob found its way out, and the tears stung. He found the exit out to a real road, to childhood, and the oil-lamp weekend cottage in

Mobberley. In Knutsford, scene of afternoon teas with aunts, he pulled up beside a call box, fed it a pound and rang Sarah's number. Sarah answered just before he gave up.

'Chris? Look, I'm just off on the school run. Any problems?'

He stared at the adverts or, rather, neat blue and white plaques, advertising space. Free enterprise was dead; no more taxi cards, French lessons, masseuses. Trespassers will be prosecuted. The cold of late October crawled through the gap, dank and sullen. He missed the foetid smell of dog ends and stale urine, which was ridiculous. Sarah was still waiting, fretful. He'd wasted sixty pence already.

'Remember when you nearly drowned? In the Roman lake, in Marple?'

She said, in Islington, puzzled, 'No. . . . How could I? I was *one*, wasn't I?'

'Eighteen months.'

'So?'

'Nothing. I'm in Knutsford. Working in Manchester for the week. Sal . . . I want the kids. I had to dump Caroline with her minder this morning. It was bloody.'

Sarah said, remote, in full charge of her own life, 'So it should be.'

Then the pips went. He found fifty pence and rang again, but the phone shrilled in an empty house. Sarah had gone to bring her children home. Now, he should ring Russell's contact in Manchester, drive to Deansgate, get the next day's interviews set up. The light was failing fast, and so was his nerve. He'd lost track entirely of Christopher Marlowe, lifestyle reporter; lived in the unhappy skin of Chris, father of Luke and the daughter he must call Caroline.

Looking out on respectable Cheshire, he saw rain. That seemed to improve matters. It was all right, almost mandatory, to be depressed in Manchester, in the rain. Feeling better, he rang Russell's contact, who was called Mackenzie and spoke fairly posh Mancunian, with Scottish top notes. In London, Russell had minions called McLeod and MacDonald, and a secretary called Elspeth Campbell. Listening to the soft, flat voice, Marlowe wondered if Russell recruited emigré Scots from habit or by accident. As for the

42

accent, he thought it might be caused by the weather. It sounded remarkably like falling rain, soft and flat.

He agreed to be at the office by five, which meant hitting the city in the rush hour, an excuse to be late. Truant, he headed for Alderley Edge, arrived in time for the shrieking exits of schoolgirls. Today, in soft rain and near darkness, he walked too tall, his present height all wrong for old memories. Roald Dahl said adults should get down on their knees, look up at the giants and know fear. He couldn't, of course. For one thing, it would be ridiculous. And his trousers, Marks and Sparks wool and polyester mix, had to last two days at least. He compromised, crouched down low, unobserved, wished leaves on the shrouding trees. But the child had gone, and the taste of ice cream on an afternoon of rainbow sun and spring rain.

Driving on to the indigo city, threaded with light, he came close to more tears. Thinking of the kids was fatal. The memory of Caro's slate eyes hurt. Coming through Styal, thinking of Bel on prison reform, he repeated, 'Caro', then 'Carrie', then 'Cara', then went back to Caro. Not Caroline, then, Bel's choice, but Caro, his beautiful, beloved daughter. He was right in the city now, or sweet suburbia, places where aunts and uncles lived; Heald Green, Hazel Grove, Bramhall. Planes cruised, barely house-high, full of businessmen or holiday people. He could, at a price, head for Ringway and buy a ticket to anywhere. Bel and the children didn't need him. If they did, he'd be with them now. When Luke was a baby, he used to take off for weeks at a time, travelling on assignment.

Coming in against the tide, he made good time into a city of too much yellow light. They'd made the Industrial Revolution into a theme park; pistons and sewers and steam trains, and high cliffs of enterprise by the Ship Canal. He felt better at once. Manchester was his metropolis, not the squalid, gaudy capital. Bel, Battersea-born, was a Londoner to the marrow. She really believed there was nowhere else. Her sort were like that. They knew tube routes to anywhere, without thinking. Parking, in the space Mackenzie had promised would be there, Marlowe faced the truth. The life with Bel was over. Dr Annabel Grey didn't need or want him

43

now. It hadn't been a mistake, though. Taking the lift up to Mackenzie's office, by the John Rylands Library, he took comfort in this. There'd been very good times. Venice, for instance, tacky sublime Venice, at midnight, making love in their fourth-class hotel. And then Luke. They'd been so smug about Luke, so idiotically pleased with themselves. Now they'd have a civilised split, sort out access and maintenance, show how it should be done.

An hour later, shaking hands with Mackenzie, heading for their cars, he knew it wouldn't do. Breaking up was a revolting idea. They would see it through somehow, give the kids the decency of two parents. Bel wasn't often unfaithful of late, except with Sam; she was too busy working her way into the credits. Bel wanted many things, and sex must take its place in the queue. He ached to go home like Mackenzie to a wife and children in Cheshire. The phone would have to do. He used to call Luke from all over Europe, except Poland – you couldn't get a line in those days. Bel had said, last week, why not a mobile phone? He took one if the situation called for it, but detested the things. Tonight, though, he wanted to summon Luke, hear his son, too far away.

There wasn't a phone free the whole length of Deansgate. He backtracked, found one at last right by the museum entrance, and the genuine article, red, with many windows, faintly smelly. Dialling the number, he felt like a boy calling his first love.

Bel answered. She sounded pert, brisk, as if role-playing. It was a game she played with students.

'Having fun?'

Marlow replied curtly, 'I'm here to work.'

He could see her, smiling, too serene. She said, sweetly enough, 'I know. Oral history and state-of-the-art reportage – speciality of the house. Seriously, I'm sure it will be very good. Your stuff is, if you try. I suppose you want to speak to Luke? He's just here.'

Marlowe waited, and waited. Finally, he snapped, yelling down the phone, 'Bloody stupid brat! Have you any idea what this costs?'

Two hundred miles away, Luke said, 'Hi.'

Marlowe, idiotic, repeated, 'Hi.' There was absolutely

44

nothing else to say. He watched the digits do their count-down.

Eventually, with seven pence left, Luke said, 'You should see my leg. Friction burns, all the way up. I skidded on the all-weather track.'

The pips went. He fed in another two pounds, and heard Bel say, 'He forgot to mention the shredded tracksuit. It wasn't even a race, just a warm-up. He slipped on a banana skin, would you believe?'

Caro wailed, the only background sound. Marlowe craved the sweet smell of her downy head, the precious, newborn smell that would be gone in weeks. Her cries rose louder.

Bel said, resentfully, 'That's your bloody daughter yelling. I'll have to feed her. She screamed for three hours this after-noon. Mrs Thing says it might be colic.'

Marlowe said, 'Allen. Her name's Mrs Allen. She isn't a thing. She looks after our daughter. Anyway, I must go, sort somewhere out for tonight. Nothing five-star, Russell's a stickler for expenses.'

The noise became deafening. Evidently Bel had picked the baby up. She yelled, 'So he bloody well should be. Your cir-culation figures are down again. You should've stayed put.'

'Going nowhere.'

He could see her smile, her particular, serene *I know where I'm going* smile. She would agree with him, and still be right.

'Yes, but the remedy lay with you, not in changing horses. You're *good*, but not often enough. Moving changed none of that. Could we have this conversation some other time?'

Marlowe looked out into starling time, a myriad beating wings and singing voices. Rare *Sturnus vulgaris* would be prized like a hill mynah. It had committed the ultimate sin, vulgarity. Like workaday journalists, starlings were two a penny. Watching the cloud of birds swirl and settle on the Refuge Assurance building, Marlowe faced his ordinary self.

Bel said, crisply, to the unseen screaming baby, 'For god-sake, shut up. I'll feed you when it's ready.' To Marlowe, she said, 'I'll have to ring off. She's purple. She'll bust her guts.'

'Where's Luke?'

'How should I know? Homework, or out with Jules.'

There was silence. She'd hung up. He pressed 'Follow-On

Call' and rang his father, but there was no answer. The old boy led a mysterious life, for ever busy. In old age, he'd become devout to the point of naivety, or like a little child. It had happened since widowhood. Marlowe distinctly remembered an acerbic dissenter, late and unwilling at Mass. His mother had been the holy one.

Marlowe stood still for a moment, staring at a brick wall, then noticed that it wasn't brick at all but rose-red sandstone, gently weathered and washed. He remembered, dimly, another city, carved in ebony, washed away. At first, with the conservatism of very small children, he'd cried for the black city. His father had a photograph of the Cathedral, taken in 1918, decently black, mourning a lost generation. Thinking of Dad was a bad move. Since his mother's death, they'd lost their interpreter. She had defined their relationship. Sarah visited with her troupe of children and good husband. Frances, nun and nurse, could do no wrong, especially half a world away. Bel was rude, the few times she came north. There'd been no meeting point, no love lost or gained. She'd said, when Luke was two, 'You go. It's you they want to see, not me.'

It wasn't, he concluded, the lack of marriage vows – his parents weren't that petty. Bel's attitude to her own family was much the same. They exchanged charity cards at Christmas, little else. Bel lived now; the past was no business of hers. She'd no time for the trivia of family life.

Older, sadder, Marlowe fought quite hard against the tears, then gave in, head down on the steering wheel, sobbing quietly. He wanted to go home.

46

Chapter Five

The last day staff had left. Those at work belonged to the shadowy night crew. Russell had been sinister, hinting at trouble as a doctor might, at the suggestion of something nasty. They mean cancer; Russell meant redundancy or, which would be less insulting, the paper folding. Both were entirely possible, but only one would be his fault. Bel was right. He should have stayed put, worked seven days a week, put himself about, shown them what he was made of. He hadn't given it long enough, lured by a fly-by-night, Bel said. It was all right for Russell: he would fall on his feet into something better. If the paper didn't collapse, new buyers might relaunch it with a spring clean. Marlowe knew exactly who sowed the seeds of self-doubt: Bel, serpentine, took pleasure in running him down. Bel, for her own peculiar pleasure, spelled out his worth: zilch. Bel had chosen him for a bright future together, and he had failed to deliver.

A man was approaching, elderly, in a blue coat and many medals, either an extra from *The Prisoner of Zenda* or the doorman. He said, gently enough, 'You all right, sir?'

Marlowe smiled at his dead grandfather. The man repeated his question. Marlow, suddenly professional, said, 'I had an appointment with Mr Mackenzie. I've just left him.'

'And you're done now? There's doors to be locked. Only them as 'as night keys to come in.'

Marlowe, all contrition, switched on the ignition and reversed smartly away from the wall. Heading for the gates, he didn't know which way to signal, couldn't remember if it was two-way traffic outside. Edging out, he saw a Chinese dragon of angry lights and turned away, left, following the man in front. Bel would laugh at such incompetence. The truth was, he hated driving in the dark, loathed the slug-trail creep of traffic. London was better at this, with the tube and taxis. Manchester offered fewer excuses. The real truth was, he hated driving. If Bel did, she'd become an eco-star, sneer as she cycled past. Delete. There'd been a report, last week, advocating that cyclists travel with their own oxygen, like divers. No, Bel, coiffed and regal, would take a taxi to Westminster, Wapping, or wherever else she was wanted. Bel owned no weaknesses, made no mistakes she didn't turn to her own advantage. Even Caroline. Bel was using Caroline right now, proof that motherhood was no barrier to anything.

The man in front was still heading north. When Marlowe, Sal and Frances were young, they drove to the Lakes every holiday. After Sal had been sick, they played pub cricket or logged registration numbers. VN was Scarborough, so the Audi was a long way from home, or second-hand. Marlowe, childlike, followed the man's every move, then discovered, by the monstrous CIS building, that she was a young woman. It was drizzling now, progressing to rain. At the next lights, she switched on her wipers. He did the same. The back one creaked up and stopped halfway. Marlowe, family man, thought Oh, shit; said aloud 'Sugar.' He tried again. This time, the wiper collapsed to the bottom and stayed there; a garage bill. He watched to see if the woman would head east. She stayed right on course, due north, Rochdale and beyond. A minute later, he saw her sidling down to seedy tower blocks. She couldn't live there, not with the Audi's August registration. Boarded windows said only the last no-hopers lived there. Social worker? Hardly, not in that model. Deciding she was a doctor, on call, he drove on.

Now he knew exactly where he was. By the old cemetery gates, he pulled in. The phone box had moved and become a shower cubicle. He had to make the call. Dad would be appalled by the idea of a hotel. He'd get to hear of it. The grapevine had many branches: prison visiting, the Samaritans, the sick, the poor, the widowed. Twenty years retired, his father's new trade was poverty, despair and grief, none being in recession. It was a wonder he'd found time for marriage and children. Twice, the first year alone, he'd grazed death: two coronaries, two anointings. Then he'd accepted the new lease of life, knew time was no longer his own. Marlowe couldn't remember telling his father the baby's name or where she was born. He'd phoned, surely? Not another word, though, all year, bar an hour in May, en route to Scotland. Few of his friends had a father still alive.

His hands began to tremble, sweating slightly, and his throat was hard. All to ring his own father. Twenty rings. Was it wrong to persist? Mother said, of knocking at doors, three times was enough. More was ill-bred. But Dad was old, a dozen years into injury time.

His father repeated the number in a voice entirely unchanged, with no old man's quaver. Marlowe said, feeling foolish, a child again, 'It's me, Chris.'

The old man became brusque, faintly hostile. 'Oh. And how is the baby?'

'Caroline? She's fine. She was this morning.'

'So you've called her Caroline.'

Then silence. Marlowe understood all too well. No card announcing the baby, giving her name. Blame the post? He liked lies, they saved needless aggro. He'd been brought up on the truth, which led to good hidings, early bed and can-celled pocket money. He said, brazen, 'Didn't you get the card?'

His father bridled. Marlowe could see him doing it, blue eyes fierce below bushy white brows.

'No card, for me or anyone else, so don't say it's lost in the post. I saw the paper. Why couldn't you write? Anyway, how is Annabel?'

Marlowe thought of cutting him off, the bullying, pernick-ety old man, for daring to treat him like a child. But he wanted approval and love more than he wanted Russell's bloody job, hacking rubbish about people down on their luck. He said, 'Sorry, Dad. I'd no idea we hadn't sent cards yet. It's been rather odd, since she was born. Bel was busy. She's back at work.'

'I see. And why are you ringing me?'

The voice had softened, only a little, offended still.

'I'm in Manchester for the week. I'm just off to find a hotel.'

His father snapped angrily, 'A hotel, is it? And what's wrong with me? It's not far. People drive miles. You'll come here. Better get a move on. The buses don't run after half past seven, not since they privatised.'

Marlowe said no, he was driving.

His father seemed relieved; distrusted public transport, what was left of it. He drove still, ferrying prisoners' wives, the old and the sick. He liked to drive very fast, thought no one else safe on the roads. He said, sharply, not trusting the boy an inch, 'Nasty tonight. Raining cats and dogs. You take care.'

Marlowe detested people who said 'Take care'. Bel always retorted, 'No, I'll walk under a bus.' But he loved his father, and that was the difference. He drove on, down a road once narrow and dark, past a blond, floodlit church with a neon cross on its tower. A flapping banner proclaimed a mission, ersatz Billy Graham. People were huddling in. Their clothes looked young – leggings, tracksuits, trainers. The few head-scarves were babushka rather than Lancashire. The young were checking out religion. Everything else had failed them. Next door to the church, there was a string of run-down shops, whining in capital orange for custom. Once, next to the brass-plated Conservative Club, there'd been Connolly's hardware, smelling of linseed and iron filings. Ransacking memory, he retrieved the wool shop, behind yellow shades in dusty summer, selling fair crew-cut men, brilliantined small boys, girls in cardigans with fancy buttons. And a greengro-cer's, with neat grass cloth below pyramids of oranges, Coxes and best Granny Smiths, potatoes that thundered down mysterious chutes. In the next street, the Co-op fired money up and down, between floors, by bullet train. He liked to revisit the vast, secret memories of childhood.

The next mile was harder, out into the strange northern wastes, only the street names familiar. The old cricket ground had spawned a monstrous supermarket, open till eight every night. No more secret forays to the off-licence for forgotten milk or sugar, and a stick of Highland toffee, going soft, for the way home. He thought, with faint disgust, of unclean

50

bacon slicers, thick with fat from quarters of ham, half-pounds of streaky, the pile of rancid, brown-edged trimmings. Irritated, he saw that the bus stop had been moved, only thirty yards or so, but the view was quite different. He fretted, for the untouchable past, turned right, into another world. Dad kept well clear of the present. Marlowe smiled, curiously happy, because here nothing had changed, except himself. The car bounced over square cobbles, never allowed tarmac. Before Highways got round to them Heritage was born. Dad lived in the 1790s, with Boney and the Corn Laws, looked out on ash and oak and beech as far as his eyes could see.

Heritage infested the park, grubbing out rhododendrons and the town's coat of arms in alyssum, salvias and lobelias, all to plant bits of scrubby woodland. Dad was disgusted; more so, when the tearooms closed. The new shop sold David Bellamy and Jonathon Porritt. Dad wanted a pot of tea for two and buttered tea cake, not a Countryside Trail and postcards of snails and toadstools. He'd written to the *Evening News*, beside himself with anger, when they dug up the bandstand and the granite fountain in memory of Alderman Lubbock.

Parking outside his father's house, Marlowe thought of running away. Bel wasted no time on the past. Away for a week, Bel would find a chat show to let the place know she was there, not slink about, anonymous.

Three knocks on the brass dolphin, and soft footfalls inside. Above, in the fanlight, hung the faded picture of the Sacred Heart. Dad still kept Mother's statues about the house, Our Lady of Lourdes and the nightmarish Sacred Heart. Christ's torn chest and bleeding, burning heart would rate 18+ in a horror video. Dad thought nothing of the kind. His Sacred Heart statue, on the hallstand, had white miniature chrysanthemums this week, and a Christmas cactus, already in bud. He came with arms held wide and kissed his son, not knowing this was now the fashion.

'And no telling me you've eaten. . . .'

Marlowe tried to remember when. The past week, past fortnight was all free space. There was only the baby, Caro,

51

and too many nights. He bent down to remove his shoes. His father wore slippers of soft leather.

'You do right. There's many walk in with, you know, all over their shoes. Filthy trick.'

He offered another pair of slippers, kept to the ways of his country-bred parents, boots off at the door. Bel kicked her shoes off because she liked to go barefoot on their idiotic cream carpets.

Marlowe sat in his mother's chair, by the coal fire, watching flames, while the old man clattered in the kitchen. Presently, he discerned too much perfection. The flames blazed up from the North Sea. There was no sign of pipes.

Old Marlowe caught his son lifting the Indian rug, 'Tea. Do your own sugar. You'll not find the pipes. All round the back. If my mother could have her time again, God rest her ... Breaks your heart thinking of it. Dad down the Labour, our Mam on her hands and knees, and anything to burn. Praying to any saint that'd listen, if only the fire would light. St Jude, by the time it got going.'

'St Jude?'

'Hopeless cases. And St Rita. I'm surprised, you not knowing that.'

'I'd forgotten. But she didn't think it really mattered, did she?'

Marlowe worded this carefully, rehearsing for tomorrow. He wanted to find out if his father still believed in this celestial demarcation – Anthony of Padua for lost property, Blaise for sore throats, Luke for doctors, and would-be saints for any miracle they could get past Vatican quality control.

His father smiled, pellucidly honest. 'Why not? She was a good woman. Loved eight of us and a man down the Labour when he wasn't coughing his guts up with gas. Why not? What will you eat? I'm not shopping till tomorrow, so nothing fancy. None of your Jambalaya or Bhuna Ghost's. I get that kind of thing at Sarah's. Beans on toast, scrambled egg, or the chippy?'

Marlowe laughed. 'Beans on toast would be great. Sarah doesn't approve of anything English. She's always wearing something handcrafted from yak hair. But she never cheats, she toils in her own kitchen instead of nipping into Marks and hiding the boxes.'

He wondered what to say next. Nothing more on Sarah, for one. Frances was off limits, halo booked like a divine gong for long service. Talking to his father was hard work. So much was proscribed, the gulf between them too great.

The older man, aware of constraint said, unnecessarily, 'I'll go and see to those beans.'

Marlowe, alone again, considered his position. In this house he was a child still, his father's son, bound by his father's rules and code of conduct, including the Nicene Creed and latest version of the Catechism. His father, far from incidentally, believed that sex outside marriage was taboo, the years with Bel one long sin of fornication. The children, oddly enough, were absolved. Ordinarily, Marlowe steered well clear of religion, but this was difficult in a house patrolled by the Sacred Heart and Our Lady of Lourdes. Images of his own unbelief hung in every room, even, defying carbon dating, a framed picture of the face of the Turin Shroud. Prodigal son, still unrepentant, he must make the best of it. At least, he mustn't hurt the old man. There was too much pain already.

Nothing in this room had changed since his mother's death. She sat, good Catholic mother, on the bench outside church, cradling Frances, the other arm around Sarah. In white silk shorts and white socks, his seven-year-old self stared into space, first communicant. For one full of grace, the child looked miserable as sin. There were three other photographs on the piano: one of his parents' wedding, one of Sarah's, and Frances on the day of her final vows. Seven. . . What had it felt like? He longed to be a child again, let the adults make decisions. That was their trade. Then his father was back with a tray, set with an Irish linen cloth and willow-pattern plates. The thin toast was cut in four triangles and the beans arranged neatly, half a large tin. In a Willow-pattern bowl, there was an EC-size-II Cox's apple and a slightly withered satsuma. The toast was spread with butter. In this house, margarine spelt poverty, not health.

The old man brought out his rosary, its carved wooden roses worn almost smooth. He sat there, praying, unselfconscious. It was October still, month of the Holy Rosary. This was his time for prayer, and nothing must change.

Marlowe, embarrassed, began his silent meal. At home, if they weren't working, the TV would be on. Bel liked being in the know. They called her for chat shows because she was news, called her back because sparks flew, sexual and political. Here, Bel would have had one role and one only, illicit mother of his children.

His father prayed on, his pale lips silently moving, until long after Marlowe had finished eating. Then he said. 'Now tell me about my new granddaughter. Any pictures?'

Marlowe said nothing, didn't trust himself, stymied by one image, Bel, walking away from him to give birth. His father touched his hand.

'You can tell me. Grown man, but you're still my son. What's wrong?'

Marlowe let his father's hand rest exactly where it was, said, 'Bel didn't want the baby.'

'And?'

He forgot, then, that he was speaking to a man of eighty-two. His father listened, Samaritan, and did not judge.

'First, she wanted to get rid of it. Then she wouldn't have me with her for the birth. Your generation didn't. Ours does, and she cut me out. She wouldn't feed the baby after the first week, and went back to work today. Caroline's hardly two weeks old.'

'And where's the baby now?'

Marlowe looked away, blinked fast, to be rid of tears. 'I'm sorry. At home, I suppose. Bel was picking her up after five. The child minder's very good. We had her for Luke, years ago. Bel's going for a big promotion.'

The old man looked at him. Marlow thought his expression distinctly odd. He said, crisply, 'And you? The baby didn't stop you coming up here, did it? She, I should say.'

Marlowe said, stiffly, 'That's different. Bel's just had the baby. She should think of Caro.'

'Is that so?'

His father stacked the tray neatly and carried it out to the kitchen. He returned with another, smaller tray: two cups, milk jug, sugar, a small plate bearing four biscuits. Marlowe, in limbo, thought again of his daughter. He could hold that small skull in the palm of his hand, crush the unfinished bones, hold all the woman who would be Caroline Marlowe in one hand. His father's response was bizarre. Defending Bel? Mother didn't nurse again till Frances was eight.

The old boy fingered his rosary again. Marlowe took strange pleasure in his father's religion, the statues, crucifixes, rosaries, and beyond these toys, the quintessential faith in a Creator. But his father had changed the script, saying, like one of Bel's friends, 'And what about you?'

Marlowe heard the whistling kettle boil.

Old Marlow said, 'I'll make that tea.'

As if anyone else could. The rule was adamantine: no one else in the kitchen, ever. In two minutes, he returned, the teapot under its hand-knitted cosy. Silent, pursing pale lips, he poured two cups. Marlowe, used to making his own, wanted to protest, not so much milk, and the milk afterwards, but that would be *faddy*, a crime verging on blasphemy. He said nothing, accepted tea sickly with milk, already tepid.

His father said, kindly enough, in broadest Lancashire, 'Well, what's to do?'

Only the old spoke like that now, his father, and all that dying breed. Gran said, *'What's to do?'*, if you came home pale and silent. Bel would laugh, her lovely, liquid sexy laugh, demand a translation. Old Marlowe stirred one spoon of sugar in his tea, waited. His son said, bleakly,

'I told you. She didn't want the baby, and doesn't now.' He added, 'Bel needs this promotion. She can't mark time, It's up or out.'

'And the children?'

Marlowe finished his tea. He longed to drain another cup, hot and strong, but, guest in his father's house, must wait until more was offered. He said, 'They're in good hands. Bel doesn't relate well to small babies.'

Old Marlowe stood up to switch on the TV. There was loud knocking at the door, muffled giggles. He said, 'Trick or treat. I'll not go. Little devils! You go. Give 'em a turn.' He settled down in his own armchair, before the TV set, and picked up last week's *Independent* colour supplement.

Marlowe opened the door. The path was full of boys. The

55

youngest child was about four, the eldest nine or ten, all tough, unloved and unlovely.

'Trick or treat, mister.'

Marlowe grinned. 'Trick. You were expecting an old man, weren't you?'

The eldest boy nodded. His skull bristled, and a thin plait trailed down his neck, rat brown. 'Yeah. They pay up best.'

'Because they're scared?'

The child nodded again. His companions looked frightened.

Marlowe said, carefully neutral, 'How many old men tonight? Or old ladies?'

The boy said nothing. Marlowe prompted him.

'Six? Ten? More?'

Silence, still, though the four-year-old boy shuffled, uncomfortable. Presently, a wet patch appeared down the front of his jeans.

Marlowe said, boldly, 'I'll do a deal. How many houses, what you've taken, and what you do if they don't pay up. Or I call the police.'

The four-year-old began to cry, very quietly. Marlowe thought of Luke at that age, knelt down, would have taken the small boy in his arms, but for what they'd think: raving poofter. He said, 'It doesn't matter. Accident. Don't worry.'

Rat-plait began to talk. Marlowe made notes. Eager, as if clamouring for a teacher's attention, the others joined in. The three middle-sized ones were West Indian, looked like brothers.

'Banger through the letter box.'

'Gate off its hinges, chuck it over the park wall.'

'Cut their washing lines. Ages, that, if it's one of they spiderwebs.'

'Dog shit, if it's Pakis. Not us, but t' big lads.'

Rat-plait added, succinctly, 'But anyway, they pay up.'

Unasked, he opened their box. Marlowe saw a five-pound note, pound coins, heaped silver, a few coppers, a franc, pesetas. There must be over thirty pounds. He said, casually, 'And what happens to the money?'

Rat-plait grinned, his teeth still chaotic, too big and too many for his thin face. 'Fireworks and prezzies. I'm getting me mum posh scent from the market. It's coming up to Christmas. Are you a cop?'

Lie? Marlowe decided against. 'No. I'm a reporter.'

'But you'll tell the cops?'

'Not if you stop now.'

It was raining again. The four-year-old in his soggy pants began to cry freely. The older kids wore denim jackets or the top halves of ageing shell suits. Marlowe offered them a lift home, but Rat-plait shook his head.

'Not in anyone's car, mister. Promised me mum. You might be a poofter.' So the rieving was sanctioned, parental warnings given. Next month, or sooner, it would be carols. Marlowe suggested they go home now and fetched his coat and camera from the car. While they were still in sight, he stalked, took aim, one band of desperadoes, three shots, until the film was finished. Then he went back to the car, unpacked his laptop, and came softly in, aware of quiet. His father had fallen asleep by the fireside. Gently, Marlowe retrieved the supplement and cushioned the old man's head with a Thai embroidered cushion. Then, while the moment lasted, he recorded the urchin raiders. . . . dog-shit, if it's Pakis. The four-year-old should be bathed and warm in his bed, milk teeth brushed with strawberry toothpaste, hearing a bedtime story – *Thomas the Tank Engine* or Roald Dahl. So often, in Luke's lost childhood, he'd not been there.

He worked steadily until after ten, fitted the lost boys to their habitat. Phone in? Hardly, in his father's house. The half-hour drive would be easy enough at this time of night. They might well use the picture, too, seven little rievers, running into the night. Without the picture, it was a slight enough story, but the pity of it appalled him.

When his father woke, in time for the *News at Ten*, Marlowe said, 'I must go out. Urgent business.'

The old man said, irate as a seaside landlady, 'And will this be every night? I usually go up by half past ten.'

Marlowe said, containing his irritation that it was strictly a one-off. 'The other work's a special project, a week of reports on poverty and unemployment. Trick or treat's fairly new, and it can't wait. Their takings were spectacular, for a bunch of snotty kids.'

57

The old man relaxed and laughed, 'Nothing new under the sun. All hell let loose, Mischief Night, when I was a lad. American, maybe, but how did it get there?' He smiled cunningly, adding, 'You really think I was born yesterday, don't you? I taught lads like them, forty years. I'd best give you a key.'

Marlowe accepted it gravely. His father, paterfamilias had given none of his children the key of the door while they lived under his roof.

For no reason he could easily define, Marlowe enjoyed the week with his father. He missed, though, the nightly seminar with Bel. Nothing escaped her, ever. She graded each day's events for herself and talked into the night. His father insisted on a nightly phone call to Bel and Luke. Luke, embarrassed and monosyllabic, barely replied. He was 'fine', the baby was 'fine'.

On Thursday night, Marlowe drove his father to the cricket-ground supermarket, filled a cart with all the food he could pile in, and paid at the check-out. The old man mustn't be out of pocket. At first, he'd refused any payment.

Marlowe said, not entirely sure of his ground, 'I'll get expenses. They expect me to eat and sleep.'

'And no matter what I do with it?'

'Of course not.'

'Mother Teresa, then. Our Trudi's eldest will see to it. She was enclosed ten years. Now she's with Mother Teresa.' He made out a professional-looking bill in a half-empty book of invoices. 'I used this when I did coaching. Not that you can ever charge the real cost. Six nights, dinner, bed and breakfast. There.'

He fell silent, then said, 'If there's room, if you can take it, there's something for the baby: the cradle. You didn't have it for Luke. There was always some reason. Anyway, there it is.'

Marlowe knelt down beside it, three hundred years old, all they'd salvaged from the forgotten past. He said, humbly, 'Caro will sleep in it. Thank you.'

He drove back on Sunday, soon after seven, almost satisfied

with work well done. Away from Bel's scorn, he was free to lay it on thick, anything but objective. Bel cared intensely about the human condition. It gave her almost physical pain to see the country or a single life badly run, but she distrusted emotion. Bel dealt in statistics, the sane, quantitative approach to human affairs. She was a realist, he supposed, clever and absolutely necessary, if things were to be done well. His father was another, neatly turning money to his own use. As for Mother Teresa . . . Someone, once, in a smart-alec column, dared to criticise Mother Teresa. Nobody would repeat that little gaffe in a hurry. Mother Teresa, said the multitude of replies, was proof of the existence of God.

Just once the first Christmas with Bel, he'd invited a neighbour from two doors down in for a drink. Harry stank of unwashed flesh and dried urine. After he had been taken home, Bel tore the covers from the chair where he'd sat, reeking, through sherry, coffee and a slice of Christmas cake. Bel had snarled, 'Never again! For godsake, leave derelicts to the professionals.' Three months later, the milkman found old Harry dead, and that was that.

Halfway south, Marlowe stopped for breakfast, rang home and asked for Luke.

Bel said, crabbily, 'You always want Luke. He never has anything to say. Waste of time. I don't suppose you want to talk to me. Some of us have work to do.'

Luke said shy, uneasy still with phones and unseen faces, 'I was just off to the common with Jules and Toby. There's a match. When will you come home?'

'Soon. In less than two hours. Is the baby all right?'

Luke sounded doubtful. 'She cries a lot and won't stop. Bel shakes her up and down, and it's no good. She still yells.'

Marlowe felt his blood run cold, goose flesh rising. There was a long word for that, horripilation. He said, quietly, 'Could you give the match a miss, Luke? Just this once? Give Bel a break? I'll be home soon.'

Anger made his hands shake. He felt physically sick, and afraid, both for Bel and the baby. Curiously, his anger wasn't directed at Bel, but inward, because the baby should not be. Her existence was his fault, his responsibility. He wanted to be with her now, hold and keep her safe, but the police were

59

out in force. One more booking, and he'd be disqualified.

Half an hour from home, he rang again. Bel answered. He heard silence all around her.

She said, faintly exasperated, 'Luke's out. He started some fuss about going, but it wasn't just rugger. There was some birthday lunch, for Toby, whoever Toby is.'

'He didn't say, last time we spoke.'

'He hadn't told me. They called for him. And we didn't have a present. I suppose you couldn't pick one up? Something for a boy of thirteen, and a card. You could fetch Luke too, I suppose. Portslade Crescent, off Portslade Road. Fifteen, maybe. There's usually balloons. I must go now.' She cut him off.

Marlowe, uneasy, rang again, heard his own voice; 'Please speak after the tone.' He drove on, fretting about why this should be. There were several possibilities. Bel might simply be working, in her office. She detested interruptions. The baby might be asleep, allowing precious working time. On the other hand, she might have gone out, leaving the baby alone. She could, of course, be fetching the Sunday paper, taking the baby for a walk on the common. This seemed the least likely option. Bel loathed pram-pushing, resented the coo of admiration newborns attract, however puce and bald. She would be working while the baby slept, too busy for the trite business of a kids' party. Sarah kept a calendar, a cluttered palimpsest of messages to herself, multicoloured, deleted, overwritten. There was a kind of logic: one colour per child, red for urgent business. Sarah would have had a present ready, a card and party clothes. Boys dressed up now, but Luke would be in whatever came to hand, ragamuffin.

Ten miles from home, he called Sarah, 'Birthday present for a thirteen-year-old?'

'Boy or girl? It's a depressingly sexist age.'

'Boy. Luke's at a party. I'm fetching him. Bel forgot a present.'

'I bet she forgot the party. It might not be a boy. Some are into sex already. Play safe. A torch. You can't lose. Kids love them, drop them, smash the bulbs, end of torch. Rechargeable and waterproof, preferably multicoloured. Try Halfords. When are you picking him up?'

Marlowe, challenged, found no memory of any time. He said, morosely, 'Bel didn't say. Now she's out, or incommunicado. What the hell am I supposed to do?'

Sarah laughed. 'Go and sort her out. No, maybe not. I wouldn't dare. Turn up at the house with extra crisps. They'll all be starving.'

'They were having lunch.'

'So? Barely takes the edge off their hunger. The parents will love you and ply you with booze. Say Luke left the present behind. They'll believe you, not him. Must go. Hordes of people piled in for lunch. The kitchen looks like . . . Never mind. Good time had by all. I don't know why . . . It simply happened. You know how it is.'

Marlowe lied and let her go. Bel entertained on purpose, wouldn't make work for herself without a clear motive. He longed to be seven or eight years old, locked safe in Sarah's uncritical love. He wanted soft arms round him, and a place for tears. Bel could offer neither. It wasn't her fault. He wanted, badly, to find the baby safe, sleeping or cared for somewhere, but it was only half past two; no time, surely, for a kids' party to end. And he had no present yet.

Half an hour later, equipped with the right torch, gift-wrapped, and a birthday card, forged with Luke's signature, he parked in Portslade Crescent. It wasn't fifteen but nineteen, identified by a bunch of two-foot-high balloons, printed: 'Happy Birthday, Toby'. Sarah was right: collecting parents were plied with booze. The stringy red-haired mother was insistent, and more than slightly drunk herself. She looked young, unfinished, no more than twenty-seven, which wasn't possible. She kissed him lavishly, brandishing a sprig of plastic mistletoe.

'Season's greetings.'

Marlow thought it was approximately Bonfire Night, but didn't try to argue. Detaching himself, he foraged about for a pot-plant for his whisky. On a marble washstand, he found an *Ikada-buki* bonsai, decorated with shreds of tinsel. Maybe the redhead really thought it was Christmas. The marble was gaudy with felt-tips. Someone had drawn rainbows in random colours, not the ordered spectrum. He couldn't feed whisky to the tinselled pine; it might be centuries old. Now she was out of sight, he could merely abandon the glass.

There were distressing sounds coming from the hall lavatory. Presently, she emerged, minus lipstick, paler, but smelling of Dior, not vomit. She clung to him for support, said sadly, 'Luke's father . . . What must you think? Drunk in charge of – God! I'm going to be sick again.'

Marlowe steered her back to the loo, only just in time, and stood there, supporting her, until the last foulness of bile. She washed vigorously, gargled with Listerine, brushed her teeth. Then, with infinite care, she reapplied lipstick, smiled as one tear fell. Her eyes were violet, but he could see the rim of contact lenses and wondered about the real colour. Her mascara had streaked, but she was still entrancing, dressed in a sort of crumpled green velvet.

She said, quite sober now, 'I promised Charlie I wouldn't, not this time. God! Don't you dare write about this. Promise. Only, kids' parties are so bloody. Thirteen's a bloody age, bit too young for sex... It's all *boring*. Even if you take them to McDonald's, or for pizzas first. Then it's the videos, and there's nothing they haven't seen already, and the loot bags, and the theme cake. Would you believe what those balloons cost?'

Marlowe shook his head, bemused. He hadn't eaten since six, and the place was littered with half-eaten toy food, canapés, pickings for greedy adults. But he felt queasy from seeing her vomit. His stomach clenched, then rumbled, loud enough for her to hear. The second time, she giggled, grabbed a tray of garish little things in aspic.

'Bel said you were driving up. You're starving.'

Marlowe, revolted, refused politely, tried distraction. 'No, I was driving *down*. I'd been working in the north all week.'

She smiled sweetly. 'Yes, I know, but Bel would say *up*, wouldn't she? Up to Town. Bel can be so peculiar. She'd forgotten all about the party. Still, she's just had the baby. Sure you won't eat?'

He said no, politely and went to look for Luke. The house was full of braying adults, mostly male, none sober. All despatched to collect their sons, while women wrote papers on the folly of welfare economics? One room was quieter

62

than the rest. Pushing open the door, he found a dozen or so boys, Luke's size. Most lay, crouched or sprawled in front of *Aliens*. Two were playing chess with red and white *Through the Looking-Glass* figures. One of these was his son, locked in a ferocious end game. Kneeling down beside the boys, Marlowe said nothing, but looked pointedly at Luke's bishop. Luke grinned, and the battle was done. The boys shook hands, very formal.

Luke said, 'Dad, this is Toby. It's his birthday.'

Marlowe accepted the cool, formal handshake. He thought of saying, 'I've met your mother', but decided this wasn't strictly true. They must have adopted him, from where, he could only guess; somewhere south of Mexico. Luke was still explaining.

'Toby's a clever clogs. He can speak a language no one's heard of.'

Marlowe said the right words, 'Congratulations' and 'Happy birthday', and pulled Luke to his feet.

'We must go. Find Toby's mother, to thank her.'

In the hall, they found the stringy redhead again, very pale, handing out bags of party loot and wrapped slices of cake. Nearer forty than thirty. He'd been deceived by the slight body, wild red hair. Then he decided it was neither, only that she looked like a hurt child. She made him take a second bag and a second slice of cake.

'For the baby . . .'

Marlowe began to explain that Caroline was newborn, then stopped, thanked her and said goodbye. Outside, in the car, Luke tipped out his trophies: a torch, pencil-thin but powerful, a wallet of felt-tips, a packet of tattoos, a tiny, die-cast Porsche, three fun-size Mars bars. At least ten quid's worth, and how many kids at the party? 'I won some games.'

This proved to be true. Caroline's bag held only one bar of chocolate and a red Ferrari. Luke said, diplomatically, 'It's a good job you brought my present. Thanks.'

'I copied your writing on the card, too.'

Luke smiled. He had a streak of pale mud on one cheek. Marlowe wondered if this predated the party. Luke said, engagingly, 'Was that a white lie? We shouldn't have forgotten. Toby's from darkest Peru, really, like Paddington.'

63

Marlowe nearly asked, Paddington who? Then he remembered, Paddington Bear, of childhood. This comforted him. The chess had been distressing, their end game so horribly clever.

Walking away from the garage, back to Wandsworth Road, he asked, 'Is Caroline all right?'

Luke dropped the Porsche, picked it up with the black and gold paint already chipped. He said, cautiously, 'I don't know how you tell. They cry such a lot.'

Marlowe made the boy stand still and wait before they went in, away from the world. 'She cries a lot? Luke, if she cries, does Bel really shake her?'

Luke hung his head, wordless. Then he said, very low, 'It was only once. I promised not to tell. So you mustn't.'

The next day was normal enough. The first Manchester piece was going out. Russell seemed well pleased, had liked the trick-or-treat rievers. All this week, Marlowe definitely existed, every day, one shock report after another. The truth was, after the first day, he hadn't been shocked at all, only surprised that poverty still smelled the same: stale urine, cooking smells, unwashed clothes and bodies. They spent the poor little they had so badly, couldn't make economies of scale. He'd spied in another supermarket, watching Volvo mothers bulk-buy the special offers. There was an offer for baked beans, practically half-price. One thrifty wife bought sixty cans, and would fill her freezer with 50 per cent extra packs of sweet corn, petits pois, ten soft-grain loaves. twenty pence off. But the great barn of a place was two miles from any estate. Pinch-faced women trailing kids couldn't carry enough to save the bus fare. They shopped on corners, couldn't make ends meet. Bel said he was going soft, preying on easy emotion. They should save, should pool their resources.

He woke from a dream about feeding the baby. Naked, he held her to his bare chest, watched by a horrified Luke.

Bel had worked into the night, and when she staggered into bed only an hour ago, she shook him awake with an order. 'Feed Caroline. It's your turn.'

'Now?'

'When she yells, idiot. No use asking for trouble. With any luck, she'll start sleeping through soon.'

Then she'd fallen asleep, quickly, efficiently, as she did everything.

Fully conscious now, Marlowe heard his daughter yelling with increasing desperation. Stumbling from the bed naked, he grabbed the first thing that came to hand, Bel's scarlet silk kimono. The bottle should only need heating, but Bel had left it out ready, in the warm bedroom. Made up when? Gastroenteritis, one more bottle-baby death. Cradling Caro, he went down to the fridge. There were no more bottles. In the sink, he found three dirty ones, and four more in her day bag. Caroline's screaming took on a new note of desperation, sad as death. Almost, he could have shaken her, but she was helpless, his daughter. Struggling, with Caro on one arm, he washed the dirty bottles and fitted up the steriliser. Then he paced the house, praying that neither Bel nor Luke would wake. Caroline fell silent, opened her eyes, glared, then opened her cavernous mouth for screams of appalling violence.

There were footsteps on the stairs, then padding down the hall. Luke tugged at his arm. 'Sometimes she sucks my finger.'

Marlow tried, and it worked long enough to boil water and mix the sickly sweet powder. Luke watched, sitting on the thirties typist's chair Bel had bought in a junk shop last week. She'd polished it bright already, cleaned the dull blue leather. Bel never waited to get round to things. If she bought paint or paper, they had to be on the wall next day or sooner.

Luke now wrapped his skinny white legs round bright steel, and said, cautiously, 'Excuse me asking, but isn't that red thing Bel's?'

'It is.'

'Oh.'

Marlowe, amused, stirring the nasty cream, watched his son think. He said, 'It came to hand. I don't *like* women's clothes, except on women.'

Luke smiled. The streak of mud was still on his face, despite a bedtime shower. On the other hand, there was a new

65

bottle of Java antiperspirant in the bathroom, another of shower gel, not Marlowe's or Bel's.

Luke said, shrewdly, 'Anyway, that's a man's kimono, so she's the transvestite, not you. But you needn't wear it just for me.'

Marlowe was shivering already, the heating off for the night, except in Caro's room. He said, amused, 'For godsake, it's November. I'm not wearing anything else.'

Luke considered this but made no comment, nor did he ask about Bel. He must have known, all his life, that they slept naked, if they slept together at all. Bel often retreated to the narrow bed in her office. This week, he was in luck, allowed to share her bed, naked. Bel, pregnant, had worn nightdresses to hide what she called the worst of the damage. This week, she was naked again, but let it be known, once and for all, that sex was off limits, for ever.

The bottles were safe now. Caro screamed and fought against the teat, then settled down to the busy sucking her life depended on. Then she fell asleep, exhausted, small round head heavy in the crook of his arm.

Luke, thirteen in five weeks' time, looked down at his sister and touched one shell fingertip. He said, looking up at his father, 'It's weird. She makes that horrible, horrible noise, but I'd do anything for her.'

Marlow put the bottle down, free now to hold Luke close. The love was almost unbearable. If the whole thing with Bel was over, it had been good, judged only by its achievements, his son and daughter.

He washed the bottle, rinsed it clean and added it to the ones in the steriliser. Then he led the way back upstairs. Luke said, formally, 'Good night,' and retired to his own room. Marlowe took Caroline back to her cot, but it was cold. Bel could say what she liked. Caro would sleep with them, warm and safe, where her life began.

He still felt ambivalent about Caroline, but it was her name, inseparable now from herself; his daughter's name. He disliked the Sophia, for no clearly definable reason. Sophia, as it happened, was his late godmother's name, but he hadn't planned to saddle his daughter with it. His child should have been Felicity, or Elizabeth. It wasn't too late to add a name,

66

but the damage was done. Bel had called her daughter Caroline as a mark of indifference or even vengeance. He remembered the words so clearly. She'd said, nine months pregnant, 'Annabel. . . One of those ringleted names, like Caroline or Belinda.'

When he woke, it was the shipping forecast, time for another feed, and his turn again, by default. Bel was up and dressed already, tapping away at the computer, not to be disturbed.

Chapter Six

Russell had the whole series on his desk, tapped the topmost feature – 'On yer bike . . . Cycle of poverty' briskly.

'Spot on, Marlowe. In the Rowntree tradition. No, I don't mean Rowntree at all, though your facts are superb. First-rate research there. May- something . . . Mayhew. Very neat, the way you take their words, then play devil's advocate, then straight back into the defence. Very neat indeed. I thought the till roll was a bit tabloid, but my wife said not at all. Any woman would understand. Why shouldn't the poor devils lash out now and again? Anyway, spot on. The reader response was terrific. One of the best things we've done.'

Marlowe nodded, said nothing at all, yet. Russell didn't like to have his monologues interrupted.

'Those eastern European pieces of yours,' Russell went on, beaming. 'You're right, of course. It's time we began to look east. Not at the Russians, or whatever they call themselves now. We've a very good man in Moscow. Let's face facts, Marlowe. . . . Macropolitics isn't exactly your line, is it? But I'd like the kind of thing we have here, moved east. The languages shouldn't be a problem for you. Anyway, interpreters are three a penny, clamouring for work. Six months' trial? You could go out alone, test the water, and then maybe get the family over later. You know the state of play better than I do. By the way, is your famous Jerzy real?'

Marlowe smiled at Russell's pretended innocence. 'Jerzy's real alright. His son used to wear Luke's hand-me-downs. I don't know about the languages; I could get by in Czech, twenty years ago. Polish too, enough to survive. Jerzy and I were at school together in Manchester.

Russell crushed his hand, signalling the end of the interview.

Marlowe thought of ringing Bel to seek her approval. She'd object, of course, make all kinds of difficulties, plead her own career, but there was a way round. She hadn't taken proper maternity leave yet. Six months, by rights; longer, with her record, surely? Some kid would be glad of a temporary post, a leg up the ladder. As for childcare, they could hire live-in help over there. Or Bel and the kids could stay put. Or . . . His brain scrambled, confused as ever by the need to include the children. Luke and Caro, son and daughter, born of Bel's lovely, long, sexy body, and here to stay. He loved them too. He grudged every minute away from his daughter; saw, greedily, the changes in Caroline after only six days away. Russell still thought of wives and children as somewhere out there, self-contained planets of their man. Russell asked, not about Bel's work, or her maverick politics, but about 'your wife and the baby'. Russell would always say 'wife'. It was easier by far to have a real wife, like Russell's, two pairs of carefully planned children, fourteen, twelve, five and three. Russell's wife would never take paid work again, volunteer woman, pillar of a society built on unpaid woman time. He left Russell's office, lightfoot, excited as a small child promised a treat. Much longer, marking time, and there might be no future.

Bel would see sense, surely? Chasing reality, he went straight back to Russell, caught up with him leaving the office. Marlowe said, abruptly,

'We didn't agree to a start date, did we?' As an afterthought, he added, 'Sir', and Russell beamed. Russell liked such little courtesies. Warsaw wasn't far enough east. He'd like, would positively relish a low bow, only his due.

But he said, amiably enough, 'Nothing too rigid. We'll work out ways and means.'

After they called her in for congratulations, Bel refused offers of drinks but agreed, provisionally, to dinner some time next week, to celebrate her appointment. Today she

69

must go early, as planned. She'd made no Plan B, not daring to hope the chair would be hers, or contemplate failure. They had so many good candidates, including three Oxbridge rising stars on the short-list... She'd met them. They were good, but, this time, not quite good enough. The future looked very, very bright.

Today she was stuck with the old order, her turn to collect the baby, drive home. They could hire a live-in nanny when they bought a bigger place. Easier all round. Seniority carried perks; Levy admitted to quite a bit on the side, from consultancy work. She had other plans too. There was nothing to hold her now, only the kids, eating her precious time. So damned unfair. Chris still thought he could swan off, regardless, like the Manchester job when Caroline was barely a fortnight old, for godsake.

Pulling up outside the Allens' house, Bel adjusted her mind, her face and her whole self, not Dr Grey, but Bel, working mother, come for her baby and to smile for Mrs Allen. She liked acting these little scenes; knew what to say. Mrs Allen, late thirty-something, had one child of her own, a boy, Luke's age, pale and skinny. Her silent, covert disapproval of working mothers was never admitted. She must like their money well enough; extra, if they both worked late. And she liked their gratitude, the soft, unspoken admission that they couldn't manage ambition without her.

Luke was home already, eating crisps and reading a horror comic. Without greeting his mother, he wandered off to fetch his rucksack, produced a crumpled letter from school about a parents' evening. He said,

'Don't come. Load of rubbish. All the parents moan. The teachers hate it too, I heard them bitching. And there's cross-country trials next week. I need new spikes. I'm sorry, but my feet grew.'

Bel looked at her son, so nearly a man, the voice uncertain, shoulders broader, hips achingly narrow. He would have a very nice body, like his father's. She liked people to be beautiful. The baby wasn't, yet, uglier, in fact, now her face had filled out like a bullfrog. Luke was clever and beautiful. He smiled for her, and drew out a crumpled painting.

70

'Here. We had to paint mothers. It's pretty awful, really.'

Bel looked. The proportions were correct, the flowing movement lyrical. It was seriously flawed, the paint uneven and streaky. But this painting of Luke's moved and danced, a joyous, female creature in rainbow colour.

'It's you, in a garden of flowers. Like the *Primavera*.'

Bel stuck it to the pinboard with a drawing pin culled from a school begging letter, remembered, briefly, her gauzy dress and eager lovemaking in the unweeded garden of a Cambridge flat. There'd been no garden since, not so much as a window box.

Luke had escaped to his room. For the past year or so, he'd avoided being alone with her, since the day he'd found Sam there. She was relieved, didn't find it easy talking to him. He was an odd child with strange, half-formed theories of life and love. She didn't like him much now, probably not someone she'd choose to know. It was an appalling admission.

Caro, fed by the minder, slept in her Karrytot car seat: good. Bel wanted to get on with some work, marking essays, second-years on population projection. There was a small, irritating difficulty over the word 'billion', which, she'd learned as a child, meant a million times a million. The Americans had devalued it to a mere thousand million. Either way, the concept of global population stabilising at around 10 billion by the middle of the twenty-first century was fairly impossible to grasp. In retrospect, she wouldn't have had Luke, and the relationship with Chris could have petered out long ago. She cut out these thoughts and set to work.

Luke said, plaintive, calling from his room, 'I'm starving.'

Bel would have snapped at him, told him to wait till supper. Then she noticed the time; twenty past seven. The baby was crying, and Chris hadn't come home. Resigned, she asked what he'd like.

Schooled in her limitations, he said, A baked potato, or even just some toast. I don't really care. I got some biscuits after school, but that was hours ago. I can get supper myself, if you like. I'll cook yours too.'

Bel discovered she was hungry enough. There were jacket potatoes, ready scrubbed, and cheese, or something. She left that to Luke, and dealt with the baby, who had begun her evening screaming. Caroline screamed more or less constantly after seven, fed or hungry, wet or dry. Chris fussed over her, paced the floor, pushed her to the Common. It made no difference whatsoever. Screaming was what Caroline did, three, four, five hours at a time. Better leave her to it: go upstairs and get on with some work. Nevertheless, Bel fed the baby carefully and changed her. With Caroline, she was entirely sure of her feelings: absolute indifference, bordering on infanticide when the screaming began. Once, she'd begun to shake the wretched little thing. Luke had seen her, begged her to stop, and taken Caroline to his own room. The distinction between infanticide and other degrees of murder seemed fair enough. She didn't dislike the baby, only, she wanted as little as possible to do with her. Chris would have to see reason on the nanny question. He'd have to.

Chapter Seven

Marlowe stood too close to the platform edge, felt the familiar insane impulse to throw himself under the next train. This was odd, because he'd never been suicidal. The idea of imminent death appalled, so much unfinished business. There was Luke and Caro, and Bel, angry and tearful, turning away, refusing to make love. Last night he thought it would be all right. After weeks of indifference and the baby's screaming, the last thing he'd expected was Bel, warm in his arms, offering her lovely body. And then she'd turned away, saying coolly, 'I'm sorry. My mistake. I don't want to after all, not with you.'

The tears came later, quiet, contained, like so much else. He'd tried to comfort her, but she'd turned away, even her tears private. Bel wanted no love or comfort from him. She'd said, with finality, 'I've accepted the chair, Chris. I won't get a second chance.'

His own, less than certain future she dismissed out of hand as not worth the upheaval, though she'd said, 'People do what they must. Go, if that's what you want to do. Hire someone for Luke and the baby. Or maybe your sister would . . .'

The board flashed up, next train, 1 minute, then came its hurtling presence. Anonymous, he barely needed to move, carried with the flow, crushed and swaying down the line, Elephant and Castle, Oval, Stockwell, one stop and then home. Climbing through moving bodies, up into darkness, he tried to feel any sense of home-coming. Hard light shone on unpainted rails, grimy tiles. Outside there were streets, and houses, only the place where they lived now. In no way was it home. Thirteen years, since they moved in, and no sense of home. . . . Crossing the road, turning left, past the pub, he wondered why. All Luke's childhood, and no sense of love. The house contained them, and that was all. Bel wasted no time on it. Everything was clean and functional. He, or Bel would prepare supper in a neat galley kitchen, looking still like a page from a catalogue.

Crossing the Common, in misty darkness, he wondered why this image was so damning. The playground was shrouded, only shapes of strange creatures, and no laughter. At weekends, on Sunday mornings, his time, there were couples who laughed as they pushed a laughing child to and fro, *see-saw, Margery Daw* . . . Lean men, with the first grey in their hair, and rainbow women, in saris, or random colour, actually enjoying the child they'd made. Bel never caught the chaos of laughing child at the foot of a slide. Last Sunday, Caro had begun howling straight after her morning feed. By ten they were all desperate. Luke, normally forbearing, said, 'For godsake, Dad, can't you do something? I've masses of homework. Take her out, please.'

Bel had escaped upstairs, to work. There'd been nothing for it but the Common, five circuits, until Caro howled herself to sleep. Bel was entirely ruthless. Unless it was her allotted duty, she ignored the baby.

Mist became rain, the lightest, laziest brand, slimy on pavements littered with vomit, chip papers, take-away clams, dog-muck. Turning up his coat collar, Marlowe longed for home, knew he had none.

The house was quite dead. It sat there, unloved in the darkness, unlit, and patently empty. Through the letter box, he could hear the shrilling phone. Instinct made him quick, twisting the key, throwing himself on the phone before whoever it was hung up. He fell, banging his wrist bone hard on the bottom stair.

He heard a woman say, sharply, 'Mr Marlowe?'

He felt sick, the other side of pain, rubbing hard to be free of it. He said, across tears, 'Yes? Sorry, I'm afraid I've just got in.'

Now he could place the voice, sharp with displeasure: Mrs Allen, hired to love Caro. She said, tersely, 'Well, it's after

seven. Getting on for half past. If you'd mentioned . . . If anyone had asked . . .'

'Mrs Allen? Look, I'm so sorry. I had a meeting. I've just
got in this minute. Bel was collecting the baby. I'll be round
for her at once. I'm so very sorry . . .'

He hard a long female sigh: trouble on the wind. Gran
sighed like that for bad news, sudden death, mortal illness.
Mrs Allen became herself, the woman he'd chosen, all love
and concern.'

'No message? She didn't ring you?'

Marlowe checked. Nothing on the pin board. Upstairs,
there might be a message; he couldn't check now.

'No. I can't see anything. Is Caroline all right?'

She was superb now, in control of something else, a drama
far better than lazy neglectful parents.

'They're both fine. Luke came round about half an hour
ago, worried sick. The baby took her bottle beautifully, and
she's asleep. Luke's with Michael, watching a video. Maybe
there's been an accident? Mrs Marlowe was driving, wasn't
she?'

Marlowe nodded, then remembered to say yes. His brain
was in turmoil, shaping words for the truth: Bel had gone. He
said, suddenly calm, 'I'll come round at once.'

Mrs Allen was on his side now, all sympathy. 'Maybe ring
the hospitals?'

Marlowe agreed, but planned nothing of the kind. If Bel
were hurt or dead, he'd hear soon enough. Which said a lot
about his priorities.

Locking up again, he walked out into serious rain, found
his own car alone in the garage. There was no need to trouble hospitals or the police. The garage was where they stored
the big suitcases, and they were gone. He was right: Bel had
gone. It seemed right and logical.

Luke said, peevishly, 'But I was watching *Dr Who*. It had-
n't finished.'

Marlowe turned left into a thread of traffic. He said, ami-
cably enough, 'You can see it again next week.'

'I can't. It's Michael's video. We haven't got it.'

'Well, surely he'll let you watch it again?'

Luke drew two Daleks on the misted window, 'No, he

won't. It was from the library. He wanted *RoboCop II*, but his mum said no. Anyway, I've seen that at Toby's, ages ago. Boring. Why didn't you come before?'

Marlowe turned left again, driving slowly, in no hurry to be home. Caro was still asleep, should be screaming by now. Luke repeated his question, raising his voice. This time, he had to be answered.

'I couldn't, because I was working.'

'Anyway, it was Bel's turn for Caro. Where is she?'

Marlowe hesitated. They were almost home now, the truth there waiting. He said, helplessly, 'She's gone.'

Luke wiped out both Daleks and said nothing at all. When they reached the house, he insisted on going in first, switching on all the lights. He ran up the high, narrow stairs to his own attic room, then into their bedroom, Bel's study, the bathroom, the small, bare parlour. In the hall, he sat on the bottom stair, watching as Marlowe carried in the car seat and Caro's bag. She slept on, oblivious.

'She's taken all the books on her desk, and her laptop. She's gone for good,' Luke said, 'I looked in your room, and all her things have gone. Nearly all, anyway. She's gone away.'

Marlowe sat down beside the boy. He tried to hold the stiff, rejecting body, but Luke would not be held, nor did he cry. Struggling to be free, getting to his feet, he said:

'It's late. I'm starving hungry again. It makes me hungry, waiting. Please turn the fire up, because this house is freezing cold. It's such a cold house. That stupid time switch doesn't work. We're always coming in and it's freezing cold. I hate being cold, all my life. I come in from school and the heat isn't on, every day. You have to put it on manual. Bel kept saying she'd get someone to fix it, but she never did. Now you'll have to.'

Marlowe was alone with his children. Luke slept on the sofa beside him, tear streaks still on his pale face. The tears had come late, wordless, quickly denied, scrubbed away with his hands. Distress, oddly enough, hadn't affected his appetite. He'd eaten a pizza, then a box of micro-chips, a yogurt, a satsuma and an apple. By some miracle, Caro slept all evening without any screaming. She'd woken up once, glared and threatened to cry, but stopped as soon as she was picked up. Now she slept, downy head in the crook of his arm. In dreaming sleep, she smiled and looked like Bel, years ago. Marlowe began to cry until his tears fell on the sleeping baby. She whimpered and moved a little. Tonight, of all nights, he couldn't face the wordless desperation of her cries. Wrapping her in a shawl, he carried her out to the hall phone and rang Sarah.

For a long time, no one answered. Then it was Sarah, guarded and truculent, saying, 'Have you any idea what time it is?'

'No,' Marlowe said blankly.

'Here's news for you then. Half past midnight. Twelve thirty-seven precisely.'

Marlowe said, 'Bel's gone.'

'What do you mean, *gone*? Not dead, I presume. No, silly question. Bel wouldn't die untimely. Far too busy. I assume she's scarpered? What did she take?'

Marlowe moved the baby's head slightly. His arm was aching. He said, as if reading an inventory, 'Clothes, lady's, size ten. Computer and VDU, boxes of disks and her new laptop. Several hundred books, one amethyst and pearl pendant, circa 1820, and one elderly bear.'

'Bear?'

Marlowe smiled, a secret betrayed. 'Oh, yes. One mangy, one-eyed, *Knopf im Ohre* Steiff bear.'

'You amaze me. So even Bel was human?'

Caro woke and stared at her father, inscrutably like Bel. Tomorrow she would be different again, but now he could see only her mother. He said, with left over love, 'Oh, yes, Bel was human. Is, I should say. Wherever she is, I'm sure she's alive and well. She left her rings.'

'Do you want me to come over?'

Marlow wanted her arms and soft breasts, his sister protector, but said stiffly, 'No, of course not. No, I just had to tell you. No one else I could tell.'

'What will you do?'

There was silence. Sarah could imagine her brother alone

in his austere white hallway. She said, 'Chris, you're all right, aren't you? What will you do?'

Marlowe moved the baby to his shoulder, felt the sweet weight of her, skin soft on unshaven skin. He said, bleakly, 'It's more what I won't do. I was going abroad – eastern Europe for six months, maybe longer. Bel got her chair yesterday. She's Professor Annabel Grey, or will be soon.' He was fighting tears, losing words.

She said maternal, no longer his little sister, 'Go to bed. It's almost one. We'll talk later. I'll come round.'

Around two o'clock, the baby woke. Outside, there were night noises, traffic, boy racers in stolen cars, angry words in unknown tongues, passing trains. Caro cried, then stopped to watch as he prepared the bottle. After hunger, she gazed up at him, fixed him with the intent stare of a newborn. Then she smiled, omnipotent, shaped the rest of his life. Tonight she wouldn't sleep in the precious cot. Marlowe made her small female body clean and sweet, then took her to bed.

He wouldn't sleep. Caro, sated, slept in his arms, making her soft newborn sounds, smiling in sleep, turning her downy head. Once, she opened slate eyes, focused on him, then slept again. For the first hour, he lay with the child in silence. Once, Luke called out in his sleep. Marlowe waited, but there was nothing more. Luke could get through the night alone. After ten minutes, though, he couldn't rest, must go and see for himself, climbing the narrow stairs in darkness. Luke lay curled in his bed like a very small child, but his duvet was on the floor. Marlowe covered the boy and left the lamp on. Darkness was Bel's rule, broken for ever.

At three, he switched on the radio for the World Service. Halfway through the news, he drifted into a kind of sleep, but woke minutes later from a bad dream of Bel with a snake head, smiling and far away. Light from outside shone straight into her laughing face. He got out of bed and turned the photo to the wall. Tomorrow, he would remove her from the house. A minute later, he thought better of it. Luke and Caro deserved their mother, not denial. The news was over now, a world he had left. That truth was busy shaping, the longer he held Caro. After the news came a quiz game, repeat of something half heard on Radio 4, while heating supper. They kept a fine repertoire of meals to heat, Chicken Marsala, Chicken Tikka Biryani, Lamb Rogan Josh, and fifty more, all neatly cartoned and timed. Bel said cooking was a waste of time and resources. She owned no gadgets. There was one small sharp knife, an electric whisk, a bread knife, nothing else. Bel was superb, never dealt in half-measures.

After five, he tried to read a Ruth Rendall picked up at some airport. He read it to the end, then considered his future. There might be more time for such small pleasures without the daunting need to succeed every day.

Caro woke at six, as if set by Truby King. She roared, hunger possessing her, small body racked with the pain of her empty belly. Clumsy from lack of sleep, he stumbled downstairs with the baby locked in one arm. She continued to roar as he prepared the bottle, squirting a little on the back of his hand, testing the temperature. Full, she forgave all, smiled and gurgled as she was changed and dressed for the day. Halfway through, Luke woke, hurtling down the stairs to the loo, falling head over heels for the last six stairs. Marlowe ran to him, but the loud yells and curses suggested nothing seriously wrong.

A minute or two later, Luke came to the kitchen in his dark-blue pyjama bottoms. He said, entirely cheerful, 'There's no clean shirts.'

Marlowe sent him back to look again. Luke returned with two crumpled shirts from the ironing basket. He smiled, holding them out.

'Heads you get breakfast, tails I iron these.'

Marlowe spread sunflower margarine on toast, watching, amused, as Luke set up the ironing board, adjusted the dial, filled the reservoir. The toast was cold long before he finished. Accepting a pristine shirt, Marlowe said, 'You're hired. Bel couldn't do better.'

'And you?'

Marlowe laughed. 'I never saw the point. I offered, but Bel said she found it relaxing.'

Luke remembered he'd gone to bed unwashed, took himself off for a shower. He stood, picked chicken, sluiced his thin body clean of the night. Last week, he'd discovered the existence of house mites and searched his bed for them,

79

repelled. Returning in a hand-towel loincloth, he said, 'Is she gone for good?'

Marlowe nodded. 'Afraid so. Sam's gain, our loss. Or vice versa.'

He'd just caught sight of himself in the mirror, cadaverous, stubbled like an old man. He tried to shave without looking too closely in the mirror. Luke watched, neophyte.

'When will I need to shave, do you reckon?'

'Not this year.'

Luke sat at the all-purpose table, still half-naked and goose-fleshed. The heating wasn't on, not due till seven.

Marlowe yelled, 'Get dressed, for God's sake. Off to your room and get dressed.'

'But what in?'

Marlow fastened his tie. He said, exasperated, 'School uniform, of course.'

'But I need clean underwear. Bel puts it out. There isn't any.'

Marlowe snapped, 'Stop being so bloody wet. You can look after yourself, surely?'

Caro began to howl. Marlowe tucked her under one arm and foraged in the clean laundry: one pair of Mickey Mouse boxers, one almost pair of black socks. Luke's school was mercifully traditional, enforcing uniform, even for the sixth form. There were six more shirts – three of his, three of Luke's – all in need of ironing.

Luke made fresh toast and ate it. Then it was almost eight. He said, looking for his maths book, 'Will I go to the same school?'

Marlowe had been next door for the paper. He looked up, puzzled. 'Of course. Five minutes.'

'I was just asking. People leave, when their mum and dad split up.'

At eight, Sarah rang, her questions delicate, determined not to intrude or hurt.

Marlowe said, 'I'm just off to school with Luke. And dropping Caro off.'

'Business as usual?'

Marlowe could see his son, huddled in grey, and his daughter, in milky pinks and blues, strapped into her seat. All around them, the walls were orchid white, a nebulous shade, chosen by Bel to give nothing away. There were no prints, no paintings, only a barometer, in fruitwood, which had belonged to her great grandmother, and the wall clock, another family piece. It had two cylindrical brass weights, and Roman numerals. Luke had learned to tell the time by this clock, and now it must go. Sarah was talking, nothing at all, only words above the din of her own happy home. She said, suddenly abrupt,

'Look, I'd better come round. This afternoon?'

Marlowe looked at his watch. Ten minutes for the school run, another ten, in bad traffic, to settle the baby. What he must say to Russell wouldn't take long, and then so many hours for living. He said, as if cheerful, 'Fine. Any time after lunch.'

Russell was smoking again, evil-smelling cheroots, like the turds of some unpleasant animal. Marlowe let five minutes pass in words about nothing, all his old trade. Outside, the morning was busy, another day to be weighed and found wanting. On the way, he'd given money to every beggar, past caring what Bel or anyone thought. One girl seemed barely twelve. He'd asked, and she claimed to be fourteen. Which meant he was probably right – she could be no older than Luke. The pity of it appalled him: so many precious children out on the streets, sex and money the root of their trouble. Overnight, his own children had become statistics: one-parent family, motherless.

Looking straight into Russell's gooseberry eyes, he said, 'I've come to give in my notice. I'll write, of course.'

Russell drew on the cheroot, eyes narrowed. He'd put on weight in the last few months, and his shirt gaped between the buttons, exposing black hair. At first he made no answer, absorbed in the act of smoking as if it were his occupation. Marlowe tried not to choke on the fumes. At last, Russell said, 'Could you explain?'

Marlowe did. He concluded, 'I don't see an alternative. Bel's leaving the kids with me. Taking the job isn't an option any more.'

'I see.'

Marlowe, sweating and dry-mouthed, listened as Russell argued. Then he said, quietly, 'No. I'm very sorry.'

Russell stood up, extending one fleshy hand. 'Then I'm sorry too. I've always liked your stuff. Tell you what, take the day off. Sleep on it. We'll talk again tomorrow.'

Marlowe had to be out, breathe again, live free. Fighting nausea, he accepted the handshake, turned and left. Out in the street, he found it was only just ten. Sarah wouldn't arrive until after one; so many uncharted hours. He walked aimlessly for an hour or more, milling through crowds. Littered around Oxford Street were desperate men peddling strange objects, unwanted even at three for fifty pence. They'd make a nice seasonal feature, quirky and sympathetic, with just a hint of villainy – where the hell did they get the stuff? He paused, a little too long, by a scrawny youth hawking crude pop-up dolls, red and white.

'Jumpin' Santa ... Jumpin' Santa ... Only a quid ... Jumpin' Santa.'

It was too late. As a street cry, it lacked poetry or wit, but he couldn't bear the look of anguish in the boy's eyes. Handing over a pound, Marlowe accepted the wretched thing and stuffed it in his pocket.

The boy said eagerly, 'How many kids, mister?'

Marlow, feeling ridiculous, couldn't get free. The toys were hideous, hair and beards askew around orange plastic faces. He said, weakly, 'Two.'

'One each? Tell you what, make it two for one fifty.'

Marlowe handed over fifty pence, took the second toy, made his escape, then dropped them in the nearest bin.

He was carried on the tide into Selfridge's by the sheer weight of bodies. Evading a blonde squirting aftershave, he looked for the nearest exit. Failing that, he tried to give the forced visit some purpose. Reading the store's inventory, he focused on one word: 'toys'. Like any father out Christmas shopping, he was carried up the escalator. Coming here was a rational use of spare time. Bel would do the same. He corrected himself, almost smiling: Bel would do nothing of the kind. Bel did Christmas in October, from mail-order catalogues. Passing the whining queue for Father Christmas, he conceded that she had a point. Whinging brats were loathsome creatures. At the grotto exit, all eyes fixed on a screeching ruckus. A waist length blonde, in sequined black velvet had swiped a present from a waif in duffle coat and denim. The blonde one's bare plump arm showed two rows of scarlet teethmarks, wet with saliva. Marlowe, amused, watched as the parents slugged it out. Luke had seen Father Christmas once, at school, and it was Dominic's dad, with jeans and trainers showing. This year, he hadn't even hinted about presents. He didn't fit any market: too young for sex, too old for Father Christmas, Baby Jesus never really an issue. Luke belonged nowhere. In the uncertain time between six and eight, he'd hedged his bets, like any wise child. Passing the display of yapping dogs and crawling baby dolls, Marlowe recalled one chilling conversation, seven years ago. Luke had said, all innocence, 'Paul gets a present from Father Christmas and from his dad and his mum and new dad, because they split up. I only get one, and it's just from Father Christmas, and it's not fair.'

Marlowe cruised about, thinking. Super Nintendo and a few more games would secure Luke's position at school. Everyone was getting Nintendo and/or a bike with eighteen gears. Bel's scorn lurked, but he was running out of time. Craven, he settled for *Duplo* finger toys for the baby, nothing for Luke. This place sold childhood, but Luke was no longer a child. Halfway to the down escalator, he turned back, bought the Nintendo, all on Visa anyway.

With a delicious sense of sin, he then queued to buy a yapping, begging, battery-driven dog. Sarah's kids would love it. Stuff Bel!

His sister was sitting on the front wall, skinny legs dangling into green ankle boots. Today, her Pre-Raphaelite curls were tightly plaited and skewered to her head with painted chopsticks. She wore a fuchsia miniskirt over black leggings, and a sweater vibrant with flowers, covering all but an inch of the skirt. She was eating chips and greeted him by offering one.

As he reached to accept, she grabbed him by the collar, kissed with salt and vinegar, and said, accusingly, 'You're late. I can't stay long. We're flat out with Christmas orders.'

Marlowe helped himself to more, suddenly ravenous,

aware of having had no food last night, and a black-coffee breakfast.

'Don't mind me' said Sarah sarcastically. Then she took another look at him. She sprang down from the wall, thrusting the parcel into his hands. 'Keep these. I'll fetch more.'

Five minutes later, she was back, eating as she walked, his ally, for ever. She said, accusingly, 'Well, where's the baby?'

Marlowe had his mouth full. Swallowing too fast, he all but choked. 'With the minder, of course. I'll pick her up after school.'

Sarah folded her chips up with care. 'Actually, I've had enough. You could microwave these later for Luke, or eat them yourself. Well, are you going to let me in? Tell me the worst?'

In Bel's immaculate hall, she dropped her scarf on the floor and let her Body Shop canvas bags fall over, spilling satsumas, grapes and chestnuts.

Marlowe saw at once that the barometer and the clock had gone. He said, coldly, 'She's been back.'

The shadows were there to see, no need for more words. Sarah reached up, kissed him again and held him close. She said, crudely, 'Shit to Bel. She always was out for herself.'

Marlowe put his own parcels down. Sitting on the bottom stair, he extracted the dog from its box and held it up. 'It's for the kids, an un-Christmas present,' he said awkwardly.

Sarah looked at it but said nothing at all. Marlowe switched the thing on. Its repertoire took it the length of the hall, stopped only by the doormat. Sarah laughed, wickedly approving.

'They'll love it. Well, what next?'

He told her.

For a moment or two, she was silent. At last, she said, hands folded as if in prayer, 'Well . . . There wasn't any choice, was there? You couldn't drag the kids out to Gdansk or Prague.'

'There are kids in Gdansk.'

She switched the dog on again. 'Yes, but not yours. They deserve one parent. What will you do?'

Marlowe saw bleakness all around, shadows left by Bel. he said guardedly, 'Not much, yet. Work out my notice. Russell said sleep on it, but I don't need to. I don't know. Pick up what I can freelance. I might get by, with a few contacts.'

Sarah pulled a face, 'Rats to that. Fair's fair. She scarpered. She left you holding the baby. Sue her for maintenance for you and the kids.'

Marlowe stared at her. 'I couldn't.'

Sarah, unasked, prised the Sellotape off the larger parcel, 'Father Christmas *will* be popular. At a price. Christmas costs. You've the tree still to get, and stocking presents. And food, and clothes, and the minder to pay. Or will you cancel her? Anyway, first things first. You haul Bel right back and sort out the loot. Make her pay.'

'Oh, no.'

'Dumbo. She's screwed around with whoever all these years. I never could make out why you stayed together. You can't even write decently when she's around. No wonder Russell wanted you out east. When you're away from Bel, it shows. You're well shot of her. I might as well warn you we won't be here to pick up the pieces. Paul's sick of propping up what's left of the NHS in London. We're moving.'

'America?'

Sarah snorted. 'What do you take me for? In the US of A, they think death's optional. No, Zambia, for a year, provisionally. He'd like to see a few more kids make it to five. He's interested in TB, and Aids, of course. I'll be working – nursing and midwifery again, if they'll have me.'

Marlowe said, sourly, 'Taking up the white man's burden? How very commendable. You always were the worthy one, far worse than Frances. Booked your place in the God slot? Or the Sunday papers? I saw the health visitor we had for Luke in a report on Ethiopia. Absolute bitch, she was. Bel said, "As if the poor bloody Ethiopians hadn't enough to worry about."'

The lie stuck in his throat. 'Absolute bitch' was Bel's language; she had resented the intrusion, Marlowe only remembered a lean Irishwoman reminding them about injections. And there she'd been, in the *Observer* supplement, trying to find a vein in a child's fleshless arm.

'That's a lie,' he said abruptly. 'Bel had a spat with her about injections. She thought Bel should take Luke to the surgery, not the nanny. We had a nanny then. Sheer hell! Three of them, the first six months. Thank God I was away half the time. Where was I?'

'Rambling. Shut up about Bel. She's the past. God knows how Caro happened. How long since you last did anything together? I've been wondering when you'd split for the past ten years.'

Marlowe said, wretched, 'As you said, God knows. Caro was an accident. I did wonder if she was mine, but Bel's current number's been to the vet. Maybe we stayed for Luke, poor little –' He stopped, smiling faintly. 'Bel would say, poor little sod. Poor Luke. He deserved better than us.'

Sarah said, almost kindly, 'I expect you were doing your best.' Then she recanted. 'No. Staying together for the kids stinks. I wouldn't, if Paul . . .'

'What about you, dragging the kids off to Africa? Kids die like flies out there.'

Sarah smiled, ready for him. 'Oh, ours won't starve, or die of measles. You needn't worry about their education either. All sorted. After a year – who knows?'

Marlowe studied his sister. She was any playground mother, if slightly raffish, only her eyes made up. She looked every day as old as Bel, but her eyes were sixteen. Her future could take care of itself. This year, Zambia, then . . . a Shetland croft? Bel liked the future mapped, obedient. It was more sinister than that. Bel thought she was in control. The accidental pregnancy had been an outrage.

Struggling to his feet, he discovered cramp in his left foot. Sarah caught him as he stumbled. She kissed him.

'There . . . And you know where we are. Any time.'

Marlowe wondered whether to return the kiss, but he was out of practice. Besides, he hadn't kissed Sarah in thirty years. He said, 'Until Zambia.'

Sarah picked up her bag, which had spilled open. He caught sight of her chaotic life, spare knickers for the smallest one, birthday invitation, shopping list, crayonned picture, shrivelled conkers, plane-tree bark, tampon holder, paracetamol and – the only extraordinary detail – a child's prayer book. He'd had no idea they went to church. Perhaps it was just the children. Bel had written once, in a lecture for first-

86

years on family limitation, that the feckless Victorian poor conceived on Sundays, while their brood was at Sunday school. He could remember exactly Caro's conception, a Saturday of bitter cold, last January, while Luke was out with friends. Caro was his child.

'Penny for them?'

'Unrepeatable.'

She fastened the bag, laughing, 'That I'm a right slut? Just you try, that's all. Speaking of which, it's almost chucking-out time at the nursery. You can give me a lift.'

After the third night, he no longer expected sleep. There was a party somewhere, invitation still logged as the evening's engagement, idiotic card still pinned to the bright-green board in the kitchen. Baby-sitters were no problem. They had five numbers on file, and any number of people for emergencies, a carefully nurtured network. It was the idea of a party that revolted him – eating, drinking, casual lechery. Near Christmas, too, there was the delicate problem of a present. He checked tonight's card. The hosts were a chaste gay couple, friends of Bel's. Their flat was full of apricot Siamese cats, gold leaf and roses. He wouldn't go to the party; displaced person. Parties were about sex and food. He wanted neither. Curiously enough, he only wanted to bath Caro, feed her, help Luke with homework, read the paper, catch up with the news on Channel 4. Later, much later, in the quiet hours, he could work.

Russell had been more than reasonable, unnaturally kind. He'd said, yesterday, 'You're not going, Marlowe. On form, you're bloody good. If we could . . .' He stopped, fumbling for words, 'Babies sleep, the older kid's at school. You can manage a weekly column? Plenty of freelancing about. Women do it all the time, six kids and syndicated worldwide. Come for a drink.'

Chapter Eight

It worked, after a fashion. After Christmas, Caro became a part-timer, mornings only, dropped off, like Luke, soon after eight, retrieved at lunchtime. The only immediate difference was that Bel no longer did her share. Twice, in the first six months, she claimed access.

On the fifteenth of May, she rang, just short of midnight. She said, briskly, 'I'd like them ready at five. OK?'

Marlow and his daughter were halfway through the last bottle. Caro opened fierce blue eyes and howled in protest.

Bel raised her voice above the noise. 'Shopping trip, Boulogne. Stocking up for parties. You can come, if you like. Sam won't mind. I'll make Luke speak French. Back tomorrow night.' Then she hung up.

Caro spat out the silicone teat and glared at her father. She howled for the next hour, not taking kindly to interrupted meals. She slept, whimpering still, for the next hour or so, then woke in a furious temper. Marlowe considered refusing to hand her over, then thought better of it. So far, they were spared the disembowelling of a dead marriage, bargaining for maintenance and measured hours with children. If he raised any objections, Bel might turn nasty. As it was, he could hand over a baby certain to grizzle all day, and Luke resentful at missing an interschool match.

Marlowe spent the day writing in agreeable peace about fatherhood. He enjoyed spending his afternoons in Caro's brave new world. Caro saw spring for the first green and lovely time. No longer strapped to his chest, she rode high in her howdah, discovered joy every day. One afternoon, she

88

broke into peals of laughter, bouncing up and down in the backpack. Marlowe, looked about for a reason, saw a flotilla of ducklings following their mother out of the long pond, but Caro still shrieked with laughter when they'd left the ducks far behind. Only then did he notice the green-haired punk, last ever Mohican, hand in hand with a girl whose matted black hair swung past her waist. She was barefoot, and there were budgie bells on her trousers. Which peculiarity made Caro laugh, he would never know. Babies had a major flaw, far worse than their incontinence or lousy table manners. They never answered a simple question. Baby care would be a pushover if only they could talk, specify wet nappy, empty belly, new tooth, boredom or temper.

When she did begin to talk, Caro said 'Mum-mum-mum' like any other English baby. Presently, though, and sooner than the books allowed, she would sit on the floor, picking up toys and naming them. She discovered tact, or copied Luke, addressing her father as 'Dad-Dad'. Marlowe began to resent their mornings apart, woke dreading the morning's hassle. The alarm was set, needlessly, for six, by which time Caro was already yelling for her bottle. By seven, Luke wandered between his bedroom, the shower and unfinished homework. By seven forty-five, nagged by Radio Four, they were loading the car with nappies, buggy, games kit, packed lunch and half-finished homework. At eight, Caro was handed into the loving, hired arms of Mrs Allen. For all he knew, Caro was already learning the Lord's Prayer, along with 'This Little Piggy', 'Round and Round the Garden', and 'Baa, Baa, Black Sheep'. Dropping Luke off ten minutes later seemed natural enough, the umbilical cord long severed. Back home, though, half an hour later, he found it quite impossible to work if there was any trace of Caro, even a half-chewed rusk. Moving to Bel's old office solved that, temporarily.

The crunch came barely a week later. At one o'clock, Mrs Allen, exultant, greeted him with Caro in her arms, then set the baby down. Caro stood there, uncertain, for a moment or two, then took off, one, two, three, four, five steps into the child minder's outstretched arms. Marlowe contrived to smile, but drove home in a rage. Caro had no right, Mrs Allen still less. Her first steps should have been into *his* waiting arms. Besides, Caro wasn't eight months till next week. The books said a year or fourteen months for walking. She couldn't have read them.

Caro didn't walk again until Luke came home from school. This time, she achieved ten wobbling steps into her brother's arms. Marlowe wrote long and angrily into the night, of serpent's teeth and thankless children. In the morning he read it through. Self-pitying rubbish, every word. Women who couldn't wait to get back to work would laugh at him. Other women would laugh, too, the kind who knew they had the best deal, the first smiles of total love, the first words, first drunken steps. He was obsessed, possessed, overpowered by one small female creature.

Bel claimed the children once more, the week before Christmas. She left Luke with Hamleys' computers and an upper limit, and took Caro off to Selfridge's Father Christmas, where Sam guarded their place in the queue with children from his last marriage. Luke, canny beyond his years and in some ways his mother's son, asked if he could take the money instead. He'd buy after Christmas, and definitely not in Hamleys. Caro arrived home with a gorilla larger than herself, clutching a bunch of felt bananas. She'd been copiously sick all over Bel's latest Paul Smith. Neither of them was requested again, even for sentimental duties. Bel, so she said, was spending Christmas abroad. Three days later, this proved more or less correct. Late at night, on 27 December, she seemed to be on Iona, in search of peace and spiritual refreshment, paid for by Channel 4. There was no sign of Sam, at least, not in the programme or credits. Marlowe watched, fascinated, discovering a strange new facet of his children's mother.

A week later, though, normality was restored. Bel was back on screen, but in Warsaw, reporting on Poland reborn. Jerzy, traitor, appeared with her, recounting his own flawless path to success. Marlowe switched off halfway through. Jerzy was his friend, not Bel's, and that, most certainly, should have been his story. He couldn't even follow it up.

In March, events took charge of his life. Mrs Allen's touch of indigestion ripened into a perforated ulcer. Finding a replacement took three days and two missed deadlines. A week later, the temporary minder went down with flu. On the Saturday, Luke, outrageously fouled, had two teeth knocked out and broke his right arm and leg. Replanting the teeth was a brisk, painful operation, but the fractures were another matter. Luke needed his food cut up, his flies unzipped, carrying up the stairs, and twenty-four-hour total care. No nanny, for whatever money, would take on a toddler and a boy of fourteen who couldn't pee unaided. Luke, in pain and occasional tears, needed his father.

Leaving Luke's bedside, Marlowe faced Russell with the truth. Russell said, dismissively, 'It's your choice.'

Marlowe agreed, then recanted. 'Choice doesn't come into it. I'm their father.'

Russell said nothing at first, playing with a pocket Gameboy. Then, shiftily, he said, 'If you had a wife –'

Marlowe cut him short. 'No wife, two kids. I should have stuck to safe sex.'

He turned swiftly and walked out, pelting back to the meter seconds before they could lock the evil yellow clamps, and drove home to relieve the fiendishly expensive emergency nanny.

Russell rang soon after eight, fed and counselled, perhaps, by his wife. He asked kind questions about the baby and Luke's accident, then came out with it. 'Listen, Marlowe. We could use a regular northern correspondent.'

'For God's sake, Russell! We live in Clapham.'

'But you're a northerner.' Russell added, snuffling a little over his own joke, 'Foreign fields always were your stomping ground. And living's so much cheaper. Think about it. Wigan, not Warsaw. Weekly report from the front.'

Marlowe said, 'Wigan's been done, I think.'

Chapter Nine

He crammed the last books into the last tea chest, leaned his weary head on its splintered wood. His left eye twitched and he felt slightly sick, sure signs of leaden exhaustion. It was twenty-five to five. The World Service chattered to itself in a corner: a play about D. H. Lawrence. The protagonists were father and son, D. H. berating Lawrence *père* for daring to marry his beloved mother.

'Fucking her, you mean? And where'd you be, without?'

Marlowe switched off, not in the mood for D. H., but the message was oddly comforting. Without Bel, no Luke, no Caro. He found the kettle at the top of another chest, with tea, coffee, three mugs and ginger biscuits. Drinking sour black coffee, he wondered how soon he could decently wake the children. Luke and Caro defined him now. Women – or, rather, mothers – had no excuse for madness, let alone suicide. They were always so necessary, with babies to deliver, children to feed, nappies to change, homework to check. Men rarely enjoyed such assurance. He waited now in suspense, crunching sugar lumps dipped in black coffee.

Caro claimed him first, her thin cry already desperate. Whether she remembered Bel or not, no one could tell. Most certainly, she screamed in anguish if she found herself alone. This morning, she was already in tears, her face mottled with grief. Marlowe kissed her with passion, let the small, wet face nuzzle his chest. Bottle-fed almost since birth, the child still mouthed and groped for the comfort of breasts, and cried, 'Mama!'

Luke stood at the door, cocooned in his black duvet. He said, abruptly, 'Is it morning?'

Marlowe checked his watch: five ten. 'That depends. What happened to your watch?'

The boy came to sit in the window. He was fully dressed in a black sweatshirt, black jeans, black socks. A skull wreathed with crimson roses stared from the sweatshirt. The ghost of his watch circled one bony wrist, white against last summer's tan. He looked down, as if expecting to see it. 'Someone trod on it in the changing room. Ten past five's morning. I'm going out for a paper.'

Marlowe opened a carton of ready-mixed feed. Modern life coped with anything: fridge disconnected, removal van due at seven thirty, cue for a carton of ready-mix. He switched on the bottle heater, wondering if Caro would really object to cold milk. No longer a baby, she had her own effective code, and would tell him if the milk was wrong. She refused to abandon her bottle, biting through teats with sharp little teeth.

Luke had disappeared already, not waiting for a veto. The newsagent's was only next door. They would be opening bundles and making up bags for the newsboys. Since the last rape, there were no newsgirls which the three redundant girls considered sexist. Mr Patel and their parents had imposed the ban.

Luke was back already, with the *Mirror* for himself, the *Guardian* for his father. Taking Caro on his knee, he began to feed her. As his small sister sucked, eyes closed in bliss, he asked, 'Isn't she a bit old for this?'

Marlowe grabbed the *Mirror*, scanned the day's sex and misery, all unforgiven. 'If she's happy, why worry? Aboriginals used to breast-feed till five.'

'But she can walk. And talk.'

'And knows what she wants. Why do you buy this rubbish?'

Luke retrieved his paper. Dad always pounced on the *Mirror* or the *News of the World*. Given a chance, Dad read the *Sport*. Turning to the TV page, he said, superbly, 'Economy. Big floppy papers waste words, forests and my time.'

93

Marlowe tried to object, but failed.

Having finished her bottle, Caro stood shaking her canvas travel cot, ready for the day. Marlowe dressed her swiftly in Osh Kosh and gaudy canvas boots, presents from Bel. His own atavistic taste ran to smocked Liberty print and patent-leather Start-Rite shoes. Bel's presents, given last week, wouldn't continue.

'Go if you must,' she'd said. 'Though what you'll find to do up there, God knows. It's a howling wilderness. The money from selling this place will be useful. Sam's flat's too small for two. I suppose you want maintenance for the kids? As for access, you know my position. It's unsettling. Hypocritical, too. Adulterous wives never used to see the kids. Besides, I'm up to my eyes in work.'

Bel always spoke in such clichés, liked words that had been weighed and not found wanting. Up to her eyes or not, she couldn't be short of money, but nor had she arranged any maintenance. Marlowe most certainly wouldn't ask. Bel seemed now a bizarre surrogate. The children were *his*, Bel's role peripheral and long over.

He slid the dungarees' brass button home and put Caro down. Small, fine-boned, with his own dark hair and eyes of brilliant blue, Caro looked superb in anything, and seemed to know it. She said, peremptorily. 'Put cot to pieces,' and stood watching as he dismantled the travel cot.

Luke pushed his duvet into a black bin liner, tied it with his old school tie. The new school wore black trousers, good, white shirts, dark-blue sweaters, silver logo, but ties were optional. He didn't want to be a man, ever, not in a job with a tie. Ties made him feel like throwing up.

Outside, there was a scrunch of brakes. Dad had the front door open. Caro was at the gate already, small and maddening. Luke wished that she was ten years older, or even his twin. Caro was someone he'd like to know, clever, good-looking, but hopelessly young. He could be her father, almost. They were a peculiar family – one man, one teenager, one baby girl. It'd be awful for her when she started to have periods. Or maybe not? The girls at school loathed talks with their mothers. Dad would just give her the info and do a run-ner. If he was still single by then.

. . . When did girls start? Twelve? Thirteen? Luke, appalled, worked out that he'd be twenty-four before Caro turned into a woman.

Five miles before the Keele services, Luke woke and asked where they were going. Marlowe said, mystified, 'To the new house, of course.' Did kids ever listen? Luke had seen estate-agent pictures of a dozen houses, had his say in choosing this one, calculated its area, cubic capacity, litres of paint needed to cover its walls.

'I know. I wanted you to say it. Nothing's real. Will we ever go back?'

Marlow felt the car swerve, came to only just in time. The night's lost sleep had come for him. Services, half a mile. He pulled in, parked next to a green 2CV, with a yellow canoe upright in the front seat. The Citroën crouched beside a state-ly Alvis tourer, 1920–something and no seat belts, even in front. Illegal, surely? He felt boring and predictable, father of two in a four-year-old Astra. Bel drove a navy-blue Austin 7, idiotic but fast enough for London, where Porsches crept at twenty. Bel liked nothing ordinary.

Wriggling from Marlowe's arms, arching her taut back, Caro said firmly, 'Walk!' The reins were still clipped to the pushchair, which was in the boot. Bel had bought an American device of handcuffs linked by curly telephone wire, for parent and child, but Caro simply lay on the pave-ment screaming. They'd given it to a neighbour. Now the brat darted from him, unbearably reckless. Luke sprinted and snatched her from under the wheels of a reversing minibus.

'Bloody stupid baby! Do you want to be dead?'

Then he carried her, piggy-back, into the mid-morning queue. Marlowe followed him and ordered breakfast.

Luke, still shaking, pushed the untouched plate away. 'I don't want to eat. Sorry, Dad, but I just don't.'

Marlowe, distressed, found his own appetite gone. Luke began to cry. Wordlessly, they rose. Marlowe released Caro from her high chair. Luke was halfway across the restaurant already, but Marlowe returned to pocket the butter and two small posts of strawberry jam, and wrap the rolls in paper napkins. Bel would scorn such frugality, but they'd be hungry later.

Outside, Luke stood very still, white-faced. He said, not turning round, 'Sorry. You can dock my allowance. My throat just closed up. I wish . . .' He stopped. Marlowe saw, not a child, but his son, another man, not to be bullied or punished.

Reaching for the boy's cold hand, he said, 'It's all right. Don't worry.'

Luke stared at the racing rivers of cars – so much speed, north and south. Every car with one more reason for moving, no one in all the world content to be still. He said diffidently, 'I don't want to be here and now. I want everything like we used to be. Three of us, and then Caro too. I hate change.'

Marlowe said, 'We weren't very happy, you know. Your mother had other plans. She wouldn't get another chance, not easily. Caro came at a very awkward time. We'll be happy now I promise.'

Luke shook his head. 'You can't say that. "Call no man happy till he dies. He is at best but fortunate."'

Marlowe, startled, could only agree. 'OK. You win. But we'll be all right.'

Luke smiled, looking suddenly, ten years older, ally and equal. He said, 'You know, I'm absolutely starving now. Do you suppose they've cleared the table? I could eat cold bacon butties, anything . . .'

Marlowe produced the rolls, butter and jam. 'No bacon butties. We'll manage with these.'

They sat down under a rowan, burdened with crimson berries, rubies, spinels, against the azure sky. Buttering the rolls without a knife was difficult until Luke produced his Swiss army knife.

Marlowe said, thoughtfully, 'We saw the Swiss army once, Bel and I. Very old men, in tin hats, marching through Lucerne with guns and horses.'

Luke picked a whole strawberry from the pot and ate it. 'In the war?'

Marlowe cuffed him. 'How old do you think I am? It was a procession for some feast day or other. I know, Corpus Christi, on our way to climbing in Austria.'

'The Body of Christ? What's that? Easter?'

Marlowe stood up, easing pins and needles. 'I forget that you don't know about these things. Corpus Christi is the Thursday after Trinity Sunday. If you know when that is?'

Luke shook his head. 'I know about Diwali and Eid and Ramadan. Corpus Christi's a new one on me. It's not in RSS.'

Marlowe was heading for the car. They'd lingered too long and must make up time. He said, fretfully, 'What the hell's RSS?'

Luke looked sly, too knowing. 'I've told you often enough. I'm missing abortion, this week. Then it's medical advances – you know, gene therapy, genetic engineering. Hitler jumped the gun. The super-race starts here. If I have kids, I'll be able to find out what they'll die of, and see if it's worth the hassle.'

'I see.'

Luke climbed into the back and buckled his seat belt. 'Did Bel have tests before Caro?'

Marlowe nodded. 'Every one. Caro passed.'

'I'm glad. I wanted a sister.'

Marlowe accelerated into the north. Curious, he asked, 'A sister?'

'Yes. Women are such a mystery. It's a pity she's so young, though.'

Azure turned black in a swift, scudding storm, rattling hailstones and swirling dervish rain. Marlowe felt light, carefree, en route to another life, with this new friend, his son.

Chapter Ten

'You didn't say there were trees,' Luke said, accusingly.

Marlowe thought of the surveyor's report. The trees were damned, obscuring light, maybe threatening the high grey wall between their house and next door. He explained this, but Luke barely listened.

'Trees are alive. You can't kill them to suit yourself. Caro will have a swing, in the ash tree. The dark room can be mine, so there.'

Marlowe sat on a tea chest, reading crumpled pages of an aged newspaper that had wrapped his share of glass and china. Bel had kept the supplement, which was historic: '1989 – the Year the Walls Came Down'. He remembered Christmas 1989 with unusual clarity. Bel had ensconced herself in the study for the entire holiday. She'd said, 'Do Christmas for Luke, if you like. Count me out. I need to get this lot sorted by next term.'

'This lot' was also known, occasionally, as the new world order, or words to that effect. Bel had felt threatened. She must learn the future, or become the past. On 1 January she left for a week in the East – Budapest, Prague, Warsaw, Bucharest – returning equipped for her new year.

Luke said, across memory, 'Dad, you've been reading old yellow paper for ten minutes. Caro's screaming and I'm starving. I'll get her, if you sort some food.'

They'd both, unconsciously, acquired this negligent phrase from Bel, but would lose it very soon. Luke disappeared, thundering up uncarpeted stairs. Caro's demented wailing stopped at once. Marlowe made his way to the shadowed

kitchen. Luke would make a far better parent. No, delete . . .
Luke responded to Caro as if she were an equal, distressed,
not a baby crying.

The kitchen was shadowed because it too had an offending
tree outside, in this case a pear. Today, the westering sun
found threads of gold in green leaves. The effect was stunning, as if stained glass could live. Only later did the eyes
adjust to see cobwebs, mouseholes and the places where
things had stood. Some of these things still lurked in a skip,
deserving death without resurrection. Sliding glass in the yellow plywood kitchen unit had a crack mended with red carpet
tape. The cupboards smelled of mice. Nothing left behind
was good, precious or even agreeable kitsch. The top-floor
flat reeked of cannabis and stale incense. He'd no idea where
to start in making this gracious wreck their own. Late in
August, up here alone, he'd bought a great oak table, in a
junkyard, stuck with gobbets of candle grease. It came from
a vestry. For another fifteen pounds, the dealer threw in four
rush-seated chairs with boxes for prayer books.

Marlowe plugged in the kettle, toaster and microwave, and
opened cans of beans. Tomorrow, he'd light the Aga, and if it
wouldn't light, he'd buy a new cooker. Buttering toast, cutting it into fingers for Caro, setting the waxy table, he felt
desolate, horribly alone. Moving should be bibulous, con-
vivial, to conceal at all costs uprooted agony. Spreading hot
beans on two slices of toast, he ached with absurd longing for
the Patels' shop, for buying the paper and a packet of
Cadbury's buttons. It was half past five: time to make Caro's
supper, then run her bath. Later, while she played, he or Luke
would cook in their sleek, narrow galley.

The past year had been gruelling. Bel had made a new life
and left them the dregs. She offered no money, demanded no
access. She'd seen Luke twice more, once for school prize
day and once purely by chance, in the Science Museum.
Caro, she'd simply discarded. It proved less easy to do likewise. Images of Bel pursued him, night and day. Bel haunted
prime time, colour supplements and the *Evening Standard*,
priestess of the new right, more Thatcherite than Thatcher
ever dared to be. Bel, maverick, fluently inconsistent,
favoured prudent euthanasia, eugenic breeding, the abolition

of family allowance and monarchy alike. Bel, it was rumoured, had been offered the next safe Tory seat, but refused to ally herself with any party. Two days ago, he'd heard her arguing that the peace dividend should be spent on Third World reconstruction, policing famine and mayhem, until right prevailed. Bel knew exactly how the world should be run, and would say so for as long as her love affair with the media lasted. It was quite impossible to imagine her with a small, smeary child with a wet nappy and wetter kisses. Bel's hour had come. Giving birth to Luke and Caro had been a mere incident in her fêted life. London, or any capital, was her natural habitat.

Luke came in, holding Caro perched awkwardly where a woman has hips. She wriggled down, stumped across pock-marked lino to her father and stood at his knee. Marlowe met the child's china-blue eyes without flinching. Bel's eyes were dark, his own grey, Luke's greenish. Caro's were a mystery until he remembered Grandad's, brilliant in the weathered face. Caro's were identical, down to the darker blue rim.

She said, without preamble, 'Hungry.'

Fed, she began to eat in the thorough way of toddlers, immersing herself in the task, filling her small mouth to capacity, raking her hair with a finger of toast. The bean sauce would congeal there, and prompt one more howling, kicking shampoo session. Luke ate like a young wolf and looked round at once for more.

Marlowe sighed. 'There's more toast. Or biscuits, or an apple.'

The kettle switched off. Luke made tea in two bizarre mugs: Black Sambo tigers, chasing tails, which formed the handles. No one had managed to break them. Dropping one tea bag in each, Luke looked around for milk and saw no fridge. Marlowe pushed a tin containing miscellaneous sachets across the table.

'Bel's a kleptomaniac. Hotel filchings. The fridge is in the living room. They wanted to knock off. I said we could cope.'

Opening three packets, Luke shook in two Czech sugar lumps, German brown sugar and English coffee whitener. He said, affectionately, 'You're hopeless, Dad. They'll charge the same. Just as well we're poor. You'd be lousy with servants.'

Marlowe watched lovingly as Caro licked her plate. Baked-bean sauce coated her hair and most of her clothes. She crowed, laughed and tried to climb into his arms. Gingerly, he transferred her to the floor.

'Grubby little object.'

Luke tipped his unfinished tea down the sink, rinsed the mug, filled it with water and drank cautiously. Then he smiled. 'It tastes of nothing at all. Or maybe water? Not Domestos, anyway.'

Marlowe picked up his daughter and wiped her sticky hands with a striped cloth. 'Bath, young lady, then shopping. Will you come, Luke, or would you rather stay here?'

Luke's foot had found a split in the nasty green lino. It ripped open, exposing flagstones. He saw, briefly, what the kitchen might be, flagstoned, rag rugs, the Aga working, more cupboards to go with the table and chairs. Fruit piled in bowls, and herbs hanging from the rack. Some people in London had kitchens like that, but they looked odd, like a cow walking down Oxford Street. The pear tree must stay, ever changing, serene in its great age. Peculiarly hungry, he slit open a sachet of sugar, crunched it up. Being consulted by his father definitely appealed. Childhood was left behind in London. He said, after a moment or two, 'I'll stay. I want to look round, get the feel of the place.'

As they left the room, Luke's hand touched his father's shoulder. Accident or caress, Marlowe didn't know, but it felt good.

Outside the downstairs bathroom, Luke moved ahead to open the door. He was smiling. Marlowe, confused, saw that his son was a young man, lean, dark, saturnine, almost fifteen. Jewish, he would be bar-mitzvah already. Half the world would call him a man. Only the fat indulgent West could prolong childhood to such idiotic lengths.

Unasked, Luke made his sister lie down on the changing mat as he stripped off her sodden nappy and sealed it up. Having finished undressing her, he sat on the edge of the great iron bath as Marlowe tested the water. Caro wriggled free, slid down the shiny white side, landing with a splash that drenched them both. She laughed convulsively.

Luke touched his father's shoulder again. This time, there was no mistake. He said, 'Relax, Dad. We'll be all right, I promise.'

Alone, Luke sat for a while reading the local free sheet. There was only one cinema, and he'd seen everything it was showing months ago. There were photographs of strange events: fat men wrestling in giant stretch-suits, thin men surrounded by sheep or dejected bulls, women in clogs and straw hats, dancing. They'd just missed a carnival. He knew no names or faces. It would be strange, walking down the street, buying *2000 AD*, knowing nobody, not even the nearest take-away. If they'd heard of take-aways . . .

He wandered out into the garden, taking five minutes to unlock the kitchen door. The key had rusted in, but at least someone had left a can of oil on the window ledge. Maybe it happened all the time? Bel would say the house smelled damp, but Bel didn't live here, and never would. Bel would moan about the garden, full of things rank and gone to seed. Things grew in wild abandon, waist-high grass for a lawn, coarse, nightmarish things in the borders. There was no sun, only a sulphurous glow from streetlamps, and the thin light of a sickle moon. Two of the coarse, fleshy plants were burs. Someone had planted nasturtiums in a cracked plastic urn, but there were no flowers, only dark leaves and leprous stems. Half buried in rank grass, he found the head of a lion. Kneeling down, he freed it, revealing the whole thing, couchant, regardant, in mossy sandstone. Below the rhododendrons, there was a bike, tyres flat, no brakes, no seat. Behind washed-out hydrangeas, there was a smell. Pushing aside undergrowth, he found the source of it, five dead newborn kittens, seething with maggots. Caro would be fascinated, but Luke wanted to cry or vomit.

He found the garden shed, swagged with ivy and Russian vine, groped in half-light until his hands closed on a trowel. Returning to the hydrangeas, he dug deep, scrabbling round roots, removing stones. He scooped the kittens into their grave, covered them with handfuls of grass, then earth. The stink went quickly. Presently, he could smell only crushed grass, damp earth and roses. Black in the darkness, the roses clung to a swaying, broken trellis. Below this stood a cast-iron bench and three strawberry pots.

Now he was back near the kitchen window, bolted lettuce and spinach, ginormous rhubarb, and the pear tree. It was too dark for picking fruit, but his hands touched lichened bark, then the limestone wall. Along the wall minced a cat, a lean, slinking creature. It jumped down into next door's garden. Someone called out, 'Chloë, Chloë, Chloë!' Luke took an instant dislike to the voice, a woman's. Shivering, he fled in darkness back to the kitchen, cursing himself for having switched off the light.

The switch, damn it, wasn't by the door but round the corner. Then the striplight flickered on and off before deciding to work. The kitchen looked ramshackle, charmless as a builder's tea hut. He moved on into the tiled hall, switching on every light. A naked bulb high above the stairwell lit a fantastic dragon, breathing fire, wild-eyed, made all in tiles, red and green. He looked for St George, but the dragon snarled alone. Opening the inner door, Luke stood in the porch, littered with drifts of gold leaves, three free sheets and a pools coupon. Illuminated, the glass swarmed with mythical beasts – gryphon, basilisk, phoenix – all green and gold. Medusa stared, evil eyes on each snaking hair. The effect was bizarre, unsettling. He knocked over a milk bottle, picked it up and placed it on the step. The glass in the outer door was only amber, bordered with roses and lilies.

The removal men must have been knackered. Dad was right to let them knock off. For ten feet, the path headed straight for a wall. Then came a bank, mounted by six steps. Then, menacing, the path headed straight for the road, almost a sheer drop. At the bottom swung a rotting wooden gate, labelled *Pear-Tree Lodge*. Holding the guard rail, Luke made his way down to street level and looked up at the silent house with its naked windows. Twenty past eight – Dad should be back soon with Caro. Long past her bedtime already. Only, she didn't have a bedtime. Dad carried her upstairs when she crashed out. Caro could ride in a piled-high cart all night, come home with the milk, sleep till mid-day. Nothing to get up for . . . Dad barely had a job now.

Luke had wondered for some time how they'd live, where the money would come from. Did Bel pay maintenance? The word made him think of drains and gutters. He pushed the thought away, but it came back. If they'd been married . . . Again, he dismissed the idea. Bel, the year he was twelve, had explained in laborious detail her case against marriage. He'd felt vaguely resentful. It wasn't supposed to be such a big deal, not any more. Half his class had parents who weren't married, but given the choice, asked to state a preference, he like the idea of marriage, 'for better, for worse, till death us do part'.

The street was full of sounds, not familiar or friendly. He didn't like the new accent, nor the tough kids on skateboards, nor the snarl as a muzzled bull terrier passed an overweight Doberman. A woman walked past, long legs sexy in black leggings, long feet bare in thonged sandals. He wanted to see her shape better, gauge breasts, waist, bum, but she wore a flapping T-shirt and had goose pimples. She might be about twenty-five, walked past him, unseeing. At school, there'd been a long, humiliating rumour: Marlowe's a poofter, Marlowe's gay – because he wouldn't touch Jo Russell's fanny, the day they all held her down. Judiciously, he hadn't told Dad or Bel about this incident. They were the kind to be up at school. Then there'd be the papers. The truth was, he'd fled, unable to bear Jo's moaning shame as they made her come. That was when it began: Marlowe's a poofter.

The sexy woman had seen him; she stopped to speak. She said, cheerfully, 'Just moved in?'

He nodded, glad of darkness, cursed his stupid stuttering speech, replied, 'Today. From London.'

'Moving's hellish. Shout if you need anything. Next door but one.' Then she said, asking outright, 'How many?'

She was scooping up children now, three of them, street kids, allowed out all hours. Luke revised her age up to thirty, then down again.

He said, warily, 'Three. Dad's gone shopping with Caro.'

'Oh.'

He wasn't imagining it. She looked like a disappointed child. To check, he added, casually, 'Caro's my little sister. My parents split up.'

Spot-on, and draw your own conclusions. She wore filigree twists of silver in each ear, silver rings on all her long, slim fingers. Halfway to bed with Dad already. Luke, expert, constructed her past: unplanned pregnancy in her teens, two more kids, then divorce and the DSS. Some of the houses in this road were still split for flats. She'd live in one, private landlord, everything falling apart. She'd be round every day, after Dad. Under the yellow streetlight, he couldn't quite be sure, but surely the two hard little peaks of nipple meant no bra? Now she was reaching for his hand. The other arm secured a child. She said, pointing to each child, 'Anna, Oliver, Max. I'm Faith. Faith Sinclair.'

Luke took her cool hand and managed to say, 'Luke. Luke Marlowe. See you.'

Faith Sinclair smiled still. 'See you.' Then she was gone.

Resisting the temptation to watch her walk away, he climbed the leaf-fallen path, up the six steps, through two doors, into the refuge that wasn't yet home. From the front-room window, he could see her still, chivvying the children home. He couldn't tell which was the girl. They looked exactly the same, shaggy-haired and dark-eyed. They wore the same clothes that kind of woman bought in London, but dirtier.

Lying on the sofa, not quite watching the nine o'clock news, he considered Faith's parting words, *see you*. They meant nothing at all, just something people said, like *au revoir*. He wanted it to mean more, to walk into her house like a friend. The people next door to Jules were like that, borrowing things, off down the pub, casually sharing kids. Faith hadn't treated him like a kid at all. He felt nicely adult, remembering her long sexy legs. In a love story, he'd invite Faith for coffee and everything would fall into place sooner or later, depending on the front cover. She exuded sex, but there were those bloody kids. Besides which, it'd be Dad she'd go for. Bel didn't want him, but plenty of women would.

The TV had reached the local news. It spoke of strange places, accidents on unknown roads, alien weather; to Luke, it felt like being abroad. Luke sighed, like an old man. He found the tea chest with goodies in and poured himself a mug

105

of cider. Then he opened the Jaffa cakes, wondering where the hell Dad had got to. Finishing the second, he heard the car in their back lane. Halfway to the kitchen, to open the back door, he began to feel ill. He felt it first as slight unease, close to nausea. Then he discovered overwhelming weakness, his bones turning to water.

That was all. Two minutes later, he was carrying Caro inside, adorably asleep in her car seat. Dad had bought bags of coal at the filling station for a blazing fire. And he was sorry about being late, but Caro had needed changing. He looked guilty, truly contrite, threading his fingers through greying hair.

'Bloody ridiculous. The baby room was in the women's loo. Could you carry in some boxes?'

Indigo, black, and shafts of broken light on fantastic shapes . . . Luke stood very still, facing fear, like a kid waking up in the dark. He said, casually, 'Is there a torch anywhere?'

Marlowe offered his pocket light. Now Luke had no excuse left. The twisted horror was pear-tree branches, shadows on flagstones. Carrying in boxes was ordinary, too banal for fear. Across the lawn and round the side of the house, to the waiting car, its boot raised, stacked full of everyday things . . . Tight-lipped, he followed the thread of light, forced himself to pick up the first box; baked beans, tinned tomatoes, free-range eggs, half a melon in clingfilm. There were four more boxes, and Dad was busy, lighting the fire, filling a bowl with water to wash Caro. Down the road, a dog barked, a cat swore. Someone kicked over milk bottles, breaking glass. A motorbike roared uphill at speed, a car door slammed. Further away, dragon in darkness, a local train rumbled across the bridge, gathering speed on its way to the sea.

Luke stacked the boxes on the floor and went out for the last one: loo paper, nappies, two-pair pack of scarlet tights for Caro. Something moved, low and sinister, coming towards him through uncut grass. He shone the torch, almost laughing in relief – a hedgehog. Upstairs, Caro howled. Dad must be trying to put her to bed alone, the way proper parents did. The weakness and nausea had gone, as if something tangible had left. Even the twisted branches looked benign, shadows of a garden tree. He carried the last box in, switched off the torch, ran upstairs to rescue Caro.

Marlowe zapped through the channels, pausing briefly to size up a horror film.

'Pathetic,' Luke said. 'Crap, honestly. About as scary as *Songs of Praise*. Less . . . Some of those born-agains terrify me. How can they be so certain? I'm not tired, though. Let's watch a video.'

Marlowe sipped Cointreau, briefly at peace with the inconstant world. Driving back, he'd composed a balance sheet. Lost; Bel, his job, the small certainties of London, a hundred or more acquaintances, few of whom had rung or called round since he split with Bel. Gained: Luke and Caro, without so much as a solicitor's letter, a ramshackle Gothic house, an uncharted future. He liked that. Bel had always ruled the future. Now, very properly, it had been returned to Fate, or even, possibly, God. He remembered, dimly, but better than other themes of childhood, the doctrine of free will. His own responsibility for the future had been restored. Separated from Bel, he'd become whole again. It was very odd, like the unfamiliar sensations of happiness.

Caro lay in his arms, small rosebud mouth working. She smiled without waking, safe in his holding arms. Did women feel like this, after the storm of birth? Very likely. There'd been pain, the muscle-wrenching agony of lifting furniture and tea chests.

Poverty disturbed him surprisingly little. His job was a small casualty when set against famine, disease or civil war. Luke and Caro deserved at least one parent. The old frenetic juggling life seemed aeons past. Glancing at Luke as he knelt by the video, slotting in some idiotic film, Marlowe wondered what they'd done, crushing his childhood into accounted hours. Luke had learned to live his own measured life, with only occasional reference to parents.

He looked up, smiling; Bel's son. Then the likeness was gone. He said, 'I'd rather not watch this on my own.'

Marlowe laughed. 'I thought you liked grisly ghastlies.'

Luke came to sit with his father, touched Caro's hand. He

was still smiling. 'Oh, safety in numbers. When you were out, just before you came back, I felt spooked.'

'Thought you were made of stronger stuff.'

Luke shook his head. 'Not tonight. Tonight, I want to be with you and Caro. Don't put her back in the cot. It feels odd, being here. My head lives somewhere else. Caro feels the same. She can't tell you, but that's how she feels.'

Marlowe quivered with guilt. Bel didn't want to see the kids. She'd said, calm and reasonable, 'True, I gave birth, but no one delivered the maternal instinct. I have none. Zilch, nil, absolute zero. No more than a cuckoo. It's hardly my fault. I think it's far better if I don't see them. Make a new life.'

Luke moved closer. The fire hadn't taken off properly, and he was cold. Marlowe offered no resistance, liking the soft weight of his children.

'One minute. I must wake that fire up. Or bed . . .'

Luke watched as his father rearranged kindling and coals, opened vents. He said, wondering,

'I've never seen a real fire before, not in a house. Smart. . . The light moves, and, oh, too many colours to say. It's not like those gas things. Lousy for the environment, though.'

With a glance at his daughter, Marlowe said, 'Stuff the environment. But we need a fireguard. Anyway, this comes out. Fetching, but inefficient. We'll have a stove.'

Luke watched credits roll. It was that kind of film, hundreds of names, down to who fed the studio cat. He couldn't zap forward, because the handset hadn't turned up yet. Holding his hands out to the blaze, he said, 'Scandinavian, with a pipe? They've got one at Jules'. Cost a bomb to have it shipped specially from Germany. Or was it Norway? I thought we were broke?'

Marlowe wanted to watch the film. Howling fear on a desolate moor was like rain in the night, soothing, infinitely safe. There wasn't a single werewolf in the room, only his son and baby daughter. He said, feeling blessed, 'There isn't much cash about. We'll live. About school . . . Monday soon enough for you?'

Luke nodded. School was precisely distant enough: three days, time to look around and see where they'd fetched up. The werewolf on the screen had drawn blood from another victim, perpetuating its bloodline. Like Aids, passed from one to another, all the way to death. There was Jon, in his class – his old class – dying of Duchenne dystrophy, marked down from conception, from his parents' meeting. He said, abruptly, 'Dad, would you call the werewolf myth a metaphor for disease? I mean, like Aids or all those genetic things?'

Marlow saw London on screen, unloved and too well known. He no longer wanted to watch, overwhelmed by sleep. He said, wearily, 'If you like.'

'No, listen, I want to know. Last week, we were working on the function of myth, for English. I thought of it then, but Jon Blake was in our group, so I didn't say it. Imagine, knowing you'll die young.'

'Answer to prayer, surely? *"Lord, let me know mine end, and the number of my days, that I may be certified how long I have to live."* Yeuch! No, seriously, I'd rather not imagine anything of the kind. Don't be so bloody morbid.'

'Jon's my age. Two months younger, his birthday's February. He'll be fifteen on Valentine's day. He's in a wheelchair now, and weaker every day. He's on A-level double maths and physics, top of the chess ladder, and he'll be dead in five years.'

Marlowe stood up and lifted Caro onto his shoulder. 'You might be dead tomorrow. Who knows? I'm off to bed. Sweet dreams.'

At the top of the stairs, he stopped, turned round and looked down on the vaulted hall. The size of this place was daunting, so much solidity and substance. Bel had chosen the Clapham house for its frugality, all space calibrated to exact needs. Bel abhorred fantasy or any other kind of waste. Their long partnership seemed more incongruous than ever.

Opening the bedroom door, he remembered, too late, that the bed was still in pieces, trussed with old climbing rope. His one Gothic whim, shining impractical brass, bought when love made the difference. Caro's cot leaned against the wall next door, tied with more rope. Her bedding was in a labelled bin liner. Bel had done her share of that, turning up, surprisingly, to help. Or grab things she'd missed? Bel had bought labels, logged everyone's possessions.

'Caro, duvet, cot bedding, waterproof sheet', the label had said, but tonight at a quarter past one, he couldn't summon the energy to fix the cot. In her scarlet fleecy suit, Caro would sleep in his arms. He shook out the duvet, lay down with his sleeping child, and slept at once.

Luke watched through to the bloody end. The werewolf's bloodline was severed, and the fire all but out. He considered shaking more coal from the plastic sack, but it was almost two. Besides, the house might burn down. Dying, the fire could still get up to mischief, spit live coals onto the rug. Then they'd all burn to death or, more likely, suffocate. When people were burned at the stake, they made the fires smoky, to be kind. Martyrs passed out before roasting, or that was the idea. The thing he really didn't fancy was torture, like the rack, or having your bits cut off, like Abelard. They held your privy parts up for everyone to see. History was disgusting. This house was quite old, 1840-something, Dad said. The weird thing was that ten rooms, attics, a cellar and all the garden cost only their share of a poky London terrace.

Climbing the wide and curving stairs, he thought of the old route to bed. The new one was more complicated. Third on the left, next to the first-floor bathroom. Moonbeams shone through the uncurtained window. He crossed the room and pushed up the middle sash. There were two more panes on either side, too narrow for leaning out. If the branch was strong enough, he might climb out, down to the silver garden. A cat, expensive, stuck-up Chloë, was sitting on the wall, eating a mouse. Outside a house across the road, a girl staggered from a taxi to be sick in a grid. Then she paid the driver and let herself in. Lights came on in the hall, then in an upstairs window. He imagined her brushing her teeth, gargling the taste of bile from her throat. She looked, in the shadows, as if she might be pretty, but girls who drank were slags.

He turned away from the window. Dad had spread the mattress out for him, with a sheet on and his duvet. No pillow . . . No matter. They'd put the bed up tomorrow. A clock, somewhere, struck the half-hour. Luke lay down, low on the floor, already in the rest of his life.

Chapter Eleven

Caro sailed a take-away tray in the market-square fountain. She'd wanted to eat the cold chips from it but agreed, after a few screams, to feed tattered pigeons. Soon her boat was lost in a flotilla of cups, straws and sodden greasy paper. Once a day, the take-aways sent spare scullions to dredge out their share. Labelled litter was bad PR. Caro's boat came from a nameless chippy with no image problems. It was half past ten, so the chips were last night's.

Caro splashed in the moving water using a chip tray to chuck water at the pigeons. Not quite two, Caro controlled the known world. In history the previous week, Luke had advanced the idea that all dictators – Saddam, Napoleon, Hitler, Henry VIII, to name a few – were spoilt brats who never had this trait spanked out of them. The idea went down well and served its purpose perfectly, deflecting the lesson from its proper course, the decline and fall of Cardinal Wolsey. Murray gave them too much bloody reading, threw essay titles at them without a word of explanation – 'Discuss the King's Great Matter'. Once a university lecturer, Murray had lost out to cost-benefit analysis. Five years on, the lessons of history were back in fashion, but Murray had been too long in the wilderness of GCSE. Luke, with regret, thought of his last essay, on Calvinism and Capitalism. It might have been an A, but he'd never know. Marlowe, L. B., had been struck off the register, one life ended. This thought kept returning, that an era of his life was over. On Monday, Marlowe, L. B., would walk into school a stranger.

A posse in green invaded the square, clipboards out, enjoying the carnival freedom of town when they should be in class. Fourth- or even fifth-years, they looked. The teacher, barely five foot three, commanded instant silence. He had dark-red hair, coarse and stiff as a brush, pebble lenses, a ginger beard and total power. Luke watched as they took orders, dividing the town between them, no time to waste and the truth to discover. They dispersed. Barbarossa followed the last girl at a distance, watchful.

Caro began to drum on the footrest, kick, kick, kick. She arched her back. This was ominous. Her lower lip trembled. Any moment now, her rosebud mouth would emit a hideous wail. Luke had been planning to take her to the library, which opened at ten thirty. Howling monsters couldn't go in, nor had he anything to quiet her.

A clipboard approached. There was no escape. Luke knew this business. Shopping-bag women were boring, tick the right boxes, thank you, ma'am. Stray males livened things up, and stray males with babies in tow were asking for it. The girl's eyes were deep-set as a Celtic carving, shadowed as if by sickness. Claws veined in blue clutched the clipboard, bloodless lips failed to smile. Anorexia nervosa, Luke thought, pitying her, like Zoë Maitland, next one up in the register, skull and bones.

The girl said, 'Good morning. Would you like to take part in a survey?'

Luke bowled the pushchair backwards and forwards. Caro postponed her tantrum to watch them both, biding her time. Across the square, a six-foot blond had seen off three already.

'Feel free.'

Caro whimpered and kicked the footrest again. The girl knelt down beside her.

'I won't be long. Promise. Honestly. It's only geography.' Taking the cap off her pen, she said, 'She's lovely. Your daughter?'

Luke stared at her, horrified. 'She's my *sister*. For God's sake, how old do you think I am?'

Caro howled. Luke glared at her. 'Shut up, you vile brat, or I'll chuck you in the fountain.'

The girl laughed, touching Caro's dark oriental hair with one thin hand. 'Sorry. I didn't mean you were old. Some people do, though. A kid in the first year had an abortion last term.'

Luke's eyes narrowed. 'Get on with it. Town survey, I mean, not your school's sex life.' Lowering his voice, he added, 'Barbarossa over there's watching us. Quick. I'm fifteen, nearly. Keeping the brat out of Dad's hair while he works. We moved from London yesterday. I'm loitering without intent. Move on.' Then he called her back, heart bouncing on the back of his throat. 'You should eat. People die of anorexia. I don't want you to. Scat! He's looking this way again.'

Caro stank and howled. She couldn't bear stinking and howled till someone sorted her out. There were kids with clipboards everywhere. They should give out stickers, like a flag day. Asking the same guy twice would invalidate their data, surely? Instead, he asked the next one for Boots. Straight ahead, then first right. Dad couldn't bear to ask the way, even in England. Last year, he'd walked in a complete circle round scrubby bits of Prague, then told the story against himself in the paper.

Struggling through awkward doors, Luke wondered again about money. They'd make out, Dad said. How? Babies closed doors, slam in your face. Caro squirmed, trying to be free of the mess. Bloody awful, really, being a baby, incarcerated 90 per cent of the time, cots, buggies, playpens, nappies, fed muck from jars.

A woman swayed past in full sail, pushing a Benetton toddler. Her belly button had popped out, stood proud in the centre of her pumpkin body. She had varicose veins, both legs bandaged like a mummy. Above the swollen insect body, her face was pale and drawn. She wasn't young, over thirty at least. For the first time, he felt pity for Bel. His beautiful mother, swollen like that, to give Caro life. Two years ago, so he was just a kid. If he'd been older, if she'd had someone to talk to . . .

He dismissed the thought, coming up to the changing room. *Fathers may use this facility. Please check with an assistant first.* In case you saw some woman's boobs? That restaurant thing on *Spitting Image* was good, when people complained about the baby breastfeeding, and they fetched a

113

tie for it. Breastfeeding was supposed to be best, but Bel wouldn't. Caro was ill all the time, nothing major, just coughs and colds, but her nose was always running, No one would sign her up for a catalogue. She looked old for her age, too knowing, thin. Lifting Caro out of the pushchair, Luke saw that her tights were stained. There weren't any in the bag Dad had packed, but there were loads of Boots freebies, even nappies. Cleaned up, Caro was summer golden still, silvery down on her arms and legs, shell-pink nails on ten fingers and toes. She smiled for him, grateful for so little; he felt ashamed. The tights couldn't go on again. Washing his hands, he remembered the cash card and shopping list. Dad even trusted him with the pin number. Fruit, free-range eggs, black ink for Dad's old Parker 51, and a paper. Add tights for Caro and forget about change from a tenner. Better get twenty pounds. Covering Caro's bare legs with his sweater, he left Boots, pushed uphill to the bank and queued self-consciously, aware of every woman's eye on him. He should make a badge: *She's my sister!* Nine eight five four; two tens; and it was half past eleven. Changing Caro took years; no wonder women came home shattered, with two or three kids in tow.

The clipboard class hadn't gone far, sentries on every street corner, climbing castle high. The castle was a real live dungeon, inmates detained at Her Majesty's pleasure. He saw the anorexic girl again, ghost white, her fingers blue with cold. That was a symptom. They'd done eating disorders in the course on personal and social development last term. You were supposed to see the school nurse – as if anyone would. Skin and bone, nearly, but sexy still, stupid cow. He must see her again . . . Barbarossa was nowhere in sight, so he crossed rattle-bump cobbles to speak.

'Good hunting?'

She stared blankly. There couldn't be two anorexics, not with long red hair. Then she said, not quite meeting his eyes, 'One judge, going to the murder trial. He didn't say, but everyone knows it's the river murder. One osteopath, any number of Japanese tourists for the castle and two Alexander-technique teachers. Shouldn't you be at school?'

Luke smirked, out on licence. 'Next week, miss.'

'Ours?'

114

He shook his head. 'Dark blue, silver badge.'

'Get you – grammar school. Sorry I spoke.'

Luke said, truthfully, 'I didn't know. Maybe Dad said, and I wasn't listening.'

The girl saw a victim and turned in pursuit, practised now, rat-tat questions, thank you, sir. Then she came back, faintly amused. 'Priest, would you believe? En route to a service, at this time of day. I don't believe in God, do you?'

'Pass.'

She came closer, smelling of peppermints. Zoë Maitland chewed gum to kill hunger. He backed away, aware of darkness all around, and Caro, crying.

The girl knelt over him. Lying on the cobbles, Luke registered pain in his head, and the sound of Caro screaming. He sat up, sick and dizzy, retching and all but collapsing again. She was placing cool fingers on his pulse, then unbuttoning his shirt. Caro screamed louder, and a crowd had gathered: shopping-bag women, mothers with prams, a couple of winos. Luke sat, head in hands, waiting for the world to be still.

The girl said, 'Keep still. You shouldn't try to stand. I'm supposed to ask if I can help you.'

Luke smiled faintly. 'Duke of Edinburgh first aid. I did the same one. Suppose I said, "No, push off, let me die in peace"? Anyway, I'm fine. I skipped breakfast, that's all. Bloody useless gawpers . . . Tell them to clear off.'

A woman stepped forward, crow in black, silvery rings on long white fingers. She said imperiously, 'Move on, please, everyone. There's no problem. I'm a doctor.'

It was Faith, taking his pulse, pulling down his eyelid – his body, her craft. The gaping crowd dispersed, cheated. Luke saw, with regret, that the girl had gone too. Close up, she wasn't skeletal. As she leaned over him, her V-necked school jumper and blouse had revealed black lace cupping small breasts. He could see her still, turning the corner, out of his life. Trying to stand up, he felt hideously sick and dizzy. Faith looked menacing. Between her and Caro's pushchair six feet of rolling cobbles swayed, like the view from a swing.

He stood up, bullied unsteady legs into making the journey, one, two, three. Holding the pushchair handles, recklessly lifting one hand to touch Caro, he said, 'I'm fine. Don't fuss. No breakfast, that's all.'

He really felt better now. Caro had stopped screaming, and the air here was like water, clear and cool, high above the traffic and clamour. Eight, no, ten men in blue overalls climbed into a dark-blue van, dangerously obedient. Another van was loaded with tools: gloves, sacks, rakes, shears, strimmers.

Faith said, easily, 'Wogs. Literally, I mean. "Workers on government service", off to clean up the river. One warder travels with the tools, two with the prisoners. They might as well be useful.'

Luke wondered how she dared. Five of the men were black, one brownish. Even Bel wouldn't say 'wogs', or not in public.

Faith was still eyeing him suspiciously. 'Have you registered with a doctor yet? Somebody should see you. Fainting isn't normal, not for a boy of your age. I'd better run you home. Or the surgery?'

Luke took a step or two, making sure he could walk. Casual, man in control, he said to the woman, 'I'm fine. I can get myself home. No need to worry my dad.' He moved on, quickly, without looking back, downhill all the way to Sainsbury's, into the sweet, hungry smell of the in-store bakery.

Caro's face was gruesome. She'd only eaten a jam doughnut. Bel would have had a fit, paranoid about E-numbers and additives, but at least the kid was asleep, thumb-in-mouth cherub. He bought fruit, free-range eggs and a pack of nappies, fifty pence off for a torn label. One-basket queue, and out into falling rain; his own bloody stupid fault forgetting the raincover. He should know by now. The rule this year was: one fine day and a week of howling rain. Sun was yesterday, the day he changed lives.

Crossing to the bus station, he remembered ink, sweated uphill again to Smith's. Then down again and into the bus station, exhausted. Their bus was about to leave. Luke struggled to collapse the blasted pushchair while Caro howled. At

116

last, a tattooed youth took pity, removed the brat, kicked the back bar, made a vast umbrella. Luke, shamefaced, muttered thanks, stowed it by the door and paid his fare. The tattooed one sat facing him, a small stubble-haired child on his knee. Caro stared entranced at the fire-breathing dragon, all in red. She pointed, making loud, eager noises, hadn't learned English manners yet. Luke read, *Cymru am Bydd*. Cymru meant Wales. Wales for ever? Red Dragon couldn't be more than twenty, judging by the fine down on his upper lip and the cloudy stubble on thin cheeks. The child was older than Caro, maybe three, and called him Dad. Luke, celibate still, thought of school, next week, exams, and years more of them, novitiate for the only life he knew. Red Dragon spoke with a soft Welsh accent, offering sweets for Caro, rainbow bright. Bel allowed no sweets ever, bought dried banana, carob bars, seedy things fit for a parrot's cage. Caro reached out pink hands for orange and green sweets. She lisped, 'Chunkoo.'

Red Dragon shook more Smarties into her hand, 'She's like you, dead spit. Buggers to fold, those pushchairs. Where do you get off?'

Luke said, 'Near the Memorial. The one like the Taj Mahal.' He added, 'We've just moved,' but the relationship was over. Red Dragon swung the child into his arms and pushed the bell for his own stop. Studying his back view – broad, bony shoulders, snake hips in black denim – Luke imagined the slight body in action, fathering that child. As the bus slowed and stopped, the boy kissed his son, quickly, before jumping him down, setting him lightly on the pavement. They walked off, crossing at the lights, down past MFI and sooty warehouses.

The bus was climbing now, a cliff-face, sheer and steep, houses clinging to the sides. He could see the place Dad called the Taj Mahal, a glistening white dome. Caro stood on his knee, hands on the window, slug trails of stickiness in her wake. She said, clearly, 'Off, now.'

Luke stood up, mystified. How did the kid know that? The answer was probably their acute visual memory. Lifting the pushchair, shopping and Caro, he swayed again, but the wind from the north kept him upright. Caro sat down, the shopping rested in its tray, one extra bag slung between the handles.

117

Like a weary woman, he began the labour of pushing uphill, stars in his eyes and pain somewhere undefined. Halfway up, he paused to draw breath, leaning over the pushchair. A bird overtook him, perched on the turquoise hat of some ancient woman. She was a bird too, kingfisher coat, legs of bone, in silk stockings, and an old woman's hunched back. Osteoporosis? Reaching their own strange house, he cursed Dad again for buying the stupid place – you needed crampons and ropes to reach the front door. Then he calmed down, thought a bit. Garage at the back, the way Dad came last night. He caught up with the old woman,

'Excuse me. How do I get round the back of these houses?'

She stared straight at him. In London, in their patch, no one over forty-five stayed around. This old bird had a face like Auden, fretted with a hundred thousand lines. Her eyes were bird-bright, dark as sloes. He'd seen the colour once before: Caro's, newborn. Maybe she was deaf? He rephrased the question, injecting more courtesy. It worked and she told him, in words of ice. Then she crossed the road to let herself into a house with great bay windows, hung with green velvet. On her side, the even numbers, the houses were on the level, needed no steps. She must have a gardener for her green baize lawn and astilbe, lavender, lychnis and love-in-a-mist, old-lady colours for her old lady's life. Next door, they had Technicolor dahlias, as if someone had spilled a paintbox; and a swing and a netball post.

He wanted to know more about the neighbours, take bearings. There were, for instance, three ways to enter the house: by the steps, by the back lane, and now this narrow, sidling ginnel. It was just wide enough to take the pushchair. Caro reached up, trying to touch the lime trees spilling gold onto grassy cobbles. He turned left at the bottom, opened the gate into the drive. The garden was a mess. There were three mossy pegs left to rot on the washing line, holding a ragged tea towel. Chloë the cat, stuck-up sphinx, sat on the wall, looking at him. Dad was at the kitchen window, cleaning it. Luke lifted his sister out and made her walk to the back door while he carried shopping. Then he went back, folded the pushchair and left it in the garage, trying to make all these actions seem real.

118

The kitchen smelled of vinegar, eco-friendly window-cleaner. In London a man came, every week, with buckets and chamois.

Marlowe washed his hands at the chipped white sink and said, 'Lunch?'

Luke sat down, taking Caro on his knee, 'Just coffee. I'm not hungry.'

Marlowe made instant, tried to remember if his son took sugar. Better to offer the sugar bowl and watch. He said, cautiously, 'What do you make of the place?'

Luke gave Caro two sugar lumps, one in each hand, bad for her. She wriggled down.

'Does it matter? We can't go back to London. There were kids in town, doing one of those fatuous surveys. You know, spot someone with a clipboard and do a runner. A girl thought I was Caro's *father*. Where's my school?'

Marlowe said, surprised, 'By the castle, overlooking the river. You saw it yesterday.'

'Did I? Bloody awful hill. Can't I go somewhere else?'

Marlowe had returned to his window cleaning. When he started, there was bird muck and cobwebs. He couldn't achieve the silky perfection of chamois, but it looked a great deal better. He hadn't cleaned a window for twenty years.

'Old age setting in?' he said, amused, 'You'll be able to use that mountain bike. Sorry, delete, no cycling to school. Rule book, don't ask me why. You'll have to walk. It's twice as far on the one-way system.'

Luke closed his eyes to make the room be still. If he drank the coffee slowly, it should work as in biology, sugar entering his bloodstream, releasing immediate energy. Instead he felt hollow nausea and struggled to his feet, staggering across the room, reaching the sink only just in time.

Marlowe held him still and waited until there was no more retching. The last spasms produced only bile, blood-streaked. Luke leaned against his father, sobbing, gagged once more, spat bile into the sink. Marlowe ran the tap to clear the mess away; it was only coffee. They moved together across the kitchen, out of time. Luke sat down, laying his head on the great scarred table. Marlowe brought him water, but the boy

119

retched again. Presently, though, he sat up, 'Sorry, Dad. Must be sickening for something.'

'You look rough. Like to go to bed?'

Luke nodded and tried to stand up. He knew better now, sitting down at once as the ground surged towards him. On the floor, Caro had him by the leg. In tears still, he longed to *be* Caro, at one with life.

Marlowe picked the baby up. She biffed him in the face, tried to bite. Tucking her firmly under one arm, he said to Luke, 'I'll get your bed made up, properly. Five minutes with a screwdriver. Are you warm enough?'

Luke nodded, shivering, 'Fine. Don't look like that, Dad. It's just a bug.'

He walked steadily enough to the hall door, across the tiled floor, up the bold sweep of stairs. Halfway up was the best place for a view of the fantastic glass, roses, lilies and creatures that never lived. The stairwell was painted Elastoplast pink, and there were holes where great chunks had fallen away. You could see five colours of paint, all chipped. The stair carpet was barely a foot wide, red and flapping loose. Marlowe, supporting his son now, vowed to rip it out before someone tripped. He saw the wood stripped bare, waxed, new carpet, dark red, or green. He steered Luke into his own room, hideous still in its disarray.

Luke said, very low, 'Could I lie down? I feel a bit faint.'

Caro wandered about the room and found the sack of her soft toys. She took no interest in her father or brother. Marlowe lay down beside his son. Presently, uncertain, like a new lover, he moved Luke's head to rest on his chest, cradled it there.

Luke said, 'I feel very strange.'

'Feverish,' Marlowe said, practically, 'You looked a bit frail this morning. I shouldn't have sent you out.'

Luke nestled closer, remembering strong arms lifting his small slippery body from the bath. He lay very still, thinking. It was early afternoon on an ordinary working day, not raining or cold, yet he was lying on a mattress in his father's arms. He could hear the steady beat of Dad's heart, caged there below the rack of his ribs. Dad was too thin, unshaven, shadows around his grey eyes. He'd eat when there was noth-

120

ing else to do, no deadline to meet. Bel never had meals ready for him, not a nurturing woman, discharging her duties, and no more. He'd known this since he was young, six or seven. Only in the last couple of years though, did he realise how very odd their life was. Bel, for instance, always bought the paracetamol, never ran out, bought the baby syrup for Caro. It was dispensed like petrol, according to need. He'd seen her when Caro was teething. Bel gave medicine like a farmer drenching cattle; one precise dose, without love. Luke took his father's hand, studied the close-clipped nails, the crescent scar between his right index finger and thumb, the blue veins, prominent still beneath lightly tanned skin. Long, slender hands, one silver ring, not on his wedding finger. He said, quietly, 'Did you ever love her?'

Marlowe moved free of his son and lay staring at the cracked ceiling. Caro had found the fireplace and was busy untwisting the screws of newspaper left there to gather soot. She was absorbed by this task, blissfully happy.

Luke said again, insistently, 'I need to know, Dad. Did you love her?'

Marlowe raised himself on one elbow, facing his son. A son on the threshold of manhood dispelled any illusions of youth one might cherish. Was this the explanation for the final break with Bel? Since Luke had turned twelve and grown tall, Bel had avoided her son.

'What would you mean by love? Separating wasn't my idea. Your mother's a remarkable woman.'

'Then why?'

Luke bit his lip and looked hard at the flor, trying to check the rigors that shook his body. Of all the times to be ill! On the other hand, he'd never get a better chance to ask. Confronting Marlowe, he repeated the question.

'Why? What's wrong with you? You're all right.'

'She prefers Sam, that's all. Knowing Bel, I think Sam gave her an ultimatum.'

Turning away, Luke saw that Caro had fallen asleep on the bare floor. He said, with difficulty, 'I don't understand you. You should be angry.'

Marlowe had fallen asleep, quite suddenly, like Caro. Luke studied his father. Their closeness now confirmed the likeness. In twenty-five years, this would be his face, his body. Next year, he'd be six foot, like Dad. Tall, dark, with this man's face. The dark hair was still thick, only touched with grey. Some people were fat and bald at thirty. Luke, confused, wanted to hold his father, take the hurt away. People should stay together. At school there was always some drama, people dumping each other. Boys either said nothing at all, or told everyone she was a slag. With girls, it was all tears and conspiracy. When he was small, and unhappy at school, he used to cry in Dad's arms, never Bel's.

Caro woke, sat up, with her hair all on end, staring round the strange room. She stumbled past tea chests and black bin liners to reach them, and pointed to her father. 'Why asleep? Sun in the sky.'

Luke looked at her warily. Caro could talk, no doubt about that. Two months ago, when they began packing books into tea chests, she'd screamed, 'Give it to me! I want to do that! It's not fair.'

Putting one finger to his lips, he said, 'Ssh! Dad's tired.'

Caro came to sit beside her brother. It was too late to worry about passing on the bug. Besides, he felt better now, nausea only a memory. If he lay still, he felt fine. The shivering had stopped. Caro was gazing up at him, her shadowed face curiously adult. She didn't look like Dad or Bel just now. He'd wondered, when Bel was pregnant, whether Dad was her real father, but he knew it couldn't be Sam. He thought with priggish distaste of his mother, Bel, screwing around all over the place. Years of cheating . . . Dad tried to make it sound two-way, but Luke, with a glance at his sleeping father, seriously doubted that. For a journalist, Dad was curiously shy and self-effacing. That was what made his foreign pieces so good. What came across was the place and the people, not Chris Marlowe. Hard to imagine him picking up a tart, or any woman.

Luke sat up, trying to ease the stiffness in his neck, but it was still there, linked to a certain dull ache. Besides his throat was sore. Lousy, lousy timing. They needed to get this shambles in order before they could devise a new normality. Caro deserved some shape to her life.

She began to whimper. Pointing to her nappy, she said, 'Wet. Change my nappy now.'

Luke glared at her. *If* he ever had kids, they'd be housetrained from birth. If Caro was bright enough to give orders, surely she could quit nappies? Caro started to rip open the tapes. Luke grabbed her.

'Hold on. I don't want your piddle on the floor.'

He changed her in the bathroom. Set free, Caro pulled off her skirt and ran half-naked through the house. Clambering up the second flight of stairs, she turned to make sure he was following, then darted on into the nameless rooms above, laughing still. Then there was silence.

The first room was empty but for an ancient doll's pram. The second held a Baby Belling with no oven door, and one ring broken. There was a grubby embroidered Afghan rug, a kettle and a condom packet. In the third room, he found Caro, huddled in a corner, white and silent. She buried her face in his sweater and began to cry.

Luke carried the terror-stricken child out onto the landing. Leaving the room, he made to close the door, but couldn't. Shifting Caro onto his hip, he tried again. This time, he saw why. The catch was broken and sticking out – nothing spooky. Yet Caro began to scream, on a high animal note of pure terror. Frantic, she clung to his hair, biting hard into his hands. Luke, in darkness, tried to reach for the light switch, but nothing happened. Looking up, he saw the perfectly logical explanation: no bulb in the green celluloid shade. More for Dad's repair list: light bulbs, door catch, tap washer. He carried Caro downstairs. She clung like a baby chimp, then wriggled free when he reached the middle floor.

The whole house was deathly cold. No wonder he'd felt ill. The heating would go in next week, not soon enough. Caro was shivering now. On the landing, he found the bin liner Bel had labelled 'Caroline's clothes'. He ferreted about for a few things – tights, a thicker sweater, the denim pinafore embroidered with mice and blackberries. Bel used to buy Caro's clothes from small, precious shops, madly expensive, hardly ever the right size. The denim thing, a goodbye present, barely covered Caro's bottom.

Rummaging in another bin liner, Luke found a sweater for

himself. Then with Caro toddling behind him, he checked on Dad.

He stood for a minute or two, holding her hand, as they watched Marlowe sleep. Then Luke fetched his own duvet, covered his father and quietly left the room.

Caro took the next stairs in her own way, bumping down, giggling. In the hall, she paused to study the tiled floor, said, in confirmation, 'Dragon.'

In the living room, Luke used the second bundle of bought kindling and a firelighter, opened the second plastic bag of coals. Caro watched as he laid them out, using smaller pieces. He'd never lit a coal fire in his life. It was like a barbecue, with coal instead of charcoal. Then, as the red flames flickered, he thought of Caro. There might be a fireguard, somewhere. There was any amount of junk left behind. No fireguard, no fire.

Caro followed him next door, into a room the estate agents had called the breakfast room. There was a folding metal guard leaning in the grate, festooned with cobwebs. This room had long windows that looked onto the garden. Beyond the next road and the Taj Mahal, dark fells rose, treeless and desolate. Outside, there was no one about. Nothing moved but the trees. If you looked the other way, you could see the town, or city, whatever it was, full of nameless landmarks. Luke bit his lips, checking tears. He was feeling weak again, sweating this time, then shivering. He wanted to be in his own room under the duvet, with London outside; school tomorrow, and the autumn term unfolding.

This room led to the kitchen. There was another, marked 'dining room' on the plan, bigger than the living room. There was even a dining table, but someone had rigged up a table-tennis net. The dining room had a filthy parquet floor and a fireplace straight out of Bel's magazines. Someone had painted it banana and blocked the grate with hardboard. On the mantelpiece, there was a half-empty box of pink tissues. There were curtains at the windows, not bad, considering the state of the house, amber velvet. But the walls needed paint or paper, the floor cried out for cleaning and polish. There was no other furniture, and the walls had light patches, ghosts of pictures.

Caro watched as he dusted the fireguard with tissues, trotted behind as he carried it next door. She stood, absorbed, as he folded it round the grate. It wasn't ideal – they should go all round with a lid affair on top – but this would have to do for now. Sitting her on his knee, he said, fiercely, 'Don't touch, ever. Very, very hot.'

Caro smiled beatifically. 'Hot. Don't touch,' she repeated.

Marlowe woke alone, in semidarkness. Under the duvet, the luminous dial on his watch said a quarter to six, 21 September. He turned over, ready to sleep for another hour or two. Then he heard Caro, struggled out of sleep. Bloody child. Bel could go to her for once. A van chimed in the street below: 'Santa Lucia', digital, loathsome. This time, Marlowe flung the duvet off, struggled to the window and discovered his mistake. Ten to six, yes, but a wet and windswept afternoon. He thought of hurrying down to buy ices for the kids, then remembered that Luke was ill. They had lain down together in here. The room, like every other in the house, was still a shambles. Bel would have licked somewhere into shape by now.

Caro charged towards her father, arms wide with love. It would have been quicker to skirt the obstacles, but that wasn't her way. Climbing over sacks and tea chests, she jumped into his arms from the back of an armchair. Diving forward, Marlowe caught her, kissed her on the mouth, nuzzled the rose-petal skin of her neck. Caro giggled, jerking away from him, the way Bel did if sex moved out of her control. The baby, though, wasn't rejecting him, touched her father's thin face with soft hands, she said, by way of explanation, 'Scratchy. Hurts me.'

Marlow took the child in his arms, noticing the different clothes. He said, tracing the line of stubble, 'Sorry, miss. I forgot to shave. And yesterday.'

Caro inspected his face solemnly, one small finger exploring the limits of his beard. She touched her own cheeks, said, mystified, 'Not scratchy.'

Luke had built the fire well. Satisfying tongues of flame rose and fell from the coals. There were only about ten lumps left in the bag, not enough for the night; an expensive way to keep warm. Marlowe, still carrying the baby, came to sit beside his son. He said, 'You should have woken me. Feeling better?'

Luke held out his hands to the blaze. 'Sort of. I don't feel sick, but my neck's a bit stiff and my throat's sore. It's nothing. We need more coal, and stuff for that Aga.'

Marlowe touched his son's neck with cool fingers. The glands were swollen. He said, 'We'd better get you to a doctor.'

Luke protested, 'It's nothing. I'll be all right. It's not mumps, I had them when I was seven. Caro's been jabbed, MMR. Don't fuss. Did we bring the fan heater?'

'Bel took it for her room in college. They still have fixed dates for the heating.'

Luke shuddered. 'Like school. They like time tables. Snow in April, tough, it's still spring. October heatwaves, same difference, the heat stays on. Can we manage another bag of coal?'

'One more, at that price. I'll find a coal merchant tomorrow and order. Bear up. The heating goes in next week.'

Luke looked troubled. 'Can we afford it? I thought . . .'

He was deathly pale, blue about the lips like an old man. The impulse was too strong to resist. Holding the boy close, Marlowe said, 'Listen, Luke. Money's tight. No BMW for your eighteenth, unless I write a best seller. But there's more than enough to live on. One column a month pays the mortgage. The other three keep us. I borrowed enough to do the place up. We could let the top floor.'

Luke said, bleakly, 'Must we? I like this place being for us, I don't want anyone else. Stand back while I chuck this coal on the fire.'

Caro stood watching. One piece of coal missed its target and fell on the hearth. She picked it up, bit it and said, wondering, 'Black stones?'

Marlowe found her jacket, zipped it on, and retrieved her shoes from the kitchen. 'Come on, old lady. We're going to buy more coal.'

Luke replaced the fireguard and stood up. The room lurched. Unseen by Marlowe, he caught hold of the mantel-

126

piece and stood very still until the world fell into place again. He said, casually, 'Mind if I come too?'

Marlowe looked at the fire. 'I'd rather you stayed here. Setting the place on fire before we've unpacked would look a touch careless. Anything I can get you?'

Luke saw the leap and fall of flames, all the colours of gold from a three-quid plastic bag. He said, 'Nothing, thanks. More paracetamol, maybe. There's only one left.'

Marlowe was already in the hall, leaving the back way, through the kitchen. The wind blew in a scurry of leaves; they danced across the tiled floor, lay still. Luke heard the car scrunch through gravel and into the next road, away into wind and rain.

Chaos had become familiar. He skirted the jumble of labelled sacks, boxes and things upturned, sat on the sofa, its shabbiness exposed without the Shaker quilt that used to cover it; Bel's own property, gone for ever. He'd known every stitch, every patient inch of that quilt, from babyhood. Bel, the prescient, had bought it as a student for a couple of quid. Everything that ever belonged to Bel was two hundred and thirty miles away at least, depending where you started counting. His mother was living her own life. Bully for her. He enjoyed a minute or two of exquisite loathing before switching on the TV. The adverts were definitely different and not for the squeamish. A bellyful of worms writhed through a cartoon cow, then the camera zoomed in on the real thing. Then back to the cow – *zap! pow! ergh!* – all worms snuffed, voice-over for the latest miracle anthelminth. After offers at a chain of strange supermarkets, the local news came on. Today, it was marginally less alien. He knew Casterton a little now, recognised the castle, then the anorexic girl. On screen, she'd gained weight but still looked slender, clipboard in hand, as she challenged a passer-by. The news was no news at all, only the survey and plans for a hypermarket, off the bypass. Cursing himself for not getting her name, he switched to Channel 4, then registered the knock at the back door.

Faith said, flowers in hand, 'I'm your neighbour. The script says I come round and invite you all to supper. Or I bring home-made soup, and bread fresh from the Aga.'

Luke laughed. 'Don't waste food on me. I threw up a cup of coffee at lunchtime. Dad's out, begging a shovelful of coal. Come in.'

Unasked, Faith made her way to the warmth, neatly stepping round bags and boxes. 'All alone?'

Luke nodded, all alone in chaos with a sexy woman. Tonight, she wore a rainforest T-shirt over black leggings. Her maenad curls were tied with a green silk scarf. Downcast, he confronted her feet, long and slender in thin black sandals. There was raspberry varnish smudged on the end of one big toe. Bel's feet were stubby, size four, with stumpy little toes.

Faith smiled, and that was dead sexy too. She said, 'Stop staring at my feet. They're shy.'

He had to laugh again. She was on the sofa now, feet up on a tea chest. It was time for her to say, 'I won't stay,' or he had to make coffee. Faith looked entirely at home, had every intention of staying. He said, to see how she'd take it, 'I should offer coffee now, shouldn't I? There's instant, if you can find another mug.'

'Or you'll have to wash up? No coffee. I'm tea-total, with an *a*, and not thirsty.'

'Sure?'

Faith nodded gravely. 'Sure. I spend my life dodging buckets of tea and coffee. Occupational hazard.'

Luke discovered her eyes, dark blue, discovered his own weakness for sloe-dark eyes. He said, feigning disappointment, 'You mean, I can't borrow your Gold Blend? Shame.'

She studied him, a practised, all-over scan, said, 'Next year, maybe. Fifteen, are you?'

Luke smiled. She was very nice to be with. He felt better, simply talking to her. He said, deciding on the truth, 'Fifteen in December. And thanks for the flowers. We'll start on this tip tomorrow. I'll tell Dad you called.'

If only the bloody woman would go, or Dad were here. He was feeling faint again, weak from sickness, and not eating. She wouldn't move. Presently, though, she swung her feet to the floor, stood up and said, 'Some other time, maybe. I saw a man drive here yesterday, with a little girl.'

Like said, formally, 'My father and sister. I'll tell them you called.'

Faith said, indicating the flowers, 'Any chance of a jam jar?'

Luke considered. 'In the kitchen?'

She followed him, found dusty jars by a red plastic plate rack, washed them out, chopped stems with the bread knife, and arranged three jars of bright colour.

'There. Three jars full, earwigs, and these. See you.'

Luke heard the car arriving. It was funny, the way people drove in character. Dad slowed down at the last minute, but the odd thing was, he'd never crashed, parked tidily. He thought of going down to help. Then a spasm of nausea possessed him. Better to keep still, hope it would go away.

Coming up and down the steep stone steps, Marlowe and Faith met, exactly halfway. There was no room to pass without touching, especially as he was carrying Caro. At this mid point, the privet bushes, not cut back for the past two years, grew right across, had to be pushed back. The whippy narrow branches brushed against the woman, scattering yellow leaves. He had to look up, apologise. And then look again. Faith, hurrying back to some other life, recollected herself first. She said, extending a slim hand, 'You must be Luke's father. We met yesterday. I've just been round doing the welcome act. Flowers and chocs. Come round for coffee some time. Not now, though. I'm on duty soon and the kids haven't eaten.'

Marlowe said, pressing himself back against the overgrown bushes, 'See you, then, Thanks for coming round.'

And then she was gone, a woman with work to do, kids to feed. He carried Caro up to the house, set her down in the hall, returned to the car, for the coal. Also, he made a mental note, *buy secateurs, cut back privet.*

A well-feathered earwig sidled across the table. Luke caught it on a spoon, tipped it out into their own garden. The woman had gone; good. She made him feel gauche. She was rather like Bel, but kinder.

'These' proved to be a large box of Swiss chocolates. The thought of chocolate made him sick again. He hung over the sink, retching. He wanted to be alone, asleep in an ordered

129

room, in a warm bed. None of this was possible: bloody, bloody unfair.

The bout of vomiting over, he swilled away the mess. Probably, he would have been ill today, no matter what, but not in squalor, in this transit camp of a house. For nearly fifteen years, his room had overlooked the common and the Long Pond. *His* room, four metres by three, measured for maths, years ago. Bed, his, Davenport desk, his, the big chest of drawers, his. On the door outside was a sign you could turn round, *Come in; Go away*. They'd left it behind, hung on its brass hook. The room in this house was immense: sixteen feet by twenty. Dad still couldn't think metric. The point was, they'd taken his life apart. People – Richard, Jules, Toby – would walk past, but that place wasn't Marlowe's any more.

Dad had put the sack of coal on the hearth, and two bundles of kindling.

'That looks so squalid,' Luke said, disgusted. 'Can't you find a coal scuttle or something? And there are sticks in the back lane, free. A woman brought flowers and chocs. Excuse me, I'm off to bed.'

Marlowe tried to call him back, but Luke ignored him, slammed the door of his allocated room.

Caro found the chocolates, said, hopefully, 'I like these, don't I?' She knocked over a jam jar of dahlias, howled, then demanded food.

Half an hour later, Marlowe plonked her, fed and watered, in front of the TV. There was nothing on – news, sport, two comedy repeats. Caro howled some more. He fed in a Muppets video, crept out and upstairs to Luke's room. The boy had assembled his bed, found a fitted sheet, his own duvet and bedding. He appeared to be asleep. Marlowe went to stand beside the bed, struck with sudden fear. Taking his son's hand, he felt for a pulse. It was light, surely too fast. The boy seemed cool enough, though, breathing softly.

Marlowe was turning away, silent with guilt, when Luke woke, staring with unfocused eyes.

'How do you feel?'

Luke's head lolled. He replied, grudgingly, 'All right, if I stay in bed. What do you want?'

Sensing rebuke, Marlowe edged away. 'Can I get you any-thing?'

Luke closed his eyes. 'No. I'd like my old life back, but that's not on, is it? You and Bel . . . You didn't ask what I wanted, did you? Leave me alone. I just want to sleep.'

'Paracetamol? Hot drink?' Marlowe stood by the bed, uneasy.

Luke turned his face to the wall, made no answer. Marlowe waited a moment or two, then left, spurred on by piercing cries from his daughter. Halfway down the stairs he found her, crimson with grief and rage. Caro clung to him, wetting his shirt with her tears. Presently, he made out the words: 'Where's you, where's you, my dada?'

Marlowe took her in his arms, resting her head on his shoulder. Caro lay there, still sobbing quietly. In the living room, he sat down by the fire, stroking her, gentle with love. He said, very low, 'I'll never leave you, Caro. Whatever it costs, if I never work again, I'll never, ever leave you.'

Caro had stopped crying. She snuffled, hiccuped, still choked with sobs. Her eyes were bloodshot, her small face pink and swollen. She stared at him for a minute or two, then touched his stubbled cheeks. 'Dada?'

'Always.'

Caro struggled from his arms, stood beside him, tugging at his hands. She was beaming now. 'Hungry. Eat,' she said imperiously.

Marlowe kissed the top of her head. 'Anything you say.'

Chapter Twelve

Low Gear, said the signs, adding, a few yards down, the cheerful logo of a skidding car. Halfway up, or down, a scarlet Escort GTi had clashed with a lamppost. Neither would be the same again, buckled metal, and trailing innards everywhere. A pink-cheeked, fair police officer was taking details from witnesses. Another, less pink, red-haired, photographed the debris and made chalk marks on the road. Paramedics had done their best with the driver, staunching blood, fitting drips. They were ready to leave. Blood and rain swilled down into a grid. Luke caught himself staring, transfixed by the routine horror. Across the road, a group of twelve-year-olds passed, trying not to look. One boy doubled up to vomit over a wall. Luke found this more sickening than the blood. The ambulance was leaving now, sirens screaming, storming uphill, to the Infirmary. Idiotic, surely, to build a hospital on a mountain? Maybe they'd been afraid of noxious humours, and agues, from the marshland? It was also an idiotic place for a school. You could abseil down; there should be a ski lift. The weird thing was, old people – seventy, eighty, living in the streets all around shinned up like chamois.

It was his second week at school: Marlowe, Luke, fourth year, or Year Ten, booked for one-year GCSE in maths, French, English and Latin. He hadn't been consulted about the school because nowhere else did Latin. Last spring, in London, he'd taken entrance exams and won a scholarship. Prudently, he'd said nothing to Jules and the rest; nor had he told Bel. Struggling up the last near-vertical stretch, he wondered what she'd make of it. Bel, surprisingly, deplored private education and hospital care. Offered a four-year wait, though, to shed one varicose vein, she paid up and shut up. Bel steered clear of all 'morons', including some of her own students. For the gifted, she was an inspired teacher. The rest, in her opinion, simply shouldn't be there. Bel explained, on the smart chat shows, that higher education for the masses was absurd. They couldn't grasp the simplest concepts. It was, she conceded, yet one more way of massaging unemployment figures. His mother, Luke concluded, walking through the stone archway, would approve of his scholarship.

In the cloakroom, he sat down for a minute, battled with leaden weariness. Ashburn cuffed him from behind.

'Knackered? you're softies, down south. Wait till you try a real hill. It's a fell run today.'

Luke cuffed him back affectionately. Ashburn was all right, and Birkett, Stansfield and the rest, not close friends yet, but easy to get on with. The absence of girls didn't seem to matter, or not much. It was peaceful. Truly, he didn't mind school. There were rules, strictly enforced, which made life a tad easier: you knew exactly where you were. They set more homework, too. No problem; Dad worked all evening, the only time he could, since Caro and the house claimed all his day. Picking up the leaden bag, Marlowe, L. B., followed Ashburn, M. K., to forty minutes of Cicero's second Philippic. Mark Antony was a right twat. Imagine the *Sun*, if someone threw up all over the hallowed green benches. *O, foeditatem flagitiosem!*

Marlowe had been painting all morning. The house had taken shape surprisingly quickly, once they'd unpacked all the bags and tea chests. Three more days, and the carpets could go down. Bel would want sanded and waxed floors, and rugs, five times the price of fitted carpets. The scarred deal floors weren't worth sanding, only the parqueted dining room. He'd stripped paint from the main staircase, taken the doors to a caustic tank. This week, he'd painted six rooms already, all silvery green, like the underside of a willow leaf. Choosing carpet had been as simple, industrial-grade coir all through the house. He could add frayed and threadbare Indian rugs later. The best junk shop had one for thirty quid last week.

133

He felt like God, halfway through the fifth day, and the end in sight.

Last night Bel had phoned, damn her. Marlowe had taken good care not to give the number, but hadn't warned Russell. The sound of her voice disturbed unwanted memories, such as lying in bed, wondering whether to make love. His desire for sex hadn't changed, it was the idea of making love to Bel he couldn't stomach. Putting it crudely, he no longer wanted to follow where another man had wormed his way in. The thought disgusted him, reduced him to quiet tears. Fifteen years too late, he wanted a faithful wife.

Caro had a playpen now, which Luke had discovered in a box room. It was made of Edwardian or Victorian walnut, with china beads. She consented to play inside it; what she would not allow was five minutes out of Marlowe's sight. He could go to the loo, but if he so much as paused to zip his flies, she howled convulsively. Now she began to shake the playpen, setting the beads swirling. Marlowe filled his paint-brush again.

'Bloody stupid baby! Shut up! Five minutes, and I'll be done.'

The beads whirled. The noise was unpleasant, like a dentist's slow drill, but the effect was mesmeric. Caro span them faster. Marlowe turned away from the dancing colour and painted on, steadily. It was good paint, thick as Greek yogurt. The first time he and Bel painted the Clapham house, before Luke's birth, they'd bought cheap stuff. It didn't just drip, it ran down the brush, along their arms, into their armpits and down their necks. It wrecked two sets of overalls. The second time, richer, they had hired a decorator. Now he could enjoy himself, relishing the sensuous pleasure of creamy paint and a soft, yielding brush. Paint was user-friendly now, and even smelled quite good. This was the seventh room, Caro's, and he hadn't tired of the colour yet; it reminded him of summer afternoons, lying on a riverbank.

At night, he wrestled with words, for ever dissatisfied. Printed, everything looked slightly better. Caro had done for the fax, emptying her beaker of apple juice into it. He'd been frighteningly close to strangling her, disarmed in seconds by her cherubic smile. He should get a new fax machine, but

134

there was no money: eaten, every penny, by removers, solic-
itors, agents and Bel. Bel had half their essentials. Replacing
every small detail was tedious. Only last night, making loose
tea because they'd run out of bags, he discovered that Bel had
nabbed the strainer. It was a Victorian souvenir of Great
Yarmouth; his godmother's. He'd never been near Yarmouth,
but Bel had no right. The list of discovered bereavements had
grown since moving. She'd taken all the photos of Luke as a
newborn. She'd even walked off with the Red Army greatcoat bought for Luke in Prague, in the scruffy market near the
football stadium, his last job abroad. Last night, he'd assembled all these resentments, drafted a piece of first-rate
bitchery. Tonight, he'd hone it a bit, devise three or four versions, send it out on spec. Bel could read all about it. And
Sam. And many more.

Caro had been busy. She'd watched intently as her father
or Luke fastened the playpen catches. She'd practised carefully, unobserved. Today, her small fingers perfected the
moves, lifted the catches. When she pushed back one side of
the pen, it collapsed. Marlowe swung round, dropping his
paintbrush. Caro had him by the leg, biting his trousers, sure
of victory. He tried putting her back. Caro, an honourable
child, let herself out at once, rather than tease by waiting till
his back was turned. Then he folded the pen, said, resigned,
'You win.'

Caro nodded, wriggled free, content to watch him finish
the last corner. There would be no more painting today.
Satisfied, she watched him squirm free of paint-crusted overalls, wash brushes, leave them in water. She said, cheerfully,
'Out.'

First they needed to clean up. Caro, after felt-tips and Play-
Doh, had to be stripped and bathed. Marlowe washed paint
from his hair, showered quickly and took Caro down to the
car. She balked, furious, kicking him hard on the shins. He
was too tired to fight back. They could walk down to town. If
they skipped lunch, ate on the hoof, there was time before
Caro's playgroup. Strapped in the pushchair, she drummed
on the footrest with small angry feet. Marlowe offered a
banana. She biffed it to the floor, then a rusk, then a chocolate biscuit. Finally, he tried asking her what she wanted.

135

Speechless with anger, she unclipped her harness, scampered to the kitchen and opened a cupboard. No good. She tried another, slammed the door in fury. Marlowe resisted the urge to spank her.

Caro looked up, smiled. 'Dere.'

She was pointing to peanut butter, which she'd tried just once before. Stamping size five feet, she pointed again, sighed an exasperated, adult sigh of contempt. Marlowe sat her on the kitchen table, spread Sainsbury's sliced wholemeal with peanut butter. Luke had bought it for peanut-butter and jelly sandwiches, his current diet. The jar was almost empty, cue for another zap round Sainsbury's. He checked a few other jars, and the fridge; all running on empty. Impossible. Luke was barely eating, Caro a baby, but the food had disappeared. Despondent, he checked the washing powder, loo rolls, soap and, as an afterthought, nappies. All in the red zone. Now they'd have to go by car, no matter how hard the brat kicked.

Folding the pushchair, he carried it and his squealing daughter out to the car. Caro kicked him in the balls. Mad with pain, he all but dropped her, refrained, just, from shaking her senseless. Dazed, he strapped her into the car seat. As the pain ebbed, Caro stared at him with troubled blue eyes. Marlowe walked round the car, sat down gingerly in the driving seat. Caro began to cry, not her usual manic howl, but true sobs of contrition.

Marlowe took her small hands in his and said, as if she'd understand, 'Pax? Listen, beautiful, cars are a pain, likewise shopping, but we're out of everything.'

Caro took a bite of her sandwich, then another. Her tantrum belonged to the past. She broke off a piece of bread and offered it to him. Marlowe accepted it gravely. If only adult disputes were so easily resolved.

Driving down the hill, he saw Faith, for the first time in a fortnight, and waved. No response. Maybe she didn't see him. He felt slighted, rejected, then disgusted with himself. Faith was the first woman he'd fancied since Bel cleared off for ever. He should be bloody grateful, reassured that all was in working order. He'd been celibate since the second month of Bel's pregnancy.

There were road works at the bottom of the hill, and traffic lights, on red till the workman finished his mug of tea. Moving away at last, Marlowe saw with relief that it was too late for playgroup. Caro had been once so far, leaving him without a backward glance to crawl down tunnels, bounce, and smear paint. There were no other men. The women eyed him covertly, talked about episiotomies, morning sickness, and going back to work. Apart from changing Caro's nappy, he'd sat alone for two hours, pretending to read the paper, listening. Then he'd written it up. It made, so he was told, an hilarious feature, but once was enough. Today was to have been her second visit. Turning to Caro, he said, 'No Mums and Toddlers, brat. Round of golf?' She was asleep.

He'd missed the one-way system, third time he'd made that mistake. Reaching the haven of Sainsbury's car park took three extra miles and a cold sweat. Lifting the sleepy child into a cart, he studied the shopping women. None looked especially desperate. Most had at least two children. One, with a child Caro's age, three-year-old twins and an eight-month bump, looked seraphic as she lobbed nappies into a cart. She contrived to tow a second cart for groceries, directing the twins by remote control. It must be oestrogen.

Marlowe filled the cart as if on a sixty-second trolley dash. Halfway through the check-out queue, he remembered nappies and began to back out.

The woman behind said, tenderly, 'Forgotten something, love? Easily done. I'll watch your trolley while you fetch it.'

He came back with four vast bales of the things, wondered what it cost to hire a wife on an hourly basis. He thought of kissing his saviour, but she too looked eight months gone, plus toddler: someone else's woman. There were none left for him.

The home run took ten minutes, door to door. It was win or lose: choose the right lane, or head for Scotland. Caro ate prawn-cocktail crisps all the way. He hadn't forgotten anything. Russell had rung yesterday, liked the new column. Luke seemed happy at school, tired but working hard. They'd unpacked their lives and almost finished painting. They were free of Bel, for ever. It felt good.

137

Carrying the first box up the garden path, he saw a folded sheet of paper secured to the door handle by the kind of rubber band postmen drop. Setting the box down by the dustbin, he freed the note. It said, in green felt-tip, 'Please ring the Infirmary at once, re Luke Marlowe.'

Chapter Thirteen

There was a signature, illegible, and the Infirmary number. He stood very still. There were no other words, no comfort or reassurance. The downstairs phone was in the hall. Crossing the silent kitchen, he could hear it ringing, peremptory. Before he could reach it, they hung up. Again, he stood quite still. Luke might be dead, and he preferred not to know.

Outside, Caro was yelling. Focusing on the one practical job to be done, he fetched her and the box of frozen food. He stowed peas, fish fingers, boned breast of lamb and burgers. Then he returned to the phone. Caro followed, thumb in mouth, unnaturally quiet. Simultaneously, the door bell and phone rang. Halfway to the door, he remembered that answerphones belonged to another life, but Caro had already grabbed the phone, dropping the receiver with a crash on the tiled floor. Taking it from her, he gasped, 'Hang on. There's somebody at the door.'

At the door, he turned this round, fled back to the phone and said, when the female voice repeated its question, 'Speaking.'

'Father of Luke Marlowe?'

There was no more sun; the roses and lilies were only dark shapes in darker leaded glass. The receiver slipped in his sweating hand. He said, obediently, 'I'll come at once.'

His first, bizarre impulse was to ring Bel. *In extremis*, kin are summoned across time and hostility; not that Bel was hostile, merely indifferent. The hospital hadn't suggested imminent death, only that Luke had collapsed during a school fell race. He turned to find Faith standing on the dragon's head. She said, 'I'll run you to the hospital, if you like. You've had a shock. You shouldn't drive.'

Caro was talking to a parrot-head umbrella left in the hall stand, jetsam from the late owners. She managed to extract the umbrella, then drag it across the hall, said, 'Put it up.'

Marlowe was about to obey, then remembered that erecting umbrellas indoors brings bad luck. He refused.

Caro said, accurately, 'It's raining now.'

Faith steered them to the front door, expert in shock, sudden illness and death. She said, on the doorstep, 'You'd better lock up.'

Twice, on the way down, Marlowe almost missed his footing, thinking of his son, newborn, and all the years since. Faith directed them down to her own car. It was a Rolls. She said, by way of excuse, 'Same age as me, appreciating daily, and the patients love it. And yours?'

He laughed. 'Boring hatchback, one dented wing, past its best. Maybe we suit each other.'

She didn't smile or protest; serve him right. They reached the roadworks. The light was red. There was no one in sight, bar the officious workman. Faith glared at him and pointed to her windscreen. At once, he jumped to attention, switched to green.

Marlowe said, resentfully, 'How did you do that?'

She indicated the badge: twisted serpent, *Doctor on Call*. 'Has its uses. About Luke . . . You're not to worry. He'll be fine.' She turned left, up a near vertical cobbled street. The Roller rolled, satin smooth. They emerged opposite the Infirmary, all shining lights and sirens.

'Motorway smash?'

Faith shook her head. 'B team. It's the accident hour. Kids playing after school, chip-pan fires and babies. Those two are maternity, first stage. Could have walked here, better for them than all that huff-puff nonsense.'

Marlowe, about to protest, remembered the three kids. Instead, he asked about Luke.

Pulling into a parking space marked *Doctors Only*, she said, 'He collapsed on the fell run. They decided to bring him here.'

Marlowe reached for his daughter's hand, touchstone, said,

140

'You mean a fit?'

Faith opened her door. 'Absolutely not. He passed out for rather too long. We decided on a few tests, as a precaution.'

'We?'

She opened the passenger door, released Caro and swung her over a puddle. The school called our surgery. They thought you might be patients.'

Marlowe looked her up and down, observing details: a cameo brooch at her throat, purple Doc Martens. Intercepting his glance, she said, demure, 'It's a bishop's ring. God knows who popped it, or why. I didn't like to ask. You're not registered with anyone. We checked all the files in town. Jehovah's witnesses, or is it Christian Science?'

Marlowe removed Caro from a puddle, where she was stamping. 'Apathy. No plumber, dentist, doctor or milkman. I meant to, one day.'

The rain decided on a work-out. Faith took his hand, pelted towards Accident and Emergency. At the entrance, they stopped, breathless, facing each other below a marble statue of Lord Shaftesbury. Faith's waist-length hair was pinned up today, decorously Victorian. She might be any age from twenty to forty. The riding habit, strictly tailored, defined every line and curve of her body. Under the heavy serge skirt, he could see and still better, imagine the curve and strength of her thighs. She might or might not be beautiful.

She said, 'Report to the desk. I'll look after Caro. It's all right, I've no surgery this evening.'

Marlowe walked through water, leaden, every step a retreat. At the desk he said, as if there might be some mistake, 'I had a message about my son, Luke Marlowe.'

The clerk said, indifferent, 'Marlowe? I'll tell Sister you're here.'

Marlowe stood by the desk, leaning slightly against it. She added, gesturing with a stubby forefinger, 'If you could wait over there, Sister will see you soon.'

Obediently, Marlowe sat down on a chair angled to encourage relaxation. Waiting for life or death, or even an X-ray, the body refuses to relax; a misericord would make more sense. Above his head, a poster extolled healthy eating. None of Luke's or Caro's favourite foods featured. Possessed by guilt,

141

he broke into a sweat that shivered from hot to cold and back again. On the other hand, Luke's collapse wasn't brought on by a surfeit of fries and Coke.

He picked up a magazine. It was for women, like nine tenths of the rest. The only offerings for men were two pristine copies of *Football Monthly* and one of the *Racing Pigeon*, several years old. Men didn't wait, certainly not alone. Men were carved up in boy-racer crashes, injured on the football field, fell off ladders or broke noses in drunken brawls. Waiting was women's work, especially since labour became a male spectator sport. He studied breast self-examination, cystitis, hormone-replacement therapy and ovarian cancer, thanking God, like an unreformed Jew, for not making him a woman.

Faith put a mug of tea into his hands, pushed him back gently into the powder-blue upholstery.

'Bloody fortune these chairs cost, and you sit like the condemned man waiting for breakfast. Caro was hungry, OK?'

Caro was eating potato hoops, a ring on each pink finger, sucking the flavour off. Then she saw the rocking horse and shot across the room, struggling unaided into one stirrup. Marlowe abandoned the tea, lifted her into the saddle. It was a magnificent beast, dapple grey, anything up to a thousand quid, commissioned or bought antique. When Luke was born, he'd wanted such a horse, but Bel said no to the expense and false aspirations. Riding was no part of her city past. Caro sat straight and true, gripped unyielding wood with her knees. Marlowe stood by, imagined the crack of one small skull, brain damage and instant death. Then Caro had had enough, slid down, without warning, safe in his waiting arms. She scampered away into a playhouse where she began to cook, stirring three smiling pans, emerged with the largest on her head to climb on his knee, sodden.

Faith saw the wetness spread across his crotch and said, with some tact, 'No spares in your bag?'

Marlowe removed Caro from his knee. He snapped at the stupid woman, doctor or no doctor. 'What bag, for God's sake?'

Smiling, Faith took herself off. The duty nurse returned, followed by another. He'd been waiting exactly six and a half

142

minutes. The second nurse wasn't Sister but an underling: student nurse Eileen Connolly. She said, in a Derry accent.

'Mr Marlowe? Would you come this way?'

Marlowe, helpless, picked up Caro. Eileen Connolly was leading him to Luke alive or dead. Only, she didn't, stopping outside the half-glazed door of Sister's office. He knocked then entered, holding Caro's hand for luck.

Sister smiled her mother-superior smile. She said, practised, 'Mr Marlowe? There's absolutely no need to worry. We'd just like a word with you before Doctor sees Luke again.'

Marlowe prayed to any god – Pluvius, maybe – that Caro wouldn't pee again, or worse. There was a knock at the door; Eileen Connolly again. She held out a nappy, 'Dr Sinclair sent this.'

Marlowe, detesting the omniscient Dr Sinclair, thanked Nurse Eileen, then waited for the verdict on his son. Bel had threatened to miscarry at thirteen weeks, had been taken in for a scan. After a week, she stopped bleeding and was sent home. Knowing that 50 per cent of miscarried foetuses are abnormal, Bel insisted on repeat scans, demanded and got amniocentesis, at twenty-five. Luke passed every test, survived a horrendous labour unscathed. Bel's refusal of pain relief had been steadfast. Nothing must hurt her child. The pity of it hurt still with a memory of old love.

Sister was saying, or repeating, 'We've done a few tests. We've found nothing obviously wrong, but we'll keep him in for observation. Has he fainted before?'

Marlowe shook his head. 'Not that I know of.'

'No history of epilepsy?'

Caro wriggled free, trotted to the desk and began to play with a paperweight. Marlowe, shaking his head again, retrieved her, answered three more questions. Luke didn't smoke, snort or sniff. End of grilling. At last, he said, foolhardy, 'Couldn't I take him home now, come back tomorrow for tests?'

The lips, wide yet thin, set in a constrained approximation of a smile. She said soothingly, 'We don't consider that advisable in your son's case. If you or your wife would like to stay . . .'

143

Marlowe extracted the glassy treasure from Caro's paw again. 'Luke's mother lives in London.'

'I see. Would you like to see him now?'

Marlowe wondered whether such a fatuous question needed an answer, said nothing, then followed her out of the room. Caro trotted along beside them. They turned right, along a diversion marked by white footprints. Theatre was green, surgical wards red, medical, blue, psychiatric, yellow, and paediatric, white. The walls were hung with signs, all sinister. He knew very well what *oncology* meant. First right from *oncology* was the morgue. Their Virgil, blissfully at home, led the way to a single room, away from the clamour of paediatric teatime. Through glass doors, he saw the bald heads and spectral bodies of children, the kind captioned *tragic*. There were parents, species *courageous*, genus *heart-broken*, giving medicine, reading stories, changing nappies. A translucent woman, or girl, no more than twenty, sat breastfeeding her baby. Two beds were screened. The ward was gaudy with totems of childhood, Postman Pat, Jess the Cat, Thunderbirds, and the earnest *Playdays* team. The staff wore cartoon overalls.

'In here, Mr Marlowe.'

Rebuked for staring, he followed the woman in. At first, he didn't see Luke at all. The room was a soap set, patients, dying, for the use of.

Sister said briskly, 'We've put Luke in isolation, until we know what the problem is. When we have the results of –' She broke off, as if seeing Caro for the first time. Picking up the baby, she said, 'Children under twelve aren't permitted to visit. In the circumstances, I'll take care of her myself. You may stay for five minutes.'

Marlowe, inspired, handed her the new nappy. She bore Caro away. Only then did he recognise his son.

Luke lay on a high white cot, attached to monitors, as Bel had been for the hours before both births. His eyes were closed, his face not pale but deathly. Marlowe had seen dead men, knew the colour of their faces. Luke had a plastic tag round his right wrist.

Marlowe suppressed a strange urge to cross himself. He stood by the bed, beyond grief, and said softly, 'Luke?'

144

Luke opened his eyes and looked like himself, pale but definitely alive. He struggled to sit up. Marlowe gripped the bedside, made the world still. Luke reached for his hand, said, cheerfully, 'Their bloody stupid idea, not mine. I fainted, that's all. Ever tried running the 10,000 metres up a cliff-face? "Fell run", they called it. Where's Caro?'

Marlowe smiled, 'Banned. Carried off by old Tin Knickers. Healthy kids *verboten*. You'll see her tomorrow.'

Luke reached for a glass of tepid water, grimaced as he drank it. He said, already patient, 'How can I? They're not allowed. There's a window, in the main ward, for waving.'

Marlowe tasted the water and vowed to import Malvern. Luke spoke as if tomorrow was accounted for: incarcerated here. Resolutely, he said, 'Where are your clothes?'

Luke's eyes had closed again. The third time of asking, he muttered, 'At school.'

Marlowe wanted to shake him. He stared at the monitor screen. It registered zero, all readings. Luke was dead? Berserk with fear, Marlowe flung himself on the bed and shook the boy violently. Luke fought back, protesting.

'Back off, Dad! I just want to sleep. Is that a crime?'

Marlowe sat on the bed, weak with relief. Pointing to the monitor he said, 'Just testing. According to that, you're dead.'

Luke's eyes closed again. He said, wearily, 'You'd better tell someone, hadn't you? If this is heaven, it doesn't rate the hype. If it's the other place, I'll appeal. Hospitals are heinous.'

Marlowe, reassured, said, 'I'll find Tin Knickers. When do I collect you tomorrow?'

Luke stared at the silent monitors. Taking his father's hand, he said, 'Ring Burke and Hare first. No, I've always fancied a Viking send-off. Tomorrow? They were talking about a week, for tests.'

Marlowe felt the hand grow limp. Dead, after all, the monitors merely prescient? Luke, lying on his back, began to snore softly. Bel snored; a great trial to her lovers. Caro, thank God, did not. Making quite sure the boy was asleep, Marlowe kissed him gently on the forehead, then left in search of Sister.

*

145

Faith drove the Rolls back by another crooked and devious route, past strange alleyways and river warehouses. Darkness fell, and with it silvery mist rolled in from the sea. Strange smells wandered about, nothing like the restaurant reek of London by night. Seaweed, he decided, then a malted, savoury smell, like dog biscuits. Looking out as they crossed the river, he saw the slimy banks and dead bicycles of low tide. The other smell slunk out of a warehouse for animal feed. High above, on opposite banks and their respective hills, the Taj Mahal and the castle watched each other. Faith said,

'I'm on morning surgery. I'll have Caro for visiting time, if you like.'

Marlowe erupted, incoherent with grief, fear and rage. The gist of it was no bloody leech-house of a hospital could have his son, even overnight. He'd fetch Luke's clothes, drive straight back and discharge him.

Faith said, carefully, 'I wouldn't, if I were you. Really, I wouldn't. You're a single parent, for one. They'll round up social workers. They might even section you, if you kick up a fuss.' She turned an impossible corner, headed down a sheer cobbled hill, turned right and parked outside his house. Marlowe said, petulant,

'I can't leave my son with that bunch of quacks. For starters, they wired him up to a duff monitor. If one of your kids was declared dead . . .'

'Luke's in good hands. Their budget's ludicrous. You should see Maternity. Some babies get to sleep in Moses' original basket. But the staff are bloody good. They'll run more tests tomorrow. If they're not satisfied, they'll send him to Manchester or Great Ormond Street. Give them half a chance.'

Marlowe, head in hands, leaned against the walnut dashboard. Caro was asleep in the back, under Faith's travel rug, which meant carrying a dead weight up all those murderous steps. He hadn't even unpacked the rest of the bloody shopping. And the rain was coming like stair rods, waves lapping in the torrent that rushed down hill.

'Sorry, Doc. I've watched too many hospital soaps. There's always at least one sheet job. You know, call the crash team,

jump-start the heart a couple of times, then they all stand
back and the sheet's pulled over. Extraordinary taboo, that,
the way we cover the dead. Luke looked ready for the
morgue.'

Faith stepped out into driving rain. From the boot, she produced a golf umbrella, rainbow-striped. Releasing Caro, she
held the umbrella against the door. Marlowe let himself out
and took the umbrella while Faith locked up. They climbed
as a trio.

At the top, Faith didn't follow them in, stood in the porch.
She said, stepping out into still-torrential rain, 'Rob's. He
should've stuck to golf. Give or take the odd lightning bolt,
it's a darned sight safer than climbing.'

'Rob?'

She was at the top of the steps already, in profile, enigma-
tic. She said with practised detachment, 'My husband. Late
husband. He died on Everest, three years ago. Glamorous on
a headstone, but walking under a bus leaves you just as dead.
See you.'

Marlowe closed the door, aware of the hideously empty
house. Caro might sleep till morning. Parts of him had
planned an entirely different end to the day. Faith was the
sexiest woman he'd chanced on in years. Better still, he'd
never met anyone like her. Bel, whatever she liked to think,
came with a marque number, was set fair to become a pillar
of the establishment: Dame Annabel Grey, vice-chancellor of
somewhere. Bel would head royal commissions or even a
ministry. Bel, if she timed it right, could trim her politics any
convenient colour. Faith Sinclair in her widow's weeds could
steal his heart with pleasure. It wouldn't happen, though.
She'd defined their relationship: doctor, patient, off limits.
Which was just as well. Besides, one thing led to another, and
he had enough children. In case he cherished any doubts on
this score, Caro woke and screamed, barely pausing for
breath, for the next hour. Then he divined what she wanted:
more of the chocolate she'd seen him buy in Sainsbury's.

Three days later, he was summoned to collect Luke. It wasn't
in the least convenient. Caro was making mud pies. Russell
had been on the phone, at seven *a.m.*, demanding this week's

article yesterday. Half an hour more, and the thing would be done. He'd have to fax it from somewhere. Russell had growled, 'Then get yourself a new one, a.s.a.p. We bloody well pay you enough.' And more in that vein. Russell in that morning mood brooked no excuses, couldn't know, of course, that *Northern Lights* was now his sole source of income.

The hospital wanted to be shot of Luke – by twelve, the voice stipulated. Luke, no longer at death's door, was occupying a precious bed, loitering uselessly on NHS property. Luke must be removed by midday, or . . . or what? Marlowe wondered. Get nabbed as an organ donor? Luke was already in disgrace for refusing to eat one mouthful of hospital food.

One last read-through, then a quick spell check, vital today, given that he was extolling the virtues of Luke's shamelessly elitist Tudor grammar school.

Caro hammered at the kitchen door. Caro, like Russell, must not be kept waiting. The computer had found four asinine spelling mistakes; his fault, no brain left whatsoever. Bel, like smart-alec Mary in the Bible, had chosen the best part. Troubled with many things, he opened the kitchen door. Caro stood before him. Three hours ago, she'd looked like a Flower Fairy. Free spirit, Caro gave such clothes the treatment they richly deserved. Mired to her jet-black fingertips, she held out the morning's casualty. Yesterday, it had been a dead bird, with maggots. She said, 'See this bleeding worm.'

He looked. It writhed, headless, oozing whatever worms use for blood. He said, not wishing to repress, 'You'd better not say *bleeding* worm.'

Caro laid it on his hand, tenderly. She said, bewildered, 'Why not?'

Marlowe sighed. 'Some people might not like it.'

Caro retrieved her pet, caressed its squirming purple body. She said, all innocence, 'Then see this bloody worm.'

Marlowe gave up, encouraged her to carry Worm to the compost heap. Caro was filthy. Russell wanted the article faxed, by midday. Luke was being evicted from the Infirmary, also at midday. It was half past eleven. Bel would lock her daughter in a broom cupboard rather than take her out like this. Caro, Luke, or Russell? There was a clean nappy on the hall stand. Thirty seconds and one baby wipe later, it was on Caro. Thirty more, and he was clipping the second strap of scarlet dungarees. They hid nearly all her filth. Sitting her on his knees, locked in a half-nelson, he clipped black nails down to shell pink. Luke's clothes were in the boot already. When the hospital said midday, they were surely not going to evict him at five past? When Russell said midday, he meant, *or else.*

GET IN LANE, ordered the overhead signs. Praying hard for a better memory, Marlowe zapped across the river, right and up a cobbled cliff-face to the market car park and the library fax. Minutes later, Russell had this week's *Northern Lights*, and some prat had blocked the car-park exit with a safari truck, complete with roo bars. They'd also left two bawling toddlers strapped in their car seats. In the back, they or, much more likely, *she* had flung a dozen or more bags: clothes, china and, of all the damn stupid things, a new camcorder, box end on show in its Dixon's bag. A small crowd had gathered, irate and righteous. At its head, a meagre woman with a frizzy perm, small eyes and the uniform of a district nurse had taken charge. Grimacing at the toddlers, she raised their screams another ten decibels. But she'd taken down the number and pressed someone into fetching the police.

'Tow 'un away, that's what,' growled a lorry driver.

A thin, fair girl dressed in cream polyester silk and a flower-strewn hat with a veil began to weep. Her mascara wasn't waterproof, but the veil screened the worst of the damage. Charcoal shadows added Goya interest to her bland young face. The scrawny little man with her wore a clump of asparagus fern and a wilting carnation in his buttonhole. Wordless, he stood cracking his knuckles until the girl protested. She was crying steadily now, but both babies had fallen asleep, exhausted. On guard, the district nurse stood by their window, though the crowd had dispersed. Resigned, they sat in their cars, listened to radios, or sloped gleefully off to the nearest pub. Two Australians suggested lifting the jeep. No one listened.

At the register office, some furious Sergeant Troy was waiting for his bride, wouldn't give her much longer.

149

Marlowe took her by the arm, steered the bride and her unhappy father out to the road. Stepping recklessly into the traffic, he pointed to the girl and to her father's buttonhole. It worked. The third car, a fishmonger's van, stopped, listened, grinned and hoisted her up. There was no room for Dad, unless he wanted a ride in the back, on ice, with the fish. Marlowe, gripping Caro's hand tightly, flagged down an empty hearse. The father was on his way. The Australians cheered; the nurse achieved a small, pursed smile. Marlowe thought of flagging down a taxi, nabbing the story, tabloid classic and a nice little filler for the local news. Then he remembered Luke. Besides, the forlorn little bride had suffered quite enough already. He couldn't imagine *marrying* Bel. Arriving together would be the only way. They certainly couldn't have trusted each other to turn up.

The police arrived, with keys and an explanation: the mother had been knocked down on a pedestrian crossing. Better and better, Russell would say, tonight's locals, TV and radio too, and a full story tomorrow. Marlowe, back in his own car, watched as a plain-clothes WPC drove away with the babies. One woke up, screamed in terror, then accepted a bag of chocolate buttons. He would *not* intrude. He'd rescued the bride, the babies were safe, the mother accounted for, dead or alive. Why should anyone else know a word about it? First to leave the car park, he faced the truth. He would mind his own business. The fish-van bride, the abandoned babies and their mother had suffered enough. In no way would he add to their grief and his bank balance. Witty little reports on the going rate for a tart from Prague to Paris, yes, gate-crashing private grief, absolutely not.

Passing the town-hall clock, he saw that it was half past twelve. The Infirmary was half a mile away by the lamppost signs, two at least on the one-way system. Ahead, nothing moved. Caro, bottomless pit, began to wail. Hunger was an outrage she couldn't bear, not for one minute. Marlowe took the car out of gear. There were police ahead, relaying news, containing passions. Presently, the driver two cars up stepped out and came to explain.

'Bad business. A woman walked under a bus at the cross-

150

ing. They need lifting gear. She's still alive. Could be an hour or more.'

Marlowe swallowed bile. The story had moved up several notches, from a filler to tonight's main news, at least locally. And he wanted, more than ever, to mind his own business. Someone else could play carrion, scavenge in this particular tragedy. Leaving Caro, he stepped out, carefully, to pass the message on. Twenty minutes later, the traffic began to move, slowly enough for the relayed news. The woman was dead.

Luke, discarded, sat in the corridor, surrounded by the debris of four days inside. He was still wearing pyjamas and a hospital robe, hideously striped, like a Nativity shepherd. They'd returned his running strip and mud-caked spikes. A crust had formed over the greenish cow and sheep muck. His vest smelled of old sweat, foxy. The rest of his luggage comprised a radio, three copies of *2000 AD*, two apples and a half-empty bottle of Ribena.

'They chucked me out. Somebody really ill needs my bed. And Sister wants to see you.'

Marlowe explained, sparing details, exactly why he was late. Luke appeared unmoved, said, 'Nobody we know, was she?' Then he added, accurately, 'Well, she couldn't be. We don't know anybody. Pics and fax in, I take it? Blushing bride, tragic death, motherless babes. And the fish van, I like the fish van. I hope the groom didn't clear off, like Sergeant Troy.'

Marlowe retrieved Caro from the Wendy house and separated her from a pink bear, three feet high. How reassuring that his son should think of Sergeant Troy. He said, brusquely, 'No pictures, no story.'

'But . . .'

Marlowe said, 'No one else's bloody business. They'd all suffered more than enough.'

Luke looked up, surprised. 'You really mean that, don't you?'

Marlowe nodded. 'I really mean it.'

'Then . . .?'

'End of my brilliant career? Very likely, unless they'll settle for a cookery column. Where's the Angel of Death?'

151

Caro had consented to stay with her brother. Sister Margaret O'Donnell clacked down the corridor, her one-and-a-half-inch heels prudently tipped. Marlowe was directed into her sanctum. She sat down, hands outstretched, body language indicating, first, her superior status, and second, her transparent honesty. She said, as if confiding a secret, 'Mr Marlowe, Luke's given us a few problems.'

Marlowe, practised listener, received the code *Mr* Marlowe, and *Luke*, formality moving swiftly to intimacy. He said nothing at all, studied a resin model of the human ear and a calendar, three days out of date; text for the day, 'Every woman should marry – and no man'. Benjamin Disraeli. He could have sworn that was Oscar Wilde; it certainly sounded like Wilde. Sister O'Donnell wore no rings on any finger; seemed made for celibacy, by default. *Virgo intacta*, he deduced, since they were sizing each other up. No one would dare to intrude.

She said, since he made no response, 'Luke was brought here after collapsing on a cross-country run. He claimed to be too weak to walk. We've carried out a few tests and, quite honestly, Mr Marlowe, we can't find anything wrong.' She stopped.

Marlowe said, since he must make some response, 'What did you test him for?'

She pursed her lips. Marlowe smiled faintly, the elusive resemblance clear. She was a dead ringer for Tenniel's Duchess in *Alice*. She said, testily, 'Luke *appeared* very unwell, very weak. We've tested for glandular fever and anaemia. And his heart. He's fine. Nothing wrong at all, physically. You can take him home, send him back to school. We do think he needs help, though. We've made a provisional appointment with Dr McKie, and we'd like to see you too.'

Marlowe said, to save time, 'You mean, a shrink? What the hell for? He was ill. I saw him. He looked like death.'

'Hyperventilation, Mr Marlowe. Luke's symptoms were self-inflicted. He may have had some minor infection recently. He mentioned a stomach upset. I assure you, he's perfectly well now, apart from refusing food. You're divorced, I understand?'

Marlowe had been about to say that refusing hospital food

proved Luke's sanity. Instead he replied, looking her straight in the eye, 'No, I'm not divorced.'

Sister pursed her thick lips again. 'But you and Mrs Marlowe are separated.'

Marlowe, enjoying himself, replied, 'No. Luke's mother and I never married.'

Contempt and righteousness sat on the desk between them. She pursued another tack. 'How often does Luke see his mother?'

Marlowe smiled, saturnine. 'That would depend on what you mean by "see". It's difficult to avoid *seeing* Bel, on all four channels and Sky. Luke's mother is Dr Annabel Grey.'

Sister O'Donnell scowled her opinion of the great and not very good. She probed again. 'There's a young child, I believe.'

Marlowe nodded, amused. 'Caroline. She's just two. He seems quite fond of her.'

The nurse snarled. 'That's not what he said. Luke seemed quite happy to be in hospital. He said it kept him away from the screaming brat. There's evidence of conflict and alienation there. You moved a considerable distance recently?'

Marlowe, virtuoso in this art, decided not to play any more. He said, 'No comment', three times in succession.

Sister O'Donnell said, 'You'll be hearing from the psychiatric department in due course. And I suggest you register with a general practitioner. It's most irregular. We can't send his notes on until you do.'

Marlowe said, suavely, 'You could give them to me. I can read.'

She ignored him, then added, pitying, 'Quite honestly, Mr Marlowe, we're inclined to consider the whole episode a piece of attention seeking, Inevitable, given his disturbed background. You'll have the referral letter in due course. You really should register with a GP. Good afternoon.'

Luke drank a cup of tea, retreated to bed. It was half past three. His room, spare as a monk's cell, could catch no more light today. He lay down on the bed and stared at the dead-white ceiling, newly painted. He'd liked it better before, cracks, cobwebs, imagined continents. If he lay quite still, it was all right. If he moved, it was freeze-frame, action replay, lead weights on every bone. Coming up the stairs, he'd stopped three times, like an old, old man. Like Grandad. He was possessed, suddenly, by the idea that Grandad would die soon, all alone. Grandma, ten years dead, was a fleeting memory, someone who had cleaned his face with her glove in church. Once, she'd bought ice cream at the tearooms in the park. They sat among the azaleas and narcissus, he with ice cream, she and Grandad with tea, milk jug and lump sugar in a silver bowl. Later, they walked home in cool green light shimmering through hundred-foot beeches, the last gracious year. After Grandma's funeral, they walked in the park again, but the tearooms had closed.

Last year, Grandad's car was nicked from inside his locked garage, found as a burnt-out wreck at the foot of the hill, near the old tearooms, where the weeping willows used to grow. Granddad walked in the park still, as if hand in hand, through all their old places. Vandals had smashed the tearoom windows and sprayed a dragon on the mossy wooden walls, green, red and gold, like a Rasta bonnet. The other graffiti were what you'd expect, sex, sex, sex, words and pictures, but the dragon was something else, Fafner, Smaug, brilliant. Someone should catch the kid who did it and get him to art school, Grandad said.

Marlowe knocked on the door. Luke said, not moving at all, 'Come in. No charge.'

His father had brought black and green grapes and a glass of orange juice on a pewter tray. Luke sat up, but the sudden movement made his head swim. He lay back, said, 'Thanks,' but touched nothing.

Marlowe sat down on the bed beside him, then felt his forehead. It was cool and dry, but his hands were like ice, blue-tinged, numb. Fully dressed, swaddled in dressing gown and duvet, Luke shivered.

'Would you come downstairs? I'll light the fire.'

Luke shook his head. 'It's too cold.'

Outside, still brave and high, the autumn sun warmed a city of light, honey-gold stone. Long rays shimmered through light branches where golden leaves still hung. In well-loved gardens, nothing would give in yet, all gaudy colour, fighting back. Marlowe, by the window, saw Faith

Sinclair leave her preposterous car, climb up to the house where she lived with those three children. The felicity of an affair or more must have occurred to her too: one man, one woman, each bereft, five children. Hostility would be promising; for *Pride and Prejudice*, read True Romance. Their current, courteous indifference was a passion killer.

Presumably there were other desirable women around, but he lacked the courage, energy or time to go hunting. The day's drama corroded in his mind: two children, crying for ever for their mother; the forlorn bride; his own acerbic dialogue at the hospital. Very likely, he shouldn't have interfered. In six months or a year, the girl might curse him. She'd hardly looked eighteen. As for Sister O'Donnell . . . He stood accused of Luke's illness, a failed father. Turning round to ask Luke how he felt, Marlowe saw that the boy had fallen asleep. One clawlike hand lay outside the duvet. He tucked it in, touching cold flesh.

Downstairs, Caro had found her way to the fridge. There was a crash, a shattering of glass, then shrill wailing. Marlowe threw himself downstairs, turning one ankle halfway down. In agony, he limped to the kitchen. Caro intact, surrounded by spilt milk and broken glass, both bottles in smithereens.

Later, a good two hours later, the floor washed, glass swept, Caro bathed and fed, he went up to see Luke again. This time, the boy had changed into pyjamas and was sitting up in bed. He said, cheerfully enough, 'I feel better now. If it weren't so cold . . .'

Marlowe drew the curtains. Night arrived earlier here. The street lights were just coming on, blue and red and gold, like new fire. Outside, there were homecomings, Escorts, Astras, Sierras, hunger, and another day ending. Children, some only three or four, roamed about the streets, trundling lumpish things in old prams. One, more refined, wore a neon mask and a tattered witch's hat. He could hear their chant, 'Penny for the Guy, mister, missis'. They added, as often as not, 'Mean old git'. Marlowe sighed for his own ordered childhood, never in the streets after dark, never begging *pennies for the Guy*. He said to Luke, as if casually, 'Did you ever collect pennies for the Guy?'

Luke opened his eyes. He'd eaten nothing, nor touched the orange juice. 'You must be joking. *If* you get any, the roughs duff you up and take it. Anyway, it's illegal. You need a licence for street collecting.'

'Did you ever want to play out, after dark?'

Luke's eyes widened. 'What's brought this on? Your little talk with Sister?'

Marlowe nodded. 'More or less. She thinks you're disturbed. And I've ruined your life. Taking you away from Bel, and everything. If I let you play out in the dark, will you get better?'

Luke took a sip of orange juice, discovered parching thirst and drained the glass. Afterwards, he said, with a trace of laughter, 'Dad, ignore her. I'm ill because I'm ill. I'm not mental, or doolally, or anything. I'm *ill*. The tests must be wrong. Besides, I didn't want to stay with Bel. She's too much. Caro and I are better off with you. London's still there.'

Marlowe sat on the bed again, willing his son to eat, gain strength. 'What about friends?'

Luke shrugged. 'Jules, Toby, Richard . . . I could phone, or write. I *like* my new school, Dad. Honestly.'

Marlowe eyed the floor, said, a little coy, 'No girls, though.'

Luke sighed. 'So? They weren't exactly queuing up. It can wait.'

Marlowe said, with unexpected candour, 'At your age, I thought about girls all the time.'

Luke laughed, sat up firmer in the bed. 'Correction. You thought about sex. The girls inside the boobs and all that didn't rate, did they? No, it's fine. I like school without girls. It's peaceful, if you must know. When can we see Grandad?

Marlowe glanced towards the door. He'd left Caro building with Duplo. Her current style was sixties brutal, erected for instant destruction. There was a satisfying crash, manic laughter. Caro was fine, Luke's request mysterious. Long past the age of affection, the boy seemed ill at ease with his grandfather. But Luke said, almost eagerly, 'It's not far, is it? Less than an hour? Could we go this weekend?' His eyes were bright, feverish.

Marlowe could hear his daughter squealing, dragging something that scraped across the hall tiles. Caro could be relied on to end intimacy. Caro's screams had foiled his last ever attempt to make love to Bel, who'd said, 'You go. Anyway, she's all yours now.'

Luke flung back the duvet, pulled on a sweatshirt over his pyjamas, stuffed his feet into shabby tigers, Christmas nonsense, two years old. He said, kindly, 'That cow gave you a hard time. I knew about the shrink. Codswallop, honestly. I'm just ill. It's nobody's fault.'

Caro was on the stairs, might teeter and fall, dash her unfinished skull on unkind stone. Marlowe fled to retrieve his daughter. They'd tried a stair gate, loaned by Faith but it was no good. Caro had sussed the catches, could climb over anyway. Caro was lethal. Taking her in his arms, he caressed the small round head, the silky dark hair. She said, peremptory, spitting image of her mother, 'Hungry. I want something to eat, now.' She wriggled free, made for the door. Marlowe pounced on her. Caro kicked him, hard, then sank her teeth into his wrist.

Luke said, laughing, 'She *said* she was hungry. I'm coming down now. There's something I want to video.'

Caro ate hugely; Luke toyed with an apple, left three quarters of it. Presently, Marlowe left them, retreated to his office, loaded a disc, sat staring at the screen. Three minutes later, it went blank, and bleeped. This happened three times. At least blank sheets of paper didn't nag. He arranged a few words in his head, tried them out. It looked readable enough, an account of a morning in town, without any of today's drama. He found a title, 'Stand Laughing By', decided, with some regret, that the reference might elude even the most ardent fans of Kenneth Branagh, or Lord Olivier. He tried quoting it in full:

> *O noble English, that could entertain,*
> *With half their forces the full pride of France*

And let the other half stand laughing by
All out of work, and cold for action.

Bump-started by Shakespeare, the rest came fluently enough:
England out of work. *Northern Lights*, once a week, stood
between him and total destitution. By day, he walked with
Caro on the edge of another world. Its citizens had never
worked, nor did they expect to. They roamed through a working day, stood laughing by, paradise regained. They could get
on very well without work. He liked 'cold for action'.
Shakespeare, like the Bible, was fair game to twist any which
way. Today, 'cold for action' meant just that. Why join in,
risking acid cruelty and failure, when the view was much better from here? Yesterday, for instance, had been a day of
pellucid loveliness, the October air cool as water. He'd
walked with Caro by the canal, fed the ducks, visited Luke,
bought fruit, kicked through heaped golden leaves. Casterton
people were busy living, with no plans for revolution. In the
market square, young Leonardo chalked his *Last Supper*,
almost perfect, gone for ever in a night's rain. The young sat
round the fountain, laughed and fed pigeons. If the extinction
of work distressed them, they bore it bravely. Nobody
starved, few seemed seriously drunk.

Marlowe finished the first draft in half an hour, went to
check on his children. Caro, jam on her face, a half-eaten
apple falling from her hand, had fallen asleep in Luke's arms.
Luke was watching Bela Lugosi's *Dracula* on video, looked
quite happy. The hospital plastic tag still circled his left arm.
It said *Luke Barlow*. Marlowe, irritated, tugged at it. Luke
rummaged in his pocket, produced his knife, cut it through,
then chucked it in the fire.

'Barlow, Marlowe, who cares?'

They sat together, happy, until right triumphed and evil
was destroyed, again.

Chapter Fourteen

On Saturday, early, Marlowe shopped alone. Gaudy with
colours of autumn, the market stalls invited pillage with their
handfuls of richly swelling shapes: pomegranates, plums,
aubergines, great cobs of golden corn. He filled two hessian
bags with carrots, corn, cauliflower and tomatoes, paid for a
whole crate of apples to collect later. By eight forty-five, he'd
done with Sainsbury's, a week's groceries bagged and boxed
in the boot. The library opened at nine; ten perfect minutes of
peace, collecting books ordered a month ago. Master now of
the devilish one-way system, he fetched the apples, and
parked outside the house at nine thirty.

Caro toddled to meet him, still in her Jemima Puddleduck
sleepsuit. Brandishing her beaker, she said, 'Drink,' then
added, practically, 'And choc.'

Marlowe knelt before her, captivated.

Caro fixed him with fatal china-blue eyes, demanding sat-
isfaction. She said, 'Where choc? Choc now, please.'

He picked her up. She smelled of talcum powder and warm
pee. He carried her up to the bathroom, filled the great
pedestal washbasin with warm water. Naked, Caro was the
loveliest female thing he'd ever seen, every curve of her light
body perfect. He washed her and swaddled her in the hooded
wrap Bel had bought two years ago. He remembered, in sorrow, her first day at home, when she vanished inside it. Now,
it hung three inches clear of the ground.

Dressed, she bumped downstairs on her bottom, made for
the TV, which she switched on to watch *Going Live*. The day
before, she'd loaded *Aliens*, unaided, watched a good ten

159

minutes before discovery. Caro was good value. He'd spent that morning writing 'Toddler Tech', sold it, on spec, by mid-day. Caro and her alarming peers would fax their nursery-school assignments: ten more ways with Andrex tubes and fromage frais pots.

But *fromage frais* was off the menu, yesterday's bank-statement said so, likewise Luke's beef quarter-pounders. Bel's civilised *let's not waste money on lawyers* deal had been eroded by the brutish traits she deplored in prime time; greed, self interest, and conservatism. Bel, nobody's wife, or mother, had discarded them, like so many men before her. Allowances promised for Luke and Caro never came. He'd written, just once. No answer. Eventually, the letter returned, marked 'Gone Away' in black felt-tip; Bel's writing. The message was candid enough. Caro and Luke, children of no marriage, were no concern of hers. He considered, briefly, war in cold print, but good manners got the better of him. Bel was simply living by her own creed; so be it.

Luke appeared at last at eleven, saturnine in black, deathly pale.

'Your El Greco period?' Marlowe said, intrigued.

Luke made himself black coffee, crunched a sugar lump. Switching from the *Open University* to *Batman*, he said, 'Dominico Theotocopoulos? Caro's always watching the Open University. She's a mutant. Like the brats who join Mensa at three. She was watching a unit on El Greco a few days ago, and Socrates for afters.'

Marlowe turned down *Batman*, said, maternal, 'You should eat.'

Luke had his head down between his knees. The coffee, untasted, stood on the hearth. He retched, stumbled out to the kitchen, stood by the sink, trembling, but brought nothing up. Marlowe, one arm around his son, guided the boy back to a chair, said, 'Delete. You should see a doctor. I'll ring Dad.'

Luke protested. 'You can't do that. He's expecting us. Just tell him I've had a stomach bug. As for bloody doctors . . .'

Tom Marlowe found his granddaughter a wicker trug, dark with age, stained purple by decades of harvest. She filled it with lizard-green beans and windfalls with tiny slugs cling-

160

ing. Marlowe followed them with carrier bags, silently cursing all mellow fruitfulness. Twice, in less than an hour, they'd stopped for Luke to be sick, retching on nothing like a pregnant woman. Caro treated fruit like Play-Doh, squidging it about, plastering her face with purple pulp. At night, he removed gunge and grot from her hair. They didn't need twenty pounds of plums, fifty of apples, great swollen cabbages. This year, there were pumpkins and sweet corn, colossal, very likely inedible. Caro tried to lift a twenty-pound monster, while his father loaded a carrier bag with green tomatoes.

'They'll ripen, if you treat them right. In a drawer, on clean newspaper, or on a window ledge.

Marlowe took the bag. His arm buckled. He said, in loving patience, 'Dad, it's too much. We can't use all these. Luke doesn't even like tomatoes.'

Tom removed gold-rimmed glasses, polished them on the corner of his cardigan. He said, without preamble, 'The boy's ill. You shouldn't have come.'

Marlowe sat on an ivy-wreathed stump. He could see one weed, a late, truant dandelion, at the greenhouse door. A child had carved its name on a tree stump, patronised by tabby slugs. Beside the stump, there was a Guinness bottle, filled with half an inch of dark liquid, and a dozen or more bloated slugs. Tom picked it up.

'One night's haul. They prefer Guinness. Canned Boddington's a damned sight cheaper, but they're snobs. *Limax maximus*, marinaded in Guinness – could there be a market?'

Marlowe averted his eyes.

His father laughed, put the bottle down beside a stone rabbit. 'You always were squeamish. The first worm you saw had you squealing in terror. Sarah ate half hers. Frances kept several as pets. About Luke . . . I don't like the look of him.'

Marlowe told the story briefly, concluded, 'Either way, it's my fault. He's really ill, and I can't come up with the right doctor, or he's shamming, and I've damaged his soul. The old termagant of a ward sister called it attention seeking.'

'Stupid cow.' The older man broke off, apologised, lit his pipe, then dismantled it. He explained, carefully extracting charred tobacco, 'Senility. I gave up years ago, after your mother died, but the paraphernalia hangs about. You and Bel . . . Excuse me, but I can't recall the precise position.'

Marlowe watched a wren fly into a world behind ivy and Virginia creeper. He said, 'We've separated, for good, this time, sold up, and divided the spoils. Caro and Luke stay with me. The mystery is that we lasted so long.' Tom snapped a runner bean in half, ate it raw, said, gently,

'I wouldn't say that. Bel's a particularly beautiful woman. Most men could tolerate a few irritating habits, to share a bed with your wife.' Marlowe met his father's eyes.

'Dad . . . You know she was never my wife. And Bel's irritating habits ran to affairs with half London.'

He stopped, uncomfortable, too many taboos broken. His father, shameless, had included himself with most men. The silence gaped. At last, carefully moving the subject on, he said, 'Never mind Bel. They seem to blame me, for moving Luke so far north, for taking him away from Bel.'

Tom crunched the other half of his runner bean, said,

'And what do you think?'

Marlowe shrugged. 'He's ill. Anyone can see that. He was sick twice on the way here. He's been ill, on and off, since we moved, can't seem to shake it off. They suggested a shrink, but he seems sane enough to me.'

Tom said, 'Really? I prefer madness myself. Who's sane? Nice people, with burglar alarms, insured against everything? Since the car business, I've stopped locking the door. They wanted to give me a new car, but I took the money instead. It's gone to a good home, the money, I mean. No car, no thieves. No-one's walked in, yet. My pension book's here, left pocket. Far more than I need. Being old pays, you know. Damned sight cheaper than marriage and raising kids. Twenty pence on the buses, old fogies rail-card, half-price haircuts. Thankyou for coming, but I'm tied up this afternoon.'

Marlowe stood up, rejected. 'You want us to go?'

A ginger cat picked his way lightly along the cedar fence, wrinkling his nose in distaste at the smell of creosote. Marlowe said, getting no answer, 'Creosote's a carcinogen.'

Tom laughed. 'So's bracken, or living in Cornwall or

Derbyshire. No, you're welcome to stay around, but I'm busy this afternoon. Might be back about six.'

Asking the old man his business was out of the question. Marlowe accepted tea, and orange juice, for Caro. His father, clockwatching, said, 'I'm off, See yourselves out. Ring if you want anything.'

Luke said, when his grandfather had gone, 'Do we have to go straight back? Could we take Caro to the park?'

Caro missed nothing. She said, eagerly, 'Park, swings.'

Marlowe took her in his arms for one ecstatic kiss, lips on soft skin, and small arms folding round him.

'You win. You and my crazy father.'

Leaving the house, he tried to lock up, but there was no key. Only then did he see that the place had been gutted. Pictures, treasures, clocks, all the small cargo of two lives had gone. He walked through the house, found one bed, four wooden chairs, a desk, a table, his mother's piano, his father's books, an Underwood typewriter, eighty years old, a small television, black and white, four plates and mugs, one pen, a toaster and a kettle. In the kitchen drawers, he found knives, forks and spoons for two. There was nothing else in the house. His mother's collection of Staffordshire figurines had gone, and all her jewellery. No pictures, no best silver, not even their own dinner service. Above the piano, a long, light space marked where the clock had hung, chiming the hours, all the days of his life.

Luke, standing beside him, said, 'So it's true. I wasn't sure.'

Marlowe sat down on one of the four Utility chairs, and stared at his son. 'True? Did you know about this?'

Luke sat on his grandfather's roll-top desk. The graceful Sheraton chair had gone and, marked only by its footprints, a Queen Anne chest of drawers. Above the chest had hung a pair of watercolours, Victorian country scenes. Biting back odd tears of regret, he said, 'I wrote to him about leaving the old house and everyone. He didn't answer for a week or two. Then he wrote and told me about this.'

'So you knew?'

Luke nodded, tried to see again the gaggle of geese, the rosy wife, baby in her arms, the cat, sunning itself on a window ledge, the collie dog, gnawing at a bone. A small girl in a sun bonnet carried a basket of eggs. When he was young, he used to pretend to live in that house, feeding the hens, collecting eggs. The woman would be his mother, sunlit, laughing. He was the big boy, eight or nine, coming down the path with a bundle of firing. He wanted, savagely, to find the picture, buy it, now, to keep. He said,

'I didn't know whether to believe him. He didn't want to tell you, in case you tried to stop him. He decided after the car. That's why I wanted to come, to see if he'd really done it.'

Marlowe looked around the bare, sunlit room. His father had been impressively thorough. Nothing of value remained, bar the piano. The photographs of himself, Sarah, Frances and Luke as babies had been stuck to the wall with Blu-Tack, the silver frames gone.

'And left the house to a cats' home, I bet,' he said wryly.

Luke tried a few chords on the piano. It was in good tune. Sheet music filled a cardboard box. The piano stool, a mahogany two-seater, had gone. He began tentatively to play *Für Elise*, one of his Grade V pieces, years ago.

'Not cats. Or us. Africa, I think. I suppose you think he's mad.'

Marlowe heard a crash, rushed to the window. Caro had knocked over a plant pot. She was eating a greenish tomato. He said, 'Oh, no, not mad. I've never met anyone saner. He might be a saint. Thank God we don't have to live with him.'

Luke giggled. 'Don't be so sure. He was talking about the homeless, and one old man hogging a house this size. Watch it, that's all. It's fatal when people start taking Christ seriously. *"Go, sell that thou hast, and give it to the poor."* Of course he's raving.'

'If you say so. Anyway, we'd better be off. He won't want to find us here.'

The day seemed unfinished. They drove back along the A6, through a string of small towns, smaller villages.

'I hate motorways,' Luke said. 'All that mindless hurtling forwards. Everywhere real is out beyond the next exit.'

'Or the one you just missed. I know. Feeling better now?'

Luke stared out at low fields of cattle, sheep on the higher

164

fells, and all contained by grey walls without mortar. The sun had left only a bloodless glow behind low cloud. He said, vaguely, 'I feel OK. Not sick, just weak. If I could sleep and never wake up.'

Marlowe, appalled, gathered speed to get Luke home.

'Slow down, Dad,' Luke said sharply, and pointed to a Model-T Ford just ahead. The driver signalled right.

'They're going our way. Overtake, slowly. I want a good look.' He opened the window, leaned out, taking in every detail, swore softly.

Marlowe nodded, all sympathy. 'No camera? Bel and I were in Rome, the year you were one. You tried to mug the Pope. One of those guards in striped knickers picked you up. No camera. Or rather, Bel had used the last shot on the bloody stupid Trevi fountain.'

Home, Luke volunteered to make supper.

'Beans on toast, toast and beans, heated-up pizzas or jacket spuds?'

'Any. Either. Can't be worse than your boiled eggs. How long did you leave them in?'

Luke laughed, living image of his mother, only, Bel wouldn't take a joke against herself. 'A minute? Minute and a half, maybe. They were all right scrambled. Which is it?'

Marlowe stretched out on the sofa, Caro beside him, asleep. 'Oh, real food,' he said happily. 'Jacket spuds. Don't use that spike contraption. When they burst, they're done.'

'I know. Easy-peasy.'

They ate in amicable silence. Afterwards, Marlowe, still hungry, fetched a bag of his father's fruit, polished an apple on his shirt.

'Not for me,' Luke said. 'I've had enough. Would you mind if I went to bed?'

'At ten past six?'

Luke lay back in the brass-studded leather armchair, closed his eyes. 'Ten past whenever, I'm shattered. I'm going for a bath.'

Twenty minutes later, Marlowe heard the gurgle and glug of Luke's bath emptying, then footsteps overhead. Presently, he went upstairs to check. Luke was in bed already, and the light out. Under the duvet, he looked pathetically young, the small boy who would beg for another story at bedtime.

'Anything I can get you?'

Luke turned his face to the wall. 'A new body, maybe.' He rolled over, gazed up at his father.

Marlowe, helpless, touched the boy's hand, then left. Caro was still asleep on the sofa. He might be free now until morning, to write, paint, fill a hundred holes with plaster, change a washer on the kitchen cold tap. Instead, he gazed at the *Radio Times* as if staring could make the offerings less dismal: third-time repeats or *The Generation Game*? He went to the kitchen to make tea and fetch the radio. Then he sat, as if trespassing, in the chair Luke had claimed, ancient brown leather with brass studs. He took a sip or two of tea, unused still to the sweetness of water from the hills. Where their old water came from didn't bear thinking about. Caro stirred, opened her eyes, smiled, and slept again. His own eyes closed.

How long had they been knocking? The noise roused him at last. Stupefied by sleep, he stumbled first to the front door, blinking in yellow light and shimmering raindrops. It had been raining heavily for some time. There was a puddle at the door, and nothing else. Inside again, he could hear knocking still.

Faith stood at the back door in black leggings, the purple Doc Martens, a man's ancient Burberry and a yellow sou'wester. She said, amused, 'Did I get you out of bed?' She walked in.

Marlowe looked down at his bare feet, long, rather thin feet with stringy tendons and no trace of summer's tan. He said, faintly hostile, 'I never wear socks indoors.'

Faith laughed, squawked, 'I go barefoot, barefoot, barefoot.' Then she laughed again.

Marlowe wondered if she was mad. The wondering showed.

She said, 'Sorry. No straitjacket, no funny farm. Ever read *The Tale of Mrs Tiggy-Winkle*?

'All too often. It was just slightly unexpected. Are you coming in?'

166

By way of an answer, Faith followed him to the living room and sat down in the armchair. Caro, for someone her size, took up an inordinate amount of sofa. Marlowe remained standing at first, with his back to the fire, then, deciding this was antisocial, sat on the floor.

The room was full of silence and Faith's scent. Alone with a stunning woman, he hadn't the faintest idea what to do next, bar rape, which was unthinkable, and the first thing he thought of. Close up, three feet from his sleeping daughter, Dr Sinclair looked more beautiful than ever. And he'd been celibate far too long. And her husband had been dead three years?

Faith looked straight at him, transformed rape into mutual consent, a shared basic instinct. Then, possibly, just in time, she said, 'You don't know the rules. You've been here weeks, and haven't borrowed so much as a cup of sugar.'

Marlowe, greatly relieved, moved a crucial three inches away from her. 'Very remiss, but we came well supplied. What happened to your kids? Weren't there about a dozen?'

Faith spread out strong hands to the fire. She said demurely, 'You can't count. Three. They're with my mother. She has them once a month. And they go to Rob's parents once a month, too. I think it's important, don't you?'

Marlowe thought of Bel and her avoidance of family life. 'Rob's parents?' Faith stared into the coral fire. Cities rose and died, eternal. She said, without looking up.

'They need to see their grandparents.' She allowed silence, then stood up. 'It won't do, you know. This isn't London. Your son managed better. At least he offered me coffee. I don't drink coffee, so make me a cup of tea.'

Marlowe led the way to the icy kitchen. Faith stood measuring it, from the red-tiled floor to the great derrick of a drying rack. She watched as he made tea, sat, for want of chairs, on the kitchen table, swinging her legs, fifteen and a half, still touching childhood, like Sarah. Bel was born adult. Faith said, 'OK, you pass. I always do a recce on people's kitchens. Friends', not patients', of course.'

Marlowe put the box of Tanzanian tea back in the vestry cupboard. 'Politically correct, responsibly sourced. Does that make me a friend?'

She nodded. 'You're no patient of mine. By the way, how's Luke?'

Marlowe put both mugs on a tray and led the way back to the fire. He said, troubled, 'In bed, asleep. Took himself off before six. They said he was malingering. They're sending in a shrink.'

Faith lay on the floor, stirring in four lumps of sugar. 'Relax. Don't look so bloody guilty.'

Marlowe had avoided the only chair, but couldn't face sitting on the floor beside her. Lifting Caro, he retreated to the sofa.

'Any biscuits?' Faith said cheekily.

He leaped up, almost spilling tea. 'Sure. Sorry, I'm not very good at this. Any particular kind?'

'Ginger? I'm being rude, aren't I?'

Marlowe fled to the kitchen, opened doors, frantic. The packet was hermetically sealed. He attacked it with the bread knife. The first half-dozen biscuits were in a hundred pieces, spattered all over the floor. He found a clean plate, tipped the rest out and returned to Faith, wishing the bloody woman would go.

She said, not apologising, 'Bloody rude of me, but I'm starving. Surgery all morning, redundant men with bad backs and no futures, sad wives who can't remember why the hell they married him, and six toddlers with this bug that's going round. What the hell do they expect me to do about it? Except, once in a hundred thousand times, it's not "this bug", but meningitis. You can't tell over the phone, you have to see them. Then driving the kids to my mother's, and I'm on call all night.'

Marlowe tried to think of something to say, but she'd merely paused for breath.

She continued, still staring into rose-red cities, 'The truth is, I want to stay the night. I won't be in your way. I'll probably be out, mostly. Once, just *once* my paediatric tutor decided not to see a feverish toddler. Paracetamol, he said, tepid sponging, ring tomorrow, if there's no improvement. Three hours later, the kid was dead. No . . . You have to go. I used to read your foreign stuff. Ace. No, honestly. Why all this changing places?'

168

Marlowe looked at her, saw fine lines around her eyes and etched about her softly curving mouth. Not as young or as case-hardened as she liked to appear . . . He said, briefly, It's a long story. You first.'

Faith sat up, hugging her knees. Tonight she was ringless, except for one pale band on her wedding finger, white gold. She said, 'Ten years ago, this was my wedding day. Rob died. End of story.'

Marlowe longed to take her in his arms and hold her till there was no more pain, ever. He said, carefully neutral, 'Bel and I separated. We never married, and she didn't want the kids. There was somebody else, and a big career move, for her.'

Faith had moved to sit in the leather chair. She said, 'And you?'

Caro thrashed about, talking in her sleep; she said, loud and clear, 'Chocolate . . .' Marlowe laughed and began to undress his daughter. He said, 'I cancelled a job in Warsaw, the day Bel accepted her chair. My boss was very good, considering, treated me exactly like a woman. Part-time, till Caro starts school. I thought it would work. Luke's almost adult. Caro's minder was fine. Then I saw Caro take her first steps, into the minder's arms, nearly sacked the woman on the spot. Then Luke broke an arm and a leg, playing rugger. It all fell apart. Try buying a nanny for a teenager who can't zip his flies. Anyway, they're my kids. End of job, virtually. My editor offered the northern column. Bel wanted her share of the Clapham house. I came here with the kids. That's all.' Then there was absolute silence. He was alone with Faith and two sleeping kids.

Faith's phone rang. Professional, she left the room, returned, barely a minute later, her face drained.

'House call?' Marlowe asked, needlessly.

She nodded, biting her lower lip. 'A death. Thirty-two, mother of a kid in the boys' class and a girl of three. Could I come back here? God knows when.'

Marlowe followed her to the door, an unnecessary courtesy. Faith kept nobody's rules. Wordlessly, she ran down the rain-washed steps to her extraordinary car. Then she was gone.

He switched the television on for five minutes; too bad it was the adverts, happy families, queened over by bossy matriarchs, stirring gravy, slaying grease. In the past ten years, he'd liked two ads, the New Zealand butter cows, and the bloke taking a demented baby for a spin in his new . . . .? He tried, and failed to remember the make; so much for adverts. Switching off, he considered music. Then he remembered. The CD player had been Bel's, overlooked when she left, claimed this summer. Shit. Radio? Worth a try, but it was some bloody arty-farty programme, homo-eroticism in Shakespeare *again*. Off, and almighty silence. The kitchen tap dripped. Caro muttered. Some prat in a GTi roared past, scattering cats and old ladies. The woman next door called her flaming cat. He wanted oblivion. It was at least twelve hours until Sunday morning. Lying beside Caro on the sofa, he thought, hopeless, of Sunday mornings with Bel, in the days when they didn't get up till three. Now he wanted to take Faith to bed, make love, slowly, beautifully, until the sadness left her eyes and they slept, exhausted. Precisely what she was playing at, he didn't know. He didn't know women any more. Maybe Bel acquired her lovers like this, walking in, unasked.

He began to take Caro upstairs, but this would leave him alone. Also, Caro had her own plans for Bel's cot, now sadly battle-scarred. Caro rattled the bars of her cage night and morning. It wouldn't last long, or hold another child. There was, though, the cradle in the front attic, full of old press cuttings.

A mouse scampered from the cradle, where it had made its nest in a royal wedding souvenir. Marlowe moved the shreds gently with his little finger. The babies were newborn, hairless, impossibly frail. He lifted the nest out, removed the cradle, crept to the door and stood there, watching. Presently, the mouse ran lightly across bare boards, stopped, sniffing carefully. Then she climbed into the nest, back with her babies. All was well.

He carried the cradle downstairs, cleaned it out with a couple of wipes, padded it with cushions. Caro fitted into it beautifully, his baby again. He switched off all lights except

170

one small reading lamp, read the paper until the fire burnt low, and then out.

Somewhere around four o'clock, the front door opened, was closed again. Marlowe woke to find Faith standing beside him, her face stark white, expressionless. She said only, 'Could I stay now?'

He looked at Caro, one thumb in her rosy mouth; his daughter. Upstairs, Luke slept. He said,

'Of course. The sofa's a bit small.'

Faith knelt on the floor, shivering. 'No. I want to be with you, in your bed.'

Marlowe lifted the heavy cradle and led the way upstairs. On the half-landing, he stumbled and all but fell. Faith put out her hand to steady him. She said, softly, 'Which door?' Then she was holding it for him, watching, as he placed the cradle carefully at the bedside. She asked for the bathroom.

While she was away, he knelt beside Caro, as if praying.

When Faith returned, smelling of tuberose, she said, 'Well?'

Marlowe indicated the bed, remembered his own unwashed state. Five minutes later, he returned to a room in darkness and a woman in his bed. Uncertain still, he kept the white boxers on, lay down beside her. She said, insolent,

'Socks? Boots?, then reached out to remove the shorts. After that, they lay still, side by side. Rain lashed against the windows, coming from the east, pitiless. Presently, she said, 'I'm not expecting sex, honestly. I hardly know you.'

In safe darkness, Marlowe smiled. 'No, of course not. Naked women come here to discuss the FTSE.'

'Always?'

'Invariably.'

After another silence, she added, 'I don't like sleeping alone. Do you?'

'It's not a matter of choice. Not for me, anyway.'

Her stillness was eerie, taut, but without Bel's coldness. Faith said, 'I couldn't bear to be alone. Do you mind?'

She was warmer now, slender and chaste beside him. She said, 'Do you mind talking?'

Marlowe moved closer to the wall to give her more space, careful to avoid touching her.

She continued, her voice breaking, so the last words came through tears, 'I thought you might understand, better than most. At least, that's the impression you give. One of your reports from Sarajevo ... I've never forgotten. There was a little girl if six in the mortuary. She'd died after having her legs blown off. You quoted Virgil. It seemed entirely appropriate.'

'*Sunt lacrimae rerum, et mentem mortalis tangunt.* Latin tags aren't my usual style. I'm glad you thought it appropriate.'

She whispered, as tears overwhelmed her, 'Sometimes, there aren't any words, in any language.'

Marlowe lay very still. Every instinct impelled him to take her in his arms, touch, kiss, make love to her. He thought better of it, forced his unwilling body to be still. He said, 'Could you tell me? Is it allowed?'

'Seal of the confessional, you mean? Medical confidentiality? I'm allowed to be human. I used to talk to Rob. He was a good listener. Since then, there's been nobody.'

Marlowe made to reach for her hand, then drew back. The power of this self-imposed chastity intrigued him. He had the strange idea that sex would bring them no closer together, rather the opposite. Maybe, some time, but there were other matters to resolve. He felt calmer now, no longer erect either, quite sure that she'd come for comfort and company, nothing else.

'Tell me?'

Faith turned her back to him. Sulphurous light leached between a gap in the curtains. She could just see Caro in the old cradle, her eyes moving for a dream.

'They'd been expecting the cancer death. Judi came home from the hospice last week. Two kids, seven and three. There would've been a third. She miscarried during chemotherapy. Six months, start to finish. It can kill young women fast. After I'd signed the death certificate and stayed with her husband a while, it was an old man with pneumonia. Ninety-one, widower, half blind, half deaf, and wakes every day raging because he can't walk. Absolutely rational, and tired of life.

172

Pneumonia would kill him gently, but the daughter begged me to get him into hospital. If I refused . . . She's nothing else to live for. I called an ambulance. They'll keep him going a few weeks, or months, but not in his own house. He was married for sixty-three years and lives in a hell of loneliness.

'Then an attack of heartburn, convinced it was death throes. One early labour, insisted on going to hospital at two a.m. Then a cot death. Eleven years of miscarriages, miscarried the baby's twin, and now this. I find it very hard to believe in a loving God. Sorry, if you're not into religion . . . Neither am I, in any conventional sense, but I believe in a creator all right. Where I stick is believing in one who gives a toss about us. Two bewildered kids motherless, a man numb with grief, and those two, cradling their dead baby. She's forty-three. The chances of another are slim. They're too old to adopt. Now do you understand why I don't like being alone?'

She turned towards him.

'I never did get used to death,' Marlowe said. 'Bel didn't say much. Untidy emotions aren't her strong point, but at least she was there. Sometimes, we'd make love, and I'd forget, for a while. Then she'd sleep, and I'd end up lying beside her, more alone than ever.'

'I don't want to make love. If you insist, I won't resist. I could hardly call it rape, coming to your bed unasked, but I'd rather not. Could you just hold me?'

Marlowe reached for her hand. Faith laid her head on his chest, lay fitted close to him. She was crying, quiet, controlled tears, lay in his arms, trusting as a child. In a minute or two, she was asleep, inviolate. Marlowe held her close, knew she should be his wife.

Chapter Fifteen

He woke alone. Caro stood howling beside him; she had unpoppered the legs of her stretch-suit. He carried her to the bathroom and ran a bath. At least she was house-trained now, a feat accomplished three days ago. While she lay partly submerged, watching the air gap in a shampoo bottle as it filled, Marlowe played with ducks. There were two species, cartoon yellow and authentic mallards, two inches long. These were his only Christmas presents from Bel, their first year together. He'd bought her a Vivien Westwood coat. In late February, though, on a day of malevolent sleet, she'd produced a scruffy manila envelope with tickets for Venice, two nights of carnival, result, Luke. Or so she said. He suspected the dates didn't quite add up, but agreed with her: why spoil a good story? Venice was the kind of thing Bel *would* do, one reason why he'd stayed with her so long. Faith would answer her blasted 'phone and rush to some bedside, waiting for take-off.

'I'm cold', Caro said.

She wasn't just cold, she was waterlogged, small fingers ridged, every inch goose flesh. She scrambled over the side, wrapped herself in his navy-blue bathrobe, and lay on the floor giggling.

Dressed, Caro demanded food. The kitchen was occupied by Luke and a skinny girl. They were reading the *Sunday Mirror* and the *News of the World*, and eating Greek yogurts. The girl was on her third. There was a smell of garlic bread. Luke said, 'This is Marigold. We met ages ago, only I didn't know she lived round here.'

Luke was toying with the last yogurt. They'd been a special offer in Sainsbury's, yesterday. Peeved, Marlowe tried not to show it, relieved, on the whole, to find his son with a girl. The young graze free in parental fridges. If Caro whinged for yogurt later, Sunday was, thank God, no longer Sunday. Somewhere would be open.

He filled Caro's beaker with water, unfolded the pushchair and set off with her for the newsagent's. There were three within striking distance. Why were English metaphors for such distance so violent – stone's throw or, yeuch, spitting? *Katzsprung* was so much prettier, and kinder – until you considered why lazy creatures like cats ever bother to spring. Turning left, then right, through sleeping Sunday streets, he longed to say all this. Caro was short on repartee or even grunts of acknowledgement. Sitting in her pushchair, deep in thought, she appeared to survey the rainy city. Presently, though, she demanded crisps, more loudly each time. Marlowe silenced her by clipping down the vinyl rain cover, parked her outside the first newsagent. He came out with two papers, two yogurts, a packet of crisps, a small bar of chocolate, and nowhere to put any of it. When he tried to slot the papers behind Caro, she roared, ripped the front page from the *Observer*. Second time round, he broke the chocolate in half. Grudging, but hungry, she gave in.

Walking home, he wondered about Luke. How much privacy was appropriate? For how long should he feed the girl, who looked positively anorexic? How much sex education had Luke registered? In the first year, their religious and social studies teacher had brought in packets of condoms, but they could hardly stage a trial run in school. Nor could he ask, outright, how far they planned to go. He consoled himself with the well-known subfertility of the anorexic. Luke's taste was interesting. Fed, the girl could be the Mucha poster for *Automne*. All that torrid hair cried out for mellow fruitfulness, ripe hips and rounded thighs. Steering past heaped dog muck, he wondered now soon Caro must enter the nasty world. All those stabbed and strangled kids were impossibly young – three, four, five, street children. He saw Caro's small forked body mutilated, knew he couldn't bear it. His, to keep safe, for ever and ever. Knowing Caro, she'd jump down-

175

stairs, practise flying from the kitchen table, shin the back wall, foil him somehow. Caro's life was all her own.

The kitchen was empty. They'd washed the yogurt pots and coffee mugs. They'd also scoffed six crumpets, some apples, and there were two Mars bars missing from a multipack, so the anorexic look was deceptive. Unless it was bulimia? He couldn't *afford* bulimia. They'd had most of the milk, too.

Caro ate yogurt, then licked the pot and her face clean. She demanded more.

'Ask your brother,' said Marlowe sourly. He was reading the supplement. They'd changed it again, without asking him. The only consolation was, he knew only one of the writers, slightly. This softened his overwhelming sense of failure. The sour tone was because he'd found a profile of Bel, pictured and captioned with Neanderthal Sam. Bel lived a forty-eight hour day, had spent last weekend in Budapest and Berlin, eating economists, or with them. The text wasn't clear on this point. He read on. Child-free, she had the nerve to say she cared deeply, passionately, about her son and daughter, *'who live in the North, with their father'*. Like Laplanders in the Arctic? He decided it was the flamboyant capital *N* that irritated him so much. Bel had always considered the north deeply suspect, populated by miners, Arthur Scargill and the Bishop of Durham.

Outside, the rain descended, ruling out the playground, ducks on the river or a walk to the Taj Mahal. It was five past eleven; thirteen hours of Sunday to go, no zoo, and the museum closed on Sundays.

Luke said, 'Won't they worry? Think you've been murdered, or raped, or something? We should phone.'

Marigold walked on, into the rainforest. He could see her climbing fast, spiralling up the airy cast-iron staircase. Flashes of colour moved and were gone, sound and colour and scent, a place of green darkness and brilliant light. He leaned against the handrail, for the world to be still. If you waited long enough, the sick, spinning feeling stopped crawling round your head. Besides, he couldn't move now, a Day-Glo butterfly had landed on his sleeve, closely followed by another. They copulated. The glassy jungle seethed with copulation, eggs and caterpillars, most hairy, all lurid. It was like a 3-D 18+ horror, sex and monsters wherever you looked. As for the insects . . . Any minute now, they'd start copulating with Marigold. She'd have ginormous caterpillars squirming down her nose and out of her ears. Or one of those hairy black things, built like a Chinook.

And the heat . . . He'd come in blue with cold, rain-lashed, smarting from hailstones in the face. Here it was thirty-four degrees, and God knows what humidity. At least the sick dizziness had passed. He climbed up to the top of the staircase and found Marigold staring into a tank. It said *Tarantula* and, in wobbly capitals, *PLEASE DO NOT TAP ON THE GLASS*.

Marigold said, 'It fancies you for lunch.'

Then he stared too, and all but fell off the top step and the little flowery platform. The tarantula stared back, eyes all over its head. It shared the tank with locusts. He didn't fancy being a locust. Either John the Baptist ate you, or planes zapped you, or they fed you to enormous spiders. He said this to Marigold, hoping she'd laugh. She did, but it was the wrong sort of laugh.

'Locust beans, dumbo. John the Baptist ate locust beans, a.k.a. carob. Health-food freak in sandals. Of course he'd eat carob. Locusts might be better. You never know till you try. Like prawns, or langoustines. Anyway, I'm sweating cobs. Let's get out of here. You have to be careful, or they try to escape with you.'

Luke edged his way round the door, into nine degrees and a northeaster, sweat to goose flesh in five seconds flat. Marigold took his hand.

'There's a video in with these tickets. Boring, I've seen it three times already, but it's warm, and they never chuck you out. Top floor of the Wedding Cake.'

Luke laughed. 'Dad calls it the Taj Mahal.'

She had his hand still, warm, sexy; thank God for girls who made the first move. She was smiling, and her teeth were a bit crooked; good. Every single teenage girl in London had a mouth full of roo bars. Kissing was lethal. You risked lacerating your tongue. Marigold was half pulling him up the stairs, but stopped, exasperated.

177

'Look, I'm not a bloody ski lift. Let go.'

Luke sat down on the curving marble stairs. Head down, breathe deep, plead with the spinning world to keep still.

'Sorry. I felt faint. It's so bloody hot in there.'

Marigold sat down beside him, lightly touched his forehead. She sighed. 'And the last time? Did you tell your Dad?'

Luke shook his head. He moved her light hand down to his pounding chest. 'No. Only, I passed out on a run. They kept me in hospital a few days, then said it was nothing.'

'Funny nothing. You look like something the cat sicked up. We could take the lift.'

She smiled now, red hair tumbling loose. Her clothes were brilliant. Today, school-free, she wore a Regency coat, like Beau Brummell, in dark green, a tiny purple skirt and sexy boots. Her blouse was stark white, with a purple scarf. Suffragette colours, weren't they, purple, green and white? He imagined sitting in near darkness, touching that hair, and more.

'I'll be all right. Don't call the lift, I hate them. I hate the way your stomach lands later.'

In less than half-light, as planned, he sat beside her, making his hands still, said, recklessly, 'There's a funny smell. Dentists or something.'

Marigold said, giggling, 'Camphor. I slap on half the Body Shop and still reek of it. That's the trouble with old clothes.'

Luke was watching a street scene, circa 1890, poverty and swarming kids, ill fed and worse clothed. One kid's nose was running like a candle. You could practically smell dead cats, sweat, unwashed bodies, pee. He had one button of her blouse undone now, one hand moving slowly inside her soft bra. Now his hand cupped her heavy little breast, touched the nipple and felt the flesh stiffen. Now it was the Coronation, sexy old Bertie turned into HM King Edward VII. How could any woman fancy that great blubbery lump of lard? Come to that, how could anyone fancy a royal, ever?

Marigold whispered something, turning towards him, kissing, mouth to mouth, and her lips opening. She whispered again.

'Have you ever, with anyone?'

Luke, shocked, thrilled, whispered back, 'No. Not yet.'

178

Marigold's hand slid down to his crotch. Tongue in his ear, she hissed, 'You could, though. Why not?'

Luke sat up and moved, the distance negligible, his meaning patent. He said, coldly, 'Where? Six inches of mud suit you? Besides, I hardly know you.'

Two women in hats, in the second row, turned to snarl, 'Shut up or get out.'

Luke, contrite, sat on his hands for the next ten minutes, watching the twentieth century slowly begin. Grandad was born before the old king died. That made him an Edwardian. Then it was Sarajevo, and the screen full of young men rushing off to die, like Great-Grandad. His name was on the war memorial in the park. They used to see it, with Grandma. People shouldn't die and leave each other alone. Then the screen was full of scaffolding, building the memorial.

Marigold whispered, 'So your dad's right, nearly, calling it the Taj Mahal.'

Luke shook his head. 'No. That was for somebody's wife.'

'Same difference. Dead and gone for ever. You look a bit better. It's stopped raining. Fancy walking back along the towpath, feed the ducks?'

Luke didn't know where to look. He'd been holding her breasts. She'd touched him down there, found his cock, erect, actually offered sex. He said, 'I don't feel that great. Another time, maybe.'

Outside, Marigold inspected him, then disappeared into the shop. She came out with a postcard of the tarantula and a small twisted stick of barley sugar.

'Prezzies. Barley sugar's good for invalids. It's coming on to rain again. We'd better go the quick way.'

'Which way's that?'

She laughed. 'Along the towpath, of course. You really don't know anywhere yet, do you?'

Luke smiled, more used to her now. Whatever else, she wasn't a slag. She'd been shaking, all the time he touched her breasts. If she was used to it, she wouldn't, surely? He said, cheerfully, 'Find your way round London, that's all.'

Marigold stopped, then ran towards the tyre swings. They were wet; as if she cared. Hanging upside down, spinning fast, she called, 'Race you across the Grand Canyon.'

She was pointing to a ladder bridge across a shallow gully. The corporation didn't allow real danger. You fell into an orange cargo net, climbed to the launching platform by net or up a shiny pole. Marigold, in falling rain, tossed her coat to him, climbed like a cat. She stood for a few seconds on the crow's-nest platform, then launched herself, lithe body swaying to right and left. Six feet short of her goal, she missed a handhold and all but fell, hanging there by one arm. When he could bear to look, she was upside down, slender legs hooked round the bars. Then her fingers touched the last bar, and she was slithering down, standing beside him, sweating slightly, radiant.

'Your turn.'

He moved through heavy water and foul air. The smell of decay was in his face.

Marigold knelt beside him, wiping his mouth. 'You really are sick, aren't you?'

Luke moved, slowly, until he was sitting up. One smell was his own sour vomit, but the other, too close, was a dog turd. He struggled to stand, leaned against the satin-smooth pole. A family was approaching, prosperous golden parents, not young, and a child of about three whose full-skirted coat reached almost to the ground.

'Let's move,' he said. 'I bet she's called Alessandra.'

'Or Leonie, or Florence, or Venetia. Those coats cost two hundred pounds, just for babies, in that shop near the Castle.'

If only he could reach the bench . . . He tried to count the steps, ten more at least, every breath a leaden effort. He stumbled and would have fallen, but for Marigold. She said, practically,

'Lean on me. Take your time. Should I ring your dad?'

Luke began to shake his head, but the world was a dizzy, mindless place, full of faces, all women, and trees, ready to fall and dash his brains out. He fell into darkness, lost the right to move his own body. Someone else arranged him. In a preserved corner of consciousness, he thought: recovery position, just like in the Duke of Edinburgh award, abandoned when he left London. She was lifting his heavy, heavy head, thwarting any attempt to choke on vomit or swallow his own tongue. He lay very still, because there was nothing else

180

he could do. She felt in his pockets, removed the wallet, found the number. Then she was stuck, unable to leave the casualty without summoning help. She knelt beside him, gently wiping his face with a cologne tissue. It felt good. He liked the fresh female smell of it, and the old memories stirring, of being very small, weak and helpless.

Presently he heard the sound of footsteps and the rattle of a dog's claws on tarmac; a large dog, to make so much noise. A man's voice, suspicious. He said, harshly, 'I know your sort', and moved on. Marigold came back, to set beside him. Luke opened his eyes briefly, to make sure it was her, then closed them again. She began to hold his hand, just as the heavier rain began to fall. They waited five minutes or longer, heard more footsteps, light, quick people, two middle-aged women who listened at first, then moved away, gathering speed, swish, swish, swish into fallen leaves.

'The Samaritan should be along any minute,' he said, smiling faintly.

Marigold laughed. 'You're not *Christian*, are you?'

Luke lay very still. If he did, the world was safe. He said, 'No, of course not, but you knew what I meant.'

She nodded. 'O.K., fair comment. Don't get me wrong, I'm not anti-Christian. Some of it's not exactly rational though.'

'Magic babies, water into wine, raising the dead?'

Marigold laughed again, because talking about religion was weird, especially in the rain, in the park, and maybe dying. She said, 'No. Actually, I can handle virgin birth. You get weirder things on David Attenborough every week. Stuff the Bishop of Durham, I *like* the idea. Cut out the middle man. Damn sight tidier than all that sweat and semen. It's the *love your enemies* stuff I can't take. Here comes a certain Samaritan. . . .'

The woman came to sit by him. She wasn't really a woman at all, thin, black, wearing a rain-spangled scarlet beret and a coat that flowed to her ankles, above a skirt that showed her knickers. He could see them through her shiny tights. She chewed gum, fruit-flavoured, vile-smelling, said, shrewishly, 'If you're setting me up . . .'

Luke closed his eyes, wished she was thirty years older. He said, with difficulty, 'She's just ringing my dad. I was sick and passed out.'

She eyed him sceptically, then said, 'You look sick. Sniffing, is it? Or drugs?'

Luke closed his eyes again; he couldn't answer. Presently, though, she knelt closer and whispered, gently, 'Sorry. Only, you can't be too careful. There's a girl in my class, epileptic. She passes out after a fit. She's OK, though, not mental. Like some iced cologne?'

Men wouldn't carry iced cologne, or tissues, cool and sweet on his wet skin . . . She'd taken off her mac to cover him, knelt there, shivering. The velvet body clung to light curves, was cut low, to show small breasts and the soft, dark cleavage between. He wanted to share the joke about the Samaritan, but decided it might be racist. She produced a glucose drink from her bag, offered it. The thought of swallowing anything made his gorge rise. He shook his head, willed Marigold to return.

'You warm enough?' the girl said.

He nodded, deathly cold, wondered idly what else she proposed to take off. She tucked the coat more firmly round him. Her nipples showed now, small and hard under thin velvet. Then he heard Marigold. The girls argued a bit, each determined to strip for him. In the end, the girl left, but she insisted on leaving the cologne stick.

'Your dad's coming,' Marigold said. 'He's leaving your baby sister with a neighbour.'

Faith shook down the thermometer. 'Thirty-four point nine. Too damned low. He's been lying out there in the rain, but even so . . . Have you rung your GP?'

Marlowe nodded. Tonight's role was familiar, mere acquiescence, as the women took charge. Faith, like Bel, knew how to delegate. Caro was back, but her own children were with another neighbour. Marlowe wondered, undressing his blue-white son, if the children minded, if they knew or cared. Luke's passivity appalled him, until he tried, gently, to remove the boxer shorts.

'Gerroff! What the hell! *She's* still here.'

Faith left the room, thought of a few million women exposed to male hands, male eyes, male lechery. There was a knock at the door, which irritated her. Chris had a perfectly good bell, clearly marked. The knock could break glass. She let McCleod in, said quickly, 'Your patient. I live two doors along, and Mr Marlowe needed help.'

Then she was gone, pushing her luck, this time, wishing the kids on Angie the third time this week.

Luke lay on the sofa, a thick sweater over his pyjamas, idiotic tiger slippers on his thin feet. The feet were lobster bright from a bath Dad kept topping up. His temperature was thirty-six point seven now and rising, which was OK. He was aching all over, cramps in his belly, and shivering. He knew very well this was a moment to savour, by the fireside, drinking sweet hot tea, Caro kneeling on the rug, playing, and Dad willing him to be well. He never dared ask, 'Do you love me?' Better left unsaid, but tonight, he felt loved. Also, this was the first day he'd ever touched a woman's breasts. He'd been right, too, about the anorexia. She'd been heading that way, counting calories, on the scales twice a day, until he told her off, and she'd stopped. Almost, possibly, perhaps, he'd saved her. His eyes grew heavy, closed in happy sleep. He had plans, most of which involved Marigold.

Chapter Sixteen

A week later, it was parents' evening, one-time focus of seething resentment, your turn or mine. On Tuesday, Marlowe had spoken to a newcomer at Toddlers, a curly faun with one earring. They were both men, alone with two children. Then the faun discovered Luke's age, pulled rank. *He* was tied to the school gate by a four-and-a-half-year-old. More than that, he didn't choose to divulge. Women would, used to allegiances based on mere sex and maternity. The faun had spent the entire two hours reading *Crime and Punishment*, a tattered Penguin copy with the back cover missing. Marlowe knew very well they should network, save each other much time and hassle, but he didn't know how. Women conspired, and he didn't know the rules. He tried, from behind the *Guardian* or *Independent*, to eavesdrop, but they were too subtle. They said PMT, meant flaming temper; talked about stitches, sleepless nights, meant lazy men, demanding sex from sore bodies, sleeping like stones when a baby cried. Several of the women ran small firms, delegated, arriving with five or six infants, toddling from nearby, spilling from Range Rovers, or those Peugots half a street long. Afterwards, they drove to Sainsbury's, queued for each other as they bought nappies and garlic bread. They went home to be efficient, with dried flower bouquets, photography, word processing, programming. He was never entirely sure which posse of kids belonged to which smiling mother. They wore scarves and shawls, flung about them with *Vogue*-ish negligence. He had no scarf, could think of no male equivalent. He was smiled at, arriving and leaving, hadn't been invited to join any of the three baby-sitting circles, or the coffee rota. Happily, Luke, though not legally responsible, was quite old enough to leave with Caro. Luke could dial the surgery or 999, change a nappy, read a story. Better still, he didn't need to sit with alien brats, unknown Alfies, Beatrices, Jacks or Charlottes. As he left, though, Luke had said, rather desperately, 'Dad . . . You won't get mad, will you?'

Marlowe had asked why he should. Luke looked sullen, hanging his head.

'I haven't really got going yet. It's been difficult. It's going to be all right, honest. Next term will be all right.'

Marlowe decided against a premature inquest. Luke's standards were high. He collected prizes each year with the casual grace of those born to succeed. After the first year and a duffing-up, prizes were accepted as something Luke did, like running, or collecting heavy-metal photographs. No one else had all Guns n' Roses, especially on Czech and Hungarian programmes.

Leaving the school, a great, wet sycamore leaf slapped Marlowe full in the face, the stalk flicking his eye so the tears came. Slamming the door, sitting, battered and breathless, he started the car, then switched off again. There were fifty at least ahead, smug couples, not detained by the steely head. He wanted, rather badly, to cry and be comforted, preferably by a woman with soft breasts and a gentle voice.

Luke's warning had proved inadequate. After the fourth teacher, the reedy, petulant classics master, Marlowe wanted to cry off. Biting back tears of impotent fury, he queued, listened, sat through five more interviews. Then it was the class tutor, teetering prudently between sorrow and anger.

'It's odd, Mr Marlowe,' he'd said, without reproach. 'Luke's entrance papers were brilliant. His London records excellent. All-round performer, no angst with maths and no slouch on the sports field. Safe bet for the honours board. And now . . . Quite honestly, he'll be lucky to scrape through with a few Es. He hasn't done a stroke of work since September.'

185

After that, he'd been kind enough, trying to blame the trauma of the move.

Marlowe had been about to leave when he remembered PE, or whatever they called it now. The queue was one bedraggled fat woman, nor was he in any hurry to go home. The fat woman took five minutes, relaxed, happy creature, and not so very fat. After Bel's tenacious size ten, he needed to get his eye in again. The woman was merely sturdy, chatting happily about hockey. When she moved on, Marlowe sat in the seat warmed by forty-four inch hips. he said, after thirty seconds of silence, 'Luke Marlowe?'

He was scrutinised by eyes used to weighing a good scrum half or a quicksilver sprinter. Becket, five foot four, head of physical education, said, without preamble, 'Mr Marlowe, your son's ill. I've seen him go downhill since September. When did he last see a doctor?'

Marlowe said, feebly, 'They did tests after that fell run. They found nothing wrong, so they discharged him.'

'Then ask for a second opinion. Blame me, if you like. Don't lay into him, for God's sake, whatever you've heard tonight. He's ill.'

A car ahead had stalled. Marlowe hoped, sourly, that it was a Mercedes, or the scarlet Jensen with idiot plates: *HAL10* Pretentious git. It should be HAL 10, quite bad enough. The car ahead flashed, then moved out, detouring right, past the swimming pool. Marlowe followed. In less than ten minutes, he was rounding their corner, uplifted by a sudden magical sense of homecoming, dark rooftops etched against lighter darkness. Moonlight silvered their own rooftop. He saw Faith parking, then climbing her own steps into the secret world behind her closed door. In there, she was Mother, feeding her children, packing school lunches. His eyes followed her, saw one arm weighed down by her doctor's bag. She hadn't seen him, evidently relieving a baby-sitter, child minder or nanny. A woman left, pelting down the steps, late.

He drove round to the back, deciding to use the garage. For insurance, he'd claimed use of an integral garage, yet parked on the road every day.

He knocked, but there was no answer. Letting himself in,

he called Luke's name. Still no answer. The living-room fire was all but out. Caro slept like a baby, cruciform. Luke lay slumped across the sofa, his breathing harsh, like a death rattle. There was a small pool of vomit on the floor, bile and saliva. He'd eaten nothing all day. One touch of the boy's weak pulse was enough.

Marlowe rang the surgery, a recorded voice said, 'The doctor is out, call back in half an hour.' Marlowe returned to Luke. Two crimson spots blazed in the boy's white face. He breathed like an old, dying man, Marlowe moved him slightly, then returned to the phone, rang for an ambulance. While waiting, he packed food and clothes for Caro, pyjamas for Luke, wished sadly for a wife.

When the ambulance came, the team took possession of Luke, fitting a mask, for oxygen. The masked body, no longer his son, was carried away. Caro, immediately wide awake, tried to run after them, calling out for Luke. Marlowe wanted to be there, breathing for his son, but common sense said, follow by car. The ambulance was leaving already. In the street, curtains twitched. He wished for neighbours to knock and care, but they were strangers. Faith's curtains twitched, like any other woman's. He could imagine her, bathing children, reading a bedtime story, no longer mysterious.

In casualty, Caro slept again, across two chairs, her head in his lap. Marlowe had been called twice, once to give Luke's details. When they came to 'religion?', he very nearly said, 'None.' Then he remembered Luke's shifty, secret baptism at his parents' church, without Bel knowing. The Asian desk clerk tapped his pen, bored.

Marlowe said, 'Catholic.'

The man checked his list. 'RC?'

Marlowe nodded, rather than argue. It might even be true. *In extremis*, old prayers surfaced: '*De Profundis*, Our Father, don't let my son die. You don't exist, but don't let my son die.' It was perfectly, shamelessly true, one did pray.

Someone came, not offering tea. There was a machine he could use. He thanked her, went on reading vintage *Private Eye*, Thatcher's deposition. A tattooed couple wandered in, the girl with a bleeding, lobeless ear. A snake, green and purple, had lost its head and flickering tongue. Packed in ice cubes, in a cottage-cheese carton, the earlobe looked dead, not human but some kind of sea creature. Marlowe thought, callously, of a nice little tabloid feature – in colour, obviously. Chaste black and white wouldn't do it justice. If Luke weren't dying, he'd write the story now, take photos right here in casualty. Painted people weren't shy. He'd seen, once, a Welsh rugger star's green and scarlet penis, emblazoned with *Y Ddraig Goch*, full splendour revealed only when erect.

But Luke was dying. The staff's gentle kindness was proof enough of that. The painted girl insisted on a local anaesthetic, left two hours later, head swathed in bandages, ear, so far as he knew, intact, passion somewhat cooled. A nice little tabloid earner, and he'd let them walk away, could at least have passed it on to a friend. Fair-weather friends. . . No one had been in touch. Christopher Marlowe was out of it, dead and gone for ever.

Around one o'clock, someone came with blankets for Caro. He was quite alone. A suspected heart attack had been and gone, with a bottle of antacid. At one thirty, he asked to see Luke. The nurse demurred.

Marlowe said, very calmly, 'If he's dying, it can't make any difference.'

When she didn't deny this, he wished the words unsaid. Instead, with Caro in his arms, he followed her to intensive care. There was no chair. He stood at the foot of the bed, watched a machine live for his son. So far as he could tell, the brain monitor read normal. he said, softly, 'Luke. I'm here. And Caro. You must get better.'

After half an hour, Caro was leaden in his arms. He made a nest of blankets on the floor, pillowed her head with his jacket. He read the notes, knives of fear turning as he read, palate haemorrhages, grossly enlarged spleen, pleurisy, coma. Staff came to observe his son, and they were kind. At half past two, someone brought him a chair. He must have slept, because it had become ten past five. Outside, a tentative world was waking. He remembered acutely, almost with pleasure, the dawn after Luke's midnight birth, lights, still, at Westminster, some all-night sitting.

He stood beside Luke now, tried to discover his son there,

188

monitored, cathetered, sleeping, dying. A car crash would have been instantaneous. He couldn't bear this slow dying. They'd done a lumbar puncture, and it wasn't meningitis. He thought of last night, wanting to rage at the boy for so much failure. Luke stirred, fighting against the tubes, then lay still.

At six, Caro woke and had to be washed and dressed. Without permission, he carried her off to a side ward, emerged to find a nurse lying in wait. She said, kindly enough, 'Mr Marlowe, we need to carry out more tests. There's septicaemia as well as the pleurisy. Luke's immune system's giving up. We'll need to check for HIV.'

'Of course. I understand.'

He found the right coins, ordered coffee from the machine, black, two sugars. It wasn't likely. He'd seen no sign, no sign at all of drugs. So far as he knew, Luke was a virgin. Fifteen years ago, Bel had been faithful enough, surely? Then he remembered her semester at Berkeley. Briefly, idiotically, he thought of ringing her, saying, 'Bel, they think Luke has Aids. Are you . . .?' Such things did, of course, happen, but there would have been signs before this, surely? He thought of Caro, toddling up and down the footprinted corridor, calling for Luke.

He drank the coffee half a lonely hour later, stone cold, bitterly flavoured with plastic. Then the sister called him. Walking through time, Marlowe came to her, carrying his daughter. The idiotic, impossible melodrama was unfolding, scripted, the truth already known, if not by him.

'As we expected, Mr Marlowe, the test for HIV was negative. We had to be able to rule that out. It's –'

He broke in, brusque, snarling. 'How can you possibly . . .?'

She took his hand and made him still in the steel-framed chair. 'The test is very quick, Mr Marlowe. HIV was unlikely, but something we have to consider these days. Frankly, we're no wiser. The enlarged spleen means there's massive infection, but at this stage, we can't say what. We'll be doing more tests. They'll be having another look at the CSF.'

'CSF?'

'Sorry. Cerebrospinal fluid. The blood tests and lumbar

189

puncture ruled out meningitis, as we told you. Other tests take longer to run. We'll be able to tell you more tomorrow.'

Marlowe said, 'Such as?' He didn't really want an answer.

'We tried glandular fever, last time he was here. It's not likely, but we'll try again. It could be leukaemia. We really don't know. I can't tell you any more just now.'

Marlowe, expert, read the subtext in her face, having seen it so often in tricky interviews. 'I could say more, but not here, not now, and certainly not to you.'

Caro had crawled under the table, playing with the woman's shoelaces. She giggled as he retrieved her.

'My daughter needs breakfast,' he said. 'Is there somewhere?'

And then, with efficient kindness, her arm touching his, he was led away.

Alone in a littered room, he sat Caro on pale-blue disposable sheeting. He made her a bib, tucking a paper towel into the neck of her jumper. Solemnly, she ate a banana yogurt, followed up with a satsuma and two Jaffa cakes. Then she needed washing again. Liberally, he used hospital cotton wool, wipes, another paper towel. At home, he would have burned the debris in the Aga. He felt a pang of guilt about landfill, then remembered the hospital incinerator. There was a box of a hundred disposable gloves by the sink. He thought of nicking a dozen – handy for decorating, or work on the car – or cotton wool and wipes for Caro. On the other hand, he recalled the vengeful God of childhood, a maths test failed when he skipped confession. Luke might die, of course, whether or not he nicked NHS gloves. Lifting Caro down, he packed the holdall. It was Luke's school bag, racing green with a gold jaguar logo. The separate zip-off compartment for sports gear was missing. He knew exactly where it was: on the floor, in the utility room, by the washing machine.

Caro escaped, tall enough now to reach handles. She toddled full pelt down the corridor, giggling, all but colliding with an empty trolley, wheeled by a porter. Marlowe wondered, professionally, if any porters were white, or unsmiling. Oncology, X-ray, mortuary, they all smiled, at least when they met someone. They met one steering a young woman, legs raised, an ominous red stain seeping through to the sheet. The porter was saying, 'Listen, love, the missus lost three in a row. Four kiddies now, bloomin pests, never a minute's peace, *and* she's six months gone.' Marlowe averted his eyes, not part of her distress. If Bel had miscarried, she wouldn't have tried again. Or would she? Bel hated being thwarted. Then he realised Caro was out of sight; only distant laughter.

Outpatients was filling up: aged bodies delivered by taxi ambulance for physio; the night's casualties. The tattooed girl was back. One part-closed black eye; two brittle old women who'd slipped on ice. He looked closer, recognised one from the house opposite, she of the perfect garden. She was with a woman in a blue Home Help uniform. Her left leg was a bad colour, indigo, and a strip of skin missing.

She said, after a moment's study, 'Excuse me, but aren't you from across the road? A boy and a little girl?'

He agreed. Just then he spotted Caro in the playhouse. She was cooking imaginary food. It was a quarter past nine, half past breakfast on an icy November morning. Caro saw him, toddled out, blue saucepan worn like a baseball cap, handle to the back. She tackled him, knee-high, said, firmly, 'Hungry.'

There was a WRVS refreshment bar, closed till 10 a.m. He asked the woman on reception where he could buy food. She gave directions to a string of shops out on the main road. It was sleeting. He had no memory at all of parking the car, remembered with difficulty last night's despairing drive. The idea that Luke was dying, *now*, possessed him. Tucking Caro under one arm, he fled back to intensive care.

Luke's eyes were closed. The machine was breathing for him. Luke's body made no effort on its own. Brazen, Marlowe read the notes, understood nothing at all, only that Luke had no fever, had arrived hypothermic. He stood there for a minute or two, watching his son. The words 'living and partly living' came into his mind. Whatever Eliot meant by that, Luke was definitely of the partly living. It wasn't his choice or his decision at all. Left to his own devices, Luke would be dead.

191

He held the boy's dry hand for a moment or two. The decision came next, blissfully simple, the right thing to do. He found some small change and made his way to the payphone. Two minutes later, he was speaking to Bel.

'Luke's very ill. He's in intensive care, Casterton Royal Infirmary. You'd better come.'

Bel said nothing. He fed in another pound, waited. At last she said, 'You think I should come?'

'To see your son alive, yes.' He added, 'He might not know you. He's very sick.'

Bel said, 'I'll take the next train.'

He hadn't expected that. Which was, of course, sheer nonsense. Bel was behaving like the normal, human woman she was, coming to her child's sickbed, maybe deathbed. He stood for a moment, watching the money run out, then hung up.

Caro had spotted the WRVS ladies, aproned, steady creatures, used to life and death. She trotted behind them into their holy kitchen, and emerged with a packet or organic crisps. He ordered coffee, paid for Caro's crisps and bought two more packets, a banana and an apple. Caro would chomp her way through this lot in a morning, and he had only two pence left. He'd have to borrow from Bel. The idea of seeing her was strangely comforting. Premature death and sickness outraged Bel. She wouldn't allow it, not for Luke.

Chapter Seventeen

Bel stood beside Luke's bed. Marlowe watched her, keeping half an eye on Caro, who was crawling under the bed. Luke didn't move. He was 'stable', not dead, not noticeably alive. Presently, his mother turned away, walked to stand near the window. Consciously or not, she stood back to camera, a lovely, nameless silhouette. She said, 'Look. . . They're doing tests. We've ruled out Aids, not that it was likely. It's not meningitis. It won't be leukaemia.'

Marlowe said, bleakly, 'You can't know that.'

Bel half turned towards him, her face a revelation. She was *angry*. She said, coldly, 'Why the heck are they testing for T.B.? He's not some homeless derelict. How you could let him get into this state is beyond me. You should have called me sooner.'

Marlowe, weary, sat down on the only chair, Caro in his arms. She had fallen asleep, suddenly exhausted, as two year olds will. Asleep, she looked alarmingly like Luke. He saw, probably for the first time, that their mouths were identical, the rose-crimson lips thin, lightly curved and wide. Every feature proclaimed kinship, the difference in sex and age mere detail. It was also quite impossible to separate his contribution from Bel's. They contrived to look exactly like both parents, with this difference; each saw the other in their children.

Long silences distressed Bel. She liked control, moving peremptorily from a dull clod to a brighter student. She said harshly, 'Why the hell didn't you let me know sooner? He's my son. I do have rights. I do care.'

Marlowe took note of the order, thought of maintenance, never paid, then thought better of it. He remembered Bel's anger, and her anguish, as they'd watched over Luke, concussed, at five, falling from a swing on the Common. He said, through leaden weariness, 'Luke was in here weeks ago. He collapsed during a fell run. He'd been off colour for a while. They said there was nothing wrong. In fact, they suggested a shrink, and blamed me.'

'You?'

'Both of us, I suppose. For splitting up, for removing him from the familiar.'

Bel moved back to the bed. 'Psychobabble, preying on guilt. The truth is, he's sick, and they haven't a bloody clue. Bunch of half-witted quacks.'

Marlowe thought, pure Bel, his woman.

When the nurse came, a few minutes later, to check readings, Bel said, 'When will you know?'

The nurse had to ignore her at first. Luke's physical processes must all be checked and any change recorded. Then she said, 'I'm sorry, dear. I couldn't really say. At this stage, there's so many possibilities. You'll have a chance to speak to Doctor.'

Bel looked at her son, then looked away quickly. She said, 'So for all you know, he's dying. You don't know what it is. You're prepared to leave him here, dying, while you faff about. I want him transferred to London. Today.'

Marlowe walked to the window, still cradling his daughter. Very likely, Bel was right. People like Bel tended to get their way. Bel would know someone, have the transfer organised. But the nurse had gone to fetch a doctor; a woman. She came at once, only halfway through rounds on the next ward. She said, 'Mrs Marlowe, there are no grounds for moving Luke. His condition's stable. Once we know what we're dealing with, we can start treatment. We can keep him stable in here, while we wait for results. We're taking him down for a brain scan this afternoon.'

Marlowe said sharply, '*Why*, for God's sake? You think he has a brain tumour?'

Again, the maternal touch, cool fingers across his hand, all routine. The doctor said, infinitely calm, 'I thought Sister

194

would have explained. We do need CT scans, for a possible brain tumour. We're concerned about the history of dizzy spells and vomiting. Had he complained of headaches?'

Marlowe said, bleakly, 'He seemed to live on paracetamol. I should . . . It's my fault . . .'

She said, peaceably, 'Mr Marlowe, we're doing our best. We can keep Luke stable while we work on this.'

Bel said bitterly, 'You mean, you can keep Luke's body alive in here, while you find out what's killing him.'

She turned back to the bed, stood beside Luke. The doctor moved on to another patient, no more or less important. Marlowe looked at Bel, tried to remember love. Once, and, given Caro's age, not so very long ago, he'd made love to this woman. The intimacy seemed indecent. He saw for the first time that she wore trousers in a suedelike material, cut close across the crotch, and a fitted tweed jacket over a washed silk shirt. So close were the trousers cut, he could see, rather than imagine the curve of pubic bone, then the flat, taut flesh, up to her deep-set navel, handspan waist. Bel didn't look like a mother, or not until he looked up, saw, in amazement, bright tears falling. Then she was in his arms, head on his shoulder, and sobbing. Marlowe stroked her cropped hair. Bel sobbed with the abandon of a baby, tears running down her lovely face, wetting his shirt, running down his neck. Making love no longer seemed unlikely at all. In another place, he would move her to lie down, cover her sad face with kisses, free her lovely body of its clothes, however smart.

He said, 'They kept saying "stable". Luke can't do a damn thing for himself. Last time, they said he was shamming, all tests negative. I should have . . . He's been ill for so long. Since we moved . . . I didn't want to leave him, even to meet your train. Caro ran out of food hours ago. Would you like lunch?'

Bel nodded. 'I've not eaten since breakfast yesterday. Classes till six, then straight to the studios. You know me, I can't face food if we're going live.'

Marlowe touched her slim hand, partly, or rather mainly to confirm the thrill of touching Bel, for the first time in over two years. He saw her shameless response, wondered if the old scruples applied. Sam looked the jealous type. Those

195

bushy-browed Neanderthals were very possessive. He said, a little shamefaced, 'We'll have to find a cash dispenser first. I'm cleaned out.'

Bel smiled. 'My treat. By the way, I should give you something for the kids. I keep forgetting.'

Marlow retrieved Caro from close scrutiny of Luke's charts, lifted her shoulder-high. She pulled his hair. Also, being at the awkward age between nappies and total continence, her knickers were wet. He'd just one pair left, pale blue with a Snow White motif. Caro knew life must go on, eating, playing, potty training, loving. Caro wasn't dying, insisted merely on total love, undivided attention. She studied Bel closely, then said, delighted, 'Bel!'

Bel, to her own surprise, lifted the baby for a kiss, lip to lip, scented and passionate. She'd once, and quite seriously, proposed aborting this person. She said, practically, 'Well, make her decent, then we'll find somewhere to eat. And I need to book a hotel.'

Marlowe looked at her oddly, echoing his father. 'A hotel? You're staying with us, surely?'

Bel looked back once at her son, then pushed open the heavy door. She wouldn't let their eyes meet.

'It's for two nights. I have to go back on Friday, first train. Lecture at eleven, classes all afternoon, then a meeting.'

Bel's schedule didn't allow for death. It was not, as Marlowe knew very well, a meeting at all, but a TV chat show. Marlowe turned for one more sight of his son. Luke's eyes opened briefly, unfocused, then closed again.

When Caro was decent, Bel tried to pick her up, but Caro, outraged, arched her taut little back and kicked hard, straight in the crotch. Her mother scowled, snapped, 'Be like that!' and let the small giggling body slide to the floor. Caro toddled straight to a wastepaper basket, excavated it, a *Mirror*, last night's *Evening Post*, a banana skin, a coke can. Marlowe pounced, upended her, whipped a pouch of baby wipes from his pocket and cleaned her grubby small hands.

Bel watched. She said, amused, 'You're so efficient. I never had the right gear. Nonstarter in the mothers' race.'

'You said it. I ran in a mothers' race once, at Luke's infant

196

school. You were busy. They gave me a thirty-second handicap.'

'Where did you come?'

Marlowe smiled, a small matter of pride. 'First, by a
minute. The skinny ones were size fourteen, and not a sports
bra between them.'

'You never told me.'

'You never asked.'

They'd arrived at a crossroads, signposts to polysyllabic
disease and decay, or the visitors' car park.

'Your car or mine?' Marlowe asked.

Bel was halfway down the steps. Over her shoulder, she
said, 'I came by train.'

'Of course. Stupid of me.'

She could see the Astra and walked purposefully towards
it. Then she saw Caro's car seat in front. This irritated her.
Watching as Marlowe fastened straps over his daughter's
squirming body, she said, 'Caro's got it right. The time to be
a baby is now. Preconceptual care, and the front seat. What
did we do with Luke?'

'Carrycot on the back seat, with a Mothercare harness.
After that, nothing. No rear seat belts in the old Beetle.'

'It's a wonder he survived. He used to be lethal in the back,
without so much as old knicker elastic holding him in.'

'Only Volvo parents bothered. He survived.'

Fastening her own belt, Bel said, flatly, 'He might not, this
time. We simply don't know.'

Marlowe wanted to see her face, discover if the catch in
that so eloquent voice was matched by tears. Bel in tears was
particularly lovely, the wetness adding a starry quality to her
bright eyes. His mind was on anything but lunch. Caro, after
her restless night, had fallen asleep. A few seconds' work
would have her out, still in the seat, still sleeping.

He said, 'Not counting McDonald's, we don't eat out. I'm
stopping here to collect some cash, then we'll go home.'

Bel didn't answer, staring out passively at the midday city,
built of honey-coloured sandstone, a quarter of it still sooty
with heritage. Currently, no one could afford a clean face.
Stone-washing stopped in 1991. She said, in idle curiosity,
'What makes this a *city*? It's hardly a teeming metropolis.'

197

Marlowe said, equally idle, imparter of useless information, 'Charter from Edward I. Don't be rude. It's been a city a damn sight longer than Manchester or Brum. It's all the city I need. Castle, cathedral, free museums, university *and* a good library.'

They were at the bottom of the hill now, climbing steeply. Faith was coming down, walking with two small children in tow. He couldn't remember their names or sexes, the latter in no way obvious from their clothes. Faith, engrossed in motherhood, didn't see him or Bel until the last-minute fleeting smile.

Bel, missed nothing, asked crossly, 'Who was that?'

Marlowe turned to park. 'Which? We passed three people, not counting kids.'

'You know bloody well. You couldn't take your eyes off her. Medusa hair, sexy bum, and kids by Murillo.'

He had to laugh, couldn't help it. 'I'll tell her, some time. She's nearly the kids' GP. I registered with someone else at the same practice.'

'I see.'

Bel let herself out into the fallen garden, all leaf mould and split gold. She added, unaccountably forlorn, 'None of my business. Is this the house? I thought you were poor? I don't pay you anything. Sam thinks I should. He can't understand you. The last ex bleeds him white.'

Marlowe handed her a key, then unclipped Caro and carried the sleeping child up the steps. Overnight, the last trees had disrobed, stood naked above golden abundance, so much dross. A late, pale rose tried to open, and he noticed, for the first time, hellebores, unearthly, unnatural, waxy things. He thought of cheap Christmas cards, sad Christmases with Bel. He said, setting Caro down by the fireside, 'I don't want money. We were friends.'

Bel sat on the bottom stair. Staring at the tiled dragon, she said, 'A bit OTT, surely?'

Marlowe smiled, 'Maybe. I like him. And the family.' He indicated the door, but the light was wrong, the glass dark. He said, with less effect, 'Gryphon, basilisk, minotaur, two centaurs and a phoenix. I'll switch the porch light on so you can see.'

198

Bel shook her head. 'Don't bother. It'd give me the horrors. Fleurs de lis and roses, that's what it should be. William de Morgan and Morris furniture. It's a lovely house, Chris.'

She used his name deliberately. Only his family called him by his given name. Marlowe, like Heathcliff, served all purposes. He didn't like the name Christopher, nor the sexual ambivalence of Chris. He wanted to call Faith by her own strange name, preferably in his arms, better still, in his bed, and no more crying.

He said, as if indifferent, 'Like to see the rest of the house?'

Bel nodded. She said, crudely, 'I'm impressed. Do you have a mortgage?'

Marlowe led the way upstairs. When he turned, halfway up, sunlight illumined the glass door and all its monsters.

Bel looked dutifully at Caro's cradle, with its gaudy crocheted blankets, then Luke's room, spare as a monk's cell. Luke's absence and the memory of him hurt.

'I'm down the corridor, and there are attics,' Marlowe said.

Bel walked on ahead of him. Once in the room, she sat down on the bed. Marlowe joined her. Thirty seconds later, Bel kicked off her shoes.

'I shouldn't have left you like that. At the time, there didn't seem to be much choice. Sam wanted a decision, one way or the other. So I made it.'

Marlowe was tired of waiting, eager all the past hour for the necessary mating. He lay down beside her. The kiss was mutual, her mouth opening for him. Bel had never been coy. Decorous, graceful, she became naked for him. Their foreplay was swift, practised and mechanical. Before they could progress very far, though, Caro's high shrieks rang through the house.

Bel freed herself, said, coolly, 'Your daughter or mine?'

But Marlow was already half-dressed, pulling on his trousers, disgusted with himself.

The day's small light had gone. As he left, Bel switched on the bedside lamp and studied the room. There was very little to see. The curtains, faded old rose, shrunk four inches too short, dated from the previous owner. Someone, God knows when, had the leisure to hand-sew every stitch of the lining.

199

A woman or a wife could add a few inches of lace. Lace and a solitary man didn't mix. She considered the problem. The curtains were otherwise quite perfect, heavy repp, faded to the exact shades of the rose and peony tiles around the fireplace.

She lay on her back, wishing for a guilt-free cigarette, followed by more sex. Only, there was the blasted brat. Try as she might, she couldn't think of the kids as hers. Just as well Caro was the dead spit of her father, far more like him than Luke. Sam hinted about reversing the vasectomy. No chance. Nine bloody months, then hellish pain. . . . Never again.

Chris was coming back, with the baby. She could hear them laughing together, father and daughter. Some of the women she knew were locked in custody battles, snarling for possession like Oberon and Titania, or dogs over a bone. She really was incredibly lucky – lucky Chris wanted them; lucky to be going places, fast. Last week, she'd bumped into Russell on the South Bank, walking past pigeon-perch Nelson Mandela. They'd gone for lunch and talked about Chris. Really, honestly, truthfully, the crunch came at the right time for him. He belonged irrevocably to the old days, a 1980s man, from before the walls came down. He needed to move on, do something else. It was the right time. Choosing to be with the kids was probably the best thing for him.

The phone rang. Bel, prescient, knew it would be the hospital, with news about the scans for a brain tumour. Whatever the news, it was already a fact. She closed her eyes, saw the newborn Luke, prayed to a God who didn't exist.

Marlowe came into the room with Caro in his arms. 'That was the hospital. Clear. There's no tumour.'

Caro bounced on the bed, higher and higher, with manic laughter. Marlowe grabbed her, made her lie down, pinned her to the bed, still laughing. he raged at her.

'Idiot! Dumbo! Fall off, crack your head, and a posse of social workers will take you into care. Get hurt, and it's my fault.'

Caro's lower lip trembled. The words meant little, but the anger in his voice destroyed her world. She began to cry, with

200

sobs and diamond tears. At once, contrite, he held her close, pleading.

'Don't cry. Don't cry. I just don't want you to get hurt, that's all.'

Caro repeated solemnly, 'Not hurt,' then beamed at him. She added, while the going was good, 'Hungry.'

Marlowe laughed, then set about dressing properly, which meant first removing his sweater and trousers. Bel, returning from the bathroom, saw him naked, the lean, almost slight body barely changed. He was fitter than Sam, taller, kinder. A nice man, or even, possibly, a good man. The only problem was, he was such a crashing bore now, living in his little world of children and provincial dross.

He said, 'It's open visiting for Luke. I try to get back, every evening. At least, I did last time he was in. Hospital's a bit like prison. They live for meals and visiting time.'

Bel wore his dressing gown, the navy-blue towelling one she always used to borrow. She said petulantly, 'Then I can have a bath. If you like, I'll put Caro to bed while you go to the hospital. It's not as if he's conscious, as if he'd know me.'

Marlowe took her in his arms, discovered rejection too late. Still holding her, he said, 'He's in a coma. A light coma. God knows how they tell. There's no knowing what he registers.'

Bel rested her head on his shoulder. She said, allowing tears, 'You go. Hospitals give me the creeps. I feel sick in the car park. You seem able to handle it. Go by yourself. You'll manage better without Caro, anyway.'

Marlowe stroked her wet cheek and licked her tears from his hand. Caro clutched at his knees, whinging to be picked up. Bel's presence confused him, disturbed too many memories. She wasn't his wife or even the woman he wanted now. Luke lay unconscious, maybe dying. Caro was the only certainty.

She smiled at him, said, patiently, 'Hungry. I want something to eat, now.'

In case he'd misheard, she repeated the request, louder.

Marlowe turned to Bel. 'Did you hear? Luke's dying, and all she thinks of is food.'

201

Bel laughed. 'Feed her, then. I like a woman who knows her own mind. We'll get on fine, won't we, Caroline?'

Halfway downstairs, and in her father's arms, Caro found words for something else that had troubled her. She said, searching his face, 'Where's Luke? Where's he gone? Where's my brother?'

Marlowe told her. Caro nodded and sorrowfully repeated, 'Hospital.'

In the kitchen, he lifted her into the high chair, gave her a piece of wholemeal bread, spread with sunflower margarine, while he sliced a banana and half an apple. That lot demolished, she was still hungry. She ate the other half of the apple, looked around for more. Marlowe gave her a beaker of water and a small handful of grapes. After that, replete, she began to climb over the side. He caught the small wilful body only just in time, before the shattered skull, broken bones, inquests and inquisitions.

The kitchen, though stark, looked stylish enough, not poor. Where the conventional ranged wall cupboards, he'd hung a rack, *batterie de cuisine,* not dried flowers. There was another rack, over the Aga, for drying clothes. The Aga was sixty years old, scarred with years of Aga cooking. The Oxo and Ovaltine posters stuck up with Blu-Tack were originals, too. On the vestry-cupboard shelves, he'd arranged four old tins and a vase of late, battered roses from the garden. The tea towels hanging over the Aga rail were clean, one scarlet, one cobalt blue. Overhead, Caro's tights, jumpers and dungarees hung like Christmas streamers.

Bel, standing in the doorway, thought it a good place to be, for them. She said, politely, 'She doesn't really know me. We'd better all go to the hospital. Could I possibly have a cup of tea first?'

Leaving the hospital, some time after nine, Marlowe said, 'I'm glad we stayed on. There was some response.'

Bel, more honest, less deluded, shook her head, appalled by what she'd seen. 'His eyelids flickered. I thought he was going to open them. Then he didn't. Don't delude yourself. They still haven't a clue.'

They had to stop for road works. The road was clear ahead,

for a straight mile, not another car in sight. Bel said, 'Shit. Go *on*. There's no one about.'

Marlowe refused, took the car out of gear. A police car pulled up behind them. He smiled but said nothing, moved on when at last the lights turned to green. At the bottom of their own hill, cones marched, cordoning off half the road. They'd appeared since six.

Bel swore again. 'They bloody do it on purpose. *And* more fucking lights.'

Caro opened her eyes and looked about. Marlowe said, coldly, 'I'd rather you didn't swear in front of Caro.'

Bel said nothing at all.

Caro had been asleep five minutes when the doorbell rang. They'd just switched on *News at Ten*. Bel nearly swore again, then put a singer across her lips. Marlowe went to the door. Even Jehovah's Witnesses laid off at this time, in pouring rain.

The huddled figure in the porch was Faith, her pale face rain-streaked. She said, quietly, 'Sorry to disturb you so late. I came to ask about Luke. How is he?'

Marlowe tried to invite her in, but she shook her head.

'No. The kids are on their own. It's just that I heard McCleod talking about the scans. I had to call in at the surgery. I . . .'

Marlowe looked at her, pale, composed, dark shadows below the deep-set eyes. He said bleakly, 'They've ruled out a tumour, but he's in a coma, still. They keep saying "stable". How the hell can they tell?'

Faith touched his hand, love without, at this point, any complicating sex. She said, gently, 'Stable means just that. He's in no immediate danger. I must go. You've got company.'

Marlowe shook his head. 'No, only Bel. Luke's mother. She came this morning. I'm not sure why. She can't bear to be with him. Or me.'

Faith's hand was still on his, healing. 'If I hear anything, I'll tell you. I must go. Imagine, if someone shopped me. Three kids alone in the house. I'd be struck off. It was easier when they had a nanny.'

Marlowe stood watching her, light and quick down the

steep steps. Now he had to go back to Bel, find words, live through another day. One thing was entirely clear. They'd made love for the last time long ago. This afternoon business was an aberration, as if checking some old, unfinished piece of work, seeing its faults writ large, not worth further effort. He was glad Caro had intervened.

Chapter Eighteen

Leaving the hospital on Thursday night, Bel said, 'I must catch the first train tomorrow. If I could ring for a taxi . . .'

Marlowe held the heavy door open for her, said, truthfully, 'Caro wakes at five. She's still on summer time. I'll take you. Then I can come back here.'

Bel stood before the cluttered notice board, wondered why people couldn't stay at home, mind their own business, or watch TV. The whole town was up to something, every night, and weekends too, car boot sales for the special care baby unit, Christmas Fayres for the hospice, the psychiatric unit, half a dozen day centres and half the world. She said, well rehearsed, 'Buy enough raffle tickets, and the Four Horsemen don't stand a chance.' Marlowe wondered how to take that. Bel liked her state control minimal, approved of self-help and sponsorship. Faith might say the same thing, but in scornful disbelief. Luke's room, Luke's bed, according to the wall plaque, had been funded by the Friends of Casterton hospital. Bel approved. Faith, almost certainly, did not. He said, 'I'll collect Caro first, if that's all right with you.'

Bel nodded, still benign. She said, 'Everyone should have a neighbour like Faith. Strings of kids, and room for one more.'

Driving back Marlowe sped through the road works just before the lights changed, and pulled up outside Faith's house. He rang the bell, realised, after waiting five minutes, that it didn't work, and knocked hard. The sound was lost in laughter and many pairs of feet thundering up and down bare wooden stairs. He waited another couple of minutes, then knocked again. Something swished across a tiled floor, and a small child opened the door. It wore a tattered poplin bachelor's gown and a mangy fur stole with too many legs and small faces. She, or he, smiled entrancingly, revealing six front teeth missing, some replacements halfway through. Marlowe said, 'I'm Caro's father. Is she . . .?'

The small one put two fingers in its mouth, whistled loud and shrill, and bellowed, 'Caro! Your dad's here.'

Caro came running. She wore two shades of green eye shadow, peacock feathers in her hair, and scarlet Chinese pyjamas. She didn't run to him, merely said 'Hello' before scampering off. Marlowe, shaken, realised that the child he'd just seen was his baby daughter, two a month ago, a person called Caro.

He wondered how much longer this would take. Bel had been sitting in the car for a quarter of an hour; had no key to the house. She would be very, very angry, for she had calls to make. Then Faith came from the kitchen in a blue and white butcher-stripe apron. She held out Caro's clothes and a wet kitchen cloth, all floury, like her own hands.

'Sorry. We were making gingerbread men. I'll dress her and wash that gunge off.'

Marlowe said, stiffly, 'I'll take her like this. Bel's been waiting outside for the past twenty minutes.'

Faith smiled. 'Goodness! How awful!' Then she said, in an utterly different voice, 'How is Luke?'

Marlowe turned away, choked by all too familiar tears. He wouldn't cry in Bel's presence, nor did he choose, yet, to let Faith see tears. He said, staring intently at the neat mosaic tiles, 'Worse. He didn't know we were there. Not a flicker. Last time, he pressed my hand. How they know he's not dead, God knows.'

Faith said, gently, 'They monitor brain activity. If he was dying, if there was any sign of brain death, they'd tell you. They'd want to discuss organ transplants.'

Marlowe said, bleakly, 'I'm afraid to sleep, in case I miss the dying. If I could stay there, always.'

Faith opened the door. He stood very still, aware of unfinished business with Bel.

'I know the ICU staff,' Faith said. 'They won't lie to you.

If Luke's dying, they'll tell you. If he's in a PVS, they'll say so. The chances are, it's one of these viruses we know sod all about.'

Marlowe was silent for a moment or two, then said, 'And can't treat.'

Taking Caro in his arms, and her clothes in a supermarket bag, he returned to Bel, who wasn't angry at all, but asleep.

In the morning, Caro yelled, on cue, at five, came scampering to his bed. Bel had taken Luke's room, enclosed by his icons. Luke's trophies were speared to his pinboard by three overworked drawing pins: piano, abandoned after Grade VI; class prizes, cross-country colours; two press cuttings of his work; a poem published by the *Observer* the previous year; a radio play, runner-up in a Radio Five competition. Bel had said, why not frame them? Too late now, unless he recovered.

Marlowe, sleep-sozzled, persuaded Caro to lie down beside him. He drifted into the best sleep of all, the brief, craven, early morning hour. Halfway through, Bel stood by the bed with coffee. There were two cups and a bowl of sugar lumps. Naked, he sat up in bed, wincing as scalding black coffee stung his hairless chest.

Bel said, 'I hate leaving you to all this. If Luke was in Great Ormond Street, or even . . . Come back to London. You could let this place. Ask for a couple of those Japanese language students. They take better care.'

Marlowe pulled the duvet round him. It had become curiously important to keep his body well hidden. He sipped coffee in silence, then said, 'Change places.'

She looked at him, trying to remember love. The only confusing factor now was Luke, still as death, and no name for his sickness. She said, more honest than kind, 'I couldn't. Really, I couldn't. The children are your business now. There's nothing I can do for Luke, not if I prayed by his bedside day and night. If it's money . . .'

Marlowe drained his cup. The coffee was excellent, far better than he ever bought now. Yesterday, the TV and press had measured poverty, one day behind a feature on Radio Four. It was interesting to find himself a pauper, officially on the breadline. Very likely, there were benefits to be claimed.

It might come to that, some day. *Northern Lights* and occasional spin-offs kept their heads above water, saved them from long thin books and small green cheques. He preferred it this way, but decided against telling Bel. Let her imagine secret resources of wit and brilliance syndicated worldwide.

'No, money isn't a problem. I earn our keep. By the way, what's a PVS?'

Bel was pouring herself a second cup of coffee. She said, 'Persistent vegetative state – braindead, I think. Luke isn't braindead.'

'Yet.'

She stood up. 'Maybe never. This time next week, he could be playing scrum half. Anyway, I must get dressed.'

Marlowe regretted, a little, not seeing her dress, remembering the way she would lean forwards to cup her small breasts in black lace. Bel's choice of underwear was simple: black or black.

He drove her to the station through howling wind and rain. They were far too early, ten official minutes and another thirty: cattle on the line. She laughed.

'That beats fallen leaves or the wrong snow. You're so rural up here.'

She looked very pretty laughing, her two crooked teeth exquisitely capped, the tiny gap gone, the pearliness improbably perfect. How much did that lot cost? Also, and this was most curious, the fine, fretted lines around her eyes and the slightly deeper ones around her mouth had gone. He looked closer. Her skin was indecently young, all life's scars erased without trace. They were almost exactly the same age. He could see, by the merciless waiting-room mirror, that he looked a good ten years older, grey in his hair, and lines etched deep about his mouth and eyes. Bel, the beautiful, clearly intended to stay that way.

Marlow shrugged. 'They should fence the line better. It's always cattle or sheep. There aren't any trees between here and the border, not near the track.'

Bel bought the *Financial Times* and started the crossword, then, looking up, said, 'You don't need to wait.'

Marlowe checked his watch and the overhead screen, which didn't agree. The railway was ten minutes out. He

208

said, hesitant, 'They won't want me before seven. It's not worth going home. If I visit Luke now, I can put in a few hours' work before evening.'

After that, they sat in silence until the train was announced. Marlowe picked up Bel's case. Someone else held the door open. Bel checked her ticket, took the case from him. The exact space between them ruled out even a social kiss. She said, and it was banal, nothing, 'Take care. Keep in touch about Luke. If there's anything I can do. . . .'

He thought, walking away, that she sounded like a distant aunt, not Luke's mother.

Caro tried to wriggle free, wouldn't hold his hand. She kicked him, stamped fierce little feet. Marlowe would have smacked her, but smothered her with kisses instead, for being his daughter.

Luke lay very still, visibly, hideously thinner, but his eyes moved under the bruised lids. Marlowe challenged a nurse.

'Why does he look like that? He'll starve to death. I want the truth. Is he dying?'

She looked scared, eighteen years old, first week on the wards, two months out of Galway, and taking an illicit short-cut to Maternity.

Contrite, he said, 'It's all right. I'll see Sister. Don't be late on my account.'

She touched his hand and said, desperately Irish, 'I'll pray for him. What's his name?'

'Luke.'

'Luke. I won't forget.'

Marlowe watched her go, poor unfledged thing and still believing. On the way out, though, he pushed open the door marked *Chapel* and sat there for a minute or two. A man of sixty or seventy knelt in the farthest corner, not weeping but very still. Guilt-stricken, Marlowe thought of his own father. Luke had been here since Monday, and he hadn't rung. He sat watching Caro rearrange candles in boxes. There was nothing she could damage or tear. The room was Quaker in its simplicity, of no denomination, a place to be still, rather than pray. He thought of praying, then decided to ring his father. To have a fair chance, prayers should come from a believer, surely? He rang three times, then hung up, just as his father, muddy boots kicked off, rushed in from the garden.

Chapter Nineteen

Luke's heart had stopped. Only briefly, but the record was there on his notes. It had started again before any staff could reach his bed, but the monitors knew what he was up to: trying to die. He was on full life support now, his condition deteriorating. They'd taken more blood, for testing. Given time, they'd reach a diagnosis.

Marlowe received the news calmly. On the way home from Caro's toddler group, he'd stopped at a call box to give Dad one more chance. The old man answered at once, as if waiting by the phone. Marlowe asked if this was true.

'Since quarter to ten. It's Luke, isn't it? I've been praying.'

Marlowe said, 'I should have rung before. He's been in hospital since Monday.'

The old man said, sharply, 'And this is Friday. Just as well there's other ways. Your mother said last night, "Pray for Luke."'

Marlowe sighed. At eighty-three, his father was nearer death than most. Ten years widowed, he lived in close and happy communion with his dead wife. Bel, the last time she ever saw him, found this so bizarre she insisted on seeing his GP. The outcome was less than satisfactory. The doctor, a singularly humble man, took his premiss from *Hamlet* – 'more things in heaven and earth' – exposing the weakness of Bel's philosophy. The old man was mentally alert, fitter than most people half his age. If he talked to his dead wife, what of it? Like his patient, Dr Leigh declared every Sunday and holy day that he believed in 'the resurrection of the body, and life everlasting'. Bel, outvoted, had to leave well alone.

211

The pips went. Marlowe found another coin, wondered how many words it would buy. His father said, as they were reconnected, 'Give me your number. I'll ring you back.'

Marlowe was ready to refuse, then realised he had one pound coin and a few pence in his pocket, a fiver in his wallet, and nothing more at all until the next cheque. He'd thought of Dad as a pensioner, but the truth was, the old boy could hardly spend half his money; state pension, teaching pension, bus pass and no garage bills. He gave the number, grabbed the receiver as a waiting woman glared.

'Sorry, Dad. I should have rung. It's been difficult. Bel was here. And Caro's kicking up a fuss outside.'

'Caroline? Could I have a word? Would she?'

Caro, allowed in, scowled at her father, who deserved it. Her hands were froggy cold and her face scarlet. A wicked little wind was up, tossing leaves, fetching hail and sleet. Marlowe had forgotten the rain cover; one of his besetting faults.

Caro said, through chattering teeth, 'Cold. I's cold.'

Marlowe lifted her up for a minute, then took the phone back. His father said, 'Death isn't the end, you know. But I should be next, not Luke. I'm praying.'

Marlowe saw an indignant foot-stamping queue, three of them. With apologies, he hung up. Outside, he said, shamelessly touting for sympathy, 'My son's in intensive care.'

English, they let him go without a word. He walked back, pushing Caro up ever steeper hills until he was rank with sweat, antiperspirant left off the list the previous week. On the doormat, there was a letter from Russell. Russell wept for him, Russell deeply sympathised, but times were hard, budgets tight, the northern office closing. In short, they would have to let him go. With, but of course, the most glowing commendations, with every confidence that he'd find another niche soon. Marlowe began to tear the letter up, then thought better of it. Times were hard, and one side had been enough for Russell's regrets. Caro could draw on the other. Caro preferred freshly painted walls, but he lived in hope of diverting her.

That evening, Marlowe found a stranger at Luke's bedside.

212

He said, not entirely hostile, 'Excuse me, but this is my son. I don't . . .'

The man extended a hand. Marlowe saw the dog collar, knew he was in for it. The priest said, 'Mr Marlowe? Philip Hughes. I'm chaplain here. Your father told me about Luke.'

Marlowe said, 'Thank you, but I'm afraid I don't believe in prayer. *Que sera, sera.* If Luke's illness leads to death, that's what will happen. All I need is the strength to live with that.'

'A Stoic? "Free me from the fear of losing my beloved child"?'

'If you like. All the same, there's no law against praying. Feel free, if you think it does any good.'

Both men stood by the boy's bedside in silence, one in prayer, the other in limbo. Old habits die very, very hard. Presently, though, Marlowe said, 'Jairus's daughter. Was she really dead, or in a state like this?'

Hughes looked at the machines that lived for Luke. 'Academic, in those days, unless Christ got to her pretty damn quick.'

Marlowe looked down at his son. Tonight, he was extremely beautiful. *In extremis?* A loathsome, bruising rash disfigured his body, but his face was clear, its pallor lily white, porcelain frail, luminous. The dark, feathery curls gave him a look of Shelley. Marlowe tried to remember a tough, grubby small boy, garden vandal, kicking down delphiniums with Jules and Toby. Luke, racing to be first off the car ferry in an unknown land; actually Boulogne. Luke, blowing out ten candles on the Rialto, the week of taking him to work, some bloody boring arty bash in Venice, and Luke's birthday in the middle of it. Then he stopped, to look at the still body of his son.

Hughes said, 'You were smiling. Don't stop. Celebrate his life. It isn't the length of our lives that matters, you know.'

Marlowe looked up and smiled faintly. '"*The days of our age are threescore years and ten, and though men be so strong that they come to fourscore years, yet is their strength then but labour and sorrow, so soon it passeth away, and we are gone.*" Luke isn't fifteen till the week before Christmas.'

Hughes said, 'He's dreaming. Look.'

It was true. Very, very briefly, the boy's eyes opened,

closed again, to move in dreaming sleep. It was, at least, a sign of life.

'Do you know all the Book of Common Prayer?' Hughes asked. 'I thought, with your father a Catholic . . .'

Marlowe smiled. 'I'm a journalist. Young reporters do funerals and memorial services; it makes the older men nervous. The great and the good still tend to die C of E. Like infants, they haven't much choice.'

Hughes had taken the boy's hand. He said, 'Luke was baptised, I believe?'

Marlowe nodded. 'Almost over his mother's dead body. I never did tell her. To please my parents. Lousy reason, but there you are. It did. Look, Father . . . The best I can manage is agnostic. *I don't know.* I really don't know. Pray for my son, if you think it will do any good.'

Hughes had turned away, ready to go. Marlowe had decided he must be all of twenty-five. Slightly more generous now, he made that thirty. He reached out to shake the man's hand. Hand-shaking was very religious these days. Church was about the only place you could legitimately dodge kisses with a firmly extended hand. He'd learned that the hard way, at too many funerals.

'This isn't my only hospital,' Hughes said. 'I'm at the Manor as well, but I'll visit Luke whenever I can. And pray for him.'

Then he was gone. Marlowe stood holding Luke's right hand, then bent down to kiss his son. Again, for the most fleeting of moments, Luke's eyes opened. He stared at his father and tried to smile, then his eyes closed again. The machines recorded life, but Luke lay still as death.

That night, Faith's house was magically still, not a sound from any child, including his own. Faith greeted him at the door with a gentle kiss on the lips, and led him to the lofty living room. The kids, all four of them, were watching *The Railway Children*. Too bad it was near the end, Jenny Agutter running into mist and tears, *'My daddy! My daddy!'* Three minutes later, the film ended and the clamour began, demands for food, drink, the loo. Caro had wet her knickers.

Faith said, 'Change her in here. It's freezing in the bathroom. God knows why they didn't fit a radiator.'

Faith's children gathered around as he stripped Caro and cleaned her with a baby wipe. Like any mother, he'd learned to carry spares. One of the boys said, 'Girls bums are peculiar. Hers is just like Anna's.'

The other added, 'When they grow up, they're all furry. Did you know?'

Marlowe nodded, wondered what they'd say next. The bigger boy said, 'Mum's brother came to stay. He's our uncle. You can see through the bathroom keyhole, and his willy had a red beard. His hair's red too.'

Marlowe said, dead-pan, 'Really?'

They tried again. 'We saw a film at school. A baby came out of a lady's bottom.'

Marlowe nodded gravely, remembering Luke, at this age. 'They do. Weird, isn't it?'

After that, they let him off. Instead, they turned to Faith, demanded food. Faith led him out, stopped outside a door with a Mickey Mouse knob. 'You can wash in there. Disneyland, but it was what they wanted then.'

He washed, scrupulously, as she stood in the doorway, then asked, 'What do they want now?'

'Dunno . . . *Thunderbirds, Magic Roundabout*, aliens and mutants. I lose track. I'm sticking with Mickey, until they paint it black.'

Marlowe laughed, 'Four years, then.'

'So soon?'

'Or sooner. Luke was a late developer. I drew the line at painting the walls. We settled for black duvet, black sheets, black curtains, black rug with cabbalistic signs in luminous paint. Gives me the horrors, but there you are. No accounting for the young.'

She said, understanding too much, 'Do you mind, then, not being young?'

Marlowe stared at her, then laughed again. 'God, no! Never again. The happiest man I know is my dad. He's eighty-three, and not afraid of dying.'

'Tell me more.'

Marlowe shook his head. 'You'll have to meet him. I rang him today, about Luke. The odd thing is, he knew already.'

Faith sat in the big kitchen chair on a cushion made like a rag rug, bands of coloured cloth woven in and out. She stood up to let in a long, tabby cat, who promptly sat in her chair, becoming circular. Marlowe wondered if she would offer tea, or coffee, wondered why she'd led him away from the kids. It was a quarter to ten, and school in the morning, surely? And what the hell were they watching now? He could hear manic noises and too much laughter. Faith said, reaching for his hand, 'Relax. They're happy. It's something innocuous.'

'They should be in bed. Caro should, anyway.'

Faith stood up and came towards him. 'On Friday nights, the rule is, they sleep where they drop. Tomorrow's Saturday, remember. No school, no surgery; I'm not on call, and the night is young. Tea or coffee?'

Marlowe refused both, didn't like the way she looked at him – too appraising. Avoiding her eyes, he said, 'Sorry, but I'm dead beat. Caro needs her sleep, too. She's been up since five.'

'Ah, but she slept for two hours while you were out. Is she allowed to eat this late?'

Marlowe smiled. 'Try stopping her.'

Faith fed crumpets into the toaster and put two pizzas under the grill. Watching, Marlowe discovered no hunger at all, or not for food. Faith's signals were confusing. She'd slept and wept in his arms, virginal. Tonight, she was detaining him deliberately. Apart from the pathetic business with Bel, he lived without sex for nearly three years. It was time, and long past time, to fight back, to return those candid, appraising glances.

No make-up or plastic surgery denied the years. Faith's transfiguring smile lit laughter lines about her dark eyes. No grey showed in her heavy dark hair, but he'd seen, in the bathroom wastepaper basket, an empty packet of *Loving Care*. So she did care, quite enough, about her looks. This was the self she wanted the world to see: older, wiser, undaunted.

She said now, over her shoulder, 'Tea, coffee, chocolate or something else?'

216

'Such as?'

'Ginger wine, cassis, Cointreau, barack, Benedictine, advocaat, amaretto, kirsch?'

'Ginger wine would be perfect.'

She crossed the room to an oak corner cupboard and produced a bottle of Crabbies. her collection of spirits was astounding.

'Half this stuff is revolting,' she said. 'In my far from humble opinion, advocaat's for cleaning drains. I take the kids abroad every year, and collect local hooch. Barack's brilliant for sore throats. One sip, and you're out for a week. It's ominously quiet in there. Let's move.'

Caro slept, spreadeagled, on Faith's sofa. Oliver, Max and Anna slept in their own beds. Marlowe sat by the fire, watching a Czech film with subtitles. He hadn't a clue what it was about. Death, possibly, rather than sex. They kept flashing in hammy close-ups of the skeleton on the Staromestské clock. It was twenty past twelve. He said, 'I really should go.'

Faith's long fingers moved through his hair. She whispered softly, 'Must you? Well, that's for you to decide. When I want you to go, I'll say so.'

Marlowe felt sweaty, unclean with too much rushing about and fear of death. He aid, diffidently, 'If I could have a bath?'

Faith led him to her own bathroom. The bath sat in splendour, fed by glistening brass pipes. Claws pawed the ground. Towels, all white, filled the airing cupboard. The loo was mounted on a dais, the pan elegant in blue and white. On the wall, there was Nick Kamen stepping out of his Levis in the launderette, a leather-clad biker on a Harley Davidson and a huge close-up of a man on a rockface. Her dead husband? By the door, there was a height chart, free with *Playdays*, and the floor was littered with ducks, an inflatable dolphin and sodden towels.

Faith said, 'Little gits. The other bathroom's full of old bikes. See you later.'

Clean and sweet, he rifled shamelessly through her cupboards, borrowed antiperspirant, then washed his shirt in Lux flakes at the great pedestal basin. There was still a reek of sweat. He used Faith's Roget et Gallet on the armpits and rinsed the shirt again. Then, belatedly, he decided to wash his

217

hair, with Body Shop mango. He hung the shirt to drip-dry on a rail above a great snaking radiator, black and shiny as anthracite. There was a red washing-up bowl, strategically placed, and three hangers. Only then did he return to Faith. It was after one. She said, amused,

'Clean at last? Then I'm off for a shower.'

She was back less than ten minutes later. She knelt down beside him before the dying fire, kissed him deliberately on the mouth. Marlowe held back, assaulted by guilt and lust, then fear. He said, all but pushing her away, 'Luke's dying . . . I must go. I'm sorry. Look after Caro, please.'

Shivering, naked under a thin sweater, he drove through the sleeping city. *Five gold rings . . . four colly birds. . .* The Christmas lights burned bright, like the spangled lights on premature trees. Santas in crude red and white sold everything from gas cookers to golf clubs. All the traffic lights ahead were against him, red as any blood, the hospital a mile away, still. They stayed red, pitiless, fully five minutes, until a patrolling police car told him to move on.

Beyond the dark walls were birth and death. A woman moaned as she was wheeled past. He felt no pity. Before dawn, she'd be sitting up, smug as a plaster Madonna, the only mother in creation. He sped on, unchallenged, to stand by Luke's bed. Luke lay very still, sleeping like Caro, in perfect trust.

The night nurse finished writing some notes, came to the bedside. She said, gently, 'Mr Marlowe. . . .?'

Marlowe turned to her, ready for grief. Luke lay so very still. No one, yet, had switched off the monitors. They needed consent . . .

He was led away to her desk, saw, for the first time, the others who waited and watched. The nurse said, 'Mr Marlowe, I did try to ring. Luke was conscious. I promised you'd be here in the morning.'

Marlowe said, 'Then he isn't dead?' He leaned against her desk, sick and dizzy, nothing eaten since breakfast. Through choking tears, he said, 'I had to come. I thought he was dying.' Then he was in her arms, without words.

She led him out to a curtained cubicle and made him sit on a metal and canvas chair. She handed out wipes, wet and dry, offered tea. Accepting tea, he waited for the woman to come back with it.

She said, 'Mr Marlowe, Luke's much stronger. We're still ventilating him, but he's begun to fight back. He wanted to speak, so we stopped the ventilator, just for a moment or two. He was breathing alone, and completely lucid.'

Marlowe said, very low, as if the words were dangerous, 'I thought it would be organ transplants. I thought he was dying.'

She smiled again, the perfect woman for this night, full-bosomed, mouse-brown hair in a sensible, womanly knot. She said, with the very faintest hint of remembered brogue, 'Crossed line with the Angel of Death?'

'Then you believe me?'

The woman had taken his hand, like a mother comforting a small child. 'Sure, of course I believe you. Middle of the night, no shirt . . . Why else would you come? Will you be getting home to bed now?'

'If I could stay here till Luke wakes?'

She looked doubtful, then said, 'If you'll scat the minute this room's needed. Are you easy to wake?'

Marlowe smiled. 'My daughter doesn't suffer sleep gladly. She's just two. I'll wake the minute you call. But if I could stay . . .'

She touched his hand, let her own rest there, firm and strong. On her left hand, there were three rings, wedding, engagement, eternity. It wasn't the kind of hand used to advertise such rings. Then she indicated the narrow examination couch, left, to return with a blanket.

Marlowe lay down. He slept deeply and dreamlessly until she came to shake him awake.

'Luke's asking for you.'

He stood by the bed in disbelief. Luke lay still as death, but he was breathing for himself. The monitors worked on, recording one more patient. If they'd made a mistake . . . Presently, though, Luke's eyes opened, brilliant in his pale face.

'Dad?'

Marlowe took his hand, remembering the tendril strength of newborn fingers.

Luke said, 'I dreamed my mother came here.'

'She did. She sends love.'

Luke tried to move onto his side, but the drips got in his way. he said, 'You know the feeling after a long day in the hills? Totally shattered, and fantastic. I feel like that. So happy. You can't believe how happy. I dreamed I met Gran, but she sent me away.'

Marlowe held the thin hand still, dismissed the dream, gratefully, as just that.

Luke said, watching him, 'This is intensive care, isn't it? Where people die . . .?'

Marlowe kissed his son, and to hell with Luke's embarrassment. He said, holding tight, 'Where people have every chance of getting better.'

Luke gripped his father's hand. Seeing the time, half past five, he said, with the selfishness of the sick, 'I suppose you want to get back to Caro?'

Marlowe nodded. Luke closed his eyes. Marlowe, angry, wanted them open again. The death's-head look was back, so much flesh lost. But he said, 'I'll be in later, with Caro.'

Chapter Twenty

Faith said, 'You're frozen. Come and warm up in bed. Better late than never.'

Marlowe stood in her hallway, shivering. 'Isn't this all rather sudden?'

She looked him up and down: lean, maybe just under six foot; dark, thick hair, frosted with grey; deep-set eyes, the colour of iron; high cheekbones above hollows. She saw, too, dark stains below his eyes, new lines around his mouth, too much pain for too long. About Luke, she dared not ask.

She said candidly touching his stubbled cheeks, 'Not sudden at all. Over two months, since the day we met. Total score so far, one measly kiss. I call that indecently chaste.'

Marlowe kept his hands to himself. 'Is screwing new neighbours one of your hobbies?'

Faith glowered, then burst out laughing. Leaning against him, she said, 'You make this so bloody difficult. What am I supposed to do? Strip? I thought it was going well, till you shot off.'

Marlowe kicked off his shoes and bolted Faith's front door. It was after six. Caro would, most certainly, wake any time now, yell for him, need feeding, dressing, the usual treadmill of loving her. No doubt Faith's kids prowled too, pitiless. But Faith had taken him by the hand, leading him, quickly, barefoot on bare wooden stairs, to the attic room where she slept. Beside the bed, she switched on soft light. The floor was bare wood, softened only by a faded Namdah rug beside the bed. The walls were stark. There were no posters or paintings, no

221

clothes scattered about the room, apart from a pair of jeans hanging over an ancient treadle sewing machine.

She stood beside him, silent, then whispered, 'Marlowe . . . What more can I do?'

Marlowe reached for her hand and let her guide him down onto the narrow bed. Then he was lying beside her, said, 'My name's Christopher. Chris. Not guilty. My parents got carried away, too many years ago. The comparison is odious. I'm not gay, failed to die young and it's far too late now. Yesterday, I lost what was left of my job.'

Faith said, 'I was afraid so. It was on the news about the Manchester office. And I was afraid you'd go back to London, and Luke's mother. She's very beautiful.'

Marlowe propped himself up on one elbow. He was against the wall. The bed was barely three feet wide. He could smell jasmine and frangipani, tenderly female. Bel wore men's aftershave, essence of tom-cat, and musk. He loathed musk, told her, often, where it came from. He said, 'Why should you care?'

Faith touched the cleft in his stubbled chin. She'd always liked cleft chins. Like Rob, like the young Olivier, before he grew fleshy. She said, abruptly, 'Because I want to marry you. I think it would work. I want to be married again, and to you. Before I say any more, how's Luke?'

Marlowe looked up at the white, cobwebbed ceiling. 'Psychic crossed wires, according to the night nurse. Luke wasn't dying. He'd been conscious and asking for me. He's perfectly lucid, and they had him off the ventilator.'

Faith took his hand. 'That's good. I'm glad.'

Marlowe said, bitterly, 'You think so? He's conscious, but he can't move a muscle. One of these viruses you know sod all about . . .'

Faith held him close and stroked his hair, as if he were one of her children. She said, quietly, 'We know so very little. Sometimes, there's nothing we can do but watch and wait.'

'For death?'

Faith kissed his cold lips, knew she would never deceive him. She said, weighing every word, 'Even when there's nothing else we can do, the machines give us time.'

He slept like a child in her arms, but for no more than an

222

hour. Before dawn, he woke again, slipped from the bed and dressed quickly. Faith woke as he leaned down to kiss her.

'I must go.'

'Luke?'

He kissed her again, discovering that they had all the time in the world. 'No. Your children, and Caro. They need to know us better. I'll take her home now.'

The phone was ringing, and there he was stuck outside with a key that wouldn't turn. Why it wouldn't turn was quite obvious. There was a lid of ice encasing the key hole, like an acrylic paper weight. He remembered, too late, a silly gadget Bel gave him, last Christmas, key warmer, sculling around a desk drawer, never used. Last year, there was no winter at all. Today was 13 November, and a ghostly white frost. He was tempted to go back, discover what Faith would do next, then recalled an old trick of his father's, learned for icy desert nights. He slid the key into his armpit and held it there a minute or two. Caro was entirely happy, sucking ice off privet twigs. Presently, he extracted the key. This time, it worked.

Inside, he rang the hospital first, in case it had been Luke. Luke was, in their hallowed phrase, stable. In that case, it must be Dad. The certainty was distressing. A year ago, or less than that, in London, it could have been any of a dozen friends, fifty or more acquaintances, new commissions. The transience of his own modest fame was alarming.

Caro found the post and tore open the only real letter, a Get-well card for Luke from school. She screamed when forced to part with it, and had to be appeased with food. She sat on the bottom stair, eating a banana, as he dialled. His father answered at once.

'Yes, I rang. I want to see Luke. I'm catching the next train. My cab's at the door now.' Then he hung up.

Just as well sex and sin with Faith was off. Marlowe did a quick recce of the fridge: two inches of suspect milk, one yogurt, two cold, cooked potatoes, a shiny lump of ageing cheddar. Dad had forsworn worldly goods, but his appetite was youthful, his standards exacting; odd that he should stay so carefully spare. Caro had seen the yogurt and demanded it, though it was hazelnut, despised fourth in a multipack. After

223

that, he dressed her with loving care. Last winter's snow suits wouldn't touch her. Anxious, he piled on cardigans under her rosy jacket, added a Swedish hat with Scandinavian earflaps. Her mittens didn't fit either.

Forty minutes to shop, before the train, and thank God for plastic. He could feed the old boy today, pay after Christmas. Nor must his father hear of the lost job or suspect even the vestige of poverty. Luke's illness was grief enough.

Driving past the hospital, Marlowe felt guilty, but there was no time to spare. Sainsbury's was kind, selling yesterday half price. And then, on Castle Hill, Caro saw gingerbread men, in the patisserie window. Gingerbread men, and blueberry tarts, with cream, for dad. . . Blueberry tarts, for Grandma's Sunday tea, butter and milk cooling in a galvanised butt outside, and the gas-works' reek creeping through smutty net curtains. . . . His father knew every hallmark of poverty, the smell and taste of it. Bel would be amazed to see how little they needed to get by. They'd live like the pound a week poor of 1910, on bread, spuds, and the occasional relish. He had six pounds, ninety-seven pence left, enough for a smallish free range bird from the market, fresh herbs for stuffing.

Two minutes before the train pulled in, he parked outside the station. The car would be the next thing to go.

His father bounded down from the train, hoisting a woman's case. Eighty-four in February, he looked unnervingly fit, twenty years mislaid somewhere. Dapper, too, in a three-piece suit, bought for a winter wedding, a charcoal grey topcoat and a bright pink scarf which looked not effeminate but dashing, a definite touch of the Regency buck, fizzing on to four score and ten. He said, as he must, 'How is Luke?'

Marlow told him.

His father nodded gravely, 'We're praying for him.'

Marlowe let that pass. 'It's open visiting for children, and in the ICU. We can go now.'

'Then the sooner the better.'

On the way, though, he insisted on stopping at the Cathedral. It was five to ten. At ten o'clock, there would be Mass, and no decent means of escape; far from it. His father chose a pew two rows from the front, in the middle of a bench. It was impossible to beat a tactful retreat. Marlowe wondered what etiquette decreed. He'd once written a *Miss Manners* spoof, but apostasy didn't rate a mention. Then, out of love for his father with his terrible, simple faith, he knelt in an attitude of prayer, agnostic still. Luke had barely been initiated. His own faith was lost, stolen or strayed, but the old man, grey head bowed, still believed no prayer went unanswered. Look at Russia, he would say, by way of proof. All those years of prayer, and now look, churches full and Communism a dead duck. Marlowe knew better than to waste breath. It would, though, be sheer hypocrisy to present himself at the communion rail. He allowed Caro to be taken, for the first blessing of her life.

At the hospital, the old man hesitated. He said, 'How many visitors do they allow? I could wait outside with Caroline.'

Marlowe said nothing and steered him in, past yesterday's M6 crash, one leg amputated already, the other doubtful. They stood together by Luke's bed. For twenty minutes, Luke lay still, but he was breathing for himself. Once, a nurse came to turn him. Five minutes later, his eyes opened. He said, with difficulty, 'Grandad!'

Marlowe's blood ran cold. The boy's voice had been clearer last night. Luke tried to raise his hand in greeting; Marlowe could see the effort, the will, quite clearly.

Luke said, and there were tears of fear in his eyes, 'Dad, why can't I move?'

Marlowe said, trying to smile, 'Cramp, I bet. Stiff from all this idling in bed.'

Luke didn't even try to smile.

Old Marlowe took his hand, saying, 'Luke, I brought you these. The nurses can change them over.' He produced a Freddy Mercury album and six other tapes. '*Monty Python, Blackadder*. You liked them. I can send more.'

He walked, purposefully, to the desk, settled the matter. They stayed ten minutes more, but Luke was absorbed, lay there, his eyes closed, listening. Twice, he laughed out loud, an eerie sound, given their surroundings. Then they left. For the whole time, old Marlowe's lips had moved in prayer.

Leaving the hospital, he said, bitterly, 'Would you sponsor me? Ten miles, for water in the Sudan?'

Marlowe agreed and signed up. He couldn't decently get away with less than ten quid.

The old man said, still bitter, 'Ten miles! I could go twenty, and there's Luke, lying in bed like . . .' Words failed him. He waited patiently for the car to be unlocked, then sat down in the back, head in hands. Marlowe was very much afraid of tears, his own, but especially his father's. They drove to the house in silence. As they arrived, the old man lifted a white, tearless face and said, wondering, 'Quite a place. I thought there'd be less money about, on your own.'

'Half the London house, and a ludicrously small mortgage to mend the holes. It was a bit of a shambles.'

Marlowe led him in through the frosted garden. Yesterday's clothes hung stiffly on the line. The Aga greeted them with a swell of warmth. Marlowe went back to the car to fetch the shopping. He said, standing at the sink, preparing the bird, 'You'll stay till Monday?' This was a device of Bel's: define a limit, well inside what you can stand.

His father said, 'No. Tomorrow night. I'm busy, Mondays.'

Marlowe didn't press for details. Better, by far, that the old boy should be so busy. Besides, a father still pressed for time allowed him to be young, dependent and needing love.

They managed the rest of Saturday well enough, with a brief evening visit to the hospital. Tom Marlowe insisted on returning to Sainsbury's, to buy crumpets, strawberry jam, Eccles cakes, and full cream milk. He didn't care for prudent semi-skim. They ate roast chicken, stuffed with fresh herbs, served with roast potatoes and sweetcorn. Caro ate a whole bowl full of grated carrot, intended for a salad. She added a dollop of ketchup, a perversion caught, no doubt, from Faith's kids. Sunday was straightforward. Old Marlowe went out to eight o'clock Mass, came back with two papers, so there was no need to explain there being only four pence left in the house. They visited Luke once, and stayed for an hour. They took Caro to the playground near the Taj Mahal. Marlowe wondered what memorial he could give his son. It was scholarships, hospices, Aids or cancer research now. Marble was out, any size, with or without cherubs, except in the Polish quarter of the cemetery. Morbid nonsense . . . Luke couldn't die; happier today, listening to tapes, smiling for

226

them, breathing alone still. They left him to it and drove back for crumpets beside the fire, watched the new Sunday serial before the seven-thirty train. As the train left, Marlowe burst into tears, stumbling out into the concourse, shameless.

Faith left him alone for a week. She'd said, 'I want to marry you. I think it would work. I want to be married again.' He would have preferred 'I love you, can't live without you', but there it was, a pragmatic, sensual, almost medieval attitude to marriage. It looked a sound enough proposition. They were, one way or another, free; so convenient that Bel never wanted marriage. They were both *compos mentis*, patently fertile. Faith had one of the few remaining jobs for life, well paid, secure. It was the idea of being marked out that jarred. He felt preyed upon. Since Luke's illness, he had little time to think of sex. Now Luke was conscious, some of the time, they knew the very worst. His sight and hearing were sound, his speech slow but lucid. Beyond that, he could barely move a muscle. Supported by two nurses, propped on many pillows, he could sit like a four-month-old baby, ready to collapse any minute. He spoke with great difficulty, rarely finishing a sentence. On bad days, he looked thirty, forty, fifty years older, slack-jawed, stubbled. Marlowe found the stubble distressing. It should have been a matter of pride – the Christmas of his first razor. Instead, he could only think, what a waste, all those hormones surging into action for nothing. They had, at last, what amounted to a diagnosis, 'idiopathic recurrent splenomegaly'. Faith said this was longhand for 'haven't a clue'. The path lab, supplied with yet another blood test, were chasing up a new idea.

At the end of the week, on the next Sunday evening, Faith came round, soon after five. She had one child with her, Anna. The boys were at a birthday party. Marlowe switched on the TV for Anna to watch, but it was *The Clothes Show*.

Anna said, kindly, 'It's all right. It's good after that, until *Songs of Praise*.'

Marlowe left Caro with her. Anna, entranced, played with the baby. Rehearsals for the infants' Nativity play were under way. Caro consented to be wrapped in tablecloth swaddling clothes, to double as a sheep, to be massacred by Herod.

Marlowe led Faith to the kitchen. She said, quickly, 'I can't stay long. The party finishes at six. I'll be late on purpose, but no more than ten minutes. She's always landing her kids on me. Max and Oliver are in the same class at school, August and September birthdays, so they go to the same parties. It's all bedlam and breakages these days. They're sick of McDonald's, so it's back to housebreaking.'

She looked heartrendingly beautiful. The curtain of dark hair hung loose, only her eyes were made up. She'd made no attempt at all to conceal lines left by tears, not laughter. She said, 'I know about Luke. I'm sorry. How was he today?'

'The same.'

Faith moved towards him, drew him into her arms and kissed him on the lips. Marlowe held back, ill at ease. He wanted Faith, no doubt about that. His body said, make love, and the sooner the better. The constraints were fairly obvious: two kids in the next room, likely to burst in at any moment; two at a party, for ten more minutes; and Luke, less than half alive, in his hospital bed. They were parents, not lovers.

Freeing himself, he said, 'Some other time?'

Faith stood very still before him. 'If you must. Only, I love you *now*. I want to be with you, whatever happens with Luke. You shouldn't go through this alone.'

Marlowe could hear his daughter's lovely, liquid laughter, like birdsong. He said, carefully distancing himself, 'But I'm not alone. There's Caro, and my father. Bel will come again, if Luke becomes worse. And all my other women . . .'

That made her smile, disbelieving. '*Other* women?'

Marlowe nodded, amused by her reaction. 'Hordes. Monstrous regiments. Mothers at Caro's playgroup. Caro's health visitor, concerned about trauma for the sibling, for godsake. Hospital social workers, assorted do-gooders. I'm inundated with women. Open the door, answer the phone, and I fall over some woman, wanting to help.'

'And do you accept?'

He shook his head, 'Their idea of help is taking Caro away.'

She'd moved away to stand by the door, listening. The children were quiet, watching the serial. Turning to him

228

again, she said, 'After Rob's death, people were always offering to have the kids.'

Marlowe said, brusquely, 'Caro's the only way I can live through this. If Luke dies . . .' He stopped, left the rest of it unsaid.

Faith was out in the hall, calling Anna. At the door, she said, 'If there's ever a right time, let me know.' She added, wickedly, 'It would be so convenient if we were married. You'd only have one woman to contend with. I'm a good catch, respectable widow, gainfully employed. Sleep on it.'

Marlowe said nothing, watched her go. Did she have to underline his jobless state?

Halfway down the steep steps, Faith turned to see him again, but it was too late, the door resolutely closed.

The second Saturday in December, Caro struggled with her Advent calendar, scrabbling with small fingers to open the door marked 12. At last, she tore at it, ripping the cardboard hinge, revealing a bunch of grapes. The calendar was Hungarian, bought cheap from the street market, like the papier-maché Victorian baubles, made in China, £1.99 for six.

Caro had fetched her mittens and salopettes an hour ago. Now she brought his sheepskin jacket, dragging it by one sleeve. She said, firmly, 'Out. Go shopping.'

Marlowe gave in, tipped the rest of his coffee down the sink, broke his toast into a dozen pieces and tossed it to sparrows on the frosted lawn. Caro trotted to the hall cupboard, dragged her pushchair out.

Marlowe said, as if she were twenty years older, 'Car or bus, my lovely? We were running on empty last night. One trip in the car, or staggering up that bloody hill with carrier bags?'

Caro looked at him solemnly, considered the options. One delicious day, soon after they moved in, he'd taken her upstairs on an open-topped bus, branch-high, through a city of towers and hills. She shrieked, delighted, 'Bus!'

Marlowe buttoned the salopettes, zipped her jacket, then took it off again, to feed mittens on strings down the sleeves. The mitts were a present from one of his women, likewise the salopettes and jacket. Caro's outgrown clothes had moved on to Oxfam, where they sold almost before the assistant could hang them on the rail. Bel's taste had been exquisite, recklessly expensive. Caro was just as warm in second-hand Marks and Sparks.

It was surprising how quickly they'd become poor, and how little he minded. He was pretty well unemployed, one more casualty of a world slump that would end one day. Nor were they any longer rock-bottom poor. Russell had been better than his word, coming up with a weekly column in a women's magazine. Women liked to read confessions of male ineptitude. Luke wasn't mentioned, not part of his brief. The role was New Man, single parent, not father of a dying child. Russell was working on that, waiting. There'd be a story in Luke's illness, either way.

Writing a shopping list, chatting to Caro, thinking, always, of Faith, Marlowe found it extraordinarily easy to forget Luke. Luke belonged to the hospital, tube-fed again, after one hopeful day of yogurt and ice cream. Luke no longer spoke, nor asked to listen to the tapes his grandfather sent. Yesterday, Marlowe very nearly didn't bother visiting. It was Caro's free swimming class, a day of nasty sleet. Afterwards, he'd wanted to drive straight home, not sit in wordless anguish by Luke's bed. The tabloid stories of agony had it wrong. After the first shock and grief, the loss of his son had become mere normality. Caro was his life, Luke no more than an incident in that life. Yesterday, they'd stayed barely ten minutes.

Caro said, impatiently, 'Hurry up. I told you, hurry up. How many times . . .?'

Marlowe laughed, scooped her up and tucked her under one arm. 'Precocious brat.'

Strapping her in the pushchair meant leaving the back way, across the garden, down the leaf-littered ginnel. He picked up a frosted leaf, showed Caro diamonds, and bare branches where frost flowers blossomed. Then, for honesty, he showed how the crystals had formed. Caro saw and listened, mastering her world. It was a day of pellucid beauty, the sky winter blue, yesterday's malice forgotten. Only the distant hills were white, beyond the city, across the silver bay. He lifted Caro up to see, saying, 'Seaside.' She looked puzzled, wouldn't repeat the word. Then he realised: in all the months since leaving London, they hadn't been to the sea, barely three miles away.

He said, 'Seaside now, on the train, while the tide's still out.'

She brought treasures for him: half a Nike trainer, a take-away tray full of small dead crabs, a Budweiser bottle, an old five-pence piece, sea-green, a mermaid's purse. Overhead, a herring gull terrorised all opposition, swooped and dived for the remains of their chips. Beyond decay and the sad promenade, there was the world's end – dunes, reedbeds and winter birds. He knew oyster catchers, Canada geese, herring gulls, nothing else. They'd walked too far, trundling the empty pushchair over rippled sand and places where old men dug for lugworms. In less than an hour they must catch the little train back to visit Luke and shop. Caro, in bitter cold, had stripped off her shoes and tights, scampered through still pools of salt water. Now she came laughing to him. Marlowe lifted her into his arms, discovered joy. Walking along the shore, he thought, in magic detail, of making love to Faith. Bel had gone, and stayed away. Faith left her own children to sit with him at Luke's bedside. And then he must stop thinking of Faith, because Caro had found a dead gull and wanted to share it with him.

Half an hour later, they were sitting on the empty train. At the world's end, it had nowhere else to go, sat in the station waiting for passengers. There was birdsong in the ivy that clothed high golden walls, chaffinches, blue-tits, deluded by the pale sun into spring songs. In summer, they made a good living, chips, take-aways, left over sandwiches. Today, there was no one else on the train. He walked up and down with Caro, and it was quite true. There was nobody else at all. At the very last minute, an old woman climbed aboard, left at the first village, without being asked for any fare. Caro was in ecstasy, shouting to cows and sheep that walked the salt marshes. The journey should last for ever, ended in little more than ten minutes. Then they must visit Luke.

231

Climbing the hill to the hospital, Marlowe faced the truth; that his love for Luke had been conditional. He'd loved a Luke who no longer existed, artist, athlete, writer, handsome son of his beautiful mother. The creature labelled *Luke Marlowe* lay on his sick bed without moving, would stink in his own ordure, without the administering nurses. Plastic-tagged *Luke Marlowe* no longer smiled, or wept, or wrote a word. If he were dying, it would be easier to love, but he was not. Cared for, guarded from every infection, Luke could go on forever, only, there was no more love.

At the main entrance, they must cross cobbles. Marlowe turfed his daughter out, grabbed her reins, jerked the pushchair's eight wheels across to the visitors' entrance. It was all routine now. Luke wasn't even in the ICU, but in a side ward. There was nothing else they could do for him. He could breathe alone, showed no other sign of recovery. This week, in triumph, the path lab had named his sickness; *Brucella melitensis*, every symptom accounted for at last. Diagnosed sooner, treated with the right tetracycline, he need never have become so ill. Septicaemia had wrought havoc with his body, the enlarged spleen swollen below washboard ribs. Luke's mystery illness had a name, and no one seemed any the wiser. Luke was an embarrassment. Patients should die, or recover. Luke did neither, remained pitifully weak, his joints swollen and painful.

The staff, once so solicitous, now greeted them with the briefest nods. He stood by Luke's bed, remembering the child, warm and laughing in his arms; so many reunions. Often, it hadn't been Bel, bringing Luke to airports, and stations, but the current nanny or minder. Today, as usual, Luke lay there, barely alive. The livid rash still mottled his body, and there was an unwashed smell. Marlowe wondered how well they managed incontinence. For the past month, he'd seen no more than Luke's face and wasted arms. Unwillingly, he forced himself to take one thin hand in his own. It felt scaly, and the long clean nails needed cutting. He took out his own nail clippers, slid a paper handkerchief from the bedside table under Luke's hand, and clipped each nail neatly short, the way he used to when Luke was small. When he was about

232

to start on the other hand, Luke's eyes opened. He stared at Marlowe, unfocused, then croaked hoarsely, 'Thanks, Dad.'

Marlowe bent down to kiss him, fighting nausea as the stench assailed him. Then he went to find a nurse. It was entirely, he understood, a matter of routine. A little over five minutes later, he was allowed back. The stench was less, but he determined to bring an air freshener next time. And it would be better, far better, for Bel never to come again.

Caro played under the bed, as usual. Leaving, she waved goodbye, but Luke was somewhere else.

Chapter Twenty-One

Bloody impossible trying not to prance in step, jingle all the way. Caro leaned out of the shopping trolley to throw in delectable things: bright stockings stuffed with chocolate, books, gaudy socks, mince pies with brandy, red string bags of satsumas, three successive bottles of champagne and a box of Tampax. He let her keep everything, bar the champagne and a box of Tampax, hesitating over the latter, wondering how soon they went off. Did tampons come with a sell-by-date, as well as lurid warnings of toxic shock? The thought of sex education inspired thoughts of Faith; one more good reason to accept her candid proposal. At the check-out, even with all Caro's help, it came to less than he'd feared. Outside, in starry darkness, there was a flower stall. He bought freesias, narcissi, scented things his mother used to love. Two bunches didn't look much. He added more, until there was no money left. Then he pushed Caro from the riverbank to their own high hill.

Faith, or somebody, was in: there were lights on inside, and fairy lights shining in the dark yew tree. He thought of leaving the flowers on her doorstep, but they would freeze and lose their beauty in one night. He should unpack, give Caro her tea, then surprise Faith. But she might go out, any minute, on call. Releasing Caro, he left the shopping at the kitchen door and walked in darkness down the ginnel until he came to the back of Faith's house. He stood there, shivering, looking for a bell or knocker, until she came to wash up at the sink. Then he knocked at the window.

Faith screamed and dropped a melamine Peter Rabbit mug

that bounced across the tiled floor. She came to the kitchen door, raging, 'You bloody, bloody stupid – Never do that again. Ever.'

Marlow, abject, tried to hide the flowers, but Faith had seen them.

'For godsake! What's going on?' She seized them from him, buried her pale face in soft colour, and came back gentler.

'No one else was buying,' he said. 'I can't bear seeing people fail. I chose these because they smell. Flowers should, or what's the use of them? What was all that about? Mad axemen don't carry flowers, nor babies.'

Faith sat him down beside the Aga. She filled a beaker with apple juice for Caro, then said, 'Ever read Grimm, with the original woodcuts?'

'Of course. No expurgated versions in our family. The two little pigs and Red Riding Hood's grandma were eaten *up*, bones and all.'

Faith came to him, one spray of freesias in her hand. 'Remember the picture of the Devil, like a goat, appearing at the window in the dark? It used to scare me stiff, reading under the bedclothes. I can't bear people looking through the window.'

'Then draw the curtains?'

The scent of freesias was all around him, too sweet, too readily female. He took the flowers from her, kissed her and held her close. There'd been just one other woman in all the years with Bel, a young, childfree translator in Strasbourg. He preferred the softer breasts of motherhood.

Faith freed herself, saying, 'Later. Caro can sleep in Anna's old cot. I'm glad you came. Sometimes, I think one more night alone will finish me. No, let me go now. Later.'

Max and Oliver, shrewd eight- and nine-year olds, knew this was a night for sabotage. Caro, obliging child, slept willingly in the borrowed cot; Anna fell asleep on the sofa, to be carried up to bed; but the boys, gimlet-eyed, watched every move, stared too long and too often. During a brief phone call, for Faith, they put on a video, a threadbare, watched-to-death Sean Connery *Bond*, and they sat through it to the final credits.

Marlowe wanted to leave, depressed by so much easy sex. The thought of taking Faith up to her own bedroom alarmed him. Her job was the last straw. Like should marry like. That, halfway through *Goldfinger*, was the first time he admitted the possibility of marrying this woman. Mere sex barely came into it, yet. The issue wasn't sex per se, if they ever got round to it, but marriage. The wonder was that Faith should be available, and wanting him. One had to ask, what was in it for her, since he had so little to give? The suggestion of marriage definitely came from her. Since then, he'd been wondering why. A casual affair would be easier, surely? – give or take four vigilant kids. He no longer needed a woman merely to survive, could manage very well without. The blatant role reversal was unsettling. Faith had made all the running. Her credentials were impeccable, brass-plated job for life. She didn't need him at all, unless one admitted the joker: love. Which was absurd, a mistake no one should make twice. He'd fallen in love with Bel, and precious little good came of it, discounting Luke and Caro. He wasn't in love with Faith, coolly assessing every advantage, every drawback. The conviction had grown slowly, measured and checked by Luke's sickness, by the demands of their children. In silent hours at Luke's bedside, they'd rehearsed the ruthless marriage vows. And it made perfect sense, for better or worse.

Faith behaved impeccably, supervised the washing of necks and brushing of teeth. When Oliver said, 'Has *he* brought a toothbrush?' she simply ignored the question.

Some time after eleven, they were alone at last. There was another phone call. Marlowe heard Faith say, patiently, that she wasn't on call tonight, heard her give the emergency number. Then she said, 'All right, Ursula, I'll be right round.'

To him, she said, 'I'll be back soon. It's the old lady across the road, can't open her heart tablets. McCleod's on tonight, but he lives miles away. She's ninety-six. There's a son, seventy-four, but he lives in Carlisle.'

Half an hour later, she was back, trembling with cold, sliding blue hands inside his shirt. She said, as her hands tingled

236

back to life, 'Cryogenics, that's her secret. She'll see us all out. The place is like an ice house. Poor love, she didn't want me to go.'

Marlowe allowed her hands to move down, volunteered a kiss, and another, remembering, at last, what to do next.

'*There*, please,' Faith said clinically.

His hand froze. He said, coldly, 'Cut out the stage directions.'

Faith silenced him with another kiss, shy and soft, only on his lips. 'Sorry. Stage-fright makes me talk. It's been so long. And you're always leaving me. Or the kids are always here. And I'm tired to death all the time.'

Marlowe stood up and took her by the hand. He knew exactly what to do now.

Around two o'clock, Caro woke in strange darkness and cried out. Nobody came. She began to howl, loud and desolate. Marlowe struggled out of sleep, discovered Faith in his arms. Any minute, Caro would wake all the kids. Struggling into his trousers, he tried to cross the unknown room in darkness. No streetlight trespassed into Faith's room at the back of the house. Halfway across, he collided with cast iron, walked on in agony, bleeding. Finding Caro was easier, from her screams and the nightlight in Anna's room. He crept back into bed, Caro in his arms. There was a stickiness below, but whatever it was could wait till morning. Caro slept with her head on his bare chest, displacing Faith, which was, approximately, what she'd intended.

It was still dark when Faith shook him awake, complaining about something. 'Bloody hell! What's all this? I woke up thinking I'd started. Nearly died of embarrassment. The sheets are all bloody.'

Marlowe looked down. There was a jagged cut on his shin, with some flesh gouged out. They found a mess on the sewing machine's cast-iron base. The bottom sheet was stiff with blood. It was only ten to six, raining hard, on a Sunday morning. Faith, composed now she knew the blood came from him, stripped off the sheet, sponged the mattress and found a new bottom sheet and a clean duvet cover. Marlowe felt a little sick at the sight of the blood.

237

'What about me?'

She cleaned the wound, studying it professionally. 'It'll be a messy scar, if you don't get it stitched.'

'And if it's stitched?'

'A tidier scar. Casualty, or should I do it now?'

He sat very still, without flinching, as she drew raw flesh together and dressed the wound. Caro slept through everything, lay between them in bed. Faith said, 'When Max was a baby, he always slept between us. I'm not sure how Oliver happened. Anna came after they both moved out.'

Marlowe laughed. 'Caro comes to my bed every morning. She'll be shocked when she wakes.'

'Then we'd better get married soon.'

Marlowe propped himself on one elbow, studied his would-be wife. Long hair concealed the small breasts until she pushed it behind her head and lay there for him. Then, shivering, she drew the duvet up to her chin.

'Enough lechery. It's too bloody cold. Besides, I need to get the kids up for church.'

'Church?'

Faith giggled. 'Your face . . . Did I never explain? We're rabid papists. No, that's a lie. I'm not very good at religion. We go for the company, unless I'm working. Sunday shouldn't be allowed. If we go out, it's all access parents, buying treats. If we stay at home, it's me and the kids, locked in with old films and the rain piddling down. No one comes near. The kids will want to go today. They make decorations for the church tree, instead of sitting through a sermon. Anna's going to light the third candle on the Advent wreath, and I'll cry. You'll have to bear with me. "O come, O come, Emmanuel" is my downfall. I can't take all that hope.'

Marlowe cupped her breasts and kissed her, hard, on the mouth. He could bear a great deal this morning, was even disposed to believe in God. He said, 'Do rabid papists invite strangers to bed?'

Faith said, primly, 'Listen, I proposed first. I want to marry you. Ancient custom bedding, before wedding. The Church used to mind its own business. Marriage legitimised the mantel children. Tea or coffee?'

Marlowe said, resigned, 'I'll get up.'

Half an hour later, the house clamoured with children, fighting to open doors on Advent calendars. Two were chocolate, one Thomas the Tank Engine, one dripping with angels and Bible texts. Caro had stolen three chocolates, including Christmas Eve, but Faith's children forgave her innocent sin. Already, they seemed quite fond of her. The sheer good sense of the arrangement was disturbing. Max and Oliver would gain a stepfather, Caro a mother, Anna, the baby sister she'd often requested. If last night was anything to go by, he had a superbly sexy lover, afraid of nothing, bar a picture in Grimm's fairy tales.

Bewildered, he found himself at Mass for the third Sunday of Advent. Anna lit a rose-pink candle on the Advent wreath. The celebrant's words rang out, '*Gaudete, rejoice in the Lord always; again I say, rejoice. The Lord is near.*' Marlowe was surprised when Faith rose to receive communion with her sons, then decided it was her business. And he refused to call last night's love *sin*. He considered praying for a miracle, but decided that one miracle was probably all he had any right to expect. Faith must be enough, and far more than he deserved. The truly extraordinary thing was, this love followed death and betrayal. More, possibly, of God's alleged mysterious ways? Bel was a lousy, impossible mother, but Bel had given birth to his children. No Bel, no Luke, no Caro.

After Mass, Faith said, 'I can't be bothered with breakfast. Let's go to McDonald's, and read all the papers.'

Halfway there, Max said quietly, man to man, 'Excuse me asking, but do you love her?'

Marlowe said yes, adding that they would marry, soon. Max seemed satisfied, and relayed this information to the others at the top of his voice.

In McDonald's, they ate hugely, on to a good thing, Big Macs, muffins, do-nuts, double large fries. The boys studied tabloid sex and scandal, compared notes eagerly. Faith and Marlowe read the adult versions, in more detail. They didn't leave till midday. Faith said, 'We might as well see Luke on the way home.'

Marlowe went in alone, leaving even Caro in the car. Today, Luke was propped up; might or might not be listening to tapes. But he smiled at the sight of his father. He'd been

239

spoon-fed, promoted once more from drips and tubes. There was a half-finished carton of plain yogurt on his tray.

'Would you like to come home?' Marlowe said.

Luke nodded and slowly, heavily, extended a thin hand. Marlowe searched in his wallet for a nail file and hacked through the stubborn plastic of Luke's wrist tag. Then he presented it to the ward sister.

'I'm discharging Luke, now.'

They tried, reasonably hard, to prevent him. Marlowe listened politely. The staff agreed, honestly enough, that nothing more could be done for Luke. They had no idea if he would ever fully recover. He no longer needed life support, only nursing care.

'Fine,' Marlowe said. 'He comes home now. If you could do anything, I'd leave him here. You can't, so he comes home.'

Faith drove her own children and Caro home, left them with a neighbour and returned with blankets for Luke. An hour later, Luke, silent, bright-eyed, sat up in his own bed, under his own black duvet. He said, through tears, 'I thought you'd left me there for ever.'

Two days before Christmas, Luke had a visitor. Faith let her in, for Marlowe was in town, collecting the tree with the children.

Marigold said, 'I need to see Luke. Tell him it's me, Marigold. Anyway, give him this. It's nothing much. I never went to see him. Hospitals turn me up.' She held out a badly wrapped parcel, gilded paper surrounding some awkward shape.

Faith went up to Luke, who was still barely speaking. She said, 'There's a girl. *Beata Beatrix*, but skinny. She wants to see you.'

Luke smiled and said, slowly, 'Marigold. Bring her up.'

Faith left them alone. Luke could, now, ring a bell if he needed the loo. He smiled, ate a little, listened to music. His grandfather had come twice, deduced, without being told, the state of affairs, dared not ask for more. His son was as happy as any man had a right to be. More, one couldn't expect, though Luke's life seemed a high price to pay. The wedding

240

was set for Candlemas Day, frail snowdrops in the Cathedral, the end of Christmastide. No, he shouldn't ask for more.

Marigold said, 'You look horrible. You look like something Drac sucked dry and spat out. I hate black sheets.'

Luke made room for her on the bed. 'No one's asking you to sleep in them.'

'No?' She sat, of necessity, very close to him, took the fleshless hands in hers. She whispered, 'I hope whatever you've got isn't catching. They'd've said, I suppose. Let me in.'

Unasked, she lay beside him under the duvet. Luke smelled good. Antaeus, maybe, or Aramis, she couldn't remember which. Men should smell good, especially in bed. Luke, no longer quite so thin, no longer disfigured by the rash, no longer incontinent, might never walk again, but looked delectable. Emboldened by the sound of the front door closing, she drew Luke into her arms and kissed him. He responded healthily enough, with deep and eager French kisses and some agreeable groping. After a while, though, she released herself. It wouldn't do to go too far, yet, especially when Faith might be back any minute. She held out the present.

'I got you this.'

Luke asked, 'Do I open it now?'

Marigold took it from him and transferred it to the chest of drawers. She said indignantly, ''Course not. No self-control, that's your problem. Twenty-fifth December, it says. You can get me a prezzie when you're better. See you.'

Then she was gone, out of his bed, downstairs, out of the house, as Faith returned, only taking a present to old Ursula across the road. Just as well they hadn't . . . All the same, he must be getting better, to go that far.

On Christmas Day, Faith slept in, after midnight Mass, and three nights on call. Marlowe drove with Caro to collect his father. The old man had steadfastly refused to come any sooner. As they drove back up the deserted A6, he said, 'Could you manage to bring me home tonight?'

Marlowe controlled a skid on black ice. He said, when it

241

was safe to talk, 'No, I most certainly could not. It's bad enough driving cold sober.'

'Then I'll go tomorrow morning, first thing.'

They drove past running deer, silhouetted against the rising sun. Marlowe sang cheerfully, '*The rising of the sun, and the running of the deer.*'

His father said, 'That's why. You've discovered love, for the first time in your life. You don't want me around.'

Marlowe turned to his father, smiling. 'Oh, but we do. It was Bel who didn't want you around. You made her feel shallow and worldly.'

'Is that what she said?'

'Her very words. She came up last week, to see Luke. She thinks I've reverted to type. Slipped down a snake, to the bottom of the board.'

'Would that be so very bad?'

Marlowe had to have his wits about him. They really had done it on purpose, cones and lights on Christmas morning. Then he said, 'What do you think?' turned left and up their hill.

Faith had invited old Ursula. It would be Christmas as it should be, ill-assorted ages and as yet unrelated people under one roof. For the life of him, he couldn't remember what they'd done last year. Nine hours ago, Caro stood before the crib, believing every word of it, ass, ox, shepherds, angels and all. The details of conception didn't worry her yet. Marlowe had decided, today, to believe in the virgin birth for good measure. Faith did, and she was a Fellow of the Royal College of Obstetricians and Gynaecologists.

Chapter Twenty-Two

A week before the wedding, there was a pilgrimage. Marlowe's tenuous faith was on hold, tested severely enough by Christmas. Pilgrimage, as a form of divine arm-twisting, had never appealed to him. He was shocked when Faith blatantly encouraged her more credulous patients to go to Lourdes or Walsingham. When he objected, she said, 'Half of them are sad and unloved. I can't cure these things. As for the sick, who knows? Even doctors allow for the placebo effect. Send Luke to Maryholme. It's only twenty miles. No one's suggesting Lourdes.'

Marlowe said they already had, adding that he'd told them what they could do with the idea. Reluctant, but preoccupied with marriage, especially the having and holding, he agreed to go with Luke. Besides, the shrine at Maryholme was Saxon or even Celtic, surely pre-Christian. The healing water, tested in accordance with EC regulations, was bacteriologically and chemically pure. Luke could come to no harm.

Luke himself, with a mind and tongue of his own again, consulted Marigold.

'You're getting better anyway. Some people I know believe in magic crystals. Some even believe in God. This is *supposed* to be the Virgin Mary. Personally, I wouldn't believe a word of it, but give it a whirl. I would, if I were you. I mean, I would if I couldn't walk.'

Luke agreed. Once, before the worst snow came, Marigold had taken him out in his wheelchair. It had been very tender, almost romantic, along the frosted riverbank below the castle. Until, that is, the cold got to his bladder, and he'd needed her help to pee in the disabled loos. If he hadn't made it . . . The idea of being permanently paralysed was establishing itself, slowly. At Christmas, he'd been grateful for small mercies, like the use of his hands. He would very much like his legs back. School apart, there was unfinished business with Marigold, all the more exasperating since Dad won himself the sexy doctor.

They travelled *en famille*, with thirty devout pilgrims, mostly past sixty, mostly female, in a coach booked from church. Luke's wheelchair was folded with others in the boot. On the way, snow began to fall, and meant business. The driver, nervous, consulted the Bishop, who sat apart, but not aloof, in the single front seat. The Bishop indicated a gritting team, but observed that the heavy snow had been promised for Scotland, not northern England. Marlowe considered this dodgy advice, given that the Met office and the BBC thought Scotland meant anywhere north of Manchester.

The snow fell faster and lay deeper. On the opposite carriageway, a gritting team had come to grief, and the road back was closed. The driver said, grimly, 'There's still the motorway. They keep that open longest. If we turn back now, we might get home, or we might hit six-foot drifts.'

They were two miles short of the shrine. One old lady, halfway through her second rosary, burst into tears. The Bishop decided two more miles would make no odds.

They arrived at the shrine to find ten or more coaches parked in a rutted, drifted field. Luke shuddered as they lifted him down into the wheelchair. Dad looked embarrassed, the way he did on parents' nights, or if you caught him kissing Faith. Clearly, he wished the whole thing over. Anyway, the Maryholme spring would be frozen. Would sucking an icicle work? The Bishop glared at him for his frivolity.

There was another bishop, a brace of Monsignori and half a dozen priests or curates. The sick looked cold rather than faithful. They lingered as briefly as they dared at the shrine, kept longer prayers for the warm little church. Luke, frozen stiff and entirely disbelieving, drank his mouthful of holy water. The cold almost broke his teeth off. In the church, even the two bishops agreed they should move on and try to beat the weather home. Luke, blue with cold, needed a pee, suffered the ignominy of Dad helping him to use the adapted bus loo. At least they hadn't dragged him down to Lourdes.

On the way home, he became aware of a tingling in his legs, not quite shivering, more like someone walking on his grave. Prudent, he decided to say nothing. Since becoming ill, he'd felt all manner of strange sensations. They had a name, paraesthesias. This was probably another. At home, he agreed to a bath, suffered the embarrassment, once more, of Dad seeing his tackle and pubic hair. The alternative was Faith, so it could be worse. The snow fell thickly outside. In the morning, Max, Oliver, Anna and even Caro would toboggan and build a snowman. It felt good, though, to be at home by the fireside, with everyone. In the hospital, he'd been expecting to die, already '*sans* everything'. At home, he was part of the family, so he couldn't die, could he? They were all together in his house tonight, because Faith was on call. The little kids were all right. Jules had twin brothers this age. Once or twice, they'd said *Dad*, by mistake. They were building with his old *Lego Technic*, because there was nothing on TV, meaning, nothing at all. Snow had knocked the transmitter out. Later, during supper, they watched old videos, *Dr Who*, then *Winnie the Pooh*, for the little ones. He was aware of great love.

In the morning, he walked from his bed to the bathroom to pee and brush his teeth. Looking down at his legs, he saw spindleshanks, wasted flesh, bones and dry, dead skin. He dressed without help, wondered whether to wake Dad. He was never entirely sure where Dad slept these days – or, rather, nights. It didn't do to ask questions. He had an idea they were in their own beds this week, a period of self-imposed abstinence before the wedding. He found his father lighting the Aga, which had chosen the coldest night of January to go out.

He said, cautiously, 'Morning, Dad. I can walk.'

This was only moderately true. The journey downstairs had taken all of ten minutes, one slow, weak step after another, clutching the rail. It was also, canonically, less than miraculous, since recovery had always been possible. Luke was a stickler for truth.

'My legs started to tingle on the way back from the shrine.'

245

Marlowe nodded. 'Paraesthesia, maybe.'

'No, not this time. It felt different. I asked to walk. I can walk. Not very well yet, but I'm out of practice. If you don't believe, it might not work. Like clapping for Tinker Bell. If God doesn't get the credit, she might cancel. Anyway, you'd better tell the hospital. I don't care why I can walk, but it feels good.'

Marigold said, lying on Luke's bed, 'If someone comes in . . .'

Luke shook his head. 'They're all playing happy families in her house. Anyway, the door locks. It was the first thing I noticed when we moved in.'

Marigold kicked off her shoes and began to kiss him, less expert than she'd like to be. She said, unbuttoning his black shirt and pulling the black duvet round both of them, 'Was it a miracle?'

Luke smiled, for once getting exactly what he wanted. 'How should I know? My legs tingled a little the day before, only not so much. I think I got better because I got better. I was ill because I caught the bug. No mysteries, no miracles. But if it makes them happy . . .'

Marigold was wondering, maybe too late, if Luke had any condoms, if she dared ask. She said, uneasily, 'I know. No point in hurting them. People are so cruel to each other.'

A fortnight later, Luke walked down the aisle with his father to wait for Faith. Caro, peculiarly good, sat with her grandfather. There were twelve people in the Cathedral, counting the priest. In the back row, behind a pillar, careful not to be seen, there was Bel. Luke, in fact, had seen her, passed by looking straight ahead. Marlowe didn't, and, since she slipped away before the end, never knew she'd been there.

Bel saw her only son walk past, tall and straight, knew her unbelieving prayers had been answered. She'd asked, very simply, for a miracle, health for her son, happiness for his father. She left the Cathedral happy, all her sins forgiven and her son healed. God, assuming the existence of such a being, couldn't do fairer than that.

You have been reading a novel published by Piatkus Books. We hope you have enjoyed it and that you would like to read more of our titles. Please ask for them in your local library or bookshop.

If you would like to be put on our mailing list to receive details of new publications, please send a large stamped addressed envelope (UK only) to:

Piatkus Books: 5 Windmill Street
London W1P 1HF

PIATKUS

The sign of a good book